MW01135765

Endurance

Gwen Sutton

ISBN: 1518719287
ISBN 13: 9781518719288
Library of Congress Control Number: 2015917526
CreateSpace Independent Publishing Platform
North Charleston, South Carolina
Published by Lift Him Up Productions, Inc.

Praise for Gwen Sutton's original novel,
All Means All, If You Believe

"An exciting read that is sure to keep readers on the edge of their seats...."

"I found the novel hard to put down, as I was eager to see what would happen next in this unpredictable and deeply emotional story."

"An incredible and suspenseful fiction novel. Very realistic and compelling...."

"A great read from a very talented author! I highly recommend the well-written novel...to readers everywhere."

--Lucinda Weeks, Readers' Favorite Reviews

"I was captivated from the very beginning of the story."

"This book is an awesome read. Kudos to author Gwen Sutton."

--Valerie Rouse, Readers' Favorite Reviews

Praise for *Endurance*

"I love this book. Loved. It."

"A heart-wrenching tale of atrocity and redemption...."

"Anyone who enjoys reading suspense, action, intrigue, stories with a strong message ...should definitely read Endurance."

--Tracy Slowiak, Readers' Favorite Reviews

"Simply a great read."

"Characters that readers will connect with, relate to and continue to think about long after the book is finished. If that isn't the hallmark of a great author, I don't know what is."

"I look forward to more from this very promising author in the future!"

--Chris Fischer, Readers' Favorite Reviews

"An emotionally charged, and at times heart breaking story.... The subject matter of this well-written book ... can move you to tears in places."

"There are plenty of surprises and twists to the story too as the battle for good over evil plays itself out."

"A brave story about atrocities that shouldn't happen. But also a story about resourcefulness, hope, courage, and endurance."

--Hillary Hawkes, Readers' Favorite Reviews

"This book reaffirms the need for the world to come together in the fight against human trafficking. Gwen Sutton delivers this message in a very compelling way."

"I was profoundly moved...."

--Faridah Nassozi, Readers' Favorite Reviews

Dedications

To my Lord and Saviour, Jesus Christ.

To my soulmate, husband, and the love of my life, Swindell Sutton. Thanks for your unwavering love and support. I'm so grateful that God blessed me with you.

To my siblings, Deborah, Rozell, and Raymond, with love. We have and will endure.

To the millions of human trafficking victims around the world.

Preface

ENDURANCE **CONTINUES THE** compelling, emotional, and inspirational story of the Jones family which began in my original novel, *All Means All, If You Believe.* When I wrote the original book, it was not my intentions to continue the Jones family saga. But God, and my readers, had other plans.

Readers wanted to know what became of the complex, endearing, and realistic characters in my original book who were blindsided by an unimaginable tragedy; but who by grace, faith, and prayer pulled through. And God led me to a story that required me to delve into dark, unfamiliar territory, in order to shed light on an abominable crime against children. I pray I've done the subject justice.

To be honest, *Endurance* was a tough story for me to write. And it may be difficult for some to read as well. However, as tough as it was to write, or as difficult as it may be to read—most of us can only imagine how painful it must be to live.

I hope that readers will not only be enlightened, engrossed and entertained by the many twists and turns in the plot of this emotional story, but will also be moved to action. We all can do something, no matter how small, to combat this appalling atrocity against children that is thriving in society among us.

Prologue

DEREKA DRIFTS SOMEWHERE between the conscious and the unconscious. She feels like she is in a dark, narrow tunnel, floating in a place that is neither here nor there. Visions of a birthday cake, candles, and colorful balloons drift like a dream across the breadth of her mind. Dereka tries to reach out and touch them, but everything seems just out of reach. She visualizes the beautiful smiling face of her mother, Serena, and hears her gentle voice and joyful laughter as they walk arm in arm across a huge parking lot. Serena is carrying a birthday cake in her free arm, and Dereka has a huge bundle of balloons.

But something isn't right. Something has happened; something horrible. In her subconscious state, Dereka feels a deep sense of fear and trepidation. *What's wrong?* she questions in her mind. *I have to find out what's wrong.* So Dereka fights her way to consciousness as if she were freeing herself from a thick net that was determined to keep its catch. But when Dereka opens her eyes, she is still enveloped in darkness. She is lying on her side somewhere in total darkness. She closes her eyes and opens them again only to be greeted by that same foreboding darkness. Fear grips her heart as she moves her head slowly from side to side, trying to get her bearings.

Dereka tries to remember something, anything that would explain where she is and why. *Let's see*, she thinks. *I went shopping with Mama to pick up my birthday cake and balloons for my party*, Dereka recalls, feeling a twinge of excitement at the thought of finally becoming a teenager. She remembers going to her mother's favorite bakery in Old Town Alexandria and picking up a chocolate cake with purple and white icing. She also recalls buying a variety of colorful balloons with "Happy 13th Birthday" written on them. She even remembers her mother laughing and teasing her about the fact that some boy who lived down the street from them, and who had a crush on Dereka, had called and asked to be invited to her party. And he wouldn't take no for an answer. The last thing Dereka remembers is walking arm in arm towards the car with her mother. But that's when things goes black. Dereka can't remember anything after that. *Why can't I remember? Where's Mama? What happened?* she thinks frantically.

Dereka tries to stand up, but something is preventing her from standing. She's in some kind of contraption, in a cramped, stuffy place. She tries to stretch out her arms and legs but can move them only a few inches in any direction. Her body is curled up in a fetal position. She uses her arms and legs to push against whatever is enclosing her, but it won't bulge. Then Dereka senses a slight moving sensation. It seems whatever she is in is actually moving. She lies perfectly still, trying to hear anything that will give her a clue as to where she is and what is happening. For a moment the moving sensation stops, and she believes she hears a deep humming or rumbling sound, like a motor of some sort was left running. When the moving sensation starts again, Dereka's body shifts sharply to one side. She listens carefully and thinks she hears the faint sound of horns and cars in the distance.

And it is at this moment that pure, unadulterated panic and hysteria seizes Dereka as she finally realizes where she is. She is trapped in the dark trunk of somebody's car. Dereka begins to scream.

Birthday Prep

(One Week Earlier)

DEREKA JONES AND her Aunt Kenya sat at the kitchen table browsing through the last of the e-vites to Dereka's upcoming birthday party. The invitations had been sent out about a month earlier, and the RSVPs were due that day. Dereka's grandmother, BabyRuth, had wanted to mail out formal paper invitations to her granddaughter's special thirteenth-birthday party. But Dereka had playfully teased her, saying, "Grandma Ruth, that's so old school. Nobody does that anymore. That was back in the olden days." BabyRuth had eventually relented, throwing her hands up in the air and saying, "I give. I can't compete with all this high-tech stuff you young folk are into. I sure miss the good old days when things were done proper."

Dereka was using her new Samsung Galaxy S6 phone, which she had gotten the week before as an early birthday present from her Aunt Jasmine, who lived in Los Angeles. A bit extravagant for a thirteenth-birthday present, in BabyRuth's opinion, but there was nothing too good for Dereka as far as her Aunt Jasmine was concerned. Kenya marveled at how tech savvy her niece was as she watched Dereka expertly use her fingers to tap, scroll, and browse her way through Facebook, OVoo, Instagram, Twitter, and a host of other social media sites popular with young adolescents and teens. To her family it seemed that Dereka was almost to the point of obsession with electronic gadgets. There was hardly a moment when she wasn't hooked up to, plugged in to, talking on, texting with, listening to, or looking at some sort of electronic device, be it a cell phone, note-book, iPod, iPad, or some other gadget.

"Well," Dereka said, looking up at her aunt while her fingers continued their dance over the keypad of her phone. "I've heard back from everybody I invited, and with the exception of my friend Marion, who will be out of town, everybody's coming to my party. Even Brandon Evans is planning to come. Brandon is soooooo cute, and popular, and smart, and nice, and fun…," Dereka said, going on and on about some boy at her school that she obviously liked. Kenya just smiled to herself as she gazed at Dereka's youthful, animated face.

Dereka was a beautiful, blossoming young girl, with cinnamon-brown skin, big brown eyes, high cheekbones, and the Jones-family-trademark full lips. She had her mother's adorable dimpled smile and her father's athletic physique and height. Her hair was long, curly, and thick, and she kept it completely natural, copying the natural way her mother, Serena, wore her hair. Although only twelve years old, Dereka already stood about five feet six, making her one of the tall-est girls in her eighth-grade class. And to the dismay of her mother and grandmother, Dereka's body was already filling out in all the right places. She had a full C-cup bosom and a round, plump, traditional African American female butt. Her good looks and friendly, down-to-earth personality made her quite popular with a lot of young, tes-tosterone-driven boys who had started buzzing around her like bees around honey.

As Kenya watched Dereka, she was amazed at how much Dereka was like her father, Derek. *Like father, like daughter,* Kenya thought to herself as her memories drifted back to the big brother she had loved so much and lost so tragically. He died just months before his beautiful baby girl was born. Derek had been the perfect big brother who had loved and cared for Kenya all of her life. After Derek died, Kenya's life had taken a downward spiral. She got involved in a sex-ting scandal with a substitute teacher at her high school, named Mr. Curtis, who conned her into trusting him. He had turned out to be a sexual predator and a blackmailer. And in an attempt to get money to pay off her blackmailer and save face, Kenya had unwittingly gotten involved with Kevin's father, a drug dealer named Memphis. It had all blown up in her face and turned into one scandalous mess.

But thanks be to God, Kenya managed to turn her life around. Now at the young age of thirty-one, she was a successful Virginia commonwealth prosecutor in Fairfax County, a highly prestigious elected position responsible for the prosecution of felony crimes. She was also engaged to an equally successful attorney named Ryan Young. Ryan worked as an estate attorney at Sampson & Peterson LLP, a top law firm in DC.

Kenya was a tall, attractive woman with beautiful African facial features, a slim build, dark chocolate skin, and short curly natural hair. She owned and lived in a high-end condo in Fairfax City.

Kenya loved her job as a prosecutor, and had quite a good reputation for being highly intelligent, thorough, dedicated, and hardworking. She was admired by her comrades and feared by her opponents. She knew, without a doubt, how proud her brother Derek would have been of her if he were still alive. *I miss you big bro*, Kenya thought, wishing he had gotten to know his wonderful daughter.

"What are you daydreaming about, Aunt Kenya?" Dereka asked, sensing something was weighing heavily on her aunt's mind.

"Sweetie, I was just thinking about your father. You know, the older you get, the more you remind me of him. You have the same sensitive, caring spirit, the same inquisitive nature, and the same sense of humor. He was really something special, and so are you," Kenya responded, smiling at the niece she had come to regard as her own daughter.

"I wish I could have known him," Dereka stated wistfully. "Tell me more about him. What was he like? What did he like to do?"

Kenya shut down her computer, giving Dereka her full attention. "Well, Derek was very intelligent and hardworking, compassionate and caring—always looking out for me and your Grandma Ruth. He liked all kinds of sports, played football in high school and college. He was also a bit of a prankster growing up, always playing jokes on me and trying to get me into trouble with Mama and Daddy. I remember one time when we were kids, he took some of my glue that I was using for a class project and put it on the handle of Mama's favorite frying pan. It stuck to her hand when she picked it up to fry some chicken. Daddy laughed so hard he cried, but Mama didn't think it was so funny. It must have taken Mama and Daddy well over an hour to unstick that frying pan from Mama's hand. They used soap and water, margarine, nail polish remover, alcohol, and Lord knows what else. Needless to say, dinner was late that night. Mama wanted to ground me for a week, but Derek finally fessed up when he saw how mad Mama was. So she grounded him instead. That boy was something else," Kenya said, smiling broadly as she reminisced.

Kenya fell silent for a moment as her face turned solemn and serious. "He was my heart, and now you are my heart," Kenya expressed as two tears ran down the side of her face.

"Don't cry, Aunt Kenya," Dereka said. She got up to hug and kiss her aunt on the cheek.

"I'm sorry, baby," Kenya responded as she wiped the tears from her face. "Now enough of this gloomy stuff. Let's get back to planning your partay."

"Sounds good to me," Dereka said cheerfully and went right back into happy chatter about her upcoming birthday, including what girl liked what boy and so on and so forth.

Three Generations of Love

THE NEXT MORNING Ruth Jones, better known as BabyRuth, was in the kitchen doing what she loved—cooking for her family. She hummed softly to herself as she went about preparing pancakes, smoked sausage, eggs, grits, toast, and coffee. It was Saturday morning, a brisk, cool mid-November day, the time of the year she liked most. She hummed one of her favorite songs, "Amazing Grace." While she hummed softly, BabyRuth thought about when she was a little girl and watched her mama, Leona, sing that same song as she went about her housework. She remembered once asking her, "Mama, why you always singing that song?" Her mother just smiled at her and said, "Oh, I guess it just makes me feel good, that's all. It makes me feel happy inside. Just like you do."

As a child BabyRuth had not understood the true essence of the "amazing grace" her mama sung about, but she certainly understood now. It was that same amazing grace that brought her through the darkest days of her life: the death of her only son. Derek's unexpected and tragic death had forced BabyRuth to use every ounce of her strong Christian faith to pull herself and her family through one of the most agonizing situations that any mother should have to endure. BabyRuth's husband, Derek Sr., called DJ for short, passed away from cancer about seven years after her son's death. Now father and son were buried side by side. "Only by your amazing grace, Lord, have I been able to carry on," BabyRuth said, looking towards heaven.

BabyRuth could hear her granddaughter and daughter moving about upstairs. Dereka and Serena had moved in to live with her shortly after DJ died. Serena was not really BabyRuth's daughter, but BabyRuth considered her to be. Serena was actually the former girlfriend of her late son, Derek. BabyRuth and Serena had gone through so much together after Derek's death and, as a result, had become closer than most blood relatives. Serena even formally changed her name to Serena Dixon-Jones, taking on the last name of the man and family she loved. She was about two months pregnant with Derek's child when he died. She was also HIV positive. Derek, not yet knowing that he himself had been infected during a moment of weakness, had unknowingly transmitted the virus to her. Not being able to live with the consequences of what he had done, Derek had taken his own life. His death had been extremely difficult for her, to the point that she almost gave up completely. But God, in his infinite goodness and mercy that endures forever, had pulled her through. Serena thanked God every day for helping her to survive what she had thought was not survivable and to forgive what most considered unforgiveable. She had gone through the storm and come out stronger, knowing that, as the Bible teaches, *"the trial of your faith, being more precious than of gold."*

"Morning, Mama Ruth. Smells good in here," Serena said as she entered the kitchen dressed in a beautiful, colorful caftan with a matching headband around her soft, natural hair.

"Good morning, sweetheart," BabyRuth responded, giving Serena a quick hug. "You looking lovely as usual." Serena was a natural beauty with caramel-brown skin, big sparkling brown eyes, and deep adorable dimples. She had a head full of soft, fluffy, natural hair, which she wore in a variety of ethnic hairstyles such as twistouts and Senegalese braids, or just pulled up freestyle atop her head like a crown of glory. And Serena was just as beautiful on the inside. She had a sweet, sensitive, compassionate spirit, and she was always looking for opportunities to help those less fortunate.

"Is Dereka up and about?" BabyRuth asked as she expertly flipped a couple of pancakes.

"I peeped in on her, and she was on the phone as usual. I some-times think that thing is glued to that child's ear," Serena said, chuck-ling softly to herself as she placed plates, napkins, and utensils on the big oak kitchen table.

"I think all the young folks are going to be crazy as Betsy bugs when they get older from all the energy waves, radiation, and what-not generated by constant use of those cell phones. Just mark my word," BabyRuth said, placing bread in the toaster.

"Mama Ruth, what's a Betsy bug anyway?" Serena asked, laughing at BabyRuth's use of the old folk term.

"I don't really know," BabyRuth confessed. "But my mama used to say it all the time, and I guess it's something that I just picked up along the way. Funny how those old sayings pass down through the generations. I guarantee you will be using that same phrase when you get my age," BabyRuth said, shaking her finger jokingly at Serena.

When breakfast was almost ready, BabyRuth went to the bottom of the stairs. "Dereka, get off that phone, and come down here and eat," BabyRuth yelled in her official, no-nonsense grandma tone.

"Okay, Grandma Ruth," Dereka quickly answered. A few minutes later she galloped down the stairs like a thoroughbred and sprinted into the kitchen, a small force of teenage energy and aura, wearing colorful leggings and a cropped purple sweater. Dereka was athletic, like her father. She loved to play basketball and was quite good at it. She could actually hold her own with the boys in the neighborhood and was on the coed basketball team at the community center.

Serena and BabyRuth marveled inwardly about how their little Boogie Boo was growing up. Boogie Boo was a nickname Serena gave Dereka when she was about two years old. As Dereka got older, she begged them to stop calling her Boogie Boo. "Please, please don't call me that in front of my friends. It's so embarrassing," Dereka pleaded. Serena, Kenya, and Jasmine conceded to her request. But not BabyRuth. She told Dereka, "Look, you're my little Boogie Boo, and you always will be. Deal with it."

The three generations of love—grandmother, daughter, and granddaughter—enjoyed a nice, leisurely breakfast together in the sunny, spacious kitchen. After breakfast Dereka cleaned up the kitchen while BabyRuth and Serena went over their plans for the day. They spent at least one Saturday out of every month doing something of each of their choosing. Today their plans included a manicure and pedicure (BabyRuth's choice), a stop by the HIV awareness center to stuff envelopes for mailing (Serena's choice), and a trip to the cosmetic store at the mall (Dereka's choice). Now that Dereka was about to turn thirteen, her mother was finally allowing her to start wearing a little makeup, starting with just a little lipstick and rouge on the cheeks. Nothing more.

"We better get a move on it," Serena said, noticing the time. "We have a lot to do before picking up Jasmine at the airport later this evening."

"I can't wait to see Auntie Jazz," Dereka said excitedly. Dereka called her Aunt Jasmine "Auntie Jazz" because she was so full of fire, spunk, and sass. "And I know she's bringing me something fierce to wear from LA," Dereka continued. "I asked her to bring me some of those Versace jeans she had on the last time she was here."

"What have I told you about pestering your aunt for things," BabyRuth lightly scolded. "Gimme, gimme, gimme. That's all you young folks think about. Remember the Bible says that *it's better to give than to receive.*"

"But doesn't it also say *ask and you shall receive.* So that lets me know I need to ask for what I want," Dereka countered, laughing.

"She got you there, Mama Ruth," Serena added, joining in on the laughter. BabyRuth just shook her head and smiled.

"Well, I'm glad you at least remember some of the Bible verses I've taught you over the years. Even if it is only the ones you can use for your own gain," BabyRuth admonished, shaking her finger at her granddaughter in jest.

BabyRuth had made it a habit over the years to teach Dereka Bible verses, starting as soon as Dereka was old enough to read. Little did BabyRuth know that those same Bible verses would one day be a lifeline for her granddaughter, who would be forced to fight for her survival in the most horrific conditions imaginable.

Lady Jazz

JASMINE MCKNIGHT READIED herself for her 12:30 p.m. nonstop flight from LA to DC. She decided to wear a Louis Vuitton black-and-red belted pantsuit that showed off her shapely figure, and black high-heeled Gucci boots. For her accessories she chose a stylish Chanel handbag, a lightweight wool Yves Saint Laurent cape for the chilly East Coast weather, and a stylish wide-brimmed black hat. Her makeup was, as always, applied to perfection, and her full, wavy black weave with light auburn streaks hung just past her shoulders.

Jasmine rarely dressed down, even when flying on a long transcontinental flight. And she didn't understand why most women on flights chose to wear baggy jeans or sweat pants, oversized sweaters, and athletic shoes, or worse yet, flip-flops. That wasn't Jasmine's style. She dressed for a flight the same way she would dress for an important business meeting, a dinner, or a night out on the town. She dressed to the hilt.

Jasmine was drop-dead gorgeous. She stood about five foot seven, and at the age of thirty-four she still had the tight body of a twenty-two-year-old, which she worked hard to maintain. She had smooth, beautiful vanilla-brown skin, big sultry hazel eyes, perfect white teeth, full puckered lips, and a body that could be referred to in old-school terms as a "brick house." She also had gorgeous hair (which she paid good money for) in all colors, lengths, types, and textures. It didn't matter which of her wide array of wigs and weaves Jasmine decided to wear. She could rock any style.

Ms. Jasmine took fabulous to a whole new level. She could literally stop traffic at high noon, or at least slow it down a bit, as one man after the other pumped his brakes to slow down and watch her strut her stuff as she moved down the street. When Jasmine walked, it seemed her hips had a rhythm all their own—like smooth jazz on a hot summer night. Jasmine was sensuous and sexy without even trying. It was just who she was, who she had always been.

But Jasmine was more than just an outer beauty—much more. She had brains and street smarts, and she used both to become a very successful businesswoman. She owned two prosperous health and beauty spas in the LA area, which she named Lady Jazz's Abode. She had plans to open a third spa in northwest DC. Jasmine selected the DC location so she could be closer to her best friend, Serena, her adopted niece, Dereka, and their family, Kenya and Mama Ruth. She already spent a lot of time in the DC area and would stay with the Joneses whenever she was in town. She loved and cherished them with her whole heart.

Jasmine's street smarts were the result of a sordid past—a past that she had long put behind her. Sometimes the memories of her past would threaten to overtake her, creating inner turmoil to throw her off her game. It was at those times that she would contact BabyRuth or Serena, who would pray with and for her and share Bible scriptures to encourage her. Jasmine particularly liked the scriptures that stated, *"But this one thing I do, forgetting those things which are behind, and reaching forth unto those things which are before. I press toward the mark for the prize of the high calling of God in Christ Jesus."* Jasmine even had the scriptures engraved on parchment paper, framed, and hung on the bathroom wall next to the mirror. That way she could read them every day as she went through her morning routine.

Jasmine was on the right path now, regardless of her past. And she wasn't about to let no devil in hell hold her back. She felt as if she owed her very life to Serena, a woman who had reached out to her years ago, when Jasmine was teetering on the cliff of total despair. A woman who would have been justified in pushing Jasmine over the cliff, but who had instead showed mercy, grabbed her hands, and pulled her to safety. You see, Jasmine was the one who had seduced Serena's boyfriend, Derek, and infected him with HIV, a disease she had contracted due to years of child sexual abuse. Serena had shown Jasmine a level of forgiveness and compassion few humans possess. Jasmine had tried, without much success, to repay Serena for literally saving her life. But Serena was the kind of woman who gave so much to others and never expected, and rarely accepted, anything in return. So Jasmine instead showered Serena's daughter with all the love, attention, and affection she could muster.

Jasmine knew that she overindulged Dereka, but she couldn't help it. She had fallen deeply in love with her the first time she held the beautiful baby girl in her arms. As Jasmine held Dereka, she sang to her the song, "You Are My Sunshine, My Only Sunshine," while the baby stared at Jasmine with wide inquisitive eyes. That song had since become their song. When Dereka was about six or seven years old, Jasmine and Dereka would sing it to each other, or sometimes just pantomime the lyrics with gestures and facial expressions. When Dereka was in the first grade, she drew and colored a smiley-face sun and gave it to Jasmine for her birthday. To Jasmine it was the best present she had ever received, and one she would always keep and treasure.

Jasmine had never thought it was possible to love another human being as much as she loved Dereka. When she was a young girl herself, love had been as elusive and foreign to her as an ice storm in Jamaica. *But that was then, and this is now*, Jasmine thought, smiling to herself as she put the finishing touches on her makeup.

A knock on the door interrupted Jasmine's thoughts, notifying her that the driver from the limousine service had arrived to take her to the airport. Jasmine opened the door and directed the driver to collect her luggage. Before leaving, she checked her handbag to be sure she had the surprise birthday present for Dereka. Although she had already gotten Dereka a new phone, she wanted to get her something more special and personal for her thirteenth birthday. Something from the heart. So she got her a heart pendant necklace, and inside the heart she had engraved the simple phrase, "You are my Sunshine."

Calm before the Storm

BABYRUTH, KENYA, SERENA, and Dereka waited at the airport for Jasmine to arrive. Dereka was so excited she could hardly contain herself. She was the first to spot her Auntie Jazz, looking as fly as ever. Jasmine was strutting down the corridor of the airport as if she were a model on the runway, her wide-brimmed black hat cocked sassily to one side. She looked as though she had just stepped off the pages of *Vogue* magazine rather than a long transcontinental flight. "Auntie Jazz," Dereka screamed, running to her, hugging her tight, and knocking Jasmine's hat off her head in the process. A middle-age white man quickly scooped up the hat and handed it to Jasmine with a smile and a wink. Dereka laughed and said, "You go, Auntie Jazz. You still got it."

"And I'm planning to keep it," Jasmine responded, striking a sexy pose. "My goodness, Dereka, look how beautiful you are. And how you've grown," Jasmine said, looking admiringly at Dereka. "Just look at you. Junk in the trunk and the whole nine. I'm going to have to beat the boys off with a stick, and don't think I won't," Jasmine teased.

By this time the other three ladies had caught up with the happy twosome. They playfully referred to themselves as the Five Heartbeats, after one of BabyRuth's favorite movies and as a symbol of their love of one another. Jasmine hugged each of them tightly, and when she got to Serena, she hugged her just a moment longer than the others. This lady was very special to her. "It's so good to see you, girl. How are you feeling?"

"Thank God, I'm feeling fine. I have my moments. There are good days, and a few bad. But glory to God, mostly good days. How about yourself?" Serena asked.

"Same here," Jasmine responded knowingly. They both could not only sympathize but empathize with one another regarding the physical, mental, and emotional trials of being young women living with HIV. They both dealt with it in different ways.

Jasmine believed living with HIV meant doing just that—living. She dated regularly and was completely open and honest about her HIV status with anyone she dated. Not just because disclosure was the law in some states, but because it was the responsible thing to do. But although Jasmine dated frequently, she chose to be intimate with only a few men she trusted and who trusted her. She took great care in keeping herself and her partner safe by taking her antiretroviral medication, always using protection, and following other safety measures.

Serena, on the other hand, chose a completely different path of living with HIV. She focused on her spirituality, her work at the HIV awareness center, and raising her daughter to fulfill her life. She had plenty of friends, male and female, and enjoyed a variety of social activities. But for now, she chose male friendship over love, and abstinence over sexual intimacy. Serena believed she had already loved and lost the one great love of her life. There would never be another Derek. So she contented herself to find fulfillment in other ways, primarily in raising her daughter.

Dereka watched the two women closely. She knew that Serena and Jasmine had a special bond between them. Always had since she could remember. But she didn't yet know the tragic understory surrounding the relationship between Serena and Jasmine. Dereka surmised that their bond had something to do with her father. Serena had promised to tell her the whole story, including the good, the bad, and the ugly, when Dereka turned thirteen, which was only about a week away. Of course Dereka had heard rumors and tidbits about something awful that happened between her father, Serena, and Jasmine. Sordid rumors involving seduction, sex, and sickness. She knew her Auntie Jazz had done something terrible. But Dereka also knew that whatever it was wouldn't affect the way she felt about her aunt one bit. Dereka loved Auntie Jazz, and all her family members, unconditionally. The capacity to love fully and unequivocally was a trait that, she was told, she got from her father.

When the Jones family females finally made their way to the baggage claim area, it seemed like porters came out of the woodwork. They surrounded the group of attractive females, jockeying for position to be of assistance, and pretty much ignored some of the other, more homely passengers. The porters smiled, winked, gawked at, and flirted with the ladies, including BabyRuth, who at fifty-eight was a tall, attractive, regal woman who could hold her own with the best of them. The porters that couldn't get close enough to them contented themselves to just admire them from afar. The male passengers standing around were amused by the porters' behavior as they continued to circle the Jones females like a pack of hungry wolves. But some of the female passengers were highly annoyed. "Hey, can I get some help over here?" a middle-aged, heavyset black woman yelled while rolling her neck and placing her hands on her ample hips. One of the older porters, looking a bit embarrassed by the whole fiasco, quickly rushed to the aid of the offended woman.

On the ride home, Dereka brought Jasmine up to speed on the plans underway for her birthday party. Serena told Jasmine about Dereka's honor roll grades, school activities, awards, and other accolades. It was evident how proud she was of her daughter, because her face lit up like a Christmas tree while she spoke of her.

"Your father would be so proud of you, baby," Serena said to Dereka, placing her arms around Dereka's shoulders. "I wish he were here," she continued, her eyes misting up a bit. Silence followed Serena's statement as each of the ladies got lost in their own thoughts about the man who had been a central figure in their lives. For BabyRuth, he was the loving and supportive son; for Kenya, the caring, fun-loving, and protective brother; for Serena, the one great love of her life; for Jasmine, regretfully the object of her desire; and for Dereka, the father she never got to know, but loved and longed for in her heart.

Once home the ladies ordered a pizza and watched the Tyler Perry movie *Diary of a Mad Black Woman*. Dereka was in seventh heaven being surrounded by the circle of women who had loved, comforted, disciplined, taught, and cherished her all of her life. She watched them closely as they talked and laughed about the movie, empathizing with some of the characters and criticizing others. Dereka admired each of these women, but for different reasons. She admired Kenya for her intelligence, strong work ethic, and resiliency; BabyRuth for her love of God and family, strength, and unyielding faith; Serena for her sensitivity, sweet spirit, and compassion for others; and Jasmine for her street smarts, business savvy, sass, and perseverance. Each of these women had taken time over the years to pass on to Dereka the best in them. And their lessons would serve her well in the difficult times ahead.

On the Prowl

LUTHER CURTIS, AKA Memphis, was back in the Washington, DC, area after almost thirteen years on the run from local authorities. Over the years, he had moved from city to city, living in Atlanta, Houston, Miami, and Detroit, using a different alias in each city. He knew it was risky to be back in the DC area, but he had to come. He had a score to settle that was long overdue, and it was time to settle it once and for all.

Memphis followed and closely watched a tight-knit group of five female shoppers make their leisurely way through the shops at Tysons Galleria, an upscale shopping mall in McLean, Virginia. His blood boiled as he watched the group go happily along their merry way. They were laughing and talking, stopping at various stores, and coming out carrying shopping bags filled with, no doubt, expensive clothing, cosmetics, and who knows what else. Memphis knew this group well, even down to the cutesy nickname they used to describe themselves. He'd kept close tabs on them over the years, waiting on the right time to strike. And now that the heat from the police had died down, he was ready to exact his sweet revenge. Of course, Memphis could have had a couple of his minions handle this situation for him. But this was something he needed to handle himself. This was personal.

Memphis trailed behind the group closely, but not too close as to arouse suspicion. He moved slowly but with purpose, like a leopard stalking its prey. He followed the gleeful group of five females to the food court area. *Five heartbeats my ass*, Memphis thought sarcastically as he took a seat on the upper level, where he could look down and easily spy on his prey without being noticed. As Memphis watched them, he took time to focus on each one closely, mentally scrolling through his list of their attributes, characteristics, likes, and fears. Yes, he had taken the time to find out over the years exactly who they were and what made them tick, or not tick. And he would use this information to destroy them.

First and foremost, there was Ruth Jones, aka BabyRuth. She was the family matriarch, the backbone of the family. The holy roller who seemingly had a direct line to God. Yes, BabyRuth was the strong one, who could pull her family through any trial or hardship. The powerhouse, the rock of the family, the strong believer that faith in God could move any mountain. *Well, we'll see how that works out for her, considering what I have in store for her and her precious loved ones*, Memphis thought to himself with a slight smile on his face. He doubted that even God himself would be able to deflect the agony he was about to rain down upon the Jones family. Memphis knew that BabyRuth had lost her only son to suicide years ago and that her husband had died from cancer. He figured that one of her greatest fears would be to lose another one of her beloved family members.

Memphis shifted his attention to Serena, the former girlfriend of the dead son, and the mother of the first and only grandchild in the family. Serena, the do-gooder. The kind, gentle, loving, and forgiving spirit. The one who had forgiven and even embraced the hussy Jasmine, who had transmitted HIV to her boyfriend and, by doing so, indirectly infected Serena herself with the virus. *But what did Serena do to Jasmine?* Memphis thought ironically. *She actually forgave the tramp and put a Bible in the whore's hands, while she should have put a bullet in her head like she deserved. What a fool*, Memphis mused, shaking his head in disbelief. But Memphis didn't really have anything against Serena. She just happened to get hooked up with the wrong family. And if something happened to her, he would just consider it to be collateral damage. Simply necessary in the bigger scheme of things.

And then there was Kenya, the true target of his revenge. Kenya was the reason his son was currently sitting in a prison cell. Because of her, Kevin had been charged with child pornography, extortion, and a number of other charges. Because of her, his son was serving a twenty- to thirty-year prison term in a Virginia penitentiary. Memphis wasn't about to let that go.

And on top of all that, the little wench had also produced evidence against Memphis regarding his drug dealing in a plea bargain deal to save her own neck. So not only had Kenya messed with his blood, his only son Kevin, but she had also made the grave mistake of messing with his money. Washington, DC had been one of his most prosperous areas for drug dealing and a lot of his other illegal activities. Memphis had been forced to shut down his DC operation and flee the area. All that money, lost. And it was all because of Kenya.

Memphis's hatred ran hot as he stared at Kenya coldly through narrowed eyes. He could hardly contain himself from pulling out his Glock 41 firearm and ending her life right then and there. But that would be too merciful, and mercy was something Memphis was in short supply of. Very short. His nostrils flared with rage as he stared down at Kenya laughing and talking as if she didn't have a care in the world. She would pay for her sins. And then some.

And lastly there was Dereka. The beautiful golden child of the family. The daughter, granddaughter, and niece they all doted on, loved, adored, and cherished. Memphis watched as they showered the young girl with affection and attention, shepherding her like she was the prime sheep in a herd. It was clear that Dereka was the center of their world. She was their heart. So that's where Memphis would strike. He would rip out their heart because he knew that once you ripped out the heart, the rest of the body could not survive. *The Five Heartbeats are about to become the Five Deadbeats*, Memphis thought, amusing himself.

He watched Kenya lean in and whisper something to the rest of the clan. It must have been amusing because they all exploded in laugher, leaning back in their chairs, waving their hands around, and just having the time of their lives. Kenya retrieved her cell phone and took selfies of the group, all smiling brightly for the camera as she snapped away. The sight sickened him. "Enjoy yourselves for now, bitches," Memphis mumbled under his breath. "Your real good thing is about to come to an end." And with that, he got up and headed for the nearest exit.

Take Care of My Child

IT WAS FRIDAY evening, the day before Dereka's birthday and big party. Serena and Dereka were at their favorite bakery in Old Town Alexandria to pick up her birthday cake. The bakery was one of a few black-owned businesses in Old Town. The Jones family made it their practice to patronize African American–owned businesses as much as possible. The owner and head baker, a hefty women in her early sixties named Lorraine, greeted them in her usual boisterous and fun-loving manner.

"How you doing today, sugar?" Lorraine said to Serena, giving her a big bear hug. "And who is the lovely young lady, as if I didn't know? Dereka, you are getting prettier by the minute. And so big. I remember when your mama first started bringing you here. You were about knee high to a grasshopper, and just as cute as a bumblebee. Now look at you. Just as pretty as a picture. You know, I got a grandson about your age. I want you to meet him. He would love to have a pretty thing like you on his arm. You got a boyfriend? Well, of course you do." Lorraine continued her barrage of words, going on and on and on. Lorraine didn't talk with you; she talked at you. Most of the time you couldn't get a word in edgewise. Serena and Dereka mainly just smiled and nodded at the appropriate times.

When Lorraine finally had to pause for air, Serena quickly asked, "Is the cake ready, Ms. Lorraine?"

"Oh sure, sugar, sure. I'll be right back," Lorraine said as she walked down the hall towards a back room, continually talking as she went. While they waited for Lorraine to return, Serena and Dereka browsed through the store to see what other items they could find for the party. Dereka picked out a bunch of purple and gold balloons with "Happy 13th Birthday" written on them. Dereka loved the color purple, and even the movie *The Color Purple* was one of her all-time favorites.

A few minutes later, Lorraine returned with a beautiful double-layered chocolate cake, with purple and white icing and *Happy Birthday Dereka* written on top. "Here you go, sweetie. And happy birthday to you. I got a feeling tomorrow is going to be a very special day for you, sweetie," Lorraine said, beaming at Dereka as she placed the cake on the counter.

"Thanks, Ms. Lorraine," Dereka exclaimed, her eyes lighting up as she looked at her cake.

After Serena paid for the items, Serena and Dereka walked arm in arm across the large parking lot toward their car, carrying the cake and balloons. Although there were several cars in the lot, one in particular caught Serena's attention. A black sedan with tinted windows was parked a couple of spaces from her vehicle. And two young men, one black and one white, were standing near the rear of the car, talking between themselves. Serena didn't know why, but she felt a sinking feeling in her stomach, and the hair on her arms stood up. The men appeared to be watching them without wanting to appear to be watching. Serena instinctively moved to the other side of Dereka in order to position her own body between Dereka and the two young men. As they passed by, Serena watched them out of the corner of her eyes, and when she and Dereka got to the car, she glanced over her shoulder to see whether the men were up to no good. But to her relief, they were talking to each other and didn't seem to be paying them any attention at all. Serena relaxed a bit and told Dereka, "Hold this, baby, while I get my keys." She handed the cake to Dereka, retrieved the keys from her purse, and turned to open the passenger-side door for Dereka.

Then it happened. In a flash both men were upon them. One man hit Serena hard on the side of her face, knocking her backward into the car. Serena temporarily blacked out, and her body slid off the car and onto the ground. The other man grabbed Dereka and held a white cloth soaked with chloroform over her nose and mouth. Dereka's eyes widened in shock as she struggled momentarily to get free before her body went limp. When Serena came to a few seconds later, she saw the two men placing Dereka's limp body into the trunk of their car. Motherly love and adrenaline propelled Serena to her feet, and she ran towards the men on wobbly legs screaming, "Noooooooo. Stop! Please don't take my daughter. Pleaseeeee don't take my baby." Then the white man took out a gun with a long silencer on it, pointed it at Serena's chest, and fired one shot. The force of the bullet knocked her backward, and she fell to the ground. She tried to call Dereka's name as she heard the car drive away, but she could only make gurgling sounds as her lungs slowly filled with blood.

As Serena lay on the ground looking up at the sky, she prayed within her heart, "Father, please take care of my child. Please take care of my little Boogie Boo. In your hands I place my baby. Thank you, Lord." And as she lay on her back, gasping for air, she saw one of Dereka's birthday balloons floating away in the sky. That balloon was one of the last things she knew her daughter had held in her hands—one of the last things Dereka had touched. So Serena kept her eyes on that sole balloon until the darkness overtook her. And she was gone.

As Cold as They Come

MEMPHIS WATCHED THE entire scenario through the tinted glass in the backseat of the black sedan. It had taken a little over two minutes flat to go down. He'd gotten a couple of his top hired hands to carry out the kidnapping. These guys were real pros and could generally pull off the most complicated and intricate jobs without a hitch. And although killing Serena was not something he had planned for, it was no major hiccup as far as Memphis was concerned. From what he could see, his boys had no choice. Serena was causing quite a ruckus trying to save her precious daughter. So she had become collateral damage.

The shooter, a guy named Marcus, turned around from the passenger seat to talk to Memphis. "Sorry I had to shoot her, man. I hit her so hard she should have been out for a few minutes. I was surprised to see her coming after us. Man, that bitch could really take a punch," Marcus said, rubbing his knuckles.

"You did what you had to do," Memphis stated in a matter-of-fact tone. "No harm, no foul."

Memphis was as coldhearted as they come. He grew up in the rough LeMoyne-Owen housing project in Memphis, Tennessee. His father was the neighborhood drunk, and his mother the neighborhood whore. So Memphis was left to fend for himself the majority of his childhood. He got started in the drug business at the age of nine. He would run drugs for some of the older gangbangers in the neighborhood, mainly to have money for the basic necessities of life, such as food and clothing. As a young boy, he sold drugs in parks, in schools, out of his home and friends' houses, and even at the local YMCA. He was a good street student. He slowly and methodically learned the culture of the drug trade and rose quickly through the ranks.

He was given the name Memphis by a ruthless drug dealer called Slice, who had taken the young boy under his wing, serving as a wheeling and dealing street-thug mentor and role model of sorts. Slice got his own nickname because he could slice a person's throat in a split second, and the person never saw it coming. No one could figure out how or what Slice used to cut someone, because no one ever saw any weapon in his hand. It was like he was a magician or something. Abracadabra—you're dead. As a young boy, Memphis witnessed Slice cut a homeless brother's throat just for asking for loose change. When Memphis was nineteen, Slice was gunned down in a drug deal gone bad. Memphis stepped into his shoes and quickly expanded the business into surrounding areas in Arkansas and Mississippi. And since he was Slice's protégé, he automatically gained a reputation for being ruthless, which he was, and he worked hard to maintain it.

Memphis never wanted a family, due to his strong hatred and disrespect for his own father and mother. They were both dead now, and Memphis had not even attended their funerals. He never understood how two people could bring another person into the world and totally neglect that person. His parents couldn't have cared less whether he lived or died. And he swore to himself that he would not bring a child into the world to experience the same loveless upbringing as he had.

Because Memphis was extremely good looking, he always had plenty of women flaunting themselves in front of him and vying for his attention. All kinds of women were attracted to him due to his chiseled, handsome face, lean, muscular physique, and charismatic, bad-boy charm. But Memphis had little respect for women, and believed most of them were heartless whores like his mama. His only uses for females were for his sexual pleasures and for making him money. He'd never intended to have a child but had made a careless mistake with a lady named Paulette, who lied to him about her ability to conceive. So, needless to say, he was furious when she showed up one day out of the blue, six months pregnant. She'd intentionally waited until it was too late to have an abortion. Having Memphis's baby was Paulette's lame attempt to hold on to him. Memphis was more upset with himself than with her. His mentor, Slice, had always told him, "Never trust a ho."

So Memphis told her to go ahead and have the baby. But she'd be completely on her own. He made it perfectly clear, in so many choice words, that he wanted nothing to do with her or the bastard she was carrying. And he meant it. Until one day he was in a restaurant and Paulette strolled up to him with the baby in her arms. "Here, look at your child. This is your child, Memphis. Look at him," she yelled. Memphis got up to leave, but Paulette blocked his path. "What kind of a man are you? Huh? What kind of man are you? You won't even look at your own son." Memphis started to slap her around for disrespecting him, but she did have a baby in her arms. Paulette proceeded to stick the baby boy right up in Memphis's face, so he had to look at him. The baby was about four months by this time, and Memphis noticed that the baby did look a lot like him. When Memphis reluctantly touched the small baby's hand, the baby grabbed hold of Memphis's little finger and wouldn't let go. Memphis tried to pull his finger away, but the little rascal held on tight. Memphis pulled harder, but the baby had quite a grip. It was as if the small baby boy was saying, "You may not want me, but I want you. And I'm not letting go."

And right then, the bond between father and son was created. "His name is Kevin Curtis," Paulette said, smiling down at her baby. From then on Memphis started supporting his son financially and spending quality time with him. He would even take the baby on some weekends, hiring a babysitter to do all the feeding, changing diapers, and such. As his son got older, Memphis wanted Kevin to live with him full time. He had thought Paulette would put up a fight about giving up her son, but found out she was more than willing to hand him over to Memphis—that is, for the right price. So when Kevin was five years old, Memphis took him in full time. He hired a middle-age Hispanic woman as a full-time live-in housekeeper and care provider for his son. She was an illegal immigrant from Mexico working to send money home to her family. She spoke a little broken English, had a sunny disposition, and loved taking care of his son.

Kevin was the only somebody in the world that Memphis gave a damn about. He started to prime Kevin at an early age, teaching him the culture of the streets and drug trade. He made sure Kevin got a college education so he'd be able to match wits with the best of them. Kevin decided to major in education and work in the school system, knowing it would be a great place to run some schemes and scams on the many vulnerable, naïve young girls. After Kevin spent a few years in the school system, Memphis had planned to bring him into the drug business full time.

But that was all ruined thanks to Kenya, who just couldn't keep her big mouth shut, Memphis reflected as he cruised along in the back-seat of the sedan. Kevin had told Kenya years ago that she would be sorry if she snitched on him. And now that Memphis had Dereka, he knew that she finally would be.

Memphis mentally calculated what would likely soon happen back at the Jones family residence. Someone from the bakery, or perhaps a passerby, would discover Serena's body and call 911 to summon the police and ambulance personnel. Then Kenya and the rest of the chummy females would get the news of what had gone down in the bakery parking lot. Memphis tried to visualize the outright horror, shock, bewilderment, and despair that they would experience. His only regret was that he wouldn't be there to see it. He was, plain and simple, as cold as they come.

The Call from Hell

BACK AT THE house, BabyRuth, Kenya, and Jasmine were in the kitchen prepping and cooking a few dishes for Dereka's birthday party the next day. BabyRuth was marinating chicken that she planned to grill out on the patio. Thankfully, the fall weather was looking to be sunny and cool, just fine for some outdoor grilling. Serena was peeling potatoes to make potato salad, and Jasmine, being no cook, was sitting at the kitchen table making a "Happy Birthday, Dereka" sign to hang in the big family room.

"What about games for the party?" BabyRuth asked.

"No, Mama. Kids Dereka's age don't want to play no games. They want to dance and have fun. They may play some video games," Kenya responded.

"What was you all's favorite childhood game?" Jasmine asked.

"Mine was hide-'n'-go-seek. We would play that for hours," BabyRuth answered, smiling.

"I loved to play May I. Y'all remember that?" Kenya asked.

"Yeah, I remember. But I liked to play doctor with the boy down the street. Because, as the doctor, you got to examine things," Jasmine said with a devilish glint in her eyes.

"Ooooh, you nasty, girl," Kenya admonished as the three of them burst into laughter.

BabyRuth tuned the radio to Magic 102.3, an old-school R&B station, and they began to sing along with some of the oldie-but-goodie classic songs by the Temptations, the Four Tops, Mary Wells, and Smokey Robinson. BabyRuth and Kenya, both wonderful singers, took turns singing the lead, while Jasmine contented herself to sing backup. During the long musical intervals, traditionally found in the middle of most old-school R&B classics, BabyRuth demonstrated some of the dances she grew up doing, like the funky chicken, four corners, jerk, watusi, and philly dog. Jasmine and Kenya tried to imitate the dances but couldn't quite get the hang of it. "That's not the way you do it," BabyRuth said to the new-schoolers. "You got to do it like this, children. Put some more hip action into it," BabyRuth instructed while she danced in the middle of the kitchen floor, putting on a grand spectacle for Kenya and Jasmine. They clapped and cheered her on, which only encouraged BabyRuth to really show off.

When the song ended, BabyRuth was winded and had worked up a little sweat. She took a gracious bow, grabbed a paper towel to wipe her forehead, and sat on a kitchen stool. "Mercy me. I'm too old for all this. But back in the day, DJ and I would dance all night long."

"Yeah, Mama, I remember. And I also remember when Derek and I were kids, y'all used to make us come into the living room and dance for company. We had to demonstrate all the latest dances," Kenya said, smiling fondly at the memory.

"Dance for company? You're kidding," Jasmine said, laughing.

"No, I'm not. And Uncle Isaac would give us both two dollars after we finished dancing, and we'd go straight to the corner store to buy candy. Those were wonderful times, weren't they, Mama?" Kenya asked.

"Yes, they sure were, baby," BabyRuth responded. "Uncle Isaac and Aunt Joyce got such a kick out of seeing you all dance. I think it's because their own son, Trevor, couldn't dance a lick. He always looked as though he was having an epileptic seizure or something when he tried to dance," BabyRuth said, laughing at the image.

"And Derek and I would give him a quarter to do the James Brown to that song, 'I Feel Good.' Once I laughed at him so hard I peed on myself," Kenya chimed in.

"Y'all know y'all was wrong for that," Jasmine chided, laughing in spite of herself at the image of Trevor doing the James Brown.

Jasmine looked at her watch and noticed it was half past four. "What time are Dereka and Serena supposed to be back with the cake? I thought they'd be back by now."

"Probably got caught in traffic. You know how crazy that Old Town traffic can be sometimes," Kenya responded.

"Want to see the surprise birthday present I got for Dereka?" Jasmine asked with a sly smile on her face. "She thinks the phone is the only gift from me, but I just had to get her something special for her thirteenth birthday," Jasmine said, digging in her handbag for the gift. She pulled out a small jewelry box and opened it. BabyRuth and Kenya gasped at the beautiful diamond heart pendant nestled in the box.

"It's beautiful," BabyRuth said, picking it up to look at it closely.

"Open the heart and read the inscription," Jasmine said with excitement in her voice.

BabyRuth opened it and read the inscription out loud. "You are my Sunshine. Love, Auntie Jazz."

"She's going to love it," Kenya said, beaming at Jasmine. "And since we are sharing, I want to show you all what I got Dereka." Kenya went to the closet and retrieved a box she had hidden in a secret place to keep Dereka from finding it. She opened the box and pulled out a blue-and-orange jersey with the number 42 on the front and D. Jones on the back. BabyRuth knew right away what it was.

"That's Derek's old Morgan State football jersey, isn't it? The one he had hanging on his wall," BabyRuth said in amazement as she gazed at the jersey.

"Yes, it is," Kenya confirmed. "I took it to my tailor and had her make it into a basketball jersey for Dereka that she can wear to practice. I wanted her to be able to wear the same jersey her father wore when he was a star running back at Morgan State. I thought it would make her feel closer to him," Kenya stated.

"What a thoughtful thing to do," BabyRuth said with tears in her eyes. "She's going to be thrilled. I can't wait to see it on her."

Just then the phone rang. "I bet that's Serena calling to let us know she's running late," BabyRuth said as she picked up the phone.

"Hello." She listened to the voice on the phone with a confused expression on her face. "Lorraine, is that you? Slow down, honey, I can't understand what you're saying," BabyRuth stated. Both Kenya and Jasmine stopped what they were doing and watched BabyRuth closely as she held the phone tightly to her ear, listening intently. "Oh my God! Oh my God! Something's happened to Serena and Dereka," BabyRuth shouted with complete horror etched on her face.

"What's happened? What, Mama?" Kenya asked in a state of near panic.

"I don't know. I can't understand what Lorraine is saying. She's crying, and I can't understand her."

Kenya took the phone from her mother. "Ms. Lorraine, this is Kenya. What's wrong? Has something happened to Dereka and Serena? Please, please, Ms. Lorraine, calm down and tell me what's happened." After a few moments, Lorraine managed to get out a few words.

"Something awful happened, baby. Just awful. Come as soon as you can. Lord Jesus, Lord Jesus," Ms. Lorraine sobbed.

Kenya dropped the phone and stared at BabyRuth and Jasmine in complete shock. Jasmine went to her and shook her slightly. "Kenya, what's wrong?" she asked tentatively, as if she was afraid to hear what Kenya would say.

"I don't know. But it's bad. We need to get down there now," Kenya responded, her eyes darting around wildly. The three ladies scrambled about in a state of panic, hardly able to function coherently. Jasmine, seeing that neither Kenya nor BabyRuth was in a condition to drive, took Kenya's car keys from her, feeling that she was in the best frame of mind to at least make it to the bakery. *They may need our help*, Jasmine thought frantically to herself. *We've got to get to them.* The thought of helping Serena and Dereka was the only thing that kept Jasmine from being totally consumed with fear and dread.

They rode to the bakery in silence, each too fearful to speak—too afraid to even think of what could have possibly happened. BabyRuth and Kenya huddled together in the backseat of the SUV, shivering and shaking like two lost, frightened kittens. BabyRuth was praying, "Lord, please let everything be all right. We need you, Lord. We need you." Jasmine drove as fast as she could, her hands tightly gripping the steering wheel. When they got close to the bakery, they could see the blinking lights of multiple police cars and at least one ambulance in the parking lot. "Oh, my Lord," BabyRuth murmured. She sensed in her spirit that something terrible had happened.

Not the Body

JASMINE PULLED ABRUPTLY into the parking lot, and the three women stumbled out of the car like zombies. They held on to each other as they walked toward the crowd gathered at the scene, none having the strength to walk on her own. As they moved closer, they saw yellow tape around Serena's vehicle. Two police officers stood next to the vehicle, looking down at something on the ground. The female detective noticed the tight-knit group of women approaching and immediately went to them. She instinctively knew, from years of experience on crime scenes, that they were close family members or friends of the victims. And one look at their distraught faces was enough to let her know that this would be one of the toughest and most heartbreaking cases ever. This case involved not only the death of a young woman but also a missing child.

"Good evening, ladies. I'm Detective Joan Davis with the Alexandria Police Department," she said, showing them her badge. "Are you family members of Ms. Serena Dixon-Jones and Dereka Jones?" she asked, standing in front of them in an attempt to prevent them from seeing the atrocious crime scene ahead.

"Yes, yes, we are. Serena's my daughter, and Dereka is my granddaughter," BabyRuth answered, trying to look around the detective for some sign of Serena and Dereka.

"Where are they? What's going on?" Kenya asked, still clinging tightly to BabyRuth and Jasmine for support. Detective Davis saw the desperation in their eyes and heard it in their voices. She knew they were inwardly pleading with her to tell them that their family members were fine. Perhaps hurt or harmed in an accident or something, but at least okay. And as much as she hated to, Detective Davis knew she had to tell them the dreadful truth right away. She swallowed hard and took a deep breath to prepare herself to deliver the horrific news.

"I'm sorry to inform you that Ms. Dixon-Jones was shot in the chest and has died from her wound. We do not currently know where Dereka Jones is, but we have issued an Amber Alert for her. A couple of witnesses said that she may have been taken by two men in a black sedan. I'm so sorry," Detective Davis concluded.

For a moment none of the ladies responded. It was as if neither their brains nor their hearts could decipher what the detective had just said. It wasn't possible; it just couldn't be. They stared at each other with dumbfounded expressions. For a long moment no one spoke, because they couldn't speak.

"No, no, please. Pleaseeeeeeeeee," Kenya said, looking to her mother to say that everything was all right. To somehow take back the horrible words the detective had just uttered.

"Pleaseeeee just take us to them. That's all we want. Please, please," Jasmine begged with a pitiful expression on her face. Kenya and Jasmine looked desperately at BabyRuth for support.

"They're okay," BabyRuth said, tightening her arms around Kenya and Jasmine. "They're okay. Don't worry, they're okay," she repeated in a complete state of denial as she started to move them forward toward Serena's car. "We just need to get to them, that's all," BabyRuth said as she continued to propel them forward. "Serena! Dereka! We're here," BabyRuth called out as they inched closer to Serena's car. But the sight before them stopped them in their tracks. They saw a body lying on the ground, covered with a white cloth. The only part of the body visible was the feet, with one shoe on and the other shoe off. They knew right away that they were Serena's feet. Next to her was a smashed birthday cake, with the partial words "Happy Birth" still intact. It was Dereka's birthday cake.

And the realization that it was Serena lying on the hard parking lot pavement covered by a white cloth, and that Dereka was missing, struck them like a lightning bolt. They tumbled to the ground, none having the strength any longer to support the others. Grief and shock consumed them. BabyRuth began to wail and cry out hysterically, "Oh God, oh God," over and over again as she lay on her back, her arms thrashing about as if she was trying desperately to reach out and pull her loved ones to her. Kenya lay face down on the pavement, her pain so great that she became physically ill. Her body started to convulse, and she began to heave violently, coughing and choking on her own vomit. Jasmine coiled her body into a tight ball—a ball so tight it appeared as if she was trying to disappear into herself in order to avoid the pain. She was whimpering as she continued to coil her body tighter and tighter, like a snake coils its body when it encounters danger. Their agony was extremely difficult to watch, even for some of the most seasoned cops and medical staff. Their pain was like a magnetic force encircling and pulling those around them into its heavy, dark realm.

Lorraine was overcome anew with sorrow as she watched her friends and patrons of over twenty years suffer from such a debilitating blow. Even a few of the bystanders were affected, rubbing their eyes, shaking their heads, and placing their hands over their own hearts. One older black woman in the crowd extended one hand towards the ladies and prayed, "Help 'em, Jesus. Help 'em, Lord." Detective Davis, seeing the fragile state of the women, summoned the medical staff to attend to them. As she bent over the ladies, trying to comfort them, she felt a single tear start a slow but steady descent down the side of her own face. She quickly brushed it away so that the other police at the scene wouldn't see it. Police are supposed to remain aloof and emotionally detached during such situations. And she usually did, but this was different. This was unlike anything she had experienced before in all her years on the Alexandria police force.

BabyRuth managed to get on her knees and began to crawl to Serena. One of the EMTs tried to stop her, saying, "Miss, I don't think you should see her like this."

"I have to," BabyRuth said as she continued to crawl forward. "I have to be with her. Please let me be with her. She needs me," BabyRuth pleaded, looking to Detective Davis for support.

The detective nodded to the EMT that it was okay. She got on her knees next to BabyRuth and said, "Ms. Jones, I can only let you see her for a moment. But I can't allow you to touch her, because the body has to be processed for evidence. We have to preserve the body until the medical examiner completes an examination. Do you understand?" Detective Davis asked. BabyRuth looked confused.

"The body? The body? But that's not the body, that's Serena. Please don't refer to her like that."

"Yes, of course. I'm sorry," Detective Davis said sincerely, looking at BabyRuth with sympathy. She and a police officer helped BabyRuth to her feet and escorted her to where Serena was lying covered by the white cloth. "Are you sure you want to see her like this?" Detective Davis asked. BabyRuth slowly nodded her head yes. The police officer lifted one corner of the cloth to reveal Serena's face. BabyRuth gasped loudly and automatically reached for Serena, wanting to hold her, but she was held back by the officer.

As BabyRuth stood over Serena, sobbing and gazing down at her beautiful face, her one comfort was that Serena looked peaceful, as if she were merely sleeping and dreaming of a happy time and place. And BabyRuth thought of the scripture that says, *"To be absent from the body, is to be present with the Lord."*

"We love you, baby. You rest peaceful now. And don't you worry about a thing. We'll get Dereka back. So help me God, we'll get her back. Don't you worry. You just rest, sweetie. Until we meet again." And then BabyRuth's legs gave way underneath her as she collapsed from grief and exhaustion. She was placed on a gurney and transported by ambulance to the hospital, along with Kenya and Jasmine.

The Devil is in the Details

WHILE MEMPHIS AND his posse cruised down the GW parkway, he went over the details of his plan to transport Dereka to the living hell where he planned for her to spend the rest of her life. Their first stop would be in southeast DC to do a quick vehicle change. He planned to change vehicles at least three times during the long drive to South Florida, stopping only at rural rest stops or gas stations as needed along the way. In Florida Dereka would be taken by small aircraft to her final destination. Life as she knew it would be over. There she would be sold into sex slavery. She'd be property, not a person, and at the whim of any pervert with the money to pay for her goods.

Revenge is sweet. Now Kenya's niece will suffer the same fate that I had planned for Kenya to suffer years ago. That is, before she got away from me, Memphis thought. Back then he had just started to dabble in the lucrative business of human trafficking, and in particular, child sex trafficking. But if he had known then what he knew now about how much money was to be had, he would have jumped in with both feet long ago. Over the years Memphis had taken the time to learn the intricacies and complexities of the sex-slave trade, and now he was fully entrenched and well connected with organizations both in the United States and abroad. He had sex houses in several major cities, including Chicago, Atlanta, New York, and New Orleans, and was considering expanding across the border into Mexico.

Memphis thought he had seen it all until he visited a couple of sex-slave houses in Mexico several years ago. Now there he had seen some rough sh*t, the likes of which even he'd never seen before. It made Memphis wonder why people believed in God, because there was no way a holy God in heaven could turn a blind eye to the type of bullsh*t that went down in those places. That's why Memphis thought people who believed in God were fools, plain and simple.

Memphis smiled to himself, knowing that he'd hit the jackpot with Dereka as far as money was concerned. A young, attractive, African American female like Dereka would bring in big bucks. Generally those who fell prey to the sex-slave trade were prostitutes, runaways, junkies, homeless vagrants, or others that Memphis considered riffraff, whom he either snatched off the streets or coerced into the business with empty promises of a better life. Someone with Dereka's looks and pedigree was rare in the grimy world of human trafficking. Back in the slavery days, Dereka would have been considered prime stock for the sexual pleasures of the slave master. She would no doubt have been one of the house slaves, serving tea and crumpets to the mistress during the day and serving up something altogether different to the master during the night, while the less appealing wenches tolled in the hot sun in the fields alongside the Mandingos.

With proper planning Memphis had scored the big payback with Dereka, and he was about to get seriously paid. His revenge plot was finally becoming a reality. He had meticulously planned every detail himself, not daring to trust anyone with such an important mission. He knew that tomorrow was Dereka's birthday and that the Jones family often patronized the black-owned bakery in Old Town. He bribed a bakery employee to provide him certain information, including exactly what time Dereka's cake was to be picked up. What Memphis learned over the years was that money talked, and for the right amount of money, you could get practically any information you wanted. Of course, the bakery employee had no idea what Memphis needed the information for. And for the money he was paid, he didn't seem to care. But just in case, Memphis had a backup plan to ensure the employee would keep his mouth shut. He deployed one of his minions to speak with the employee and let him know that if he said anything, anything at all, he'd be implicated in the kidnapping scheme himself or, worse, end up floating face down in the Potomac River. Memphis doubted that the employee would talk, but he'd gotten a little extra insurance to make sure that he kept his silence. Memphis planned everything, right down to the nitty-gritty. Because, as the saying goes, the devil is in the details.

• • •

When the black sedan pulled into a garage in southeast DC, Memphis and the others could hear the young girl screaming and thrashing about in the trunk. He glanced at his watch. They were right on time to switch vehicles. A white minivan with rental tags was parked in the garage. They would use the van for the next few hundred miles before switching again. "Get her ready," Memphis directed his men. One of them grabbed a black leather bag, and they both exited the vehicle. When they popped the trunk open, Dereka was temporarily blinded by the bright light flooding in from a bare overhead light bulb. She placed her hands over her eyes to shield them while her eyes adjusted. Slowly the images of the two men came into focus. Frightened, Dereka scooted backward into the trunk as far as she could. When the men reached for her, she hit and kicked at their hands, striking one of the men square on. He yelled, "Son of a—"

"Leave me alone," Dereka screamed as she continued to hit and kick at them. "Get away from me! Where's my mama?" After some effort the men were able to grab hold of Dereka's arms and legs. They roughly pulled her out of the trunk and dropped her on the hard concrete floor. One of them sat on her legs to restrain her, unzipped the black bag, and took out some thick gray tape and rope. They proceeded to tie Dereka's arms and legs together. "What are you doing? Where's my mama?" Dereka cried out, trying desperately to free herself.

"Shut the f*ck up!" the black man yelled. He then placed a wide piece of tape across Dereka's mouth.

Dereka continued to thrash around. Then she heard the car door open and close and heard heavy footsteps coming her way. Dread crept up her spine as she realized there was someone else there. The first thing she saw was a pair of high-polished men's shoes. Her eyes slowly moved upward, taking in black dress slacks, a black leather blazer with a gray sweater underneath, and finally the face of a black man with dark shades on. He was tall—at least he looked tall from Dereka's standpoint on the floor. The man bent down on one knee towards Dereka and removed his shades. He had smooth dark-chocolate-colored skin, piercing jet-black eyes, a neatly trimmed salt-and-pepper mustache and goatee, heavy eyebrows, and full lips. To Dereka, he looked to be about her Grandma Ruth's age, which would place him in his late fifties. He smiled at her, revealing perfect, sparkling white teeth. Dereka could even smell his breath, which was minty fresh.

He's smiling at me, Dereka thought. *Maybe he's here to help me.* She stared at the tall, dark, handsome man and waited anxiously for him to say something.

"Hello, Dereka. I'm Memphis. It's nice to meet you. I've been waiting for this moment for quite some time," Memphis said in his deep baritone voice.

Dereka looked perplexed. *He knows me? What does he mean, 'waiting for this moment'?* she thought. *Who is this man, and why would he be waiting to meet me?*

"I see you're confused," Memphis stated. "And I guess I owe you an explanation. Well, all of this has to do with your Aunt Kenya. You see, me and your Aunt Kenya go back a ways. And it's because of your Aunt Kenya that my son is in a prison cell right now. And because of your dear Aunt Kenya, I'm wanted by the police. And even worse, because of your sweet, kind Aunt Kenya, I've lost a lot of money. A whole lot," he restated for emphasis.

Memphis stood up and dusted off his pants leg before continuing. "So you see, your Aunt Kenya owes me a great debt. And I had planned for her to pay that debt years ago, but she got away. My mistake. I should have been more careful. But I've got you now. And you won't get away. You'll pay for your aunt's sins and then some. And by your pain and suffering, your whole family will suffer. And it's all because of your dear Aunt Kenya. So you can thank her for ruining your life." Memphis paused and looked at Dereka with a pensive expression on his face. "But wait a minute. You won't be able to. So I guess I'll have to do that for you," he added with a soft chuckle. He looked down at her with a sly smile. "Hey, I know it's not fair that you should have to pay for something you didn't do. But life's not fair, as you will soon find out, my dear."

Memphis turned to his two employees and said, "Finish up here. We need to move." He took one last menacing look at Dereka before getting into the van. One of the men removed a needle and a small bottle filled with clear liquid from the black bag. While he filled the needle with the clear liquid, the other man grabbed Dereka by her right shoulder. When she realized they intended to stick her with the needle, she tried to struggle free, making loud squealing sounds through her tape-covered mouth. Dereka was horrified of needles and hated even the small ones used for flu shots and school immunizations. And the needle these men had was huge compared to those.

"Hold her still, man," the one with the needle said. The other man placed his full weight against Dereka's body and bent one of her arms back as far as he could. The pain was so excruciating Dereka had to lie still. She felt something being tied tightly around her upper arm, and then felt a sharp pierce as the needle was roughly jabbed into her arm. Dereka felt a burning sensation as the fluid flowed into her body. She quickly drifted off into sedated darkness.

Let Me Hold You

DETECTIVE DAVIS LEFT the scene of the crime around ten thirty. She was dog tired as she drove home, and emotionally drained after spending hours at the scene interviewing witnesses, speaking with the medical examiner and forensic investigator, and searching the parking lot for evidence. Detective Davis also spoke briefly with a few grief-stricken family members, who, having heard about the tragedy, rushed to the scene. One of the family members, BabyRuth's brother Isaac, provided her with a recent photo of Dereka. Detective Davis had photos and identification retrieved from Serena's and Dereka's handbags and cell phones, left at the scene. She knew time was of the essence, and they had the best chance of finding Dereka within twenty-four to forty-eight hours after her abduction. After that time, the trail generally went cold, sometimes for years, other times forever. She planned to follow up with the Jones ladies as soon as possible to talk about possible suspects and gather information. As a mother herself with a teenage daughter, she truly empathized with their plight and shuddered to think what she would do if her own daughter went missing.

Detective Davis had learned that it was the owner of the bakery, a lady named Lorraine Bedford, who discovered the body. Shortly after Serena and Dereka left the shop, Lorraine was in the bakery kitchen putting the finishing touches on an anniversary cake. Working next to the big picture window, Lorraine looked out the window and noticed a couple of Dereka's balloons floating high up in the sky. Thinking that the young girl had somehow lost control of the balloons, Lorraine quickly grabbed another bunch and hurried out to the parking lot to give them to Dereka. It was then that she discovered Serena lying on her back with a red blood spot slowly spreading across her chest. Lorraine screamed loudly, attracting the attention of several of her employees and a few people passing by.

One of the employees immediately called 911, and the police and ambulance arrived within minutes. Detective Davis had questioned Lorraine and a couple of witnesses at a pet shop across the street, but it seemed no one had seen or heard much of anything. One man thought that he had heard a woman shouting but wasn't sure because he was actually inside the pet shop. Another witness said that she had noticed two men standing by a black car when she went into the bakery. But none of them, including Lorraine, had heard a gunshot or anything resembling the sound of gunfire. That's when Detective Davis knew that this was not a random act of violence, but a targeted act against the mother and her child.

Detective Davis surmised that the kidnapping of the young girl was probably the primary objective, and the killing of her mother was incidental. The mother no doubt had died trying to protect her child. From experience Detective Davis knew it was a highly coordinated and well thought-out plan that had been executed by profession-als who had left little evidence behind. She instinctively knew there would be no fingerprints, no DNA, no footprints, and no identifiable tire tracks. In other words, there would be no smoking gun that could lead to a quick arrest or resolution.

It pained her to think about what the family would have to endure. And for some reason she couldn't yet explain, Detective Davis felt a special bond with the three women who had been so deeply wounded by this unimaginable tragedy. It was if an atomic bomb had exploded in their hearts and souls. It was painful to watch, and even more pain-ful to think about what could possibly happen to the missing young girl.

Detective Davis thought about her own daughter, Angie, now sixteen years old. Although they had been close when Angie was younger, over the years they had grown apart. Detective Davis knew that it was mostly her fault. She'd been so busy with her career she had let her relationship with her family suffer. And although she had made detective in record time, it had come at the expense of her marriage, which ended in divorce, and had resulted in an estranged relationship with Angie, her only child. At times she questioned whether it was all worth it.

When Detective Davis got home, she found her daughter in the living room, in her pajamas, watching a raunchy reality show on TV. She immediately went to her and pulled her into a tight embrace. Angie, unaccustomed to the uncharacteristic display of affection from her mother, started to pull away.

"What's the matter with you?" Angie asked, looking at her mother with a perplexed expression. Detective Davis pulled her daughter close again.

"Nothing. Nothing's wrong," she responded, holding her tight. "I just need to hold you for a minute. Please, Angie, just let me hold you for one minute." And Angie did.

It's Crying Time

THE FIRST THING BabyRuth saw when she woke up the next morning in the emergency room was her older brother Isaac, sitting in a chair and looking at her through red, puffy eyes.

"How you doing, sis?" Isaac asked, trying to force a smile on his face without much success. The memories of the previous day flooded into BabyRuth's mind, and she quickly closed her eyes, attempting to block them out.

"Please, Lord, don't let it be true. Please, Lord," BabyRuth prayed inwardly, hoping against hope that it was all just a terrible nightmare. But the memories became more vivid with each passing minute. She saw the vision of Serena's lifeless body lying on the ground next to Dereka's birthday cake. Such a sight didn't make sense to her. The vision became unbearable, so BabyRuth opened her eyes quickly in an attempt to escape. But there was no escaping. "Why? Who could do such a horrible thing? Why?" BabyRuth cried, moaning and shaking her head vigorously, still in shock and disbelief.

Isaac sat on the bed next to his sister and took her hands into his. "Just let it all out, baby sis. Go ahead and cry. Just let it all out." Isaac knew his words were of little consolation. But he could think of no words that would be appropriate at a time like this. So he just sat there with his sister and listened to her cry. And he cried with her.

BabyRuth looked up at her brother with a pleading expression. "Dereka? Did they find Dereka?" she asked.

"No, not yet. But I spoke briefly with the lead detective last night, and she assured me that they would do everything they can to find her."

"You know, today's her birthday. She's thirteen today. We had a big party planned for her."

"I know," Isaac said sadly. "Joyce and I made some calls last night just to be sure everyone was aware of what happened. We also stopped by your house and picked up a few personal items for you, Kenya, and Jasmine." At the mention of Kenya's and Jasmine's names, BabyRuth began to get out of the bed.

"I need to see them. Where are they?" she asked, struggling to get on her feet.

"No, no, you need to just rest right now, baby sis," Isaac said, helping her lie back down in the bed. "Ryan is with Kenya. He's been with her all night. And Joyce and Trevor are with Jasmine. Most of the family's out in the waiting room. They'll be in to see you later, after you get some more rest. I'm going to check in on Kenya and Jasmine. I'll be back a little later. Rest now," Isaac said, kissing BabyRuth on her forehead.

After Isaac left, BabyRuth lay in the bed and stared out the window. She felt dead inside, like her spirit and soul had departed her body. It was horrific enough that such a beautiful, loving, spiritual young lady like Serena was taken in such a tragic and brutal way. And then to not know where Dereka was. To not know whom she was with or what was happening to her—it was intolerable.

BabyRuth's heart ached so much she felt it would implode in her chest. It was the worst kind of agony anyone could ever experience. She pictured Dereka somewhere alone and frightened. And she began to speak softly to her, hoping that somehow her little Boogie Boo would sense the love and comfort coming from her grandma. "Dereka, sweetheart," BabyRuth said softly. "I know that you're scared and feel like you're all alone. But you're not. We are there in your heart, just as you are in our hearts. You know I love you more than life itself. We'll find you, baby. You just hang in there. We love you so much," BabyRuth said as tears ran down her face. "And happy birthday, sweetheart. Happy birthday, Boogie Boo." And BabyRuth broke down and cried.

When Kenya awakened to the real-life nightmare of what had happened to Serena and Dereka, she cried while Ryan held her and tried to comfort her. Jasmine cried with Aunt Joyce and Trevor by her bedside. The family members gathered in the waiting room huddled together and cried. Neighbors and friends of the Jones family wept as they laid flowers, cards, and balloons on their front porch. Serena's parents cried while they waited in the airport for their flight to DC. Her coworkers at the HIV awareness center and many friends cried at the loss of such a special human being. Classmates and friends of Dereka's cried as they gathered at each other's houses, at the mall, and at Dereka's school. Their faces were filled with shock and sadness as they received or shared the news via social media. Their pastor and the church members prayed and cried as they congregated together at the church for a special prayer service for the Jones family. A lot of people cried that day. It was crying time.

Please Don't Be Dead

MEMPHIS AND HIS partners in crime arrived in Arcadia, Florida, around eight o'clock the following morning, tired from the long ride from DC. The only reason Memphis made the trip was to oversee the exchange of Dereka personally. They took her to a small private airstrip in a rural area located about 175 miles northwest of Miami along the coastline. The airstrip, once used by legitimate businesses to transport cargo, had long ago been commandeered by a notorious crime organization known as Los Chomas, and it was now used primarily to illegally import drugs from other countries into the United States. The organization was a drug trafficking, paramilitary organization that was also heavily involved in the prosperous human trafficking trade. They used the same successful structure and strategies they'd used for years to illegally transport drugs to now illegally transport young girls and women for sexual exploitation. Different members had specialized areas of responsibilities, including laborers, transporters, financiers, and enforcers.

Memphis used his connections within Los Chomas to arrange the exchange of Dereka for top dollar. He knew the organization well owing to his long-term drug dealings with them, and he was confident in their ability to make Dereka disappear without a trace. The group was highly organized, consisting of a core criminal group and a specialized criminal support system, which was run with military-like precision. Even Memphis did not know who was really in charge of Los Chomas, because these so-called drug lords, aka kingpins and drug barons, were kept well insulated by their organizations.

Dereka, still zoned out from the drugs she had been given, was moved into a small wooden building near the airstrip. She woke up around a quarter to eleven, lying on her back on a long table. Her arms and legs were tied together with rope, and a large piece of tape covered her mouth. The only other furniture in the small room was a couple of wooden straight-back chairs. There was a coffee pot on top of a small refrigerator in the corner. Dereka could hear the low hum of conversation coming from outside the closed door. She also heard the loud roar of what she assumed was an airplane either taking off or landing. The sound was so loud it seemed the plane had flown right over the building.

Memphis entered the room and closed the door behind him. Dereka's eyes widened in fear as he approached and loomed over her. He had a slight smile on his face as if he was looking at something amusing. "Good morning, sweetie. Did you sleep well?" Memphis asked mockingly, arching his eyebrows in a questioning manner. He sat down in a chair next to the table. "Well, of course you did, because that was some powerful sh*t my boys pumped into you." He retrieved a pocketknife from his leather blazer's inside pocket. Dereka's eyes widened when he pressed a button to unlatch a sharp, shiny blade. "Don't be scared, Dereka. I'm not going to hurt you. You don't have to worry about me," Memphis said as he expertly cut the ropes loose from Dereka's arms and legs. She rubbed her arms, which were sore and red from the ropes. She started to remove the tape from her mouth, but Memphis stopped her. "Let me get that for you, love," he said as he callously ripped off the tape, causing Dereka to yelp in pain. "Oh, did that hurt?" Memphis mocked. "Well, you may as well get used to pain because where you're going, there'll be a whole lot of pain, my dear."

Dereka's eyes darted around wildly. "Where am I? Where's my mama?" Dereka asked with defiance in her voice. She wanted to get away from this man and this place as soon as possible. She wanted her mama.

"Well," Memphis said, pausing for effect. "I hate to be the one to break the news to you. But she didn't make it. Your mother died trying to save you," Memphis stated accusingly, trying to make Dereka feel as if her mother's death were really her fault. Dereka gasped as if someone had punched her in the gut. For a moment she just stared at Memphis with her mouth hanging open in shock, her eyes wide in disbelief.

"You're lying," Dereka screamed at the top of her lungs. "Why would you say something like that? You're just trying to scare me," she yelled.

"I'm not trying to scare you, but you have a right to be scared," Memphis responded as he got up to leave. He walked to the door and turned to look at Dereka with a wide grin on his face. "Oh, by the way, happy birthday, Dereka. This is your thirteenth birthday, isn't it? I guess thirteen really did turn out to be your unlucky number." Memphis chuckled as he went out the door.

Dereka sat on the table stunned. "He's lying, he's lying," she repeated over and over. *Mama's not dead. She just can't be.* Dereka pulled her knees to her chest and rocked back and forth, telling herself over and over that her mama was not dead. But deep down in the very far corners of her heart, she sensed that it was true. Because she knew if her mother were still alive, she would be with her right now. There was no way her mother would have allowed her to be taken by this awful man. No way her mama would have left her all alone. There was just no way. Her mother's love was too strong. She would have fought tooth and nail to protect Dereka, even if it meant losing her own life.

And as the realization that her mother had died slowly took hold in Dereka's mind and heart, she collapsed onto the floor. "Mama, please don't be dead. Pleaseeeee, Mama, don't be dead. Mama, pleaseeeee," Derek cried out to her mother as if somehow she could will her back to life. She became so overwhelmed with grief, anxiety, and sorrow she began to hyperventilate. She struggled to catch her breath and began to thrash about in a total sense of panic. She soon became lightheaded and felt a tingling sensation in her fingers. The last thing Dereka heard before she lost consciousness was footsteps coming toward her.

God Is

LATER THAT AFTERNOON BabyRuth and Jasmine were released from the hospital. The doctor decided to keep Kenya another day for observation because she was having unusual fluctuations in her blood pressure. Isaac asked BabyRuth and Jasmine to stay at his house for a couple of days, feeling it would be too painful for them to return home just yet. He wanted them to wait until the pain had somewhat subsided. Jasmine took him up on his offer, but BabyRuth graciously refused. She wanted to go home; she needed to be home.

Isaac droved BabyRuth to her house and turned off the ignition. "You sure you ready for this?" he asked, secretly hoping that she'd change her mind and go with him. BabyRuth was silent for a moment as she gazed at the home where she had shared so much happiness with her daughter and granddaughter.

"Yes, I'm sure. I know you're concerned about me, but this is something I need to do right now."

"I understand," Isaac said with some hesitancy. "But you call me if you need me. You hear me, baby sis?"

"I will," BabyRuth assured him, trying her best to put his mind at ease. "I love you, Isaac," she said and hugged him tight before getting out of the car.

"Love you more," Isaac replied. He waited until his sister was safely in the house before reluctantly driving away.

BabyRuth entered the familiar living room and sat on the sofa. Sorrow and pain covered her like a dark, thick cloak. Thankfully, Isaac and Joyce had cleared away the birthday preparations, knowing that they would only serve as a painful reminder of the celebration that had been planned for today. *I'm not going to make it*, BabyRuth thought sadly. *I'm just not going to make it through this.* She immediately got on her knees to pray, because she knew that was the only thing that could save her.

But prayer didn't come easy. She was hurt, disappointed, and wounded, and she just didn't understand how God could have allowed something so awful to happen. So BabyRuth began to question God. She knew it was wrong, and that she had no right to question him, but she did it anyway. She desperately needed answers that only he could give. "Why, God? Why did you let this happen? How could you do this to us? Wasn't it enough that I lost Derek? I thought that would be the single most trying thing that I would ever have to face. And now this, Lord! Why? I just don't understand. Haven't I shown you my faith? Haven't I been tested enough?" BabyRuth questioned, pausing to hear God's answer. But God was silent.

"You know that Derek's death almost destroyed me, almost destroyed the whole family. It took all that I had to survive that and to pull my family through. And now, I have nothing left to give. I can't bear this too. I just can't, Lord," BabyRuth confessed. She listened for God to speak to her, to provide the answers she so greatly needed. But God remained silent.

BabyRuth continued her fervent quest for answers from God. After all, she was his faithful servant. She felt that he owed her an explanation. "Why take Serena, Lord? Such a beautiful, gentle, kind person, she didn't deserve to die that way. All she ever did in her life was love and care for others. And she loved you most of all. It's just not fair, Lord. It's not fair!" BabyRuth cried out in distress. "And how could you allow something like this to happen to Dereka? She's just a child, Lord. A sweet, innocent child. You could have stopped it. You have all power in your hands. You could have intervened. So why didn't you? Why, Lord, why?" BabyRuth shouted out defiantly at God, clearly laying all the blame squarely at his feet.

BabyRuth continued to cry out and vent her anguish and frustration towards the Lord. For hours she questioned and demanded answers. She just didn't understand how a merciful, just, loving, and all-knowing God could have allowed such a cruel and appalling thing to happen. Didn't he care? He had to know what this would do to them. So why didn't he stop it? BabyRuth needed God to speak to her in a loud and clear voice so she could have some resolution, so she'd know how to go on. But there was no word from God.

BabyRuth began to pace frantically throughout the house. She spent hours wandering from room to room, pacing and moaning, until she eventually ended up in Dereka's room. She picked up a pajama top that Dereka had left lying on the bed. She put it to her nose and breathed in the scent, which smelled like Dereka's favorite lavender-and-honey soap. BabyRuth cried as she held the pajama top to her face, mixing in her tears with Dereka's scent.

BabyRuth lay down on Dereka's bed. "Lord, I place myself completely at your mercy," she whispered. "All my strength is gone. So have your way, Lord. Let your will be done, not mine. I don't know why this has happened, but I know where my help comes from. *My help comes from the Lord, who made heaven and earth.*" And when BabyRuth humbled herself before the Lord in this way, that's when she heard his voice. But it wasn't a thunderous roar from the heavens like she'd expected, but rather a still small voice that spoke to her heart.

And all God said to her was, *Be still and know that I am God.* When she heard those words in her spirit, BabyRuth immediately began to feel the peace of God trickle down through her body, from the top of her head to the soles of her feet. And she knew it was the peace spoken of in the Bible—that *peace of God, which passeth all understanding.*

But God didn't answer her questions as to why what happened had happened—because he didn't have to. All he did was remind

BabyRuth of who he is. He is God. Even in the most horrific circumstances, he is still God. And he *is the same yesterday, today, and forever.* And the same God that got her through past trials would get her through her present trials. He'd done it before, and he would do it again, because he is God. And that, in and of itself, is enough.

Nothing Beats a Failure, But a Try

WHEN DEREKA REGAINED consciousness, she was lying on her back on the table. She noticed that daylight was fading, so she must have been out for hours. An oxygen mask, similar to the ones found on airplanes, had been placed over her nose and mouth. For a moment she just lay still, breathing deeply through the mask. Her eyes filled with tears when she thought about her mama. It was hard to believe that she was gone, that Dereka would never see her sweet face again, hear her laughter, or enjoy the comfort and security of her unconditional love. The pain was so unbearable Dereka didn't know whether she'd survive it, nor whether she even wanted to. But as she stared up at the ceiling, Dereka could feel her mother's presence and hear her voice telling her how much she loved her and encouraging her to be strong. And she realized that if her mama had died for her, the least she could do was to live for her mama. "I love you, Mama," Dereka murmured softly. "I'll try to get through this. I know you would want me to be strong. I'll try hard, Mama. I'll do it for you. I promise."

Dereka sat up groggily, removed the mask from her face, and looked around the bleak, dreary room. This was not where she was supposed to be on a special day like today—her thirteenth birthday. She closed her eyes and tried to imagine the birthday party that had been planned for her. In her imaginary party, her mother was alive and well, laughing and making sure that she and all her friends were having fun. Her Grandma Ruth was in the kitchen serving up lots of good home cooking. Her Aunt Kenya and Auntie Jazz were playing music and dancing, trying to keep up with all the young folks. And she herself was opening birthday presents, blowing out candles on her cake, gossiping with her girlfriends, and making eye contact with the cute boys there. Her imaginary party was all that and a bag of chips.

But her imaginary party abruptly came to an end when Memphis entered the room with two men who appeared to be Hispanic. One man was dressed in military fatigues and had a huge assault rifle slung over one shoulder. He was a fierce-looking muscular man with dark penetrating eyes, a broad nose, and a shaggy beard. The other man was tall, slim, and clean shaven. He was stylishly dressed in a black suit, gray shirt, and gray-and-black striped tie. The tall, slim man looked Dereka over closely and nodded his approval to Memphis.

"Welcome back, Dereka," Memphis stated. "Glad you came around in time to board your flight." *Flight*, Dereka thought, her heart skip-ping a beat. *They're flying me somewhere.* Memphis took out a small camera and pointed it at Dereka. "Say cheese," he mocked as he snapped the photo. "Just a little memento for your family to remem-ber you by," Memphis stated, turning and walking a few feet away with the tall, slim Hispanic man close on his heels. The man with the assault rifle stood next to Dereka and just stared at her through dark, cold eyes. He gave Dereka the creeps. She could heard Memphis and the other man talking between themselves and saw the tall man give Memphis some money. The two men shook hands to seal the deal, and the tall man left the room.

"Well, Dereka," Memphis said, walking back to where she was sit-ting on the table. "This is where we have to part ways. But I'm leaving you in good hands, with my dear friend Luis," Memphis stated, plac-ing his hand on Luis's shoulder. Luis was a transporter for Los Chomas. His job was to transport the human commodity (mostly young girls) from one location to another, and to do so without great harm to the commodity that could lessen its value. Luis took his job very seriously and had lost only one girl in his six years as a transporter. A young girl, about twelve years of age, had slit her own wrist with glass from a broken bathroom mirror. The value of the young girl's worth had been taken out of Luis's pay, and he vowed to himself he would never lose another one. And he hadn't.

"I'll take good care of her," Luis said, grinning and moving in close to Dereka to get a better look at her. She could see his yellow, tobacco-stained teeth and smell his stank breath.

"I'm sure you will, my friend," Memphis responded. He looked at Dereka intently for a moment. "Well, I guess this is the beginning of the end for you. *Adios, esperso tengas una buena vida*, or, in other words, good-bye, and have a nice life," Memphis said amusingly to Dereka. Then he took an exaggerated bow and sauntered out the door.

• • •

After Memphis left, Luis sat in one of the wooden straight-back chairs and propped his feet up in the other chair. He took a cigar out of his pocket, lit it, and inhaled deeply. For a while he just sat in the chair and smoked the cigar, seemingly oblivious to Dereka. After he finished the cigar, he threw it on the floor, snuffed it out with his boot, laid his head back, and closed his eyes. Dereka was afraid to move or make any sound that would attract attention to herself. The lingering smoke in the air from Luis's cigar made her nose itch, but she willed herself not to cough. As it got darker outside, the lights near the airstrip came on, casting scary shadows on the walls.

Soon Dereka heard snoring sounds and realized that Luis had fallen asleep in the chair. She knew this was her opportunity to try to escape. Memphis had said something about putting her on a flight somewhere. *If they put me on that plane, I may never get back home. This may be my only chance to get away*, Dereka thought. She didn't know what to do, but she had to do something. It was now or never. If she could just make it to the door and get outside, perhaps she could run somewhere and hide until daylight, or maybe flag down a car, or run to somebody's house. Her grandma always told her, "Nothing beats a failure but a try." So she had to at least try.

Dereka's heart raced as she slowly got off the table. She could feel her legs trembling beneath her. She listened carefully to the sound of Luis's snoring to confirm that he was still asleep. She took off her shoes and walked slowly towards the door. She could tell that the door was slightly cracked from the thin slat of light shining through from outside. Dereka held her breath as she moved passed Luis. She could feel her anticipation mounting as she crept closer and closer towards the small sliver of light shining through the door's crack. *I'm almost there*, Dereka thought, trying to calm her nerves and force herself to keep walking softly and slowly. *Just a little further. I'm almost there.*

Just as Dereka reached the door, she sensed movement behind her and felt a sharp pain in her back between her shoulder blades. The pain was so severe she fell to the floor, writhing in agony. She looked up and saw Luis looming over her with the assault rifle in his hands. He jabbed her again with the butt of the rifle, roughly grabbed one of her legs, pulled her across the room, and dumped her in the corner. "You have just failed your first test," Luis said, looking down at Dereka with a smirk on his face. "Have you not heard the saying, 'Every closed eye ain't sleep'? That was just a test to see if you would try to escape. A test that you failed miserably. There'll be other tests. Fail them, and you'll suffer much worse." Luis returned to his chair and got back into his bogus sleep position.

Dereka cowered in the dark corner of the room, her back still throbbing with pain from the butt of the assault rifle. But she didn't regret that she had tried to escape. She regretted only that she had failed. And she knew that if the opportunity to escape came again, she'd take it. Because she would risk anything to get back home.

The Lord is my Shepherd

DEREKA FELL ASLEEP on the floor, curled up in a ball in the corner of the room. She woke up about an hour later to the loud sound of an airplane flying over the building. Her back was still aching slightly with pain. She looked up and saw Luis standing over her. "Wake up, sleeping beauty," he teased. "It's time to go." He grabbed her arm, pulled her to her feet, and ushered her out the door. He held on tight to Dereka's arm to prevent her from trying to escape. And of course, he had the assault rifle slung over one shoulder.

A small airplane glided down the narrow airstrip and sputtered to a stop a few feet from where they were standing. The plane was a Piper Aztec light twin-engine aircraft with room for six people and ample cargo capacity. Such light aircraft were very popular with drug traffickers in places like Mexico, the Caribbean, and Central and South America. They used the small planes to smuggle tons of cocaine to various destinations in the United States. These planes could fly for about 1,800 miles and stay airborne for eleven-plus hours with standard fuel systems. If there was a need to travel for longer periods of time, the pilot would either refuel at a predestined transshipment point or simply equip the aircraft with a collapsible rubber fuel bladder, which could easily be disposed of after the fuel was used.

And now that many crime organizations were expanding into human trafficking, these light aircraft were also used to illegally transport victims both in and out of the United States. Organized crime groups were very crafty and always looking for new criminal ways to enlarge their finances, authority, and power. And the sexual exploitation business suited them just fine.

A middle-age white man wearing khakis and a blue sweater got off the plane and walked towards them. He greeted Luis warmly and gave Dereka only a passing glance. The pilot's name was Bill, and he was a former Continental Airlines pilot who had been recruited by the crime organization. American citizens, including ex-military, commercial and private pilots, and others, were often recruited and paid huge sums of money to purchase and illegally fly planes for crime organizations. The pilots flew primarily in the dark of the night, flying at low speeds and altitudes to avoid detection. Most of the planes were equipped with the most sophisticated communication systems the crime organization's money could buy, including communication scramblers, beacon-interrogating radar, and long-range navigation instruments. The pilots even used special night vision goggles to be able to fly the aircraft at night without lights.

After a few minutes, Luis began to move Dereka towards the small plane. "I have to go to the restroom," Dereka said, giving him that "I got to go bad" look. She really did have to go, but she also wanted to do anything to keep from getting on that plane.

"Okay," Luis responded, directing Dereka to one of the three Jiffy Johns next to the building. "Leave the door open," he demanded as he stood next to the door, shining a flashlight inside. Dereka was embarrassed to go in front of him, but she had no choice. Afterward Luis took her onto the plane and strapped her to one of the four passenger seats. He secured the seat straps with a small lock. After checking the straps to ensure Dereka was fastened in tight, he went to the back of the plane and retrieved a bottle of water and a ham-and-cheese sandwich from a cooler. Without a word, he handed the items to Dereka and got off the plane. Dereka was famished because she had not eaten or drunk anything for over twenty-four hours. The hunger pains in her stomach prompted her to rip open and devour the sandwich and gulp down the water.

For the next thirty minutes or so, Dereka sat on the plane and watched Bill and Luis smoke, laugh, and talk between themselves. She tried to loosen the straps around her, but to no avail. She wondered what they were waiting for, and it wasn't too much longer before she found out. A black SUV came out of the darkness and stopped beside the plane. Two men got out of the front seat, and one of them opened the rear passenger door. To Dereka's surprise, three females were taken from the backseat and immediately boarded onto the plane. They seemed to be just as surprised to see Dereka as she was to see them. Two of the girls appeared to be around Dereka's age, and one appeared to be a little older, around sixteen or seventeen. In a way Dereka was glad to see other girls; at least she was not alone. But the look of fright and terror in the girls' eyes tore at Dereka's tender heart. She felt sorry for them even though she was in the same predicament as they were.

Once the other girls were strapped and locked into their seats, the pilot and Luis took their seats in the cockpit. Luis turned around to address the girls. "Stay calm during the flight. And do not talk or attempt to communicate with each other in any way," he cautioned. "If you do, there will be hell to pay." All the time he was speaking, he kept his hand on the assault rifle, but mainly for show to strike fear in the young girls' hearts. Luis was no fool; he knew bullets and planes don't mix. So he also had a powerful stun gun with him just in case he needed to discipline one of them during the flight.

The ride on the small aircraft was frightening and harrowing. The small aircraft swayed and bumped around so violently Dereka became nauseous. She thought she was going to throw up the sandwich she'd just eaten. And because the plane was flying without lights, it was pitch dark. The only light was the dim light coming from the controls in the cockpit. Dereka was terrified that the plane was going to crash into the ocean and they would all drown. Or worse, crash into land and burst into flames. All kinds of wild, scary thoughts raced through her mind. She could tell the other girls were scared also, because she heard a couple of them crying.

As Dereka stared into the darkness, she thought about all the times when she was a little girl and became afraid of the dark. She would run into her mother's room crying that the boogieman was hiding in the dark corners, under the bed, or in the closet. Her mother would always take Dereka into her arms and calm all her fears. Sometimes her mother would read her a bedtime story, choosing mainly to read Christian bedtime stories about Moses, Daniel, David, and Jesus. One of Dereka's favorite stories came from a book titled *The Lord Is My Shepherd*, an illustrated children's book of the Twenty-Third Psalm. BabyRuth had given her the book as a Christmas present when Dereka was about four years old. Dereka would snuggle under the covers and look at the pictures of children, sheep, churches, and villages while her mama, or sometimes grandma, read the psalm. To calm her fears, Dereka began to recite the psalm softly to herself.

> *The Lord is my shepherd;*
> *I shall not want.*
> *He maketh me to lie down in green pastures:*
> *he leadeth me beside the still waters.*
> *He restoreth my soul:*
> *he leadeth me in the paths of righteousness for his name's sake.*
> *Yea, though I walk through the valley of the shadow of death,*
> *I will fear no evil:*
> *for thou art with me;*
> *thy rod and thy staff they comfort me.*
> *Thou preparest a table before me in the presence of mine enemies:*
> *thou anointest my head with oil;*
> *my cup runneth over.*
> *Surely goodness and mercy shall follow me all the days of my life:*
> *and I will dwell in the house of the Lord forever.*

After her mother finished reading the psalm, she would always say, "See, Boogie Boo? You have nothing to be afraid of. The Lord is your shepherd, and he'll always take care of you." And Dereka would snuggle up next to her mother and sleep like a baby until morning. The wonderful memory brought Dereka some measure of peace during her frightening plane ride to an unknown destination.

He's Back

BABYRUTH WOKE UP the next morning in Dereka's bed, still clutching Dereka's pajama top in her hands. She immediately began to rejoice and praise the Lord for the revelation she had received in response to her prayers. "Thank you, Father, for helping me once more. Thank you for giving me what I need to carry on," she prayed. Later that morning BabyRuth drove to the hospital to check on Kenya and learned she'd been cleared for release. When she got to Kenya's room, Jasmine and Ryan were already there. BabyRuth embraced Kenya and just held on for a while. Then BabyRuth asked everyone to join hands. And right there in the hospital room, BabyRuth prayed for her family. After she finished praying, she looked at them and said, "Now let's go home."

Ryan escorted Kenya and the others to the car in the parking lot. BabyRuth gave him a big hug and thanked him for being there for Kenya. He had been with her since she was admitted to the ER and had barely left her side. "You're a good man, Ryan," BabyRuth said. She considered Ryan a godsend and was looking forward to having him as a son-in-law one day.

"Thanks, Ms. Ruth. I have to go now, but I'll be by later to check on Kenya," Ryan responded. He hugged Kenya and kissed her lightly on the lips. "You all right, baby?" he asked with a worried expression on his face.

"I'm okay, honey," Kenya responded. "And thanks for being with me," she added with the smallest hint of a smile.

"I wouldn't have it any other way," Ryan stated sincerely. He gave BabyRuth and Jasmine a hug and kiss on the cheek before leaving.

No one talked much on the ride home. BabyRuth knew Kenya and Jasmine were mentally preparing themselves to return home without Serena and Dereka. When BabyRuth parked the car, she turned to Kenya and Jasmine. "Now I know it's going to be tough to walk through those doors. But we've got each other. And we got Jesus. We can do this. We'll do it together," BabyRuth said, squeezing each of their hands, trying to give them a portion of the strength she felt within herself. Once inside they went straight into the kitchen and collapsed in chairs around the table. "I'll make us some coffee," BabyRuth said, getting up to prepare the coffee. Kenya and Jasmine just sat silently at the table with their head in their hands, neither having the words to express the pain that was in their hearts.

BabyRuth listened to the many messages left on the answering machine. Most of them were condolences and expressions of sympathy from family and friends. However, one of the calls was from Detective Davis. She wanted to speak with them as soon as possible as part of her investigation into Serena's death and Dereka's abduction. "I'll call her now," Kenya said, anxious to help with the investigation. But as she was about to make the call, her cell phone beeped, alerting her of an incoming text message. She didn't want to answer it but thought that it may be Ryan texting to check on her or just to say "I love you," as he frequently did throughout the day. But when Kenya looked at her phone screen, she saw an unknown number displayed. Curious, she opened the text message, read it, and gasped loudly.

"Oh my God, oh my God," she shrieked in panic. Jasmine and BabyRuth looked at Kenya with fearful eyes.

"Is it about Dereka?" Jasmine asked hesitantly. "Has something happened to her? Have they found her? Is she—" Jasmine stopped short. Kenya shook her head no vigorously and read the text out loud.

Finally got u. R U sorry?
M.

"He's back," Kenya yelled, near hysteria.

"Who's back?" BabyRuth asked.

"Memphis. This message is from him. It has to be. Mama, you remember that drug dealer I turned in years ago. The one who turned out to be the father of my substitute teacher, Mr. Curtis, who went to prison. His name is Memphis, and he's back. He's behind all this. He must be. That's why he asked are you sorry, because they always said I'd be sorry. I thought he was gone for good. But he's back."

Lord Have Mercy

BABYRUTH CALLED DETECTIVE Davis immediately, and the detective arrived shortly after receiving her frantic call about a possible suspect. When Detective Davis walked into the Jones residence, she detected a deep sense of dread, anxiety, and fear in the air. Whatever these ladies had discovered shook them to their core.

"Thank you for coming so quickly," BabyRuth said. "We think we know who killed Serena and took Dereka. Show her the message, honey." Detective Davis took the phone from Kenya and read the message,

"Finally got u. R U sorry? M." She pulled out a pen and pad to take notes. "Tell me what you know about this person."

"I met him years ago when I was in high school. Everybody called him Memphis, but his real name is Luther Curtis," Kenya informed her. She went on to tell the detective the whole sordid saga of her involvement with the unscrupulous Kevin Curtis and his equally corrupt father. And how, in a quest for revenge, Memphis had drugged her and attempted to kidnap and sell her into the sex-slave trade. "This is revenge against me. Serena's dead because of me. And Memphis took Dereka to get to me. This is all my fault," Kenya lamented.

"Don't you blame yourself for this. Don't you dare. This is the evil deed of an evil man. You were a victim yourself, honey. This is not your fault," BabyRuth stated. She turned to Detective Davis. "How do we get Dereka back?"

Detective Davis took a deep breath before answering. "I have to be honest with you—it won't be easy. We have very little to go on from the forensic evidence left at the crime scene. These guys are criminal professionals. I'm sorry to have to tell you this, but based on my experience, and in light of what Kenya just revealed about Luther Curtis, it's highly likely that he'll attempt to do with Dereka what he failed to do with Kenya. There's a rapidly growing crime in this country called human trafficking, and it's possible that Dereka may become a victim of this crime."

"Human trafficking. Oh my God!" BabyRuth exclaimed. "You mean Dereka could be forced to...to..." She couldn't continue.

"Yes, it's possible that Dereka may be used for sexual exploitation," Detective Davis said solemnly, completing the sentence that BabyRuth couldn't.

Deep down within their subconscious, each of the ladies had known what could happen to Dereka. They feared she could be raped and forced to do unspeakable things. But the very thought of it had been too vile to fully take hold in their minds and hearts, so they'd suppressed it. Now the detective's words about human trafficking sent their worst fears spiraling to the forefront of their psyche. And realizing that their Dereka, their heart, someone so precious and innocent, could be subjected to such brutality and ugliness was just absolutely devastating.

BabyRuth emitted a deep guttural groan and collapsed to her knees, Kenya laid her head down on the table and sobbed mournfully, and Jasmine doubled over and groaned as if she were in physical pain. Detective Davis waited patiently for the ladies to recover, her own heart aching for them. Jasmine was the first to speak.

"Where do we go from here?" she asked.

"We've gotten a few leads from the Amber Alert we issued, and we're following up on those. Now that I have the name of a suspect, that will give us some direction. Because Luther Curtis has been on the run from authorities for years, I'm certain that he has a new identity. These types of criminals are as slippery as eels and use multiple aliases and identities. They know and use every trick in the book to avoid capture," Detective Davis stated.

"Where do you think he's taken her? Could she still be in the area?" BabyRuth asked.

"It's possible, but highly unlikely. Sometimes trafficking victims remain in the same area, but those are generally victims who are runaways, dropouts, or have unstable home environments. Since Dereka has a loving family and a stable home structure, it would be too risky for him to keep her close by. He'd want to get her far away from this area as soon as possible. That's why the FBI is involved in this investigation. They assist in kidnapping cases where the victim is a minor and has likely been transported across state lines," Detective Davis responded.

"What is this human trafficking all about? I've heard about it on the news a lot lately, but I must confess, I really don't understand it," BabyRuth admitted.

"Nothing to be ashamed of. A lot of people don't realize just how massive and destructive this crime is. Human trafficking is a global, extremely complex industry, and it's on the rise. It has often been referred to as modern-day slavery because humans are bought and sold for the purpose of sexual slavery, forced labor, or commercial sexploitation. Reports vary widely in regards to the number of victims because it is such a hidden murky business. But it's safe to say that there are millions of human trafficking victims worldwide, and nearly half of those victims are children between the ages of twelve and fourteen years old," Detective Davis stated.

"Dereka just turned thirteen," Kenya conveyed sadly.

"I know," Detective Davis responded, pausing and looking at Kenya with sympathy before continuing.

"I want to be up front with you about what we may be dealing with here," Detective Davis continued. "Human trafficking is big business right here in the US, and it's been referred to as the second fastest growing criminal industry in the United States, next to the illegal drug industry. Major cities such as Los Angeles, Miami, Houston, New York, and Las Vegas are among the top human trafficking jurisdictions. But this crime also occurs in other, more unlikely places, like Saint Paul, Minnesota, and Oklahoma City, Oklahoma."

"But how can this be? How can such a foul and disgusting business be allowed to thrive right here in this country?" Jasmine inquired.

"Well, it's all about the money. Human trafficking is a multibillion-dollar industry, generating between thirty and thirty-two billion annually worldwide, with between five and nine billion of that being generated right here in the US. That's why drug traffickers are getting into human trafficking. These criminals have little regard for the victims; they see nothing but dollar signs. And Internet websites like Craigslist and Backpage.com are sometimes used by traffickers to buy and sell young girls and boys. Legislators are doing what they can to stamp out this crime, but I'm afraid the criminals have the upper hand," Detective Davis acknowledged.

She spent the next couple of hours at the Jones residence, providing what little evidence she had so far in the case. She also questioned them about any other suspicious people or events in the days or weeks before the tragedy. She asked Kenya to turn over her cell phone for a few days so she could try to trace where the text message was sent from. After Detective Davis finished, BabyRuth walked her to the door. She moved in close to the detective so that Kenya and Jasmine would not be able to hear their conversation.

"Give it to me straight. How does things look for finding Dereka? Please tell me the truth. I need to know the truth," BabyRuth whispered.

And as much as Detective Davis wanted to reply with a positive response, one look into BabyRuth's eyes told her that this woman needed to know the truth. She needed to know the cold, hard facts in order to prepare herself for what lay ahead. Detective Davis leaned in close to BabyRuth and uttered, "I'm not going to lie to you—things don't look good at this point. My gut tells me this may take some time. But I promise you, I'll do everything I can to find your granddaughter."

"Thank you for your honesty," BabyRuth mumbled, letting the tears flow freely down her face. BabyRuth closed the door and leaned her forehead against the door for support. She stood there for a moment, took a long deep breath, and sighed, "Lord, have mercy on us. Lord, have mercy."

Hiding in Plain Sight

MEMPHIS MANEUVERED HIS way through the streets of DC with relative ease. He had a smirk on his face because he knew by now Kenya had received his text message. He also knew that the family would turn the text over to the police to try to determine who sent it and from where. But it would do them no good. Memphis was one step ahead of them. He always used prepaid cell phones to conduct his shady business activities. Prepaid cell phones were the best thing since sliced bread for people engaged in illicit activities. They were a crook's dream because they were practically impossible to trace. All Memphis had to do was walk in virtually any major retail store or even a gas station, purchase the prepaid phone, use it to conduct his business, and dispose of it afterward. No contract, no credit check, and no ID required. Terrorists, gangbangers, drug dealers, human traffickers, cheating husbands and wives, and anybody with something to hide were the biggest proponents of prepaid cell phones. The phones were worth their weight in gold, as far as Memphis was concerned.

Memphis crossed over the Fourteenth Street Bridge into Virginia and made his way to the city of Fairfax. He pulled his car into the garage of a luxury high-rise apartment building on Willow Crescent Drive. Memphis knew the police in DC, Maryland, and Virginia were looking for him, so he figured the best place to hide was in plain sight. They wouldn't think he had the balls to return to the DC metro area after what he had just done. But Memphis's balls were as big as they come. Just for kicks, he chose an apartment within several miles of the Fairfax Police Department. The location also provided him an opportunity to be within close proximity of the Fairfax Judicial Center Building on Chain Bridge Road, where Kenya worked as a district attorney, so he could also keep close tabs on her comings and goings. Plus the apartment was occupied mostly by older, white, upper-class residents who kept to themselves and went out of their way to avoid black people, especially a tall black man like him. Memphis would be pretty much left alone by the residents. Just the way he liked it.

When Memphis entered his apartment, the first thing he did was take a long, hot shower. Afterward, he trimmed his mustache and goatee. Memphis marveled at his reflection in the mirror and how different he looked now than thirteen years ago, when he'd lived and run his drug business in DC. Of course, some of the change in his looks had come with age, but most of it was intentional. Back then he was clean shaven and wore his hair in a close-cut fade. Now he had grown a goatee and mustache and had a clean, shiny bald head. He had put on some weight, but mostly muscle from working out. And he was never without his trademark aviator shades. His look was so different that he doubted that Kenya herself would even recognize him if he stood next to her in line at the coffee shop she stopped at each morning before work. *Maybe I'll do that one day just for the hell of it*, Memphis thought to himself, smiling at his image in the mirror.

When Memphis finished primping, he relaxed on the big, comfy sofa in the living room and looked approvingly around the beautifully decorated apartment. He had given a couple of his employees detailed instructions to furnish and equip his apartment with the best money could buy. He pulled out his new fake driver's license and work ID badge for inspection. He had used his new credentials for his flight back to the DC area, preferring to fly into BWI airport in Baltimore rather than DC National. Less security, he supposed. His latest alias was Keith Jackson, a sales consultant with Jackson and Mahoney Marketing LLC in Fairfax, Virginia. He liked his new run-of-the-mill name and job title. To the average joe, Memphis would seem like just another hardworking, law-abiding citizen trying to make his way in the world like everybody else. He'd paid good money for his new credentials and knew they would hold up under scrutiny.

Memphis turned the sixty-two-inch flat-screen TV to the sports channel to watch a football game. Life was good.

Get Used to It

AFTER THE SMALL aircraft landed on a bumpy dirt road in a heavily wooded area, Dereka and others girls were loaded, like cargo, into the covered bed of a large pickup truck that was waiting at the end of the road. They were forced to sit on the floor, two on each side, and Luis again warned them not to talk or try to communicate with each other in any way. It was still dark outside, and it was stuffy and musty inside the enclosed bed of the pickup. The girls also had a hard time sitting upright as they were jostled about by the bumpy, rough road.

Dereka didn't know where they were or where they were headed. But she knew she was a long ways from home. *How will my family find me?* she thought. She was so afraid she could feel her heart beating wildly in her chest. Dereka knew from talks with her mother, grandma, and aunts that there were evil men in the world—men who liked to kidnap, rape, and kill young girls. She'd been cautioned as a very young child to look out for people like that. She was told not to walk home from school alone, never to accept rides from people she didn't know, and not to allow anyone to touch her inappropriately, among other things. And for the most part, Dereka had followed these instructions. But here she was with these strange men, in this strange place, stuck in the back of a stuffy, smelly truck. She just didn't understand. Memphis had said it was her Aunt Kenya's fault, but she knew that was a lie. She knew that her aunt loved her immensely and would never do anything to put her in harm's way.

As daylight broke, Dereka got a better look at the other girls. The one sitting next to Dereka was a white girl, with wavy shoulder-length blond hair, and appeared to be about Dereka's age. On the opposite side was a very slim white girl, with long, straight dark hair and large eyes that looked huge in her thin, delicate face. The older girl, who looked to be about sixteen or seventeen years old, looked Hispanic. Her dark hair hung just past her shoulders, and she had high cheekbones and full lips. All the girls, except the blond-haired one, made eye contact with each other. But no one spoke, out of fear of retribution.

The girl next to Dereka cried constantly. She was terrified, as they all were. Dereka wanted to say something soothing to her—something that her mama or Grandma Ruth had said to her when she was scared. Something like, "Don't cry, everything's going to be all right," or perhaps, "There, there, it's not as bad as it seems." But deep down, Dereka knew that everything was not going to be all right, and the situation was indeed as bad as it seemed. Perhaps worse.

The truck slowed and came to a stop in a small clearing in the deep woods. The girls were allowed to get out of the truck and relieve themselves nearby, and were told to sit on the ground beside the truck. They were each provided a package of peanut butter crackers and a can of tropical fruit drink. Luis and the driver, a big burly Hispanic man, sat on some logs near the edge of the woods while they ate sandwiches and drank canned beer. They spoke low and mainly in Spanish, so Dereka could not make out what they were saying. She and the other girls quietly consumed their peanut butter crackers and juice.

When the men finished eating and drinking, the big, burly truck driver stood up and let out a big belch. He patted his huge belly and walked over to the girls with a devilish grin on his face. He walked around them, inspecting them closely, before settling on his victim. It was the older Hispanic girl. He grabbed her by the arm and started to pull her into the woods. She screamed and struggled to get away, but he continued to drag her deeper into the wooded area until they disappeared from sight. Although Dereka and the others could no longer see them, they heard the girl's heart-wrenching screams and knew she was being raped. Dereka placed her hands over her mouth and murmured, "Oh my God. Oh my God!" The blond-haired girl started crying and shaking uncontrollably, and the slim, dark-haired girl just stared towards the woods, her eyes about twice their usual size.

Luis casually walked back over to where they were sitting on the ground. He lit a cigarette and took a couple of puffs. "No need to be worried. He's just breaking her in," he said nonchalantly. "She'll get used to it. You all will."

Finally the screams stopped, and a few moments later the man and the girl emerged from the woods. The girl's clothes were disheveled and torn. Dirt and grass were in her hair and on her face and clothes. There were also bloody cuts on her face and hands. She kept her head down and would not make eye contact with anyone. Once they were back in the truck, she curled up in the corner, shaking and crying. The brutal rape of one of them solidified their worst fears of what was ahead for all of them.

The Tip-Off

THE NEXT DAY BabyRuth received a call from Detective Davis saying they'd gotten a promising tip on the Amber Alert hotline regarding Dereka's whereabouts. BabyRuth, Kenya, and Jasmine waited on pins and needles for the detective to arrive. Before Detective Davis could even knock on the door, Kenya yanked it open.

"You said there's some news about Dereka," Kenya said excitedly.

"Yes," Detective Davis responded, taking a seat on the sofa. "Now I don't want to raise your hopes too high, but we got a promising lead. We got a call from Mexico City, Mexico. The caller saw a young African American girl about Dereka's age in a truck with two men. They were in an area known for drugs and prostitution. He saw them when they stopped at a gas station. What made the caller suspicious was that the young girl looked scared, and she looked a lot like the photo of Dereka in the Amber Alert. The caller described her as wearing a black-and-pink striped sweater and pink leggings."

"That's what Dereka was wearing the day it happened. I remember telling her she looked pretty in pink," Jasmine exclaimed.

"Do you think it could be her?" BabyRuth quizzed the detective.

"Well, like I said, I don't want to get your hopes up too high, but it's possible Dereka was taken to Mexico," Detective Davis answered cautiously. "Mexico City is a large destination country for sex trafficking victims. Forced-prostitution rings are common throughout the city.

And since Luther Curtis is a known drug dealer, he probably already had contacts in Mexico. It just makes sense that he would make use of those contacts to transport Dereka out of the country."

"What do we do now?" BabyRuth asked.

"I'll travel to Mexico City and work with authorities to follow up on the lead. We've already turned over the evidence from the phone call to the FBI," Detective Davis stated.

"Why don't we go to Mexico City too?" Jasmine said eagerly.

"Yeah, we can pass out flyers on the street and ask people if they've seen Dereka," Kenya concurred.

"No, that's not a good idea," Detective Davis interjected. "The prostitution rings in Mexico are run by brutal crime organizations. They are a dangerous group, and I don't want you to put yourselves in danger."

"I don't care about the danger, as long we find Dereka," BabyRuth countered.

"I know you want to help," Detective Davis replied patiently. "But going to Mexico City and handing out flyers on the street may actually harm our investigation. If Dereka is there, the last thing we want to do is tip off her captives that we are hot on their trail. If they feel like we are closing in on them, they may actually move her elsewhere," Detective Davis pointed out.

"Oh, I hadn't thought about that," Kenya said, disappointed they couldn't help.

"But it's just so hard to sit around waiting and not be able to do anything," BabyRuth said, exasperated.

"Look, I know it's difficult. I can only imagine what you all must be going through. But if Dereka's there, we will do everything we can to find her and bring her home. You have my word on it," Detective Davis asserted.

• • •

Meanwhile, across town, Memphis was already calculating his next move. He knew the police department had been tipped off that

Dereka was in Mexico. How did he know? Because he was the one who had provided the tip. Well, not him personally, but he'd paid a contact in Mexico City to phone in the information about Dereka being seen there. Memphis had even provided his contact with the photo he had taken of Dereka so that he would be able to describe her accurately, right down to what she was wearing.

Memphis tipped off the police that Dereka was in Mexico because Dereka wasn't in no Mexico. It was all a hoax to mislead the authorities and allow more time for the real trail to Dereka's whereabouts to grow cold. Dereka was actually in Colombia, South America, under the control of a Colombian drug and human trafficking organization. The Colombian organization's capacity to take her to a place deep in the jungled and mountainous terrain of Colombia had made them the perfect choice for Memphis to guarantee Dereka's utter entrapment.

Providing the phony tip that Dereka had been seen in Mexico City was a stroke of genius as far as Memphis was concerned. He knew the authorities would be going full speed ahead following up on the lead. *That ought to keep them spinning their wheels for a while*, Memphis thought, marveling smugly at his own cleverness.

La Casa de Placer

THE GIRLS WERE driven deeper and deeper into a thick-jungled area, traveling on narrow dirt roads that twisted and turned in all directions. Wherever they were headed seemed to be totally isolated. *Even if I was to escape, where would I run to?* Dereka thought warily. *I would never find my way out of here.* Finally, just before dark, they arrived at a huge three-story gray stone building, surrounded by a high barbed-wire gate. The building had once been used as a stash house and hideout for Pablo Escobar, the infamous, brutal Colombian drug lord who wreaked havoc in Colombia during his reign from the late 1970s until his death in l993. It was now known as "La Casa de Placer," which translates in English as "The House of Pleasure." However, it could be more appropriately described as the House of Pain. It was a sex-slave house, one of several such houses Los Chomas owned for the sexual exploitation of young girls, mostly in the form of child-sex tourism. La Casa de Placer was located in a treacherous jungled area in northern Colombia. It was about a two-hour drive from the resort city of Cartagena, Colombia, a top tourist destination renowned for its beautiful white-sand beaches and clear blue water. Unfortunately, the scenic beauty of Cartagena belied a dark ugliness lurking within its boundaries. Cartagena was a magnet for foreign child-sex tourists. Men traveled from far and near for sexual trysts with the exotic, beautiful young girls in Colombia.

Most of the foreign sex predators were successful businessmen from the United States, Canada, Italy, Australia, Germany, Egypt, Japan, and other countries. They traveled to Colombia and paid big bucks to indulge their sick pleasures. Los Chomas catered to their customers and even arranged transportation to and from their facility. They used a phony adventure tours company as a cover to hide their true purpose. The men who patronized La Casa de Placer were extremely secretive about the place, lest their sick sexual trysts with young girls were exposed. Thus, the House of Pleasure was one of the best-kept secrets near Cartagena. Some of the men, on vacation with their families, would tell their wife and kids that the daytime jungle walking tours or nighttime riverboat trips they went on were too dangerous to take them on due to the deadly lizards, poisonous frogs, or lethal, venomous snakes they may encounter. But the truth of the matter was that the men themselves were the deadly, poisonous, and lethal creatures who preyed upon the defenseless young girls at their mercy.

La Casa de Placer had a reputation for having only high-end or upscale girls, the kind of girls the affluent foreign sex tourists were willing to pay top dollar for. Pretty, young local and foreign girls were the specialty at La Casa de Placer. But Los Chomas also had other sex houses for other specialties, including one with young boys. Hell, they didn't care what went on within their walls, as long as the perverts who partook of their wares had enough money to spend. There was really no level too low for them to stoop to.

Dereka and the other girls peered with trepidation at the big gray stone building. An armed man in a military-type uniform opened the gate to let the truck through. Two men came out of the building. One stood well over six feet, was clean shaven, with dark close-cut hair and a long protruding face. The other was shorter and stockier, with long dark frizzy hair and a thick mustache. The men were brothers, ruthless criminals named Diago and Mario Tavaras, known locally as *los hermanos sin alma*—the brothers with no soul. They were raised by hardened criminals to be hardened criminals, and in that respect, they were fourth-generation criminals. Their familial roots run deep in organized crime.

Well educated and well-traveled, the brothers spoke multiple languages, including Spanish, English, Portuguese, Italian, and even some African native languages, including Yoruba. Los Chomas recruited the brothers to set up and manage La Casa de Placer, and they ruled the house with an iron fist. Their fluency in languages and reputation for brutality had made them the perfect choice. The brothers spent three out of four weeks a month at the house and occupied the main level. Each one took one week off per month, but not the same week, to splurge in the nearby resort areas and enjoy the fruit of their labor. Diago actually had an ex-wife and two children who lived in Medellin, Colombia, an innovative, thriving corporate city renowned for its culture, tourism, and education. He spent his time off there with his children. Mario never married; he saw no need for such trivialities. He spent his free time with wild women, drinking and gambling in the luxurious casino hotels in Cartagena.

After speaking briefly with Luis, the brothers ordered the girls out of the truck. Once inside the building, they were led up a narrow flight of stairs to the second level. There the girls were forced to strip naked in a long narrow hallway and stand against the wall. Their clothes, shoes, underwear, jewelry, and any personal belongings whatsoever were taken and placed into large plastic bags. It was the first step in their depersonalization and humiliation. The girls stood against the wall, crying while attempting to cover their nakedness.

Diago, looked intently at each of the girls as he prepared to give them his standard speech for new property. He was the older brother and the brains of the operation. "Save your tears. They mean nothing here. You are now the property of Los Chomas. You belong to us. You will do well to forget your past life in the States. Your family and friends no longer exist. They are dead to you. You are dead to them," Diago stated as he paced back and forth in front of them. "You are slaves. Sex slaves. Your only value is your bodies. If you please your customers and serve the House of Pleasure well, your life here will be tolerable. If you do not, your life will be a living hell. The choice is yours," Diago stated, pausing to let what he'd said sink in. "The men who come here pay well for your services. Consider these men your masters. They own you, at least for a time. Your job is to pleasure them. Do not speak, unless you are spoken to. That's the golden rule. These men are not going to help you. They are here for one reason and one reason only: pleasure. I hope I have made myself clear," Diago said, concluding his statement. He turned and walked away a few steps before turning back around, smiling at the girls, and saying, "Welcome to La Casa de Placer."

The Breaker

AFTER DIAGO LEFT, Mario, the brawn of the operation, took over. "Cause trouble and you will be punished. I will punish you," he said standing closed to each of the girls and staring into their eyes to get his point across. Mario stood in front of Dereka for a long moment. "Luis told us you tried to escape," he said, looking directly at Dereka. "Put this one with the Breaker tonight," he directed the armed guard. *The breaker?* Dereka wondered. *What's the breaker?* But the Breaker wasn't a what; it was a who. The Breaker was an extremely demented, sadistic man who was often used to break in the new girls, particularly the girls who the brothers felt were strong willed and needed to be taken down a peg or two. He was called the Breaker because one night with him was usually all it took to break a girl's spirit, render her submissive, and bend her will to their will. The Breaker actually got off on inflicting pain. He was one of La Casa de Placer's most loyal customers and paid good money for the opportunity to indulge his sadistic appetite for breaking in young, vulnerable girls.

The guard placed the girls into separate rooms and locked the doors. The room Dereka was in contained a bed and a small table with a lamp on top. Dereka looked around desperately for a way out. She knew the door was locked, and the guard was likely still in the hall. There was only one small window in the room, and it was covered with iron bars. Dereka sat on the bed and burst into tears. She was absolutely horrified. She was a thirteen-year-old virgin, and she was about to be raped. *How can this be happening to me?* she thought, shaking her head in disbelief. Just the thought of such a gruesome act was incomprehensible.

Dereka sat in the room alone for what seemed like an hour more. Then she heard the sound of men's voices and footsteps coming down the hall. In a panic, she jumped off of the bed and hid under it, pressing her body in the corner against the wall as far as she could. She heard the door being unlocked and heavy footsteps as someone entered and closed the door. Dereka held her breath, not wanting to make a sound. The person moved closer to the bed, and she could see his huge black lace-up boots.

Dereka heard the bedsprings squeak as the man sat down and removed his boots. After he removed his clothes, he got on his knees and peered under the bed. He had a sunburnt, ruddy red complexion, a broad nose, dark piercing eyes, and a shaggy beard.

"Come out, come out, wherever you are," he taunted Dereka, grinning at her and revealing a mouth full of tobacco-stained teeth. He reached for Dereka, but she kicked his hand away and tried to scoot further back out of his reach. "Ahhhhhhh, a feisty one," the grinning man said. He roughly grabbed Dereka by one of her ankles, dragged her from under the bed, picked her up, and body-slammed her onto the bed.

The Breaker lived up to his reputation that night. He proceeded to rape Dereka with viciousness and brutality. But Dereka was a fighter, and she fought back as best she could. She kicked, bit, and fought him until all her strength was gone. However, her fighting seemed to only accelerate his violent, unforgiving attack. Dereka screamed out in pain as the Breaker pounded and pounded with violent thrusts into her delicate body. To silence her screams, he placed one of his rough hands over her mouth, partially covering her nose in the process. Dereka could barely breathe. She gasped for air, moving her head from side to side, trying desperately to catch her breath. Mercifully, she lost consciousness.

A Quilted Tapestry of Tragedies

DEREKA WAS AWAKENED the following morning by the feel of something wet and cold on her face. She opened her eyes and saw a girl was sitting beside her on a bed. The girl was wiping blood from Dereka's face with a damp cloth. Visions of the previous night's horror flashed through Dereka's mind, and she closed her eyes tightly. She didn't want to wake up and face the awful truth of what had happened to her. She just wanted to go back to sleep and fade away in nothingness.

"Are you all right?" the girl asked as she continued to wipe Dereka's face softly. Dereka looked up and saw the girl looking down at her with concern etched on her face. She had a beautiful exotic look and appeared to be of Asian origin but mixed with another race that Dereka couldn't identify. Her hair was long, black, and shiny, and it hung nearly to her waist. She had slightly slanted eyes with long lashes, a slim face, and small lips.

Dereka tried to sit up but collapsed on the bed as spasms of pain cascaded throughout her body. Her nose was bloody, her lips were bruised and swollen, and she could barely move her right arm. She felt a painful burning sensation between her legs that made her grimace in pain. "Where am I?" Dereka croaked through her extremely dry throat. The girl picked up a glass of water from a rickety table and put it to Dereka's lips to sip.

"They brought you here late last night. They keep us here in the basement," the girl answered. Tears rolled down Dereka's cheeks at the memory of her violent rape. "It's okay to cry," the young girl said as she dabbed at Dereka's tears with the damp cloth. The cold damp towel felt soothing against Dereka's skin, and she attempted to smile to show her gratefulness to the young girl who was showing her kindness.

"Would you like me to help you to the bathroom to get cleaned up?" the girl asked. "We only have one small bathroom, so it's best to get up early while the other girls are still sleeping." Dereka nodded yes and looked around at her bleak surroundings. The basement was a large open space with dirty gray concrete walls and floors. Twin-size cots were lined up against the walls on both sides of the room, and all of them appeared to be occupied. The exposed ceiling above revealed a mass of jumbled electrical wires and water pipes. The basement was completely underground with no windows. Two bare light bulbs dangled on chains from the ceiling.

With the girl's help, Dereka was able to painfully limp down the narrow corridor between the beds to a small, cluttered bathroom with a toilet, sink, and makeshift shower with a dingy plastic shower curtain. After helping Dereka shower, the girl gave her a gray cotton button-front dress to put on and a pair of dingy white cotton panties she got from a cabinet under the sink. "Here, put these on," she said. "We only get a few panties to share, so we have to wash them and hang them there to dry," the girl said, pointing to a wire clothesline running across the length of the bathroom with several pairs of panties hanging across it. Then she handed Dereka a jar of a clear Vaseline-like substance. "Put this down there," she said. "It will help the pain and healing."

As Dereka, with the girl's help, limped painfully back to her bed, she noticed that most of the other girls were now awake. They were either sitting quietly on their beds or talking in small groups of two to three. Dereka looked around for the three girls who had been brought there with her. She saw two of them, the slim, dark-haired white girl and the Hispanic female, huddled together on a bed on the opposite end of the room, looking scared and sorrowful. The girl with the blond hair was in a bed directly across from Dereka's. She was lying still on her bed, staring up at the ceiling, obviously in dire distress. All of them had experienced a horrific night, but none as abominable as Dereka's with the Breaker. She collapsed a few feet from her bed, and several other girls joined in to help carry her the rest of the way. They sat with her on her tiny bed or stood by as Dereka sobbed uncontrollably. They tried their best to comfort her, just as they had been comforted by others when they first came to this deplorable place. Because all they had now was each other.

• • •

When Dereka was all cried out, the other girls left her alone with the young Asian girl. "I'm Sun-Yu. That's my little sister, Jia," Sun-Yu said, nodding at a very young girl staring at them as she lay quietly in her bed. "Jia means 'beautiful,'" Sun-Yu added. The young girl looked to be only about eight or nine years old, and she had the saddest eyes Dereka had ever seen on a little girl.

"Hi, Jia," Dereka said softly, looking into Jia's big, dark sad eyes. Jia stared at Dereka but didn't speak.

"She don't talk much. Not since we came here," Sun-Yu interjected. "We're from China. You're American, aren't you? You're from the United States?" she asked.

"Yes. I'm Dereka. I live in Alexandria, Virginia."

"Nice to meet you, Dereka."

For the next hour or so, the two girls shared their personal stories of how they came to be at trapped in the wretched house known as La Casa de Placer. Sun-Yu was born in Beijing, China, and lived there with her mother and younger sister. Her mother, who had learned to speak fluent English as a child, taught and tutored students in English out of their home. Sun-Yu didn't really remember her father very well but was told he was a French businessman who had worked on assignment in China for a while. Her mother, Lihwa, met him at a nightclub and fell deeply in love with the handsome French man.

Their love affair lasted only a few years and ended abruptly when the girls' father left them shortly after Jia was born. Their mother struggled to raise her two children alone. And because single motherhood in China was still considered taboo, she was shunned by her family and society. She taught her children English at a very young age because she always planned to take them to the United States for a better life.

And true to her word, Lihwa worked and saved up enough money for their airfare to the United States. Sun-Yu had just turned twelve, and Jia was eight years old. Both girls were very excited to be going to the promised land their mother had talked so much about. During their layover in Colombia, while their mother had gone to a snack shop to get them something to eat, two ladies approached the young girls. The ladies were frantic and told the girls that their mother had taken ill and had been taken to the hospital, and that the girls needed to come with them right away. They said they would take the girls to the hospital to see their mother. But instead the ladies had handed them over to two men, who took them to La Casa de Placer and left them there.

"That was about a year ago, I think. It's hard to keep up with time here," Sun-Yu said.

"A year! You've been here a whole year?" Dereka said in shock.

"I think so. But I know my mother is looking for us. She will come for us one day. That keeps me going," Sun-Yu proclaimed, her eyes misting as she spoke of her mother. It was clear she loved and missed her dearly.

"Have you tried to escape?"

"Those who try to escape are caught and punished bad. Three girls tried to escape about a month ago. They were my close friends and wanted me to go with them. But I was too scared. They made it out of the basement, and one of them got out the front door. A guard shot her in the back while she ran away. She died, and they buried her out there somewhere. The other two were taken to the shed and beat. They were never the same after that. The guards took them away one night; we don't know where. We never saw them again."

"Oh my God," Dereka murmured. They were both silent for a moment. "How have you survived here a whole year? How can you stand it? How can you stand being...?" Dereka could not say the words.

"It's very hard, especially in the beginning. When you're with the men, just imagine you're someplace else. Think of something that made you happy once. I think about fun days at home with my mother and sister. It helps, a little," Sun-Yu stated sadly. She continued, "But I feel sorrier for Jia than myself. I wish I could protect her. But I can't," Sun-Yu confessed as she sat on the bed beside Jia.

Dereka learned about the other girls enslaved there—the young, exotic beauties that the Tavaras brothers had gone to great lengths to collect, as if they were assembling an assorted box of rare couture chocolates for their perverted customers to taste and devour. Two of them, Camila and Gabriela, were from the impoverished area surrounding Cartagena. They'd been lured to a resort hotel under the pretense of an open call for teen models but had instead been abducted and sold to Los Chomas. There was Milena from Brazil, who had been coerced into prostituting at a Brazilian brothel and eventually sold by her pimp. The girl named Emma, from London, was literally snatched off the street shortly after getting off a bus she'd taken home one night from a friend's house. Catarina was a high school student from Spain who had traveled to Colombia on a school summer trip to learn about South American culture. She was drugged and raped at an after-hours party she'd sneaked off to attend. She was moved from one sex house to another before ending up at La Casa de Placer. And Sophia, a young girl from Verona, Italy, vacationing in Cartagena with her family—she was taken from a hotel elevator one night while going to get a late-night snack from a vending machine.

In all there were twelve girls, including the four new arrivals, enslaved in the basement of the huge gray stone building. The other new arrivals included Crystal, the blond-haired white girl. She'd gone to a hotel in Charlotte, North Carolina, to see a guy she met online. But the guy, who turned out to be one of Los Chomas's top sex traffickers, kidnapped and turned her over to Luis for transport to Florida. Lydia, the slim white girl with the long dark hair, was a runaway who was seized from the streets of New Orleans. And lastly there was Selena; born in Mexico, she'd lived mostly in Brownsville, Texas, where her mother, an illegal Mexican immigrant, worked as a domestic servant. The male members of the household sexually abused the young, beautiful Mexican girl for years, before the head of the house sold her to a Los Chomas trafficker for a huge sum of money.

The girls were a diverse group of local and foreign girls, representing an array of ethnicities and languages, ranging in age from nine to seventeen. Many of the girls spoke English as a primary or secondary language, but three spoke only Spanish or Portuguese, the primary languages of South America. All these girls had different stories and journeys of how they came to be locked away and trapped like animals in a dank, dreary basement and exploited for the sexual pleasure of perverts. Their stories were like a quilted tapestry of tragedies, weaved and woven together by the common threads duress, deception, and despair.

My Soul to Take

ABOUT MIDMORNING A guard, assault rifle in tow, came down the basement steps carrying a large pot. It was mealtime for the girls. A heavyset, elderly Hispanic woman lumbered down the steps behind him. She was Esmeralda, the great-aunt of the Tavaras brothers who slaved in the house as a cook and housekeeper. With little family to speak of, Esmeralda lived at the mercy of her two nephews, who treated her more like a charity case than family. She lived on the main level in a small windowless room near the back of the house. The brothers worked Esmeralda to the bone, day in and day out. They also warned her not to speak to the girls or attempt to help them in any way. They used intimidation and threats of bodily harm to ensure the elderly lady knew and stayed in her place.

The girls' meals were served in a separate room at the far end of the basement. The room, which served as their kitchen, contained a large wood table with two long benches on each side, a huge commercial-type sink, and a couple of huge trash bins.

"It's time to eat now," Sun-Yu told Dereka as she began to help her up from the bed. Dereka didn't want to get up, because any movement still caused her great pain. But Sun-Yu encouraged her to eat. "We only get two meals a day, sometimes just one. So you need to eat," she said. Emma came over to help Sun-Yu take Dereka to the kitchen. The rest of the girls were already lined up with plastic plates in hand. As they filed, like prisoners, past Esmeralda to be served, the elderly lady looked at them through kind, crinkled eyes. The armed guard stood nearby and watched everyone carefully.

Today their breakfast consisted of a thick creamy cereal made of maize and a piece of bread. They used cups to get water from the faucet. The girls' meals generally consisted of either maize, rice, legumes, or potatoes, with a piece of bread and water to drink. But Esmeralda at least tried to make their sparse food taste decent by adding various spices. Occasionally they were given fruit, like papaya or passionfruit, but no meat of any kind.

After the girls finished their meal, Esmeralda and the guard went upstairs, leaving them alone—that is, until the first tour bus of customers arrived. The adventure tours bus arrived twice a day, sometimes more often, but generally twice. It came around noon and again at night. The paying customers' package deals included transportation to and from their hotels, the girl or girls of their choice, a mask to cover their faces if they so desired, and condoms upon request. Since these men were mainly educated, rich, foreign tourists with wives and children, they were more inclined to use condoms than not. But not all did. And if one of the girls became pregnant, which sometimes happened, she was taken to a doctor in a nearby remote village for a forced abortion. The girls referred to the so-called doctor as "the butcher" because he used crude instruments and techniques to perform painful abortions without the benefit of sedatives. It was a harsh and brutal procedure, which one girl actually didn't survive.

Once the customers arrived, either Diago or Mario would come to the basement with one or both guards to round up the girls. They never called the girls by name but referred to them as sluts, whores, or bitches. The brothers spoke primarily in English since most of the girls spoke it as a primary or secondary language. But they also barked their commands in Spanish and Portuguese, depending on which girl their orders, or rage, were directed at. If any of the girls moved too slow or hesitated in the slightest, she was punched, kicked, slapped, and sometimes choked. Mario especially seemed to enjoy terrorizing them.

The girls selected to pleasure the customers were taken to bedrooms on the second and third floors to perform their duties. The guards waited in the hallway until they finished. The number of girls selected to serve depended on the number of customers to be pleased. On busy days, it was not unusual for one girl to pleasure three to five men.

After breakfast Dereka spent some time getting to know some of the other girls. At noon, right on schedule, Mario and a guard came down to retrieve the girls for the afternoon tryst with the customers. Due to her physical condition, Dereka was given a reprieve for the day. She wouldn't be given many such reprieves. She grieved as she watched the other girls being taken at gunpoint to and from the basement at noon and again that night. Mario even kicked a couple of the girls who he felt were lagging behind.

As Dereka lay in the bed in the dark alone that night, she felt as though she were sinking in quicksand, suffocating and going deeper and deeper with each passing minute. She longed for her mama, grandma, and aunts. "What am I going to do?" Dereka asked them, knowing they could not answer or help her. "I can't do this. I just can't," she admitted. As she pondered her fate, she recalled something her Grandma Ruth used to say all the time: "When all else fails, pray."

So Dereka painfully struggled to her knees to pray, something she'd admittedly begun to neglect to do over time. When she was a little girl, she used to pray often on her knees beside her bed with her mama. But as she got older, her bedtime prayer moments were replaced with TV, phoning friends, texting, Facebook, Instagram, and other social media activities. Now as she bowed on her knees, she didn't really know what to say. So she decided to recite the very first prayer she remembered saying as a small child.

> *Now I lay me down to sleep,*
> *I pray the Lord my soul to keep,*
> *If I shall die before I wake,*
> *I pray the Lord my soul to take. Amen.*

Dereka got back into bed and thought about the words to the prayer she had just uttered. In retrospect, it seemed like such a morbid prayer for a child to pray, talking about dying in one's sleep and such. But the prayer seemed appropriate to Dereka now in her present predicament. Sadly, she actually wanted to die before she would wake, and prayed the Lord her soul to take.

He That Endures

IT WAS THE day of Serena's funeral—a day that BabyRuth, Kenya, and Jasmine dreaded with all their hearts. Almost a week had passed since the tragic event that took both of their loved ones away—one lost to them for forever, the other only momentarily, they hoped. As the ladies dressed in their bedrooms, they each tearfully tried to prepare themselves to make it through the service. Heavy on their hearts was the fact that Dereka was still missing—not there to say her final good-bye to her mother.

BabyRuth sat on the edge of her bed, fully dressed with her Bible in her hands. She prayed that God would help them be strong. "Be with us, Lord. We need you. We can't make do it without you. But we can do all things with you," BabyRuth said as tears rolled down her cheeks. "This is a heavy burden to bear, Lord," she continued. "But I have learned to lean on you, Lord. I know you're here, Lord. I know you haven't left us. And I'm thankful for that."

Upstairs in the bedroom, Kenya could hardly get dressed due her sorrow. She tried to apply her makeup but gave up because it kept running down her face, mixed in with tears. Kenya even briefly thought about telling her mother and Jasmine to go without her. She wasn't sure whether she could handle Serena's funeral. But Kenya knew she had to go. She had to do it for Serena and for her brother Derek. He'd want her to be there. She picked up an old picture from the dresser of Derek, Serena, and her at the beach in Ocean City,

Maryland. Derek and Serena had been seniors in high school and had taken Kenya to the beach for her fourteenth birthday. Kenya looked at their faces, so full of life and love for each other. They were both gone much too soon. Kenya willed herself to be strong for them. She took a deep breath to steady herself and continued to get dressed for the service.

In the bedroom across the hall, Jasmine stared out the window, looking at nothing in particular. It was a beautiful, sunny autumn day, but to Jasmine it felt like doomsday. She sighed deeply, grappling with the loss of her friend Serena, a friend who had been kind, loving, and merciful to her. She and Serena had become more like sisters over the years, and she loved her daughter as if she were her own.

The warmth of the bright sunshine coming through the window reminded Jasmine of her and Dereka's favorite song, "You Are My Sunshine." She reflected on the last line of the song, which said, "Please don't take my sunshine away." But sadly, someone had taken her sunshine away, and it hurt like hell.

BabyRuth's voice in the hallway interrupted Jasmine's thoughts. "Kenya. Jasmine. It's time to go," BabyRuth said as she softly knocked on each of their bedroom doors. Once downstairs BabyRuth took each of their hands in her hands. "I know this is going to be difficult. But we just have to remember where our strength comes from. Like it says in Psalm forty-six, *God is our refuge and strength, a very present help in trouble.* So remember God is with us, and we have each other," BabyRuth said as she embraced each of them tightly and kissed them on their cheek. And with that they left to say their final good-byes to the woman who had become their daughter, sister, confidante, and, most of all, their dear friend.

• • •

Reverend Robert Edwards, affectionately called Pastor Bobby by his congregation, sat in his office preparing himself to preside over Serena's home-going service. He'd been up most of the night thinking about what he could say that would be of comfort to her family, her friends, and church members. He believed strongly that sermons provided during home-going services were more for the living than for the deceased. Pastor Bobby had done hundreds of funerals and eulogies in his many years as pastor of Mount Lebanon Baptist Church. But this one was particularly difficult for him owing to the tragic and sudden way Serena died and the fact that her beloved daughter was still missing. Pastor Bobby and his family were very close to the Jones family and had enjoyed many Sunday and holiday dinners at their home. He had always been struck by the love, warmth, and genuine affection between the family members. They were such a happy, joyful, and loving group. That this happened to them was bewildering and heartbreaking. Even he, the pastor, struggled internally with the why of it all.

Now Pastor Bobby sat in his office, looking at the notes he had prepared the previous night for the sermon and eulogy. But he felt God moving within his spirit and leading him in a different direction. All the things that he would traditionally say at funerals, words such as "The Lord don't put no more on you than you can bear" or "Your loved one's gone on to a better place," just didn't seem sufficient. As Pastor Bobby prayed and meditated before God, he received a new message from the Lord. He stood up, put on his robe, picked up his Bible, and made his way to the sanctuary.

BabyRuth, Kenya, and Jasmine sat on the front pew in the church, clinging tightly to each other. Serena's adoptive parents, Sarah and Jerome Dixon, sat on one side of them, and Kenya's fiancé, Ryan, sat on the other side. Sarah Dixon was so distraught she could barely sit up straight. BabyRuth reached out and placed her hand gently on Sarah's shoulder in a gesture of support and comfort. Sarah looked at BabyRuth through tearful eyes and gave her a small smile of gratitude.

The church was packed to the brim, and even the overflow rooms were overflowing. Those that could not get inside the church stood outside in the parking lot to express their sympathy for the family and their love for Serena. The choir and soloists sang several soul-stirring songs, including one of Serena's favorites, "Going Up Yonder." Family, friends, and church members made tributes, a wonderful eulogy was read, and a slide show of photos was shown.

The congregation waited with anticipation for the sermon. Pastor Bobby stood in the pulpit and looked out at the family and friends gathered there. He directed the congregation to turn in their Bibles to Matthew 24:13 and read the single scripture, *"But he who endures to the end shall be saved."* Pastor Bobby went on to preach a powerful message about endurance and how God wants us to endure unto the end. He talked about how Daniel endured the lion's den; how Jonah endured the belly of a whale; how Shadrach, Meshach, and Abednego endured the fiery furnace; and how Job endured the loss of all his worldly possessions and his children. Then Pastor Bobby brought it home by preaching about how Jesus endured the cross. How Jesus endured the lashes, ridicule, hatred, and even death. How he died and was resurrected—not that he would be saved, but that we would be saved.

By this time practically the entire congregation was on their feet, lifting their arms high in the air as they shouted praises to the Lord. Some shouted for joy, some cried, some jumped and hollered, and a few just sat in their seats and rocked back and forth.

"Endure, Jones family," Pastor Bobby shouted as he prepared to bring his sermon to a close. "Endure, Dixon family; endure, friends; endure, church. Trust in the Lord. He will carry you through. *Look unto Jesus the author and finisher of our faith, who for the joy that was set before him endured the cross.* And by the grace of God, you can endure. By the grace of God, you will endure."

BabyRuth, Kenya, and Jasmine stood on their feet, faces lifted upward as they cried and praised God. The Lord had spoken through the man of God and given them a message of hope and endurance. It was just what they needed to hear; it was food for their weary souls. After the service, when they walked out of the church, their steps were a bit surer, their hearts a little lighter, their minds clearer, and their spirits lifted higher. Because with God's help, they knew, they could endure until the end. And they hoped and prayed that Dereka would endure.

In Bed with the Devil

DEREKA WAS IN bed with the devil. That's the only way she could describe the man who was on top of her, grunting and groaning. He was wearing a face mask to conceal his face, and only his beady eyes were revealed. The men who hid behind the masks did so likely to pretend that it wasn't them but someone else performing these vile sex acts with children—not them. After all, these men were mostly respectable husbands, fathers, brothers, doctors, teachers, clergy, and such. They were wealthy foreigners on vacation, some with their families, in beautiful tourist resort cities such as Cartagena or Medellin, and would never do something as despicable as rape young girls at a sex house.

Dereka loathed all the men who defiled the bodies of the young girls enslaved there. But she was particularly disgusted by those who masked their faces. They didn't even have the guts to reveal their faces to the young victims they demoralized. *At least own up to the wretched varmint that you are*, Dereka thought bitterly. As far as she was concerned, they were slivering villainous cowards wearing masks while they indulged their depraved true nature. Afterward, they could remove the masks and go on pretending they were decent human beings.

Dereka stared up at the ceiling while her masked assailant assaulted her body. Mentally she transported herself to another time and place, as she often did when in bed with the devil. As far as she could tell, she'd been at the house ten days. Ten brutal, horrific days.

To keep track of time, Dereka used her fingernails to scratch small marks underneath the long wooden table. One mark for each day she was there. Each mark she made was like a stab to her heart, for each mark symbolized a day of intense misery, the likes of which she had never thought possible. There were times when she wanted to just give up, to throw in the towel, to just go to sleep and never wake up. But it was at those times that she could sense her mama, grandma, and aunts encouraging her to be strong, to never give in and never give up. So Dereka felt she had to keep going, if not for herself, for them.

Dereka focused her attention intently on the water stains on the ceiling, the brownish stains left from water leaking through the roof on heavy rain days. If she happened to be on the second floor instead of the third, where there were no water stains, she created them in her mind. Tonight there were several stains on the bedroom ceiling for her to focus on. The stains gave her something to concentrate on instead of the appalling reality of what was happening to her. She liked to make-believe the stains were images of the strong women in her life. Dereka pretended the biggest water stain was her Grandma Ruth, wearing her fuzzy pink robe while sitting in her favorite chair reading the Bible. Another water stain with edges that resembled wings was her mother, Serena, as an angel in heaven. The stain with the wide curve at the top was no doubt her Auntie Jazz, wearing one of her wide-brimmed hats and flashing her signature dazzling smile. And the long, narrow stain with a dark circle near the middle was Aunt Kenya. The circle represented her big, endearing heart.

Who would have thought that water stains on the ceiling could have such meaning and purpose in someone's life? Ordinarily they would not. But for Dereka these simple water stains helped her to visualize the women she loved, and who she knew loved her. They helped her to disconnect her mind, which was still able to roam free, from her body, which was not. So she stared at the water stains on the ceiling, day after day and night after night, while she was in bed with the devil.

My Mother's Child

AFTER TWO WEEKS in Mexico City, Detective Davis was without any solid leads as to Dereka's whereabouts. She had worked with Mexican authorities to successfully track down the man who called the hotline about possibly seeing Dereka there. After intense interrogation, he admitted that it was a hoax and that he'd been paid to place the call. But he refused to say who paid him, out of either loyalty to or fear of the individual. They arrested and charged the man with providing false information to authorities and hindering a police investigation. But it was clear he would rather take his chances within the court system than be labeled a snitch and suffer a worse fate.

BabyRuth, Kenya, and Jasmine carried on as best they could. Thanksgiving and Christmas came and went, but there were no festive celebrations. Kenya was still staying at home with BabyRuth. The three ladies went to church on Christmas Day and cried and prayed. BabyRuth put up a small Christmas tree so in case Dereka came home for Christmas, she would have a tree. But she didn't come home.

After the holiday season, BabyRuth returned to her job at the Veterans Administration. It helped to keep busy. Jasmine reluctantly returned to Los Angeles to check in on her health and beauty spas. Although her manager had done a great job keeping things running smoothly, Jasmine's input was needed on some important business matters that had come up. But she planned to return to Virginia as soon as she could. She felt closer to Dereka there. And she wanted to be there when Dereka was found and came home.

Of the three of them, Kenya was having the hardest time coping with what had happened. Her mind and heart were overcome with anxiety and guilt. She falsely believed Serena's death and Dereka's abduction were her fault. Memphis had done it to get to her. "Why couldn't it have been me?" Kenya questioned out loud. "I would have gladly changed places with either of them." The heavy burden of guilt she felt drove her deeper and deeper into depression. She would lie in bed sometimes for days at a time, barely eating or drinking except when her mama forced her to. BabyRuth did the best she could to lift her spirits, but Kenya appeared to be slipping further and further away. Her fiancé, Ryan, stopped by every day, sometimes several times a day, to check on her. He brought her flowers, teddy bears, her favorite latte, or anything he thought would cheer her up.

Kenya had met Ryan about a year before in the lobby of the Fairfax Judicial Center Building, where she worked. She had literally bumped into him while rushing off the elevator to a meeting. He'd stopped to help her pick up a few of her items that had fallen on the floor. Kenya was immediately attracted to the tall, handsome, well-dressed, polite man. They exchanged business cards and had lunch the following day in a nearby park. Kenya learned that Ryan was a self-made man who had beaten all odds to succeed in life. He told her that he was born in Detroit and raised by a single mom in the Islandville community in the east side of the city, an area once regarded as one of the most dangerous neighborhoods in America. His mother died of breast cancer when he was only fourteen years old. With no family willing to take in the young teenage boy, Ryan was placed in foster care, going from one home to another until he was eighteen.

Determined to succeed, he studied hard in high school, worked his way through college, and earned a scholarship to the University of Detroit Mercy School of Law. While there he was mentored by a law professor, who helped him get a position with the law firm in Virginia where he currently worked. Kenya was touched by Ryan's story and admired his tenacity and determination. Their relationship progressed rapidly, and they became engaged about eight months later. They had not set a date but had planned to do so soon.

Now, with all that had happened, Kenya could not think about marriage, or much of anything. All she did was wallow in her guilt and shame that her actions had somehow caused the tragedy. Not even Ryan's constant love and attentiveness seemed to have an effect. BabyRuth waited patiently for Kenya to come around, coddling her and pampering her day after day. But one day BabyRuth decided it was time to show her daughter some tough love—for her own good.

BabyRuth marched into Kenya's room early one morning and snatched the covers off her. "Are you a tail?" BabyRuth asked. Kenya looked up groggily and saw her mother staring at her with her arms folded across her chest.

"Am I a what?" Kenya asked, not understanding what in the world her mama was talking about.

"I said, are you a tail?" BabyRuth repeated.

"Am I a tail? No, I'm not a tail, Mama. What are you talking about?" Kenya asked, puzzled.

"Well, if you're not a tail, then why are you acting like one? My Bible tells me that *we are the head, and not the tail, and we shall be above only, and not beneath.* Well, Kenya, looks to me like you've crawled into bed with your tail between your legs, blaming yourself for something that's not your fault."

"But I can't help the way I feel," Kenya said, her eyes watering. BabyRuth sat on the bed and pulled Kenya into her arms.

"I know it's hard, sweetheart. It's hard on all of us. But we just can't lie down and give up. We've got to remember who we are, and whose we are. We are children of the most high God. *We're the head, and not the tail.* Now enough of this lying around feeling sorry for yourself. You're better than this. You're stronger than you know. And we're going to get through this thing together," BabyRuth assured.

Kenya looked up at her mother and saw strength, hope, faith, and love reflected in her mother's eyes. She smiled at her mama and said,

"You're right, Mama. I am better than this. I'm strong. I have to be. Because I'm my mother's child."

"That you are," BabyRuth responded, smiling down at her daughter.

•   •   •

Kenya went back to her own place and returned to work later that week. She was warmly welcomed back with a surprise breakfast celebration in the conference room. Her staff, supervisors, and colleagues had missed her terribly and anxiously anticipated her return. Kenya was respected by her supervisors, admired by her fellow attorneys, and well-liked by her staff. She was particularly close to her assistant, Trevon McLemore, a young man she'd met while performing volunteer work with a legal aid and support program for formerly incarcerated young black men. Most people would have given up on someone like Trevon, a troubled young man who had been in and out of the juvenile and prison system since he was nine. But Kenya, with her big heart for the underdog, saw something in him that no one else had seen. She saw potential. So she took him under her wing. Kenya exposed him to positive male role models at her office, provided him summer jobs, and invited him to Sunday family dinners at BabyRuth's house. Now Trevon worked for her full time as her assistant, and he was also enrolled in an online criminal justice program.

Kenya took Trevon to a working lunch at a nearby restaurant to review her upcoming caseload and catch up on the latest office gossip. They laughed and talked for about two hours, each of them relishing being in the company of the other. But someone was watching them—someone with an ominous agenda. Memphis sat at a table in the corner, watching Kenya and Trevon with a smirk on his face. *She has no idea what's coming next*, he thought as he bit into his pastrami sandwich.

Come Out Swinging

JASMINE SAT AT her desk in her big corner office on the eleventh floor. She had been back in LA about a week and handled all the pressing matters at hand. She looked around at all the business awards and photos of herself with famous VIPs in the sports and entertainment world. Just a few weeks ago, the awards and photos had brought her a great sense of pride at what she had accomplished. But now all she felt was a void in her heart and spirit. Her whole world had been turned topsy-turvy. And all because of one man with a vendetta against her friend Kenya. It was because of this Memphis character, this scum of the earth as far as Jasmine was concerned, that their world had been shattered.

The more Jasmine thought about what Memphis had done, the more her blood boiled. Soon Jasmine was inwardly calling him every foul name in the book, reverting back to the street language she used growing up in the tough streets of Baltimore. She called him a trifling bastard, lowlife son of a bitch, drug-dealing demon, piece of rotten sh*t, and many other obscenities that came to mind. She knew name calling was childish and futile, but she did it anyway. It was her way of venting her frustration and anguish at all the pain and heartache that scoundrel had caused.

Jasmine got out of her chair and began pacing the floor like a tiger pacing around in a cage. She was a fighter, always had been. And she could feel her fight returning, her resolve building as she paced. *"The devil is a liar,"* Jasmine said out loud as she continued to pace back and forth. And as she paced, a plan of action began to take form in her mind. She sat back down at her desk, eyes narrowed, hands clenched, and mentally began to hatch a plan. She got on her computer and began typing out the details. Jasmine stayed at her office late into the night, compiling data and performing Internet searches. Shortly after midnight her plan had taken form. She sat back and let out a deep breath. Jasmine felt a great sense of peace and assurance concerning what she was about to do. And that let her know, beyond a shadow of a doubt, that it was what she had to do.

Jasmine's plan was twofold. First, she would sell one of her spas to generate some working capital. She decided to keep one spa so she'd have something to pass on to Dereka when, not if, they found her. That way Dereka would have something of her own to build upon later in life. Jasmine knew that selling her main Lady Jazz Abode spa would be easy because one of her major competitors had been trying to get their greedy hands on her lucrative spa operations for years. The company had made several very generous offers to buy her out, but she'd always turned them down cold. As a matter of fact, she'd been rather offended that they even thought she would sell either of her babies. But that was then, and this is now.

With money from the sale, Jasmine would help fund and work with a human trafficking rescue organization to find and rescue Dereka, and as many other young victims as she could in the process. During her Internet research, Jasmine learned of an organization called Operation Undercover, a private organization in Richmond, Virginia, that conducted undercover rescues at hotels, sex-slave houses, illegal brothels, illicit massage parlors, and other places in major US cities and abroad. Volunteers in the organization often posed as buyers seeking to purchase young girls, or customers seeking sex with minors. Sometimes they would pose as men throwing a bachelor party looking to pay for sex with young girls, or as vacationing frat brothers with a propensity for young girls. They conducted raids to rescue the victims and capture and arrest the perpetrators, and also to covertly gather credible information that could be used by local authorities to successfully prosecute the offenders in a court of law.

The brave men and women who volunteered for this covert work in the organization put themselves in considerable danger. The pimp, madams, and organized crime groups that ran these sex-slave operations were violent beyond belief. If discovered, the undercover volunteers could be tortured or kidnapped themselves, or, even killed. But that didn't stop the volunteers from choosing to wade boldly into the murk and the mire of the sex-slave trade to save children. They did it because they had a heart for the young victims caught up in the repugnant business of sex trafficking. Somebody had to do something to help them. And they were that somebody.

Early the next morning, Jasmine phoned BabyRuth and Kenya to tell them of her plans to help find Dereka. They were immensely touched and moved that she would make such a sacrifice. Later that week Jasmine met with her attorney and representatives from her competitor's company to discuss her plan to sell her main spa. The company made her an offer on the spot—a little less generous than their previous offers, but generous just the same. Jasmine left the meeting with her head held high, shoulders squared, and determination in her step. Memphis had thrown a sucker punch and knocked her off her feet, at least temporarily. But Jasmine was up before the count of ten, and she had come out swinging.

Family by Default

IT WAS NOW mid-January, and as far as Dereka could tell, she'd been in captivity for about two months. For the most part, the holidays had come and gone without so much as a passing glance. And even Christmas would have faded into oblivion if it had not been for Esmeralda. One morning a few weeks ago, the girls had discovered small pieces of meat mixed in with the thick pot of maize that Esmeralda served them for breakfast. They had looked at each other in surprise. "Feliz Navidad," Esmeralda said, giving them her big snaggletooth smile. That had been their only reminder that it was Christmas. Other than that, it was business as usual.

The girls tried to support, encourage, and nurture one another as best they could. Dereka considered them her family by default. They occupied their minds in their spare time to keep from totally losing their sanity. They enjoyed teaching each other simple phrases in different languages. Dereka learned to say "I love you" in Spanish (*Te quiero*), Mandarin (*Wo ai ni*), Portuguese (*Eu te amo*), and Italian (*Ti voglio bene*). She tried to say it at least once a day to every girl in their primary language. She hoped it made them feel better. It sure made her feel better.

And because they were not provided books of any kind, they taught each other what they knew in regard to math, geography, history, and other basic studies. They were not provided paper or pens, so they improvised by using small pieces of dried-up soap to write on the walls or floor. But they were careful to wash away the writings before Mario or Diago saw them, fearing that the men may cut back on soap rations if they knew the girls were using the soap for learning. As it was, they didn't get much in regard to personal hygiene items. Each of them received one toothbrush and comb, and they shared meager monthly rations of soap, toothpaste, deodorant, and a few other necessary items.

Although all the girls were close, tighter-knit groups of friends formed within the larger group. Dereka's inner circle of close companions included Sun-Yu and her little sister, Jia, Lydia, and Emma. The only girl that kept primarily to herself was Crystal, the one with the blond hair who was part of the four girls, including Dereka, taken from the US. Dereka had reached out to Crystal several times, but she chose to stay to herself. Crystal cried in her bed most of the time, or just stared into space. "She may not make it. I've seen girls like her before. They give up. Can't take it," Sun-Yu told Dereka one day.

Dereka sat on the bed braiding Sun-Yu's hair into a twist style she learned from Aunt Kenya. Sun-Yu was engaged in one of her favorite pastimes—talking about her mother. "My mother is very beautiful," Sun-Yu said with pride. "She has the prettiest milky skin, sparkling black eyes, and long black shiny hair that hangs down her back. And she always wear red dresses and bright-red lipstick. She loves red; it's her favorite color."

"She sounds like a very special lady. I hope I can meet her one day," Dereka stated wistfully.

"Oh you will," Sun-Yu answered confidently. "She will come for me and Jia, and I will make sure she takes you too. I will not leave you here," Sun-Yu said, smiling at Dereka.

"I know you won't," Dereka said, choking back tears. "And I won't leave you or Jia or anyone here when my family comes for me. When one goes, we all go," Dereka stated earnestly.

Sun-Yu abruptly hopped off the bed and headed for the kitchen area, motioning for Dereka to follow her. "I want to show you something," Sun-Yu said as she moved one of the heavy trash cans. She got on her knees and used her fingernails to remove a loose piece of concrete, reached into a small space, and retrieved something wrapped in toilet paper. It was a gorgeous red scarf with blue and white butter-flies painted on it. "This is my mother's scarf. She gave it to me to hold for her at the airport before we were taken. I want to give it back to her when she comes for us. Isn't it beautiful?" Sun-Yu gushed.

"Yes, it is," Dereka replied, feeling the soft silkiness of the scarf.

"No one knows it's here but Jia, and now you," Sun-Yu said as she tucked the scarf securely back into its hiding place and replaced the concrete block.

"I won't tell anyone," Dereka whispered.

When Dereka and Sun-Yu returned to their beds, Jia motioned to Dereka that she wanted to play a game Dereka had taught her. Jia still did not talk but communicated through motions and nods. If she really needed to say something, she'd whisper it to Sun-Yu to say for her. It was clear that Sun-Yu loved her little sister dearly and tried her best to mother her. Dereka loved Jia too, and it broke her heart to know that Jia, at only nine years old, was subjected to the same deg-radation and depravities as they were. Dereka spent as much time as she could with Jia and even taught her a few simple games she used to play herself as a child.

Playing games may seem like the most unlikely of pastimes con-sidering where they were and what they were forced to do. One may ask, how could they even have the mind or desire to play? But playing was actually therapeutic for both of them. It helped Jia to enjoy one of the simple pleasures of childhood in the midst of unthinkable mon-strosities. And it helped Dereka to provide to another child a small source of the pleasure she had experienced as a child. Playing games with Jia made Dereka feel normal, at least for a time.

One of Jia's favorite games was Which Hand Is It In? Dereka con-cealed a button in one hand, put both hands behind her back, and showed both fists to Jia so she could guess which hand the button was in. They played this game for a while, and Lydia and Sun-Yu even joined in to try to help Jia pick the right hand. But their family play-time soon came to a sudden end when Mario and the guard came down the basement stairs to collect the girls for the evening's ser-vice. The devil's trolley of demons had arrived.

A Greater Purpose

JASMINE, KENYA, AND BabyRuth sat in the conference room of the Operation Undercover's headquarters office in Richmond. They were meeting with Douglas Wright, the founder-CEO, and Sheryl Adkins, the mission coordinator. They were there to discuss the possibility of Jasmine working with the organization. After Douglas explained their overall mission, vision, and goals, he asked Sheryl to talk about one of their recent rescue efforts in Haiti.

"With so many homeless children still living on the streets or in tent cities, Haiti is a prime destination for sex traffickers. Last month we rescued twenty-two victims from a prostitution and sex-trade house in Port-au-Prince. Our volunteer workers posed as potential buyers looking for young girls between the ages of nine and thirteen. Our team met with a man who handed them a menu of sorts that had pictures of the girls along with their ages, and whether or not they were virgins. He said the virgins cost more than the 'used girls,'" Sheryl informed.

"Oh, my Lord," BabyRuth murmured under her breath.

"On the day of the rescue, the team hid small cameras and micro-phones on their bodies and clothing while they toured the sex house to inspect the girls for purchase. The Haitian police waited outside in specially equipped vans. Fortunately, we've been able to invest in state-of-the-art surveillance equipment, including wireless mini-cameras and microphones that can be disguised as necklaces or watches or discreetly hidden in the ear, eyeglasses, and such. Once the exchange of money actually happened, the police moved in. We're thrilled that twenty young girls and two boys were rescued as part of that operation," Sheryl said with pride.

"What happens to the children after they're rescued?" Kenya asked.

"That's a good question, Kenya. In some instances we're able to return the child to his or her family if appropriate. If no acceptable family or guardian can be located, our rescue support team works with local family services to place each child in a safe environment. We also have volunteer therapists and psychologists who provide some counseling services. We do the best we can, but it's difficult, particularly in places like Haiti where family services are so over-burdened," Sheryl admitted. She continued, "When we first start-ing doing rescue work, we discovered that sometimes the children themselves are being treated like the criminals who enslave them. The victims, mostly women and girls, are sometimes arrested, inter-rogated, prosecuted for prostitution, and sent to juvenile detention or prison. That's why before every rescue operation, we work with family services organizations to make sure the children will have a safe place to go."

Douglas took it from there. "In a perfect world there would be no sex trafficking victims because there would be no sex trafficking vic-timizers. The customers are mainly men from every walk of life who pay to rape, assault and abuse young children. But unfortunately the world is not perfect, and the demand for this vulgarity is growing. That's why organizations like ours are so important. We're a non-profit organization that rely solely on donations to rescue children caught up in the sex-slave trade. And we're so grateful for your gen-erous donation to help our cause," he stated, referring to the huge donation Jasmine had already made, and Kenya's and BabyRuth's contribution as well. "And we'll do everything we can to help find your granddaughter and niece. Our hearts go out to you, and to every young person and family caught up in the heinous child sex traffick-ing crime."

"When can I get started?" Jasmine asked anxiously.

"There's a process that every volunteer worker must go through," Sheryl responded. "Our standard procedures include conducting a criminal background check and requiring that each potential worker undergoes psychological counseling."

"Let me be blunt," Douglas interjected. "This is dangerous work, and you may literally be putting your life on the line with each undercover rescue. That's why we generally have the local police accompany us. And we teach our volunteers advanced self-defense techniques. We've been fortunate that no one with Operation Undercover has been seriously injured while performing their duties, although we've had some close calls," he acknowledged.

"It's mentally and emotionally draining work. There have been times when we've had to walk away from the situation, often due to lack of cooperation from local authorities. We can't save all the victims, but we can save some; that's what keeps us going," Sheryl added with a smile of satisfaction.

After the meeting Jasmine spent about an hour completing the necessary paperwork required as part of the screening process. During the drive back to Alexandria, the ladies were quiet, each lost in her own thoughts about the road Jasmine was about to embark on. BabyRuth and Kenya were hopeful that Jasmine would be able to find Dereka and help other young girls. But they were concerned that Jasmine might be placing herself in harm's way. And to be honest, Jasmine was a little nervous about the undercover work. But she knew she had to do it. It was her way of honoring Serena, the woman who she felt had saved her life. Back then Jasmine didn't understand why or how Serena forgave her. But Serena always knew that God, in his infinite wisdom, brought them together for a greater purpose. Now Jasmine knew exactly what that purpose was. She would find her dear friend's daughter and bring her home, or die trying.

A Brighter Day Ahead

IT WAS NOW three months and counting, in Dereka's estimate. And God only knows how she'd made it so far. However, Crystal finally gave up. She broke. She just couldn't take it anymore.

One afternoon when Diago and the guard came down to get the girls for the customers, Crystal refused to move. "Get out of bed, you lazy slut," Diago demanded. But Crystal didn't budge. She just stared at him as if she were looking right through him. They dragged her out of the bed, kicked and punched her, but she only curled herself into a ball and cried. Crystal didn't even comply when the guard pointed the assault rifle to her head and threatened to shoot her. Dereka tried to intervene, but she was hit hard in the stomach with the butt of the rifle and fell to her knees in excruciating pain. Sun-Yu and Lydia helped Dereka up, their own faces wet with tears at the cruelty to their friends. Because the customers were waiting, Diago decided to leave Crystal alone for the moment and take the other girls to the waiting guests upstairs, who had paid good money for them. "Stop crying, you pathetic sacks of sh*t. *Deja de llorar lo patéticos sacos de m*erda*," Diago ordered as the girls filed past him, wiping the tears from their faces.

Later that evening, Dereka sat on the bed beside Crystal and combed her hair gently. It was a small gesture, but it seemed to soothe her a bit. As she combed Crystal's hair, Dereka hummed softly, like her own mother used to do when she combed Dereka's hair. She hummed a song she was told was a favorite of her great-grandmother Leona. She thought about the words as she hummed the soothing melody.

There'll be a brighter day ahead,
For Jesus has said.
By him we will be led,
There'll be a brighter day ahead.

Soon Mario and a guard came storming down the basement steps. Mario's face was set in a grotesque grimace that made him look like the devil himself. They dragged Crystal out of the bed and took her up the stairs.

"They're taking her to the shed," Sun-Yu stated sadly.

"The shed? What's the shed?" Dereka asked, although deep down she was afraid to know.

Emma answered, "It's a small wooden shed where they take us for punishment. They torture us there. They use electrical wires, needles, hot iron, tools and stuff to inflict pain. They like to target our sensitive parts, like nipples, belly button, eyes, and the bottom of our feet. They try not to scar our bodies too much because bodies are not useful if they're all scarred up."

Their talking ceased when they heard Crystal's piercing screams. It was the most heart-wrenching and terrifying sound that Dereka had ever heard. It became so agonizing that Dereka and some others placed their hands over their ears to try to drown out the sound. If it were the brothers' intention that the screams resulting from their skilled torture would be a deterrent to help keep all the girls in line, in that respect they succeeded. It had the effect of placing fear in the young girls' hearts and compliance in their spirits.

Finally the screaming stopped, and Crystal, barely conscious, was brought back to the basement and dumped onto her bed. The other girls tried to take care of her, but Dereka was the only one that Crystal allowed to even touch her at this point. No one knew why, but they assumed it was something about Dereka's spirit that was comforting and kind. Dereka wiped the blood from Crystal's nose and mouth, placed cold wet towels on her breasts and stomach, and rubbed the clear Vaseline-like substance on the burn marks on the bottom of her feet, her fingertips, and her earlobes. She then sat with Crystal until she was summoned to make the evening rounds. And when Dereka returned, she sat with Crystal some more. The other girls started calling her Angel Girl or *Niña Ángel* because to them, that's exactly what she was.

The next morning, when Dereka went to check on her, it was clear Crystal was dead. The girls cried as they stood or knelt around her bed. "Let's say a prayer," Dereka said, taking the hands of those around her. The girls formed a circle around Crystal's bed. Dereka prayed that Crystal was at peace and that her suffering had ended. Then she prayed for the rest of them. She prayed for "a brighter day ahead."

Slow and Steady Wins
the Race

WHEN ESMERALDA AND the guard came down with food later that morning and discovered Crystal dead in her bed, the guard summoned the Tavaras brothers. Diago was visibly upset with his brother that Crystal had died. But it was not because the life of a beautiful young girl had ended. It was because their valuable commodity was no longer capable of producing any return on investment. Diago yelled loudly at Mario, ranting and raving in Spanish, about how he should have been more careful. "You were not supposed to kill the girl, for God's sake. How can she make money if she's dead?" Diago yelled. He then looked down at Crystal with disgust etched on his face. "What a waste," Diago said, shaking his head.

The brothers left the basement, directing the guards to dispose of the body. They unceremoniously dumped Crystal's body into a huge plastic trash bag and lugged her up the stairs. Crystal, one of God's treasures, was being treated like Satan's trash. Dereka and the others cried as they watched their friend being taken out in a black trash bag to be buried somewhere in the dense Colombian jungle, her remains likely never to be discovered. It just didn't seem fathomable that a beautiful young girl could have ended up this way. She had made the foolish mistake of trusting a guy she met online and ended up dead in Colombia in a black trash bag.

The girls had never gotten to see the vibrant, free-spirited, fun-loving teenager that Crystal had been in her life prior to her entrapment as a sex slave. They had never gotten to know the real Crystal Theresa Jenkins from Charlotte, North Carolina. The Crystal with the loving family and numerous friends back home who were hoping and praying that she return to them. But for them that day would never come.

Dereka kept the comb with strands of Crystal's long blond hair in it. She asked Sun-Yu whether she could keep it in the secret place with Sun-Yu's mother's scarf, and Sun-Yu eagerly allowed her to. Dereka hoped someday she'd be able to find Crystal's family and give the comb to them. It wasn't much, but it was something that could help to bring them some comfort and closure.

That night as Dereka lay in her bed alone in the dark, she could not get the image out of her mind of Crystal's body being hauled away in a trash bag. And she vowed in her heart that she would not end up that way. She would return to the ones she loved, and who loved her.

But how was she going to survive the living hell she was in? It just didn't seem possible. Dereka thought about something her grandma used to say all the time: *The race is not given to the swift, nor the battle to the strong...but to those who endure to the end.* It brought to mind the time she ran a half marathon with her Aunt Kenya and Auntie Jazz about a year ago. They had spent about three months preparing for the race and were in prime condition. Before the race her aunts had warned Dereka to pace herself so she wouldn't run out of gas. But on the day of the race, Dereka had bolted out of the gate like a wild stallion, leaving Kenya and Jasmine in her dust. In her youthful cockiness, she'd wanted to show off and beat her two older aunts. She visualized herself crossing the finish line miles ahead of them, arms raised high, the crowd cheering. But sure enough, by around mile seven or eight, Dereka ran out of steam. She had to slow down to a fast walk instead of running, sweating and panting hard as she went. Kenya and Jasmine not only caught up with her but passed her by, laughing at her in the process. "Slow and steady wins the race," Kenya had shouted to Dereka as she cruised past.

Dereka smiled slightly as she thought back to that day. Slow and steady was the way to go. And that's how she would run her race right out of the hell she was in. Slow and steady, to the end. And she would make it to the finish line.

Like Father, Like Son

KEVIN CURTIS SAT in the prison yard with his ace boon coon, a guy named Parker, who was also his cellmate. Kevin, having now been in prison for about twelve years, was feeling no pain. *Hell, I didn't have it this good on the outside*, Kevin thought as he watched his fellow inmates lift weights and play basketball in the yard. He'd had a relatively easy prison life, due primarily to his father's ruthless reputation and connections with prison guards, wardens, and other prison officials. Kevin enjoyed privileges few other inmates did, such as plenteous access to contraband, including drugs and cigarettes, and easy work details.

Kevin knew all about his father's act of revenge against his old nemesis, Kenya Jones. He'd heard Memphis kidnapped her niece and sold her to a crime organization in Colombia, where she was a sex slave. One of Memphis's most trusted workers, who visited Kevin regularly in prison, kept him informed of all the criminal happenings in the outside world. Kevin was thrilled to learn that Memphis had finally gotten even with Kenya. And he applauded his father's use of Kenya's niece to settle the score. The kidnapping of Kenya's dear dead brother's child no doubt dealt a debilitating blow to her and her entire family. As far as Kevin was concerned, it was about time someone took them uppity Negroes, referring to the Jones family, down a notch.

As was their usual custom during their one-hour recreation time in the prison yard, Kevin and Parker were engaged in one of their favorite pastimes. It was a barbaric betting game they created to pass the prison time and keep things interesting. They would bet on things like which of the new inmates would be the first to be raped, or whether this or that inmate would get shanked by the end of the week, or whether this or that prisoner would even make it out of prison alive. Betting on the horrific fates of their fellow inmates was a sickening hobby. But they found it amusing. They bet cigarettes, candy, and other menial material things, but the biggest prize for them was the bragging rights of being able to outwit one another, of being one up on the other.

"That's another one for me," Kevin said, smiling and stretching his legs out in front of him. "I told you that mf'er Jerome wasn't going to make it out of here alive. I was laughing when they carried his punk ass out of here this morning. I couldn't wait to gloat," Kevin said, grinning like a Cheshire cat.

"Yeah, man. I never would have called that one. Mean as that dude was, I didn't think anybody would be able to waste him," Parker said, shaking his head.

"What that make us now? About fourteen to five?" Kevin asked with a smirk on his face.

"Something like that. Man, you one lucky son of a bitch," Parker said, giving his friend a fist bump.

"Luck has nothing to do with it, my brother," Kevin responded as they got up to return to their prison cell.

And Kevin was right about that. Luck had nothing to do with his winning ways. But cunningness and a cold heart did. What Parker didn't know was that Kevin was stacking the deck in his favor to ensure that the person he betted on indeed was the one to be raped, shanked, beaten, or even murdered. But Kevin didn't carry out the gruesome acts himself. He was too weak for such violent things, fearing he might end up getting hurt himself in the process. Kevin actually bribed other inmates to do his bidding for him, providing them with food, cigarettes, drugs or whatever it took to guarantee he'd win the bet.

Kevin would let Parker win one every now and then, just to reduce suspicion that he was cheating at their crazed betting game. But that didn't happen often, because Kevin liked winning too much and went to great lengths to arrange the grim outcome in his favor. He didn't give a rat's behind about who suffered as a result, as long as he came out on top. He was as cold as ice. Like father, like son.

The One Called Scrappy

IT WASN'T LONG before Crystal's bed was filled. About a week after her death, the guards dragged another girl down the basement steps. She came down kicking, screaming, fighting, and cussing. They threw her on the floor, but she was up as quick as greased lightning. And she was fighting mad. She charged the guards, swinging her fists, kicking, spitting, and scratching. One of the guards, having had enough of her shenanigans, hit her full in the face with his fist, causing her to stumble and fall on her back. The blow stunned her temporarily. But before long she was back on her feet, running up the basement steps after the guards, who had already left and locked the door. She pounded her fists against the door, yelling and swearing at the guards. The cuss words flowed effortlessly from her lips, sounding like some kind of warped poetry. Every other word was *mf this* or *mf that*. She had a mouth on her. The other girls just stared at her in amazement, their eyes wide and mouths hanging open. They were totally enthralled by the gutsy girl. She was the real deal.

When she tired of her assault on the locked door, she finally noticed the other girls standing around looking at her. "What you mfs standing there looking at me for? Come help me break down this damn door!" she demanded. Nobody moved. "Can't you dumb-ass bitches hear?" she questioned, giving them attitude.

"We hear you," Dereka replied on behalf of the girls. "But it's no use. You're just going to get yourself killed, and maybe get others killed in the process."

"Once we tried to break the door down with a bed frame," Sun-Yu added. "They blew smoke under the door, making us think the house was on fire. Very scary. We have nowhere to run. Another time they filled the basement with awful-smelling gas."

"Who are these sorry mfs?" the girl asked. The other girls took the time to school the spunky newcomer on where she was and the horrific things she'd be forced to do. Sophia brought her a cold wet towel to hold over her nose to stop the blood flowing as a result of the hard punch in her face. The spunky newcomer was Regine, a member of a Dominican American street gang based in Bronx, New York. The gang members often traveled to Colombia to buy cocaine to smuggle into the United States.

Regine was a striking beauty. She had smooth cocoa-brown skin, thick, curly shoulder-length hair, jet-black eyes, thick lashes and brows, full lips, and perfect white teeth. She was heavy on the top and slim on the bottom. Her parents, both Dominicans, had immigrated to the Bronx when Regine was five years old. Her father was abusive to both her and her mother, and it was he who introduced Regine to the gang life when she was nine.

Regine had come to Colombia several days before with a couple of male gang members to purchase cocaine to sell back in the United States. They met with three men who were supposed to be connected to the same Colombia drug cartel they'd dealt with several times before. But the men turned out to be imposters and robbed them instead. So much for honor among thieves. In the ensuing shootout, both of Regine's fellow gang members were killed, along with one of the Colombian men. The other two men had held Regine captive for a few days, drugging and assaulting her repeatedly, before selling her to Los Chomas.

On her first night there, in an effort to break Regine's feisty spirit, the brothers put her with the Breaker. But she was time enough for him and did a Mike Tyson on him by biting the tip of his ear off. After that they took her to the shed, but this time Diago executed the punishment, not wanting to trust Mario since his fiasco with Crystal. Regine came back bruised and battered, but she still managed to limp around, cussing and swearing revenge at "them dumb bastards." The girls nicknamed her Scrappy because of her fiery, spunky, give-them-hell attitude. The brothers did everything they could to break Regine, but she refused to be broken.

Dereka wondered how she could possibly stand so much pain. She even thought that Regine may have congenital analgesia, a rare disease where people don't feel physical pain. One day Dereka asked Regine, "Why do you keep fighting? How can you stand all that pain?"

"These mfs can't do sh*t to me that hasn't been done before," Regine responded with a faraway look in her eyes, as if she was reliving painful memories. "When you been through as much hell as I been through, you become immune to pain. You just learn to fight through it," she added.

The next day Regine was dragged from the basement by the guards, and the girls never saw her again. But she went out the same way she came in, kicking, screaming, cussing, and fighting. And although she had been there only a few days, Dereka and the others missed the one they called Scrappy.

Coming for You Sunshine

AFTER WEEKS OF preparing herself mentally, physically, and emotionally for the crucial task of rescuing child sex trafficking victims, Jasmine was ready for her first assignment with Operation Undercover. She'd undergone all of the psychological testing and background checks, taken all the recommended self-defense training and role-playing workshops, and received spiritual counseling from her pastor. The organization selected Miami as Jasmine's first assignment for several reasons. They had a great working relationship with the Miami authorities and had already completed a couple of successful rescues there. And because Miami was one of the top US cities for sex trafficking, it was highly possible that Dereka was either in Miami or had passed through the city on her way to another destination. So it was as good a place as any to start their search for her.

Jasmine felt butterflies in her stomach as she rode with BabyRuth and Kenya to the airport. There she'd meet up with the rest of the undercover team for their flight to Miami. She reached in her purse and unfolded a piece of paper. It was the smiley-face sun picture that Dereka made as a present for her. *I'm coming for you, Sunshine*, Jasmine thought as she carefully folded the picture and placed it back into her purse.

Kenya maneuvered the car through the heavy DC rush-hour traffic. "How you feeling? Are you scared?" Kenya asked, glancing at Jasmine.

"Well, not scared, but I am a little anxious. I feel prepared, but I know it's going to be difficult," Jasmine admitted. BabyRuth leaned forward from the backseat and placed her hand on Jasmine's shoulder.

"I hope you know how grateful we are that you are doing this for Dereka. And we're going to be praying for you every step of the way. You just remember Psalm twenty-seven, verse one, *The Lord is my light and my salvation, whom shall I fear? The Lord is the strength of my life; of whom shall I be afraid?*"

"Thanks, Mama Ruth. I'll remember," Jasmine responded, squeezing BabyRuth's hand.

They dropped Jasmine off in front of the terminal and said their tearful good-byes. Because Jasmine would be undercover, she could not have much contact with them while on assignment. And they were all committed to secrecy about Jasmine's work because discussing it with others might put Jasmine and her team members in danger.

"God bless you, baby," BabyRuth uttered as she hugged Jasmine tight.

"We love you," Kenya added, encircling her arms around BabyRuth and Jasmine. Jasmine choked back tears as she walked away from her friends. She glanced back over her shoulder and saw them still standing there, holding hands, as they waved to her.

When Jasmine arrived at her gate, the other three team members were already there. The team consisted of Greg Hawkins, an ex-CIA agent, Pamela Moore, a part-time college professor, and Anthony Perkins, a business owner and fitness guru. The team greeted Jasmine warmly and made small talk until time to board. They knew not to talk about their undercover rescue work in public, because you never knew who was listening. During the flight Jasmine listened to gospel music on her iPod.

After they landed and checked into the Miami hotel, they met in Greg's suite to discuss their assignment later that evening. Although everything had been planned weeks in advance, the team spent the next three hours or so going over every detail of the rescue assignment. They were to meet with a guy known as Ace, a hustler and pimp at an alleged sex house in the Liberty City area of Miami. They'd pose as sex traffickers with an organized crime group from Reno, Nevada, looking to buy underage girls to work in a brothel. Greg had already met with Ace several times in Miami to talk about their collaborative and lucrative proposition. Greg, posing as the head honcho at a Reno brothel, informed the pimp that he was willing to pay top dollar for girls between twelve and fifteen years old but wanted to bring his partners along to inspect the merchandise. Just to ensure they were getting the cream of the crop.

The meeting was set for nine o'clock. Greg, Pamela, and Jasmine would meet with Ace, while Anthony conducted surveillance with local police in a nondescript van parked nearby. Once the money was exchanged, the police would move in. Since the safety of the girls and the volunteers was of utmost importance, code words would be used to let the police know when to move in, or not. If the rescue was deemed unsafe for the girls and team, it would be called off and rescheduled later. Family services had been notified of the rescue and were prepared to shelter the girls and provide other assistance as needed.

Since Jasmine was a first-timer, the team took special care to ensure she was ready for the task. "Jasmine, this is heart-wrenching work. It's not for the faint of heart. Seeing the condition the victims live in, and knowing what they've been through, can be very emotional. But it's critical that you do not break character by showing pity or feelings for the victims before the rescue is complete and everyone's secure. That would be a dead giveaway and could put the team and the entire rescue in jeopardy. You must portray yourself as a detached, heartless buyer of girls in the sex trade. Even if your niece is among the victims, stay in character. And try to signal to her to play along with the pretense. We've been trained to expect the unexpected and deal with whatever goes down. Are you sure you're ready for this?" Greg asked.

"I'm ready," Jasmine confidently stated.

"Okay, everybody, that's it for now," Greg said, concluding the meeting. "Go back to your rooms, and get yourselves prepared for this evening's rescue mission. Relax, listen to music, read, sleep, pray, or do whatever you need to do to get in the right frame of mind. We'll meet in the lobby promptly at eight p.m."

When Jasmine returned to her room, the first thing she did was get on her knees and pray that God would give her the strength, courage, heart, and whatever else she needed to do the work set before her. She knew she couldn't do it without the Lord. But as BabyRuth often told her, she could *do all things through Christ*. And that gave her all the confidence she needed.

Such Things Ought
Not to Be

PROMPTLY AT NINE, Greg, Pamela, and Jasmine pulled up in front of a large two-story white wood frame house. The surveillance van was parked nearby, and family services staff were waiting in another van parked around the corner at a local store. "Time to rock and roll," Greg said as he checked his wireless micro-camera disguised as a watch on his wrist. He also had a mini-camera hidden in the band of his Stetson hat. Jasmine's recorder was hidden in a silver-and-black bangle necklace around her neck, and Pamela had a mini-camera in her stylish eyeglasses.

"Let's go rescue some girls," Pamela stated, giving Jasmine a reassuring nod. The three of them strutted boldly up the rickety steps to the house. Greg was pimped out in a black suit, burgundy shirt, and Stetson hat. The ladies were dressed provocatively stylishly, had their long hair flowing, and wore heavy makeup. They definitely looked the part of high rollers from Reno, right down to the spacious, shiny black SUV with tinted windows. Their fake names were Tommy, Dee Dee, and Rhonda.

Greg knocked sharply on the door, and immediately a dog, sounding rather ferocious, started barking loudly. A stocky black man, around twenty-five or so, with a neatly trimmed goatee and mustache, cracked the door open and looked suspiciously at the three visitors. "We're here to see Ace," Greg stated in a serious tone. The stocky male said something over his shoulder and then opened the door for them to enter.

Three men were sitting in the cluttered room, drinking liquor, smoking weed, and playing cards. The dog continued to bark at them, circling around and lunging at them. "Get that mutt out of here," a slim guy lounging on the sofa demanded. The stocky man that opened the door grabbed the dog roughly by the collar and dragged it down the hall.

The slim guy was Ace. He lazily got up off the couch and gave Greg a half man hug. "Tommy! My man," he said, grinning from ear to ear. Ace stood about five feet seven and probably weighed 140 pounds soaking wet. His nose seemed much too broad for his slim face. He had a scanty mustache and dirty matted dreads, and when he smiled, he showed much more gum than teeth. "Good to see ya, bro," Ace said, giving Greg some dap.

"Good to be seen," Greg responded, returning dap. "This is Dee Dee and Rhonda, the ladies I told you about. They're here to check out the girls and make sure we get what we pay for," Greg said, cocking his head to one side. His mannerism had now completely changed from a kindhearted humanitarian to a coldhearted pimp daddy. *He's good*, Jasmine thought.

Ace leered at Jasmine and Pamela. "Good evening, ladies," he said, grinning hard, showing even more gum than Jasmine had thought humanly possible. "Welcome to my humble abode," Ace drawled, taking a small bow. Pamela sashayed past him, took a seat on the saggy sofa, and crossed her legs.

"Can we see the girls now?" she asked crisply.

"Ahhhh, a lady after my own heart. Wanna get right down to business. But first thangs first. Y'all don't mind if we frisk y'all, do you? You can never be too careful in this business. I need to make sure y'all not wired or carrying weapons. I don't allow no weapons in my crib. 'Cept my own," Ace pointed out, instantly changing from a grinning buffoon to a hard-nosed crook.

"Sure," Greg responded. "We got nothing to hide." Ace's buddies did the frisking. Jasmine felt like she was going to throw up as the man's grubby hands touched her body, paying special attention to her breasts, thighs, and behind. But she forced a seductive smile on her face. "You do have a way with your hands," she said mockingly as she took a seat beside Pamela on the sagging sofa.

"Okay," Ace said, rubbing his hands together. "Time to get this show on the road. Go get the girls," he demanded. While they waited for the men to return from upstairs with the girls, Jasmine could hear her heart beating loudly in her chest. She even wondered whether Ace or the others could hear it. She wasn't sure how she would react when she actually saw the girls. Could she handle it? She looked at Greg and Pamela, who appeared to be as cool as cucumbers. *Get it together,* Jasmine willed herself inwardly. *Jesus, help me get through this*, she silently prayed, taking deep breaths to calm herself.

Soon the men returned with three girls, two black and one white, walking between them. Jasmine's heart dropped when she saw them. They looked so young. One of them looked to be only ten or eleven years old at the most. They were wearing black sports bras and boy-cut panties. They lined up in front of the group as if it was routine, hitting their marks like actresses on a stage. Two of them stared down at their feet, not daring to make eye contact. But one, who appeared to be the oldest, stared directly at the group, rolling her eyes and sucking her teeth. She was obviously pissed.

"What am I doing here?" she snapped, looking directly at Ace. "I don't want to go with them. I want to stay here with you." It was clear the young girl had developed some type of sick love bond with her enslaver, no doubt from months or years of trickery, coercion, and mind manipulation.

"Shut up, ho. You ain't got no say in this," Ace snapped back. "Well, here they are. This is all I have right now in the thirteen-to-fifteen age range," Ace said as if he were selling used cars rather than actual human beings. Pamela got up and walked around the girls as if inspecting them.

"No virgins in this group, I assume," she said as she continued her inspection.

"Nah, but this one here," Ace said, pointing to the youngest-looking girl, "she ain't been used that much yet."

"So you say," Jasmine stated in a matter-of-fact tone, joining Pamela in looking over the girls. *My God, my God*, Jasmine thought to herself. *This really is modern-day slavery, and these girls could well be on the auction block. They should be in school, going to the mall with friends, attending parties, or doing normal girl things. Not here in this hell hole being sold like cattle.*

While Pamela and Jasmine continued their feigned scrutiny of the girls, two guys, obviously customers, came down the stairs and nodded slightly to Ace as they went out the door. "So what's the deal? Are we gonna do business or what?" Ace asked, turning his attention to Greg and ignoring Jasmine and Pamela. It was a "man thang."

"Well, ladies?" Greg asked, soliciting their approval.

"Let's do it," Pamela answered.

"But not for top dollar," Jasmine interjected. Haggling over price was not uncommon in the sex-trade business, and they did not want to appear overly anxious. Greg looked pensive for a moment.

"I'll give you fifteen hundred for that one," Greg stated, nodding at the youngest. "And a thousand each for the other two. That's thirty-five hundred for all three."

"No can do," Ace shot back quickly. "These hoes are worth more than that. Hell, they can pull in hundreds of dollars a day. Besides, you can sell them later yourself for much more money. That's the good thang about this business. You can sell drugs once, but hoes can be sold over and over again. I wouldn't be selling 'em myself now, but I'm trying to help you out. You came to me, bro," Ace stated, trying to look offended.

"All right, all right, five thousand for all three. That's my final offer," Greg stated, standing up as if he was ready to walk.

"Now you talking," Ace said, giving Greg his full-gums grin.

Greg took an envelope out of his inner jacket pocket, retrieved five crisp thousand-dollar bills, and handed the money to Ace. Ace held the bills, one by one, up to the light as if checking to ensure they weren't counterfeit. "Nothing personal, bro. But I been burnt before," Ace stated as he examined the bills.

"No problem. Totally understandable," Greg stated coolly. After Ace was satisfied the bills were legit, he held out his hand to Greg for the customary handshake. Greg obliged. "You the man," Greg stated, vigorously shaking Ace's hand. But unbeknownst to Ace, Greg had just given the authorities the predetermined code words that it was okay to move in. Greg engaged Ace in small talk about how great it was doing business with him and how he'd spread the word in Reno about Ace to throw some business his way. Within minutes all hell broke loose as the cops burst through the door and swarmed the house. Greg, Pamela, and Jasmine immediately surrounded the screaming, frightened girls and took them out of the house. The police quickly apprehended and handcuffed Ace and two of his crew. The stocky man actually made it out of the back door but was captured by police stationed outside.

"You F*cking set me up, you punk-ass bitch. I can't believe this sh*t," Ace shouted at Greg as he was dragged out of the house.

In all, seven girls were rescued that night. Besides the three being offered for sale, three other girls were found upstairs, and one was discovered in the basement. Their ages ranged from twelve to nineteen. Six men were arrested, including Ace, his partners in crime, and two male customers. One customer was actually captured while trying to escape through a second-floor window wearing only his black checkered drawers.

The team and the girls waited outside with the family services reps while the police searched and secured the house. Jasmine held on tight to the youngest twelve-year-old girl, who was crying hysterically. Jasmine rubbed her hair and wiped away her tears. "It's okay, sweetie. You're safe now," Jasmine said soothingly. Her name was Relika, and she had been brought to the house about a week before by a family member and left there to pay off a debt.

When it was time for the girls to leave with family services, Relika didn't want to let go of Jasmine. She was afraid she'd be taken to another awful place and abandoned. And Jasmine didn't want to let go either, so she held on tight.

"You have to let her go now," Pamela whispered softly to Jasmine as Greg gently removed the girl from her arms.

"Letting go is part of the process. She'll be taken care of," Greg assured.

Jasmine cried when the family services van rolled away, and she kept crying all the way on the ride back to the hotel. Greg and Pamela understood her tears because they too had shed many tears, particularly at the start of their rescue work. The tears were of joy that the girls were rescued from sexual degradation, but also of sorrow that these rescues were even necessary in the first place. Such things ought not to be.

Got to Laugh to Keep
from Crying

AS BABYRUTH BUSIED herself in the kitchen, it was hard for her to believe one year had passed since Dereka went missing. One year since the atrocious tragedy had taken from her two of the people she loved most in the world. BabyRuth recalled something her favorite Aunt Ethel used to say often: "Time don't wait for nobody." *How right she was*, BabyRuth thought. *Times takes us all along for the ride—no matter what.*

By this time Jasmine had completed three additional successful rescues with Operation Undercover, two in Miami and one in Houston. And over forty children had been rescued as a result. But still no Dereka. Detective Davis continued to work the case diligently, following up on any and all leads. But now the leads were few and far between. Kenya used social media sites like Facebook, Instagram, and Twitter to keep Dereka's name and missing status in the public eye. She also worked closely with the National Center for Missing and Exploited Children to try to locate Dereka. But nothing so far. And at times it was unbearable.

"How long, Lord, how long?" BabyRuth said out loud as she paused for a moment to talk to the God she served. "Lord, I'm waiting. Waiting on you. You said that *they that wait upon the Lord shall renew their strength; they shall mount up with wings as eagles; they shall run, and not be weary; and they shall walk, and not faint.* So Lord, I'm just waiting on you. That's all I know to do."

Tomorrow was Dereka's fourteenth birthday, and BabyRuth was determined to celebrate her granddaughter's special day. But she wanted to do it the day before her birthday—the day that she went missing. She was making her granddaughter the most elaborate birthday cake ever. She hummed softly as she carefully removed the last two layers from the oven and set them on the table to cool before icing. She gathered the ingredients and began to make the buttercream frosting Dereka liked so much. Jasmine was in town for the weekend, and she and Kenya were coming over later to help BabyRuth celebrate Dereka's birthday. At first they had been reluctant, not knowing whether they were up for any celebration. But BabyRuth had persuaded them to participate. "Dereka would want it this way," BabyRuth had told them. And when they thought about it, they knew BabyRuth was right.

Kenya and Jasmine arrived around seven o'clock, just as BabyRuth was putting the finishing touches on the cake. And it was a work of art. Kenya's and Jasmine's eyes lit up with delight when they saw it.

"Oh, Mama. You outdid yourself," Kenya exclaimed.

"Wow, Mama Ruth. Now that's a cake," Jasmine supplied. The cake was five layers high with beautiful pink and purple flowers around each layer. The top layer had fourteen pink and purple candles on it and was decorated with pink and purple candy sprinkles. Jasmine laughed when she read the writing on the cake that said, "Happy Birthday, Boogie Boo."

"It's beautiful, Mama. Dereka would absolutely love it," Kenya declared. BabyRuth beamed with pride at the compliments.

"Yeah, I put my foot in that one," she joked. "Now you all set that food on the dining room table," BabyRuth said, pointing to platters and bowls of food on the kitchen counter. "I'll bring in the cake."

Kenya and Jasmine gathered several bowls and platters and went into the dining room. BabyRuth carefully lifted the large cake and moved towards the door. But just as she was about to enter the dining room, Kenya rushed back into the kitchen to gather more food and ran smack-dab into BabyRuth. The beautiful cake, BabyRuth's work of art, went crashing down to the floor. Kenya gasped audibly and said, "Oh my God, Mama, I'm so sorry." Jasmine placed her hands over her mouth in shock as she looked from Kenya to BabyRuth to the smashed cake, her eyes wide. For a while BabyRuth just stood there looking down at the ruined cake. The cake she had made special for her granddaughter's fourteenth birthday. The cake she had labored over for hours in the kitchen. The cake she had meticulously decorated in Dereka's favorite colors. The cake that was now lying in a messy heap on the floor at BabyRuth's feet.

Kenya and Jasmine waited on edge for BabyRuth's reaction. And then BabyRuth began to laugh. Jasmine and Kenya looked at each other in confusion, and then looked at BabyRuth. *Has she lost it?* Jasmine thought.

"Mama, are you all right?" Kenya asked timidly.

"Honey, I'm all right. Sometimes you just got to laugh to keep from crying," BabyRuth said, laughing harder and harder. And soon her laughter became infectious. Kenya and Jasmine found themselves smiling and then laughing right along with her. Then BabyRuth scooped up a big hunk of cake in her hand and headed towards Kenya with a mischievous glint in her eyes.

"Oh no you don't," Kenya said, scooping up an equally large chunk of cake in her hands as well.

The three ladies then engaged in an all-out cake fight. They chased one another around the dining room table, slipping and sliding on icing and smashing cake into each other's faces, hair, and clothes. They laughed and played like carefree children. Whenever they stopped laughing, they looked at each other, covered with icing and cake, and burst into laughter all over again. After they tired themselves out, they sat at the table. "What would Dereka make of all this?" BabyRuth said as she took a piece of cake off Kenya's face and ate it, causing them to laugh. They laughed and laughed some more. Because that's what you have to do sometimes: laugh to keep from crying. They had cried so much, and they'd cry much more. But this was their time for laughter.

An Angel in Hell

DEREKA SAT ALONE at the long table in the kitchen area. It was very early in the morning, still dark outside, and all the other girls were asleep. Dereka liked to arise early, shower, and just sit alone in the kitchen. It was the only time of the day she had to herself, and she used the time to think, pray, and just be. As far as Dereka could tell from her makeshift calendar underneath the wood kitchen table, today was her birthday. She had not told anyone about her birthday except Sun-Yu. Her eyes watered when she thought about her last birthday, and how she and her mama had gone to pick up her birthday cake. That day tragedy struck without warning or reason. That day life, as she knew it, had ended.

A big black water bug crawling up the wall caught Dereka's attention. She watched the water bug slowly but steadily make its way up the wall, crawl to the corner, and squeeze through a crack in the ceiling. Dereka found herself envying the water bug. At least it was free. It had found its way out of the basement. She even wished she was that water bug and could squeeze herself through the small crack to escape the living hell she was entrapped in. *What has my life come to that I envy a water bug?* Dereka thought sadly.

After a while she heard the other girls moving around and thought she heard Lydia call her name. When she went back into the main area, the girls were standing together with mischievous smiles on their faces. The girls began to sing:

Happy birthday to you.
Happy birthday to you.
Happy birthday, Angel Girl.
Happy birthday to you.

Jia ran to Dereka and gave her something wrapped in toilet paper. The others gathered around her and hugged and kissed her while wishing her a happy birthday.

"Open your present," Catarina prompted. Dereka slowly peeled off the layers of toilet paper and discovered a small angel figure made out of a bar of soap.

"Esmeralda gave us an extra bar of soap so we could make it for you. Camila did most of the work. She used her fingernails to sculpt it," Emma stated. Their gesture of love brought tears of joy to Dereka's eyes and touched her heart.

"It's lovely," Dereka said. "Thank you all so much. I will always treasure this," she uttered, her voice so choked with emotion she could hardly speak.

The small angel figure made of soap was just what Dereka needed to lift her sagging spirits. They thought of her as an angel, but she felt they were her angels sent from above. As Dereka looked through her tears at the delicate soap figurine, she thought about a scripture she had learned in Bible camp one summer: *For he shall give his angels charge over thee, to keep thee in all thy ways.*

She placed the angel figurine in the secret place in the wall with Sun-Yu's mother's red scarf and Crystal's hair comb. Dereka knew that if she had been home for her birthday, she would have received many lavish, expensive gifts from her family. But none of those gifts could have been more special than the angel figurine made from soap she'd received from her new family.

A Business Scheme

LATER THAT MORNING Mario, instead of Esmeralda, came down with the guard to bring food for the girls. It was the first time that Dereka could recall that Esmeralda did not bring the food. Mario dropped a heavy pot on the table and shouted at the girls to line up. As they passed by him, he dumped a huge spoon of yellowish foul-smelling mush on their plates. The girls frowned and looked at their plates in disgust. "You'll eat it or starve," Mario barked at them and headed back up the steps.

Sophia was the first to taste the mush, and rushed to the sink to spit it out. "That's awful," she said.

Emma put her plate up to her nose and sniffed. "It smells like sh*t. I'm not eating this." Dereka tasted hers and almost puked. The girls threw the food in the trash. It was better to go hungry than eat whatever that was.

For the next few days, Mario or Diago came with the guard to bring the girls food. But still no Esmeralda. The food got a bit more tolerable, but not by much. The girls forced themselves to eat what they could, just to keep from starving. They missed Esmeralda's food terribly, but they missed Esmeralda even more. In her own quiet way, she had shown them kindness. Dereka felt the old lady was as much a victim of the Tavaras brothers' cruelty as the girls were. One morning Dereka gathered the courage to ask Diago where she was. "Dead," he responded without emotion. "Died in her sleep. She was old. It was time. We'll get someone to take her place. Until then you'll make do with what you get."

Later that night Dereka thought about what Diago had said about getting someone to take Esmeralda's place. What if she could convince them to let her do the cooking and cleaning? It would at least give her a chance to get out of the basement, and perhaps get help for them. Stuck down in the basement, they were totally powerless. But if she could get access to the rest of the house, who knows what she could discover to help them?

And Dereka knew how to cook and clean well. Her Grandma Ruth had seen to that. When Dereka turned eleven, BabyRuth thought it was high time she started helping out around the house. But Dereka had other ideas. By this time she had started "smelling herself," and all she wanted to do was eat, socialize, and lounge around with friends. Serena called it her "prima donna phase" and was willing to just let her be. But BabyRuth wasn't having it. She was old school and believed children needed to learn the value of hard work.

So one summer morning, BabyRuth had found Dereka still sleeping like a baby in her bed at well past noon. "Get up, lazy bones," BabyRuth said as she snatched the covers off her. Dereka had tried to retreat back under the cozy covers, but BabyRuth snatched the covers right off the bed. Then she had marched Dereka, still in her pajamas, into the backyard and showed her an ant hill. "Now look at these ants," BabyRuth said. "The Bible says consider their ways, and be wise. They don't have a master or overseer telling them what to do. But they know how to work and provide for themselves. You see how busy they are? There's not a slacker in the bunch. Are you going to let a little ole ant outdo you?" BabyRuth asked with a half-smile on her face. Dereka poked her lips out and crossed her arms. *How dare Grandma drag me out of bed to look at some ole ant hole*, Dereka thought to herself. But she knew better than to say anything out loud to her grandma.

Dereka bent down over the anthill, determined to prove her grandma wrong. She saw what looked like hundreds of tiny ants scurrying around frantically, going to and fro as if their very lives depended on it. *There must be at least one slacker among all of these ants*, Dereka thought, peering closely at the ants. But try as she might, she could not find one loafer in the heap. Not one slouch. For some reason, that lesson about the ants had resonated with Dereka that day. And she'd gotten off her high horse and started helping around the house, determined not to let no little bitty ant best her.

So Dereka knew she could handle the work. The hard part was to convince Diago to let her do it. She knew he'd be skeptical of her request because of a past situation she'd heard about. The story went that there was a time the brothers would force the girls to cook and clean for them in addition to pleasuring the customers. It was their way of getting the best bang for their buck by using the girls for forced labor and sexual exploitation. But one evening, as fate would have it, the brothers noticed a strange odor coming from their food. After tasting it, they'd become suspicious and actually made the young girl who prepared the food eat it herself. Within moments she had begun to convulse and vomit violently, and within the hour she was dead of cyanide poisoning. She had tried to poison the brothers by putting a pesticide that she'd found under the kitchen sink into their food. After that episode, the brothers used the girls strictly for the business of servicing the men.

Thus, Dereka knew she'd have to fool Diago into trusting her. And knowing that the brothers considered themselves shrewd businessmen who saw the girls as no more than property for profit, she decided to play the "what's best for the business" angle. And she would also stroke Diago's ego. Her Auntie Jazz had always told her, "Stroke a man's ego, and he'll go anywhere you lead him."

●   ●   ●

When Diago came down the next morning, Dereka broached the subject of replacing Esmeralda and doing the cooking and cleaning.

"Why would you want to do that?" he asked, looking at her suspiciously.

"So we can eat better and stay healthy. If we don't eat well and we become sick, we cannot pleasure the customers. And if we cannot pleasure the customers, you will lose money. Right?" Dereka asked. Diago stared at Dereka intently, and she could almost see the wheels turning in his head as he pondered what she said. Dereka continued her con job. "I'm glad that you came down this morning instead of Mario. I tell the girls all the time that you are the smartest brother. Much smarter than Mario. You make all the decisions. I admire that," she stated, smiling at him and trying her best to sound sincere. But Diago still looked skeptical. So Dereka decided to play her final card. "You told me I was here to serve the House of Pleasure. I've accepted my place here. But I can do more than pleasure the men. I'm a hard worker. I can cook and clean. Let me prove my worth." Diago was silent for a moment longer.

"Okay, fine. You want to cook and clean. So be it. But you better not try anything. The last one of you that tried something is in her grave. Just remember that," he warned.

For Granted

THAT DAY DEREKA took over the housework for La Casa de Placer. Until then Dereka had not seen the main level of the building, which was larger and more lavish than she'd expected. It included a huge kitchen, a spacious living room, four large bedrooms (one for each of the brothers and two guards), an office, and few smaller rooms in the back where Esmeralda had stayed. It made Dereka's blood boil to see how large they were living while she and the other girls lived in squalor underneath their feet in the dank, dreary basement.

Dereka worked her fingers to the bone day and night, cleaning, cooking, and doing laundry. She cherished the opportunity to make decent, though plain, food for herself and the other girls. Although the refrigerator and freezer were stocked with various meats, including chicken, beef, fish, and sausages, she was forbidden to use any of it for their meals. Such delights were to be savored only by their self-appointed masters and overseers. The girls' food, which Mario jokingly called "the dog food," was kept separately from the masters' provisions. Dereka did what she could to spice up the maize, potatoes, legumes, rice, and bread that made up the majority of their meals, just as Esmeralda had.

Dereka was accompanied most of the time by a guard. The only time she got to be alone was when she went to empty the trash can in the big bin in the backyard. Sometimes the guard would stand at the back door and watch her, but most times, especially if he was preoccupied with one of his adult magazines, he'd let her go alone. Today was one of those days. "I'm going to take the trash out," Dereka said to the guard as he sat engrossed in the magazine. He waved her off as if to say, "Stop pestering me." She figured the guards knew she had nowhere to run anyway even if she wanted to. The house was surrounded by a high barbed-wire fence, which was impossible for her to climb. And even if she were able to make it over the fence, there was nothing but dense jungle for miles and miles. There was nowhere to run.

Dereka took the trash outside and immediately began to dig through it to see what edible food she could find. The brothers and guards ate well, and they often threw away a lot of good food. Dereka rummaged through the trash, knowing she had only a few minutes before the guard would become suspicious and come looking her. She discovered several large chunks of sausage she had used for the brothers' meal the previous night. She sniffed it, and it smelled okay, so she quickly took a big bite. She savored the flavor of meat in her mouth again. Dereka wanted to take some to the girls but was afraid the guard would catch her with it, and she would get in trouble. It seemed they would rather throw good food in the trash than share it with the girls, whom they jokingly referred to as the animals in the basement.

While Dereka bent over the trash can and hurriedly gobbled down the sausage, she recalled all the times back home that she too had thought nothing of throwing good food in the trash, either because her eyes were too big for her stomach, or it wasn't quite what she wanted to eat at the time. She had taken so much for granted. "Lord," Dereka whispered as she wiped her mouth clean of any remnants of food before going back into the house, "if you just get me out of this dreadful place, I promise you that I will never *ever* take anything for granted again."

• • •

Over time Dereka managed, as were her intentions from the beginning, to manipulate the brothers into trusting her more. As a result, she was given more freedom around the house and was often left alone while she did her mundane household chores. She took advantage of what freedom she had to make life a bit more tolerable for her and the other girls. Sometimes she hid meat at the bottom of the huge pot of potatoes, rice, or legumes she prepared for their meals. She also sneaked fruit and vegetables, extra soap, and personal hygiene items to them. But Dereka had to be careful because the guards were always lurking nearby, ready to pounce at a moment's notice.

Dereka's typical day included rising early, long before daybreak, to shower and dress. One of the guards would come for her and escort her to the kitchen to prepare the morning meals. After that she would strip down all the beds and haul the bedding to the laundry room off the kitchen. To Dereka, stripping the beds of their soiled and stained bedding was the hardest of all her chores. The sight and smell of the sheets soiled with semen, sticky condoms, and sometimes blood was like rubbing salt in her wounds. It was a tangible reminder of their daily degradation as sex slaves.

In the afternoon and late evening, before the customers arrived, Dereka had to place pitchers of cool water on the tables in the bedrooms in case any of the men wanted to quench their thirst. After all, these were high-end, well-paying, mostly foreign men, and the Tavaras brothers catered to their needs. Dereka often thought about doing a "Miss Celie" from *The Color Purple* by adding a little spit to the water pitchers. But she was afraid she would get caught and be punished. Besides the men took so much from her and the other girls she didn't want to freely give them anything, even her own spit.

In exchange for her hard labor, Dereka was given a reprieve from servicing the customers in the afternoon, but she still had to "pleasure" the men at night. In a way Dereka was grateful for the hard work she did during the day so that at night, when she was with the men, her mind and body would be so tired and numb she wouldn't feel anything.

Parole My Ass!

TIME PASSED, AND it was now over two years since Dereka was abducted. BabyRuth, now retired from the federal government, and Kenya carried on as best they could. Everyone kept telling them life goes on. Keep the faith. God has it all in his hands. Sometimes they would catch themselves smiling and enjoying themselves, and would feel guilty. They didn't feel they had the right or the privilege to enjoy themselves while Dereka was still missing and likely suffering unspeakable horrors. Sometimes Kenya would find her mother sitting in a chair in the living room, just staring at the front door. "Mama, why are you staring at the door?" Kenya asked her once.

"I'm just hoping that any moment, Dereka will come walking through that door as if nothing has happened. And we'll all wake up and discover it's just been a bad dream. I know it's crazy to think like this. But it keeps me going," BabyRuth replied. And Kenya had sat down beside her mother and stared at the door with her, each blinking back tears.

Now Kenya sat in her office looking over a witness deposition for an upcoming case. Her cell phone rang, and she saw it was her mother calling. "Hi, Mama," Kenya said cheerfully.

"Kenya, honey. I just got a call message from the Victim Information and Notification System," BabyRuth said, her voice in a panic. "The message said that Kevin Curtis will be eligible for parole in March of next year."

"Eligible for parole? But how can that be?" Kenya asked incredulously.

"I don't know, honey. The automated message said his parole eligibility hearing will be in March."

"Mama, I have a friend at the Victim Services Unit. I'll call her to see what's going on. Don't worry, Mama. I'll talk to you later."

"Okay, honey."

Kenya called her friend and discovered that it was true that Kevin Curtis would be eligible for parole early the next year. His original sentence of twenty to thirty years had been reduced to fifteen to twenty-five years under the Good Time Credit program, which allows an inmate's sentence to be reduced for good behavior. And Kevin, having served the minimum time by then, would be eligible for parole.

Kenya was livid when she hung up the phone. She slammed her hands down hard on her desk. "This can't be happening," she shouted. Her assistant, Trevon, hearing the commotion in her office, peeped his head through the door.

"Everything okay in here?" he asked, a worried expression on his face.

"Come in and shut the door," Kenya stated briskly. Trevon hurried in and took a seat next to Kenya's desk. "Kevin Curtis is eligibility for parole. His parole hearing is in March," Kenya stated, exasperated.

"You're kidding," Trevon responded with a shocked look on his face. Because of their close relationship, Kenya had shared with him all the sordid details about Kevin and Memphis.

"Do I look like I'm kidding?" Kenya responded, her eyes wide.

"That's messed up," Trevon said, shaking his head.

"Yes, it's messed up. And I got to do something to make sure that lowlife stays in jail," Kenya stated.

"What can I do to help?" Trevon offered.

Kenya looked thoughtful for a moment. "Print out the bios of the Virginia parole board members listed on their website. Also print out all the board's decisions over the past twelve months. I want the charts that show the name, age, sex, race, et cetera of the inmate, whether or not parole was granted, and the reasons for the board's decisions. I'm going to use the information to start working on an opposition letter against granting Kevin's parole. I want to submit it to the board as soon as possible. Also get the Victim Input Program office on the phone. I want to put in a request to appear in person and present our case before the board."

"I'm on it, boss," Trevon responded as he left the office.

Kenya was aggravated the rest of the workday at just the possibility of Kevin getting out on parole. There was no way in hell she was going to allow that varmint to roam free while her niece was still missing. "What kind of justice would that be? No kind of justice," Kenya said out loud. She was fuming. "And I swear to God, I'm going to do everything in my power to see that he rots in prison. Parole my ass."

Swing Vote

LATER THAT NIGHT Kenya sat up in her bed in her nightgown, carefully going through the information that Trevon had downloaded from the board's website, including the board members' bios and parole decisions. Ryan, who was spending the night at her place, was lying next to her reading a sports magazine. He'd been so encouraging and supportive to Kenya, and she was grateful to have him in her life. When she'd told him earlier about Kevin's parole eligibility, he seemed to be just as upset and appalled by the news as she was.

After a while, Ryan put down his magazine and started kissing Kenya's bare legs. "Honey, I know this parole thing has you all tensed up. Let me help you relax," he said with a sly smile as he moved behind Kenya to massage her shoulders.

"I'll be with you in a minute, baby," Kenya said absently, continuing to concentrate on the papers. "I'm using this information to determine how to focus our opposition statement. Now from what I can tell from the bios and the decisions, two of the board members are likely conservative Republicans, two liberal Democrats, and one an independent. Now based on the political persuasion, I think that two of them would likely be in favor of parole and two against, leaving one, the independent, as the swing vote." Kenya picked up a folder and passed it to Ryan. "He's Lawrence M. Kilpatrick III. Forty-five years old and lives in Vienna, Virginia, with his wife and four children.

Looks like he's had quite a distinguished career serving in the general district and circuit courts in DC and Virginia."

Ryan opened the folder and scanned the bio. "Hey, wait a minute," Ryan said, looking intently at the photo included with the bio. "I think I know this brother," he stated.

"You know him?" Kenya said, shocked. Ryan continued to read the bio.

"Yeah, Larry Kilpatrick. I don't know him personally. He's a client at the firm where I work. I helped him with some estate planning last year. We set up a living will for his family. If I recall correctly, he has two sons in college and two daughters in high school. He seemed to be a pretty cool dude. We had lunch a couple of times," Ryan stated, still looking at the bio.

Kenya was surprised yet intrigued that Ryan knew Mr. Kilpatrick. What were the odds that her fiancé would actually know a member of the parole board? Kenya knew the ethical thing to do was to stop the conversation right then. The ethical thing was to contact the board's office as soon as possible and disclose the fact that her fiancé had a working relationship with a board member. This type of disclosure was sometimes necessary in order to avoid even the appearance of any conflict of interest. Doing so would give the board the opportunity to decide whether the board member in question should be disqualified from participating in the case. Kenya knew that disclosure of any and all relevant information regarding the case would be the ethical thing to do.

But when Kenya considered the misery that Memphis and his scumbag son had caused her and her family, she thought, *To hell with ethics.* If compromising her ethics would get some measure of justice for Dereka, then so be it. "Tell me what you know about Mr. Kilpatrick. Anything and everything, no matter how small. A person's preferences say a lot about them, even down to the type of movies they watch, music they listen to, or books they read. I can generally tell by a person's lifestyle preferences which way they will vote," Kenya said, relying on her years of court experience with jurors and judges. "And," Kenya continued, "depending on his preferences, I can

deduce whether he generally leans conservative or liberal, and prepare my opposition statement accordingly. I want to make sure this
swing vote swings our way."

"I bet if you greased his palms, you could swing his vote any which
way you want," Ryan said jokingly, laughing so hard he nearly rolled
off the bed. But Kenya didn't laugh. She sat still for a long moment
in deep thought. Ryan had just joked about bribing a board member.
She knew he was playing around, but his joke struck a chord within
her. Perhaps this was just what she needed to secure the swing vote.
Kenya knew, in her mind, that it was ludicrous for her to even be
thinking about bribing a public official. To do so would be a crime. But
Kenya wasn't thinking with her mind; she was thinking with her heart.

Ryan looked at Kenya strangely. "What's the matter, sweetheart?" he asked in concern. Kenya knew what she was about to ask
of Ryan was unfair to him and would be disastrous for both of them
if they were discovered. But thoughts of Dereka's pain and suffering,
along with the death of her friend Serena, totally robbed Kenya of
her ability to be logical and rational. So Kenya asked the question she
wouldn't have ordinarily asked in a million years.

"Do you think you can get him to take a bribe?" Ryan sat up
straight and looked intently at Kenya.

"What are you talking about? I was just joking around. You didn't
really think I was serious, did you?"

"No. But I am. Dead serious," Kenya replied, looking Ryan straight
in the eyes. And he realized she was serious.

"Kenya, honey, you know I love you, and there's nothing in the
world I wouldn't do for you. But bribing a public official? That's
insane! Do you realize what you are asking me to do? Do you know
what could happen to us if we're discovered?" Of course Kenya knew.
After all, she was an elected commonwealth prosecutor for the state
of Virginia. Bribery of a public official could lead to prison, fines, dis-
barment, scandal, and who knows what else. "How could you even
think of doing such a thing?" Ryan asked as if he was in shock.

"Why shouldn't I?" she cried, leaning back against the headboard.
"Why shouldn't I do everything I can to make sure that monster

doesn't go free? It's because of him that one of my best friends is dead and my niece, who I love with my whole heart, is missing. God only knows where she is and what she's going through. When Memphis took Dereka, he took a piece of my soul. And I don't want his son, that waste of a human being, to get out of prison while Dereka is still missing and suffering," Kenya cried.

Ryan reached for Kenya and held her in a tight embrace. She looked up at him with tears streaming down her face. "What would you do if it was someone you love?" she asked softly. "Wouldn't you do anything and everything you could to make sure that person received some measure of justice? Dereka is being held somewhere against her will. She could be dead for all we know. I pray she isn't, but it's possible. I couldn't live with myself if the one person primarily responsible for her suffering is allowed to go free. I just couldn't."

Ryan was silent for a long time, thinking deeply about what Kenya had said. After a while he finally answered, "I'll do it."

Hooked the Big Fish

KENYA WAITED NERVOUSLY in her office for Ryan's call. It took a couple of weeks, but Ryan had arranged a meeting with Mr. Kilpatrick. He pretended he wanted to talk to him about estate planning. During the meeting Ryan was going to cautiously broach the subject of Kevin Curtis's parole eligibility. If Mr. Kilpatrick seemed willing to talk about the case, Ryan would do a little fishing to see whether he would take the bribery bait. The fact that Mr. Kilpatrick had two children already in college, and two likely preparing for college, was a plus. Ryan planned to use the high price of college tuition as the bait in the hook to reel Mr. Kilpatrick in. In regard to the dollar amount to offer, Kenya had left it open. She had money in the bank, a hefty 401(k), and an inheritance from her father's estate. And she would spend as much as necessary to keep Kevin in his cage.

But Kenya was extremely anxious about the meeting. What if Mr. Kilpatrick got highly offended by the bribe offer and decided to call the authorities right then and there? They were taking a huge risk, one that Kenya hoped, and even prayed, would pay off. A knock on the office door made Kenya jump. Trevon opened the door and strolled in with a big cup of coffee in one hand and a stack of folders in the other.

"Ready to go over my research on the McDermott case?" he asked, sitting in the chair in front of Kenya's desk.

"Okay," Kenya responded absently, reaching for the folders and setting them to the side.

"What's the matter, Kenya? It's that parole board hearing, isn't it?" he asked, taking a sip of his coffee.

"Yeah," Kenya said, letting out a deep sigh.

"Do you need me to help you with anything?" Trevon asked eagerly.

"No, but thanks," Kenya confirmed.

"Well, you know I'm here for you," Trevon stated.

"Yes, I know," Kenya responded.

For a moment Kenya thought about telling him about her bribery scheme. She was so nervous she needed to confide in somebody. Although Ryan had cautioned her not to talk to anyone about their plans, Kenya felt like she would explode if she didn't tell someone. And she trusted Trevon. Over the years that he had worked as her assistant, he'd proved to be a true friend and confidant. "I have to tell you something, Tre," Kenya said. "But you have to swear that you will not tell anyone, or try to talk me out of it. Deal?"

"Oh, this must be good, boss," Trevon said. He sat on the edge of his seat and rubbed his hands together, thinking it was just some juicy office gossip. But the solemn expression on Kenya's face let him know she was deeply troubled. "Deal," he responded seriously, giving Kenya his full attention. Kenya proceeded to tell Trevon of her and Ryan's plans to bribe a member of the parole board. He listened to her intently, not interrupting her once. When she finished, he said, "Wow, Kenya. That's some heavy stuff."

Kenya's cell phone rang. "I got to take this. It's Ryan," Kenya said to Trevon.

"Okay," he said, quickly leaving her office.

"Ryan, how'd it go?" Kenya asked anxiously.

"Let's not talk over the phone," Ryan cautioned. "I'll come over to your house later and fill you in." When Kenya hung up, she was somewhat relieved. At least nothing catastrophic had happened at the meeting.

Ryan arrived at Kenya's around eight that evening. "Well, what happened?" Kenya asked as soon as he was in the door. Ryan sat on the sofa and motioned for Kenya to join him. "Well, he didn't take the bait, but he didn't swim away either. I think he needs some time to think it over. Being from this area, he remembered the scandal that sent Kevin to prison. He also knew about your niece's kidnapping. He seemed genuinely saddened by this—having two daughters himself. We talked in circles a lot, trying to feel each other out. I guess a guy in his position has to be concerned that someone's trying to set him up. But I could tell by the look in his eyes he knew what was up. We shook hands, and I left. Now we'll just have to wait and see what happens."

But they didn't have to wait long. About a week later, Ryan called Kenya and told her he was on his way to Mr. Kilpatrick's house for their follow-up meeting. Later that night, he stopped by Kenya's to fill her in on the meeting's outcome. "Well, he took the bait. He's willing to vote against parole eligibility for Kevin Curtis. And, like you, he believes his vote will be the deciding vote. He all but guaranteed the outcome. But due to the large risk he's taking, he's demanding a fairly hefty payoff. He wants a hundred thousand in cold hard cash—no wire or bank transfers that can be traced."

Kenya was silent for a moment. *This is really happening*, she thought. They had gone fishing and hooked a big fish. She knew what they were doing was wrong—knew it was absolutely preposterous. Kenya could hear her mother's voice in her mind saying, *Don't do it, baby. It's not worth it. Leave in it God's hand. Let him work it out.* But she shook it off. When it came to seeking justice for her niece, Kenya didn't care about right or wrong.

Peace Be Still

IN THE DAY of my trouble I will call upon thee: for thou wilt answer me. That was the scripture on BabyRuth's mind as she drove to church early Sunday morning. The news of Kevin's parole eligibility weighed heavily on her mind and heart. And the continuing agony of her grand-daughter being missing was excruciating at times. BabyRuth needed to be in the house of the Lord, to feel his presence deep down in her soul. When she got to church, she ran down the center aisle and fell down on her knees at the altar. She couldn't wait for the tradi-tional altar call that usually happened at the end of the sermon; she needed a special touch from God right then and there. And as she wept and prayed before the altar, BabyRuth sensed others gather-ing around her, laying hands on her, and praying for and with her. She heard Pastor Bobby's voice rising and falling as he prayed fervently, along with the others, for dear Sister Ruth. They prayed that God would comfort her, strengthen her, and sustain her. As they prayed, BabyRuth began to feel the power of God moving within her spirit. And soon her tears of sorrow transformed to tears of joy.

BabyRuth rose to her feet, lifted her hands toward heaven, and praised the Lord with all might. Others joined her, lifting their voices in praise. The church pianist began to play some good old-fashioned Holy Ghost music, and practically the whole congregation began to clap, sing, dance, and shout before God. They had themselves a hal-lelujah good time. It took quite a while for things to calm down a bit.

And once, when it appeared that things had settled down enough to begin the regular service, one of the old mothers on the front pew stood up and shouted, "Oh Glory," and they started up again.

Finally the Holy Ghost dust settled, and the pastor was able to preach the sermon. His sermon was titled "Bridge over Troubled Waters," and it was food for BabyRuth's weary soul. He preached about how in every person's life there will be some troubled waters to cross. But we have a bridge. He spoke of how Jesus said, *In the world ye shall have tribulation: but be of good cheer; I have overcome the world.* Jesus is our bridge. He went on to tell how the disciple Peter, by faith, stepped out on the water and began to walk toward Jesus. But when Peter took his eyes off Jesus and focused on the troubled waters, he started to sink. And that's what happens when you focus on your troubles, and not on the Lord. Lastly, Pastor spoke about how Jesus was in a ship with his disciples when a great storm arose, and how the disciplines looked at the troubled waters and feared for their lives. They went running to Jesus like scaredy-cats, saying, "Don't you care if we die?" But Jesus calmed the troubled waters with three small words: *Peace, be still.* The point of the pastor's message was that Jesus will be our bridge over troubled waters. All we have to do is step out on the bridge of faith and cross over.

When BabyRuth walked out of the church that afternoon, she felt like a different person from the one who had walked in. Her faith was strengthened; her hope renewed. She marveled at how God knows exactly what we need, and when we need it.

Wanna Bet

KEVIN WAS IN the prison cafeteria eating dinner with his boy, Parker, and a few other inmates. He was upbeat about his upcoming parole hearing, having no doubt it would be granted. After all, he was a first offender, with a spotless time-in-prison record. No misbehavior infractions whatsoever, since he paid others to do his dirty work for him.

"In a few months, I'm out of here. And you mf'ers can kiss my black ass good-bye," Kevin joked.

"I hate to admit it, but I'm gonna miss you," Parker said, his mouth full of mashed potatoes.

"Yeah, it won't be the same without you, man," another inmate chimed in.

"Well, I'll be in touch. I'm not gonna leave my boys hanging. I'll be taking over some of my father's operations. I'm sure we can do some things together," Kevin said with a wink and a smile.

"But who am I going to play the game with after you gone?" Parker asked, referring to their sick pastime of betting on the fates of guards and fellow prisoners.

"Don't know, bro. But I'm sure you'll find somebody. Just make sure it's someone you can beat. Right now I'm up twenty-one to seven. That's pathetic," Kevin said, laughing.

"Yeah, you one lucky mf'er. But your luck gotta run out one day. As a matter of fact, let's make a little wager right now. I'm willing to bet you don't even make it out of here alive," Parker stated.

"Man, you must just like losing. Ain't nobody in here crazy enough to touch me," Kevin said, knowing full well his father's reputation, and his bought favor with the guards, provided him all the protection he needed.

"Yeah, but you forgetting about Loco Larry," Parker responded, pointing to a guy at another table who was watching them and mumbling to himself. Loco Larry was a prisoner named Larry Watkins who wasn't quite all there. The inmates called him Loco Larry because he had a habit of following other prisoners around while mumbling to himself. He'd even attacked a few inmates and hurt a couple of them really badly. Now, for some reason, Loco Larry had begun stalking Kevin.

"That fool's crazy, but he's not that crazy," Kevin said.

"I hope you're right. But that nutcase is getter crazier by the minute. The last dude he attacked almost didn't make it. And now he's eying you. And wacko as that Negro is, I think you good as dead. So how about that bet," Parker said, holding his hand out for Kevin to shake.

"You on, mf'er," Kevin replied, slapping Parker's hand. "But if you win, I'm dead. What do I get if I win?" Kevin asked.

"What you want?" Parker replied.

"Well, there's not much you can give me that I ain't already got. Sooooo, all I want is for you to literally kiss my black ass on my way out the door. In front of everybody. I want you to kiss it real good," Kevin said, cracking himself up.

"You got it," Parker replied.

On the way back to their cells, Kevin had to pass by Loco Larry's table. Loco Larry stared at Kevin with a demented expression on his face and mumbled something unintelligible. *Hmmmm*, Kevin thought to himself. *This prick just might be crazy enough to try something after all.* A couple of days later, Loco Larry was found strangled to death in his cell bunk. And it had cost Kevin only a few grams of cocaine that he had smuggled in, a couple of packs of Marlboros, and a hefty supply of ramen noodles.

A Little Birdie Told Me

BABYRUTH STOPPED BY Kenya's office around noon for lunch. She'd noticed over the past couple of weeks that Kenya was acting peculiar. She knew Kenya was upset about Kevin's parole hearing, but BabyRuth sensed something more was troubling her. So she wanted to check in and make sure she was all right. When BabyRuth arrived at Kenya's office, Trevon was working at his computer in the reception area. He greeted BabyRuth warmly.

"Hi, Ms. Jones. Nice to see you again." Trevon stood up to give her a quick hug.

"Hello, Trevon. Is Kenya ready for lunch?" BabyRuth asked.

"Her teleconference is running a little late, but she should be finished soon. Have a seat and make yourself comfortable. Can I get you something to drink?"

"No, thanks. I'm good. And don't let me disturb you. Just keep doing what you were doing. I'll read one of these magazines while I wait," BabyRuth said. She picked up a copy of *Black Enterprise* and took a seat on the leather sofa.

While scanning through the magazine, BabyRuth glanced at Trevon from time to time. He'd been to her house for Sunday dinner a few times but she didn't know him well. She did know about his shady past and that Kenya, with her big heart for the underdog, had taken him under her wing and helped him turn his life around. That was just Kenya's way. And BabyRuth knew Kenya was close to Trevon, and she suspected that Kenya confided in him. So she decided to ask him whether he too sensed that something was bothering her.

"Trevon," BabyRuth said as she approached his desk. "Can I talk to you for a minute about Kenya?"

"Sure, Ms. Jones."

"Have you noticed that she's been acting jumpy lately? She seems really nervous about something. I know we have a lot going on with Dereka still missing, and the parole hearing. But lately she's been so secretive, and that's not like her. Do you know what's going on?"

"Well, I know she's stressed about the parole hearing. Perhaps that's all it is," Trevon responded, looking down at some papers.

"Well, that's what I thought at first. But I think there's something more. Has she mentioned anything to you?"

"No, Ms. Jones," Trevon responded, keeping his eyes downcast. *Hmmmm*, BabyRuth thought. *He knows something, but he's not telling. That's why he can't look me in the eye.*

Kenya rushed out of her office and gave BabyRuth a big hug. "Sorry to keep you waiting, Mama. That call went longer than expected."

"No problem. I was just chatting with Trevon," BabyRuth said.

"Let's go. I'm starving," Kenya said, hooking her arm under BabyRuth's and walking towards the door. "Be back in an hour or so, Tre," she yelled over her shoulder.

Kenya took BabyRuth to one of her favorite Thai food restaurants nearby. Because Kenya was a highly regarded elected official in Fairfax County, a lot of people in the restaurant recognized her. She was greeted warmly by the restaurant staff and patrons. During lunch BabyRuth decided to question Kenya to see whether anything was amiss. Of course, Kenya denied that anything was wrong, other than being stressed out about the parole hearing and preparing the opposition statement. But Kenya knew she had to be careful. Her mother was very perceptive and could usually tell when she was hiding something. And Kenya definitely didn't want her mama to find out about the bribery scheme. So she quickly changed the subject to lighter topics. They had a very enjoyable lunch together, which was rare considering all that was happening in their lives.

After lunch Kenya and BabyRuth walked back to the Judicial Center Building. Trevon pulled into the parking lot just as they were crossing it. He got out of his car with a McDonald's bag in his hand. "How was lunch?" he asked, pulling french fries out of the bag and stuffing them into his mouth.

"Very nice," Kenya responded. She gave her mama a quick kiss on the cheek. "Got to get back to work. I'll call you later, Mama," Kenya said, walking back to the office with Trevon.

"Bye, Ms. Jones," Trevon stated, still avoiding direct eye contact with her.

"Take care, Trevon," BabyRuth said as she watched them walk away, chatting between themselves.

On the drive home, BabyRuth was feeling better about Kenya. Of course Kenya was anxious and out of sorts. They all were. And who wouldn't be, with all that was happening. When BabyRuth got home, she sat on the sofa to sort through her mail. Among her mail she found a white envelope with her name and address typed on it, but no return address. *This is strange*, BabyRuth thought as she opened the envelope and pulled out a one-page typewritten letter that stated,

> Someone close to your daughter may not be
> who they appear to be. Trouble may be on the horizon.
> Keep a watchful eye out.
>
> Birdie
> (A little Birdie told me)

What is this about? And who is this Birdie? BabyRuth thought, shaking her head and rereading the letter. She didn't know what to make of it. Perhaps it was just some crank letter related to Kenya's high-profile job as a prosecuting attorney. Unfortunately, prank letters and phone calls were occupational hazards that came with being a high-profile prosecutor. BabyRuth had talked to Kenya many times in the past about getting more security. Kenya had installed a sophisticated security system in her condo, and she felt that was sufficient.

Generally, violence against prosecutors, although it did happen, was rare.

BabyRuth thought about turning the letter over to Detective Davis to investigate. But she didn't want to distract her from focusing her time and limited resources on finding Dereka, especially if the letter was a farce. So she put the letter in the end table drawer and decided she would keep a watchful eye out. And while she was watching, she'd pray.

The Lady in Red

DEREKA EVENTUALLY PERSUADED the brothers to allow Sun-Yu to help her with the chores from time to time. Requesting Sun-Yu's help was not only Dereka's way of providing her friend some time out of the dreary basement; it also allowed them some special alone time to bond. And while Dereka appreciated the help with the work, it was Sun-Yu's company she cherished the most.

Today, as they cleaned the second-floor bedrooms, Sun-Yu was talking about her beautiful mother, who always wore red. Dereka never tired of hearing Sun-Yu talk about her mother, because it was the only time her friend seemed truly happy. Sun-Yu was still convinced that someday her mother would come for her and Jia. Dereka went down the hall to retrieve the laundry bag for the soiled bedding from the supply closet. As she walked down the hall, she heard voices in the living room below. Dereka looked around to see whether a guard was nearby but saw no one. She got on her knees and started crawling to a secret place she'd discovered by accident, which allowed her to spy on the people below. It was a small space in the corner near the top of the stairs that was completely concealed by a high solid board. There was a small cutout at the bottom of the board that allowed her to see and hear people gathered in the room below. Most of the time there were men, probably Los Chomas members, talking loudly in Spanish or Portuguese, and Dereka could barely make out what they were saying. But this time was different. Dereka thought she heard a female voice, speaking in accented English.

When Dereka reached her secret place in the corner, she looked through the crack and saw several people sitting around. Her heart almost stopped. There on the sofa, sitting between Luis and another man, was a lovely Asian woman. She was petite and had long shiny black hair and beautiful porcelain-like skin. And she was wearing a long red silk dress. Dereka knew right away that it was Sun-Yu's mother, the woman she had heard so much about. She looked just as Dereka had pictured her. Dereka crawled out of the space as fast as she could and ran down the hall to find her friend.

Dereka found Sun-Yu stripping sheets off one of the beds. "Sun-Yu, I think your mother is downstairs," Dereka said, out of breath. At first Sun-Yu looked at her with a puzzled expression on her face. "Your mother. I think I just saw her downstairs," Dereka repeated. But Sun-Yu just blinked her eyes in confusion. Although she had often spoke of her mother coming for them one day, the reality of it actually happening wasn't registering in her mind. "Come with me," Dereka said, grabbing Sun-Yu's hand and leading her down the hall. When they got to the end of the hall, Dereka placed her finger to her mouth to motion to Sun-Yu to be very quiet. They both got on their knees and crawled to the secret space. When Sun-Yu looked through the crack, she opened her mouth wide in surprise and started nodding her head vigorously, indicating that it was her mother. Her mother had come for her and Jia. Sun-Yu started to stand up, but Dereka pulled her back down, shaking her head no. *Wait*, she mouthed.

They could hear Sun-Yu's mother speaking with her beautiful accented voice, which sounded like music to the young girls' ears. Sun-Yu was so excited Dereka had to place her hand over her friend's mouth to keep her from shouting out loud. But soon the girls' joy turned to outright horror as they listened to her mother's words. She was asking for more money for the value of her daughters. It turned out that Sun-Yu and Jia had not been abducted from the airport, as Sun-Yu thought. Instead, their mother had actually sold her own daughters to Los Chomas. She had traveled on alone to the United

States and married a rich white man she met through a mail-order Asian brides' website. The mother had lied to the man, saying she had no children. Now, Sun-Yu's mother, cast aside by the rich white man for a younger, more beautiful Asian woman, had traveled back to Colombia to solicit more money for her daughters.

"Have my girls not served you well?" she asked, flashing a dazzling smile.

"Yes, they have. And we paid you well for them," Mario responded.

"But since I have been in the States, I learned that I could have gotten much more money for them," she added.

"But a deal is a deal," Diago interjected.

"But you gentlemen wouldn't want to take advantage of a lady," she added, batting her eyes flirtatiously at them.

"I tell you what," Diago said, leaning back in his chair. "You bring us one or two more pretty Asian girls, and we'll pay you well. More than before." His words seemed to appease her.

"I'll travel back to China now, and see what I can do," she said, standing up to leave. Luis and the other man followed her out the door.

Dereka felt something wet on her hands. That's when she realized she still had her hand over Sun-Yu's mouth, and the wetness was Sun-Yu's tears, which were rolling freely down her face. They crawled out of the small space, and Dereka had to practically carry her crying friend down the hall and lay her on a bed. "I'm so sorry," Dereka said, choking back her own tears. Sun-Yu couldn't speak; she could only sob. Dereka smoothed her hair and tried to think of something comforting to say. But she had no words. The only thing she could think to tell her friend was "I love you." So that's what she told her.

Dereka left Sun-Yu alone in the room, while she continued to clean the other rooms. She didn't want them to get in trouble for falling behind in their chores. *Oh my God, oh my God! How can a mother sell her own children?* Dereka thought. From what she knew personally about a mother's love, selling a child to the horrors of sex slavery was something her heart just couldn't absorb. *It has to be the ultimate sin,* Dereka thought.

But what Dereka didn't know was that such disgusting behavior by mothers, and fathers also, happens more than one might think. In poor developing countries such as Cambodia and India, selling daughters for sex is a widespread problem. Mothers who trade their daughters for sex claim they do so because of poverty and debt. Some mothers even get medical certificates of virginity in order to haggle for a higher price. In these countries, because of the low value placed on female children, daughters are sometimes viewed as property to provide for the family.

But the repugnant behavior of selling daughters for sex happens not only in poor or developing countries; it also happens in the most developed and prosperous countries, including the United States. Like the mother in Nebraska who prostituted her three daughters, ages seven to fourteen, to men at truck stops, or the mother in Indiana who sold her four-month-old infant to a pedophile. The sexual exploitation of daughters by their own mothers is a disgusting and appalling reality.

When Dereka went back later to check on Sun-Yu, she was surprised to find her up and working. "Su-Yu, are you all right?" Dereka asked.

"Yes, I'm fine."

"Are you sure?"

"Yes."

"Do you want to talk about it?"

"No."

"Well, why don't you go to the basement and rest? I'll finish up here."

"No, I'm fine. I'll help you. Besides, the men will be here soon."

Later that night, after the customers had gone, Dereka found Sun-Yu sitting on the floor in the basement kitchen. She had her mother's red silk scarf in her hands.

"It's so soft," Sun-Yu said with a faraway look in her eyes. "Just like my mother's face. I remember her skin was so soft when I touched her face," Sun-Yu added.

"Yes, I'm sure it was," Dereka responded, not knowing what else to say.

"Jia must never know. Promise me you won't tell Jia," Sun-Yu pleaded.

"I won't tell her. I won't tell anyone. I promise," Dereka replied. Then she sat on the floor beside Sun-Yu for a while.

The next morning Dereka arose long before dawn, as usual, and made her way in the darkness to their tiny bathroom. Once there she pulled a chain to turn on the overhead light. And the sight Dereka saw before her was so chilling and incomprehensible it knocked her off her feet. She landed hard on the concrete floor. She saw her dear friend Sun-Yu hanging from the wire clothesline, her face distorted in a grotesque grimace. Her mother's red scarf was around her neck. Dereka screamed.

You My Sister Now

WHEN THE OTHER girls heard Dereka's harrowing screams, they ran to the bathroom to see what was wrong. Shocked by the sight before them, some screamed, some gasped, and others fell to their knees, covering their faces with their hands. One girl, Gabriela, was so stunned and frightened by the sight she ran screaming up the basement steps and clawed at the door, trying to get out. The oldest girl, Milena, actually had the presence of mind to try to take Sun-Yu's body down. But she couldn't do it alone, and the other girls were too distraught to assist. When Dereka saw Milena struggling to remove Sun-Yu's body, she got up to help. But then she saw Jia, still standing near her bed, looking scared and confused by the pandemonium. Jia slowly began to walk towards the bathroom to see what was happening. Dereka pushed her way through the girls, grabbed Jia, and carried her back to the kitchen to prevent her from seeing her sister in such an awful way. She placed Jia, now eleven but small for her age, on her lap and rocked her back and forth.

The girls continued to scream in a panic. Their commotion quickly brought Diago, Mario, and both of the guards, guns drawn, to the basement. They pushed their way through the crowd of girls gathered at the bathroom door. When they saw what had happened, the brothers were terribly upset at the loss of their valuable property. The guards ordered the girls away from the bathroom and told them to sit on their beds. Mario took a pocketknife and cut the red scarf tied around Sun-Yu's neck. The girls heard a thud as her body dropped to the floor. One of the guards went upstairs and returned a few minutes later with a big trash bag. The guards placed Sun-Yu's body in the trash bag, just as they had done with Crystal's, and dragged it up the steps.

Dereka remained in the kitchen with Jia, shielding them both from having to witness the pitiful sight of Sun-Yu's body being removed like trash. Dereka gently placed Jia in a chair next to her and held her small hands. "Jia," Dereka said with tears in her eyes. "Your sister has gone to a better place. She's with the angels in heaven now. I know she'll be happy there. But we won't see her again. Do you understand?" Jia didn't speak but only stared at Dereka, an even greater sadness in her eyes. One lone tear slid slowly down Jia's cheek. It was the only time Dereka had ever seen her cry. Dereka gently wiped the tear away. "You my sister now. I'll take care of you," she promised.

Some of the other girls began to gather in the kitchen area, visibly shaken and confused by Sun-Yu's tragic end. Dereka took Jia back to her bed, laid her down, and placed the covers over her. "Rest now," she said. When Dereka returned to the kitchen, the girls, knowing how close her and Sun-Yu had been, bombarded her with questions.

"What could have possibly driven her to do it? Sun-Yu was always so encouraging and hopeful. And how could she have left her little sister Jia, whom she loved with her whole heart? What happened?" they asked, looking to Dereka to provide them some explanation— some relief from their heartache. And even though Dereka knew what had driven her friend to the breaking point, she kept her promise to Sun-Yu not to tell anyone what her mother had done.

"I think it all became too much for her. And she just...gave up," Dereka said. And that was the truth. It was of little comfort to the girls, but it was the best Dereka could offer at the time.

• • •

Business went on as usual that day in La Casa de Placer. Little kept the men away. When Dereka returned to the basement late that night, she found Jia sitting on the basement steps, waiting for her. When Jia saw Dereka, she ran and hugged her tightly around the waist, as if she was afraid that she would lose Dereka too. "It's okay, sweetie. I'm not going to leave you," Dereka assured as she walked Jia to her bed. And although Dereka was drained physically, mentally, and emotionally, she stayed with Jia for a while, lying down beside her on the tiny bed. A familiar song came to Dereka's mind, a song her mother used to sing to her on summer nights when they would sit together in the backyard and gaze at the stars. And Dereka, in her beautiful soprano voice, began to sing that song softly to Jia,

> He's got the whole world in his hands.
> He's got the whole wide world in his hands.
> He's got the whole world in his hands.
> He's got the whole world in his hands.

Dereka ad-libbed the second verse.

> He's got me and you in his hands.
> He's got our sister Sun-Yu in his hands.
> He's got me and you in his hands.
> He's got the whole world in his hands.

Singing the song comforted Dereka because it helped her to mentally transport herself to the tranquil surroundings of her own backyard. Dereka didn't know whether Jia understood the words of the song, but it seemed to calm her too. So Dereka continued to sing to Jia, until Jia fell asleep.

Someone Who Cares

DEREKA WAS HAUNTED in her dreams by the sight of her friend's lifeless body, suspended in air, with the red silk scarf around her neck. Where once sleep had brought her some measure of escape from the barbarity of sex slavery, now she was robbed of even that small release. She went through the motions of her day like the zombies she used to watch in horror movies—lifeless and emotionless. The loss of Sun-Yu, her closest friend in the house, left her teetering on the brink of despair. The only thing that kept Dereka going was her strong desire to look out for Jia. Dereka spent practically all of her spare time with Jia, trying to keep the young girl's mind occupied as much as possible—to provide her some escape from their unfortunate reality. She sang songs to Jia, taught her lessons, and played Jia's favorite game, Which Hand Is It In? Jia never seemed to tire of playing that game. Jia became Dereka's salvation because she gave Dereka purpose. Jia needed her, and that made Dereka feel her life wasn't totally worthless.

Today, as Dereka did her daily chores, her movements were heavy and lethargic. She went into Esmeralda's old room to dust and sweep. She cleaned it only occasionally, just to keep the cobwebs away. And Dereka enjoyed being in Esmeralda's space. She still missed the old lady who had shown them kindness. Dereka opened a drawer in the nightstand and saw a string of rosary beads. She had seen the beads around Esmeralda's neck from time to time. Dereka placed the beads in her pocket to keep as a memento. She planned to put them in the secret place in the wall with her other small treasures. Esmeralda's rosary would be a great addition. Dereka wished that she had something personal of Sun-Yu's to remember her by. And then she realized that she did. She had Sun-Yu's little sister, Jia, to care for.

When Dereka finished cleaning the room, she was so drained she took a moment to lie down on Esmeralda's bed. *Will this torment ever end?* Dereka questioned in her mind. As she lay there, Dereka felt all hope leaving her body and evaporating into thin air. She wanted to reach out and grab it, but she didn't have the strength. So she just lay there and watched her hope fade like a dimming light. She was at her lowest point since her captivity, and she was finally giving in.

A noise startled Dereka, and she sat straight up on the bed. She listened carefully, her senses keen, ears at full attention. Then she heard it again, and it sounded like it was coming from the next room. Dereka had been told by both Mario and Diago not to ever go into that room. She didn't know what it was used for but assumed they used it to store drugs and other valuables. Dereka had often seen Mario entering the room with boxes and bags of stuff.

Dereka jumped when she heard the noise again. Yes, it was coming from the room next door. Something or someone was in there. She knew it wasn't the brothers or the guards because they were all downstairs. Curiosity got the best of her, and she wanted to see what or who was making that noise. Dereka had always been a curious child. Her Grandma Ruth used to tell her all the time, "Curiosity killed the cat." Well, since she wasn't a cat, she didn't think much of that old folk saying. Dereka tiptoed to door and looked up and down the hall to see whether the coast was clear. All seemed well, so she tiptoed to the next door and placed her ear against it. Yes, there it was again—that same noise. She knocked on the door but got no response. Dereka cracked the door open a bit and noticed a very dim light in the room. Letting her curiosity get the best of her, she pushed the door open wide and walked in.

Dereka nearly jumped out of her skin when she saw an elderly lady propped up in a bed, smiling at her. She placed her hand over her mouth to keep from shrieking out loud. "Come in, little one. Don't be afraid," the lady said. Dereka didn't move. "I am Vittoria Rodriguez García. But you may call me Ms. Vee. I am Esmeralda's older sister. I used to help her around the house. Until I got too old to be of much use," she stated. The mention of Esmeralda's name, and the serene expression on the elderly lady's face, reassured Dereka that she had nothing to fear. She walked hesitantly towards the bed. "And who are you?" Ms. Vee asked, looking at Dereka inquisitively.

"I'm Dereka."

"Ahhhh, Dereka, the one they called *Niña Ángel*. Esmeralda told me all about you and the others. She loved you very much. And through her stories of you, I have come to love you too," Ms. Vee responded.

Dereka sat down next to Ms. Vee. "How long have you been here?" Dereka asked.

"For quite some time," Ms. Vee responded.

"Who takes care of you?" Dereka asked out of concern for the elderly lady.

"Esmeralda did. But now that she's gone, poor dear, I take care of myself. They bring me food once a week, which I fix for myself," Ms. Vee said, pointing to two small, old rusty appliances in the corner. "I'm an old lady, so I don't need much. Now enough about me. Tell me about you, little one," Ms. Vee said.

Dereka told Ms. Vee that she had been kidnapped the day before her thirteenth birthday. She poured her heart and soul out to Ms. Vee, just like she would if she were talking to her Grandma Ruth. As Dereka talked about how hard it was to be separated from her family, and how much she hated and dreaded being forced to be with the men, she began to sob. Ms. Vee took Dereka into her arms.

"There, there, little one," she said over and over in a soothing tone. "I know it's tough, but you can't give up. I sense something in you. You're stronger than you think, little one. So don't give up." Dereka snuggled against Ms. Vee, who smelled slightly of mothballs and rubbing alcohol. It felt so good for Dereka to be in the comforting presence of a kind, older woman. It also made Dereka realize that she couldn't give up; she had to get back to the women in her life that she loved so much.

When Dereka was all cried out, she sat up and wiped her eyes. "I have to go now, Ms. Vee. But I'll come back to see you soon."

"But you be careful, little one. Don't let them catch you here. They like to keep me hidden away. They said I talk too much," Ms. Vee said, winking at Dereka.

"I'll be careful," Dereka assured her.

"And I will keep you in my prayers. You take care, little one," Ms. Vee said. Dereka left Ms. Vee's room with a slight smile on her face. Just a moment ago, before she had met Ms. Vee, she was at her breaking point. But now, after confiding in and being comforted by the gentle elderly lady, she felt much better. She felt stronger. Like she could go on a little further. "Thank you, Lord, for Ms. Vee," Dereka whispered as she hurried to complete her remaining chores.

Bigger Fish to Fry

IT WAS THE day of the big payoff, and everything was set. Kenya had managed to obtain the $100K in cash she needed to secure Mr. Kilpatrick's vote to deny Kevin's parole. The money was securely locked in a portable home safe she'd purchased. In order not to raise suspicion as to why she needed so much cash, Kenya cleverly withdrew the money from three different sources. She withdrew $10K from her checking account and $40K from her savings account, and she cashed in a $50K CD, not thinking twice about the early withdrawal penalty. And just in case there were questions from nosy bank personnel about why she needed so much cash, Kenya concocted a story of how she'd found her dream car on Craigslist, and the seller would only accept cash. But thankfully, no one questioned her, so she didn't have to tell that lie. Not that it mattered much to Kenya at this point. What was a little lie in comparison with bribery anyway?

Kenya was too nervous to work, so she called Trevon at the office that morning, faking illness. Although he knew about her bribery plans, she didn't even tell him that today was the big day. Kenya sat at her kitchen table staring at the safe while anxiously waiting for Ryan to arrive with the final details for delivering the payment to Mr. Kilpatrick. Ryan, her knight in shining armor, had personally worked out all the details. Kenya felt guilty for placing her fiancé in such a precarious position. He was really going out on a limb for her, and she constantly told him how much she loved and appreciated his unwavering support. Ryan had even offered to give her some of his own money to make up the $100K, but Kenya refused. This was something she had to do herself. This was for Dereka.

Kenya unlocked the safe, took out the cash, and laid it on the table. She thought it strange that $100K in cash was not nearly as much money as she assumed it would be. Kenya had pictured herself walking out of the bank with a big briefcase full of cash handcuffed to one wrist, as she'd seen in many a TV movie. But in actuality, $100K in cash was very compact, consisting of five one-inch stacks of hundred-dollar bills. The five stacks would fit neatly in a large manila envelope that she could carry in a large purse. *So much for the credibility of the movies*, Kenya thought as she placed the cash back into the safe and locked it.

Kenya's cell phone rang, and she noticed it was her mother calling. BabyRuth had been blowing her phone up all morning. It was as if she knew something was up. Kenya ignored her mother's calls, which was something she never did. But she just couldn't take the chance of speaking with her right now.

Ryan arrived at Kenya's around a quarter past three, looking stressed and flustered. "Sorry I'm late, baby. It's been one of those days. I got some good news and some bad news," Ryan said, sitting down at the kitchen table.

"Give me the good news first," Kenya responded.

"Well, everything is set for the payoff tonight. Mr. Kilpatrick has arranged for his accountant, who is also his brother-in-law, to be at the Fyve Restaurant at the Ritz-Carlton in Pentagon City at seven. His accountant's name is Scott Logan. Here's a picture of him," Ryan said, scrolling through his cell phone and showing Kenya a photo. "He'll take the cash," Ryan continued, "and place it in Mr. Kilpatrick's various accounts. I get the feeling they've done this kind of thing before. His accountant-slash-brother-in-law is likely getting a little something for himself out of the deal."

"I can't believe this is actually happening. I must admit I'm nervous. But it will all be worth it when Kevin's parole is denied," Kenya stated, mostly to convince herself that she was doing the right thing.

"Now, for the bad news," Ryan said hesitantly. "I got a call from my supervisor on the way over here. She was scheduled to go to Boston this evening to teach an estate-planning seminar. But her daughter just gave birth, so she asked me to go in her place. I have to catch a six forty-five flight, so I won't be able to go with you to meet with the accountant. I'll be gone for about two weeks. I stopped by my place and packed on my way here. That's why I was late. What are the chances of something like this happening at a time like this?" Ryan stated, rather peeved.

"Oh, no. I have to do this by myself?" Kenya responded, her voice panicky.

"I tried to get out of the trip, but my supervisor's depending on me. I can call Mr. Kilpatrick and try to move the meeting to another time," Ryan offered.

"No, no, don't do that. I want to get this over with. I can handle it," Kenya replied.

"Are you sure? I'd really prefer to be with you."

"I'm sure, but thanks for the offer. You've done so much already. And I truly appreciate it."

Ryan and Kenya spent the next thirty minutes going over the details of the meeting. Kenya was to arrive at the restaurant promptly at seven o'clock and ask for Mr. Logan, who would already be seated in the dining area. During the course of their meal, Mr. Logan would casually remove some documents from his briefcase so as to make it appear as though they were just having a legitimate business dinner. He'd then engage in small talk while they ate dinner, and during their chitchat, Mr. Logan would ask Kenya whether she had something for him. At that time Kenya would give him the envelope with the cash, which he'd place in his briefcase. Then they would go their separate ways. Deed done.

Ryan left Kenya's around half past four to head to the airport. He hugged her tight and asked her to call him later that evening with an update. "And please don't tell anyone else about this," Ryan cautioned. "The less people who know, the better for us."

"I won't," Kenya said, not letting him know that she had already told Trevon.

After Ryan left, Kenya prepared herself for the meeting later. She even got on her knees and prayed that things would go well. Her phone kept ringing off the hook, but Kenya continued to ignore her mother's calls. Kenya suspected her mother was concerned about her not answering her phone or returning the calls. But Kenya couldn't worry about that now. She had bigger fish to fry.

Oh No He Didn't

BABYRUTH LISTENED TO the ringing of Kenya's phone and left another voice message. "Kenya, I know you're home because I called your office earlier, and Trevon said you were home sick. Are you okay? Call me as soon as you get this message, sweetie. It's important. Love you."

BabyRuth hung up the phone and looked at the clock. It was now a quarter to six, and she had tried to reach Kenya all day. Not only was she concerned about her being sick, but she had also received another letter in the mail from this Birdie person. BabyRuth, not willing to ignore the warnings any longer, wanted to show Kenya the letters and discuss what to do. Should they give them to Detective Davis, take them to the police station, or what? Also, BabyRuth had a strange suspicion that Kenya was hiding something, and she was determined to find out what it was.

BabyRuth sat on the sofa and stared at the two letters she received from Birdie. Both letters alluded to impending danger and deception from someone close to Kenya. *What if these letters are legitimate?* BabyRuth thought. *Who's this person close to my baby that would want to cause her harm?* The first person that came into BabyRuth's mine was Trevon. BabyRuth knew that Kenya confided in him and trusted him implicitly. *Could he be the one? He's been acting strange and secretive lately too*, BabyRuth thought. She knew about Trevon's shady background as a juvenile delinquent, but she tried not to hold that against him. After all, as a Christian woman, she knew that, by God's grace, people could change. But she also remembered something her father used to say all the time—that a leopard can't change its spots. So in the back of BabyRuth's mind, she thought Trevon may be the person that Birdie was warning her about. "Lord, forgive me if I'm wrong, but I believe that boy is up to no good," BabyRuth murmured.

After calling Kenya two more times, she decided to drive over to Kenya's to check on her and show her the two letters from Birdie. On the way to Kenya's, BabyRuth stopped at a local deli to pick up Kenya's favorite vegetable soup, hoping it would make her feel better. While BabyRuth stood in the long line, waiting to place her order, she spotted Trevon sitting at a table in the very back of the restaurant. His back was to her, and he was crouched over his computer working intently on something, but she was sure it was him. *What's he doing here?* BabyRuth thought, knowing that Trevon generally worked much later at the office. The hairs stood up on BabyRuth's arms as she watched him sitting in the corner, hunched over his computer at the back table, as if he was trying to be inconspicuous.

Once BabyRuth placed her order, she decided to approach Trevon just to say hello and see whether she could figure out if he was up to something. She tapped him on the shoulder. When Trevon looked around and saw BabyRuth, he slammed his computer lid down so fast it made BabyRuth's head spin.

"Oh, I didn't mean to disturb you, Trevon. I just wanted to say hi," BabyRuth said, looking at Trevon strangely.

"No problem, Ms. Jones. I was just...uh...working on...something. You didn't disturb me," Trevon responded, looking uncomfortable.

"Well, I'm on my way to Kenya's, but I have a little time for a quick visit," BabyRuth said, taking a seat at the table. But just as BabyRuth's bottom hit the seat cushion, Trevon was up in a flash with his computer in hand.

"Sorry I can't stay, Ms. Jones. I gotta go. I've got something to take care of." And before BabyRuth could respond, Trevon was headed for the door. BabyRuth stood up, placed her hands on her hips, and muttered under her breath, "Oh no he didn't," as she glared after Trevon. *You can run, but you can't hide*, BabyRuth thought as she picked up her food order and walked to her car. She arrived at Kenya's around half past six, but Kenya was already gone.

The Moment of Truth

KENYA WAS A nervous wreck as she drove to the restaurant to meet with Mr. Kilpatrick's accountant. She could feel her legs trembling. As she got closer to the restaurant, she thought about backing out. She could just turn around, go back home, and forget the whole thing. But that may mean that Kevin Curtis would likely be out on parole in a few months, as free as a bird, whereas Dereka was trapped God knows where and suffering immensely. And there was no way in hell that Kenya could allow that to happen. So she kept driving. There was no turning back now.

Kenya pulled up in front of the hotel and gave her keys to the valet parking attendant. She held tightly to the large shoulder bag with the envelope full of cash as she walked across the elegantly decorated hotel lobby to the restaurant. Once there she asked the maître d' for Mr. Scott Logan's table. "Yes, right this way, Ms. Jones," the maître d' said, as if he was expecting her. He led Kenya to a table near the back of the restaurant, where Mr. Logan was sitting, looking exactly like the picture Ryan showed her. He smiled when he saw her and stood up to shake her hand. He had a very amicable, laid-back way about him.

"Nice to meet you, Kenya," Scott said.

"Nice to meet you too, Mr. Logan," Kenya responded.

"No, please call me Scott," he said, motioning for her to take a seat. The waiter came over immediately to serve them. "You hungry?

I'm starved. I'm having the beef tenderloin. It's excellent here," Scott continued.

"Great. I'll have the same," Kenya told the waiter without even looking at the menu.

Kenya's stomach was in knots, and eating was the last thing on her mind. While they waited for their food, Scott removed some papers from his briefcase, just as planned, and placed them on the table in front of Kenya. Scott then engaged in small talk about his work as an accountant, the nice weather, world events, favorite vacation spots, his children, and other things. He was really quite good at continuous chatter, and all Kenya had to do was smile and nod from time to time. Which was great because she was too anxious to do much more.

After the food arrived, Scott's chatter continued until they were nearly finished eating. Kenya began to wonder when he was going to make his move. She could feel beads of sweat forming on her forehead and just wanted to get it over with and go home. He must have read her mind because he stopped the chitchat and looked Kenya directly in the eyes.

"Do you have something for me?" he asked cordially. Kenya's heartbeat quickened. This was it. The moment of truth. It was do or die. Kenya looked around apprehensively at the other restaurant patrons, who were not paying them any attention whatsoever. Her hands were shaking as she reached into her bag and removed the large envelope. She placed it in on the table in front of Scott.

Scott looked at the envelope and leaned in close to Kenya. "Before I pick up the envelope, my client, Mr. Kilpatrick, wants to be absolutely sure you're all in. He's taking a big risk and wants to be sure you really want to do this. Once I pick up this money, there's no turning back. These funds will secure my client's vote against parole for Mr. Kevin Curtis. My client's almost positive that with his vote, the parole will be denied. But there are no guarantees, Kenya. Do you understand?" Kenya nodded yes and look squarely at Scott.

"Do you know what Kevin's father did?" she asked rhetorically. "He abducted my niece as revenge for my turning in his son when he tried to blackmail me when I was senior in high school. And I don't know where she is, or what's happening to her. Do you have any idea how that makes me feel? So yes. I want to proceed. I'm doing this for Dereka," Kenya stated adamantly. Scott looked at Kenya with sympathetic eyes, picked up the envelope, peeped inside, and placed it in his briefcase. Kenya let out a deep breath. *It's done*, she thought, sitting back in her chair to relax a bit.

But Scott's next action shook Kenya to her core. He stood up, and his entire demeanor changed from an amiable, sympathetic person to a stone-faced professional. "Kenya Jones, you are under arrest for attempting to bribe a public official. You have the right to remain silent. Anything you say can and will be used against you in a court of law. You have the right to an attorney," Scott stated, reciting the entire Miranda rights. Kenya stared at him in astonishment. *This can't be happening*, she thought, shaking her head in disbelief. She heard movement to her right, looked up, and saw a uniformed police officer. The officer directed Kenya to stand up and place her hands behind her back. After handcuffing her, he took her arm and led her outside, past stunned restaurant patrons, to a waiting police car with lights flashing. Someone must have tipped off the media regarding the impending arrest of the popular commonwealth prosecutor. News reporters and camera people jockeyed for position while shouting questions at Kenya. She stared wide eyed at the frenzy of reporters and cameras around her, looking like a deer caught in headlights.

On the ride to the police station, all kinds of questions raced through Kenya's mind. *What happened? What went wrong? Did Mr. Kilpatrick change his mind and turn me in? Did someone else? But who?* "Oh my God, oh my God," Kenya murmured to herself. She knew that her career, her reputation, and her life, for that matter, were ruined. Devastated, Kenya collapsed on the backseat of the police car and cried hysterically.

Enough Is Enough

BABYRUTH WAS DOZING in her comfy chair when the ringing of the phone woke her. *This better be Kenya finally calling me back. That girl got some nerve ignoring my calls*, she thought as she went into the kitchen to get the phone.

"Mama, I'm in trouble," Kenya said frantically.

"Kenya, I've been trying to reach you all day. Trevon said you called in sick. What's wrong?" BabyRuth asked.

"Mama, I can't tell you over the phone. I'm at the police station. Just get here as soon as you can. Please, Mama," Kenya urged.

"Police station! What are you doing at the police station?"

"I'll tell you when you get here. Are there any reporters outside the house?"

"I don't know. But why would reporters be outside?"

"I'll explain when you get here. Please hurry, Mama."

"I'm on my way."

If it ain't one thing, it's another, BabyRuth thought as she drove to the police station. When she arrived, she was shocked to see a large group of people outside, and several TV news vans. As soon as BabyRuth stepped out of her car, she was surrounded by reporters yelling questions at her and shoving microphones in her face.

"Ms. Jones, is it true your daughter tried to bribe a parole board officer?"

"How do you feel about your daughter, the state prosecutor, being arrested for bribery?"

"Ms. Jones, did you know what your daughter was up to?"

"Any comments, Ms. Jones?"

BabyRuth stood in place, trying to shield her face from the flashing bulbs. Kenya's attorney drove up, got out of her car, and quickly escorted BabyRuth into the police station.

"Deborah, thank God you're here. What are they talking about? They're saying Kenya bribed somebody. Bribed who? Do you know what's going on?" BabyRuth bombarded Kenya's attorney with questions.

"Not yet, but I'm going to find out. Wait here," Deborah responded, leaving BabyRuth in the waiting area while she walked briskly to the front desk. Deborah was one of the best criminal attorneys in the DC area and had been close friends with the Jones family for years. She'd played a key role in assisting them through Kenya's sexting scandal with Kevin Curtis years ago. BabyRuth was confident in her abilities to handle this crisis.

About an hour later, Deborah returned to the waiting area to update BabyRuth. The solemn look on her face told BabyRuth that something disastrous had occurred.

"What is it, Deborah? Where's Kenya? Can I take her home?" BabyRuth asked anxiously.

"No, I'm afraid not. Let's go outside," Deborah said, wanting to get away from prying ears.

"But what about Kenya?" BabyRuth asked.

Deborah gently took BabyRuth's arm and said, "Please come with me."

Once outside, Deborah escorted BabyRuth through the remaining news reporters to her car and let BabyRuth in on the passenger's side. Deborah got in on the driver's side and took a deep breath before speaking. "I hate to tell you this. But Kenya is being charged with bribery of a public official, which is a felony. They're saying that she attempted to bribe a member of the Virginia parole board, a Mr. Lawrence Kilpatrick, to vote against Kevin Curtis's parole. She attempted to pay him a hundred thousand in cash. The police were tipped off and conducted a sting. Kenya was arrested at a restaurant when she gave the cash to a police officer posing as a representative of the board member. That's all I know for now," Deborah concluded.

BabyRuth was stunned. "Lord, Jesus. Lord, Jesus," was all she could say. Deborah reached out and took her friend's hand.

"I know this is tough, especially with all your family has been through. But I'm going to do everything I can to get you all through this. Kenya will have to spend tonight in jail, but there'll be a bail hearing at nine in the morning at the courthouse. I'm positive you'll be able to post bond so Kenya will be released."

"How is she? Did you talk to her?" BabyRuth asked.

"I spoke with her briefly. She's holding up. She told me to tell you she's so sorry. She's more concerned about you right now than herself. I told her I would take you home and pick you up in the morning on my way to the courthouse. We can swing by and get your car then," Deborah stated.

"That's okay. I can drive myself home," BabyRuth said, opening the passenger door. Deborah placed her hand on BabyRuth's shoulder to stop her.

"No, you're not okay to drive. Let me take you home. I don't mind. We all need a little help sometimes," Deborah added, smiling slightly. BabyRuth closed the car door, sat back, and finally allowed the tears to flow.

"Thanks, Deborah. You're a good friend," she whispered.

When BabyRuth got home, the gravity of Kenya's predicament hit her like a ton of bricks. She dropped on the sofa. She was spiritually, mentally, emotionally, and physically drained. "Lord, enough is enough," BabyRuth cried out in anguish. "Enough is enough."

Never Saw It Coming

MEMPHIS HAD A broad smile on his face as he watched the ten o'clock news. There was Kenya, in handcuffs, being placed in the back of a squad car. The news headline read, "Prominent Commonwealth Attorney, Kenya Jones, Arrested for Bribery of a Public Official."

Memphis chuckled to himself. His plan had worked out even better than he had imagined. His employee had really outdone himself on this one. Had gone above and beyond the call of duty. Memphis knew he had selected the right person for the job. Someone who had been able to successfully infiltrate Kenya's inner circle and gain her trust. Someone to spy on her and report to Memphis Kenya's every move. And together, Memphis and his employee had set the ultimate trap to catch Kenya in the fowler's snare. Kenya was so gullible and trusting. Had been that way since she was in high school. Trapping her had been relatively easy. *Like taking candy from a baby*, Memphis thought with a smirk on his face.

Memphis had already planned to reward his employee richly for this job, and now he decided to throw in an extra bonus. He picked up his cell phone and punched a speed dial number to call his employee, who answered immediately. "I just saw the news. Excellent job. I'm really proud of you. I'll have a little something extra for you when you stop by in a few days. See you then," he said, hanging up and redirecting his attention back to the breaking news.

Memphis could hardly contain himself as he listened to the story of Kenya's arrest for allegedly bribing a parole board member. "The dumb wench was trying to keep my son in jail. And she actually thought she could get away with it," Memphis said out loud, shaking his head. But Memphis had gotten the best of Kenya again, and this time was even more satisfying than the last. Because this time Kenya could end up in jail, like his son did when she turned on him. This strike was against Kenya personally, not a family member, as with her niece, Dereka. This blow would ensure Kenya's complete and total humiliation. Her reputation would be ruined, her name dragged through the mud. This was indeed the sucker punch of all sucker punches. And she never saw it coming.

I Smell a Rat

THE NEXT DAY Deborah and BabyRuth sat in the courtroom waiting for the start of the bail hearing. BabyRuth gasped when she saw her daughter escorted into the courtroom looking haggard and shell shocked. After the prosecutor read the charges against Kenya, Deborah presented her case for Kenya's bail. The prosecutor didn't object to the request for bail, and it was granted. After BabyRuth posted bail, Kenya was released.

As suspected, there was a media frenzy outside the courthouse. The arrest of the popular commonwealth attorney was huge news, and every media source in the area wanted a piece of the action. Deborah tried to appease the media by assuring them of a full statement once all the facts of the case were determined. "However, we have no comment at this time," Deborah stated as she shepherded BabyRuth and Kenya to their car. "I'll meet with you all in a few days to discuss the facts of the case once my investigators work their magic," Deborah stated. Her top-notch team of investigators were like hound dogs when it came to sniffing out facts. "In the meantime, keep a low profile, and don't talk to anyone about the case. That includes family and friends," Deborah cautioned.

Suspecting that the media was likely camped out at Kenya's condo, BabyRuth persuaded Kenya to stay with her for a few days. The two of them rode in silence. BabyRuth glanced at Kenya from time to time, and it pained her to see the hurt, distress, and humiliation etched on her daughter's face. But on the other hand, BabyRuth was also terribly disappointed and appalled by Kenya's behavior. *How could she do such a thing? Bribing a parole board member? What was she thinking?* BabyRuth thought. She just didn't understand how her daughter could be such a brilliant and talented person intellectually but totally lack good judgment, logic, and plain common sense in other respects.

When they arrived at BabyRuth's, there were a handful of reporters there. BabyRuth held tightly to Kenya as they hurried past them and entered the house. They plopped into chairs at the kitchen table, each looking as sad and sorrowful as lost puppies.

"Want me to make you something to eat?" BabyRuth offered, not knowing what else to say or do.

"I'm not hungry, Mama," Kenya responded, her shoulders hunched over and head down. She was too embarrassed to even look in her mother's eyes. Kenya knew her mama was extremely upset and hurt by her actions, and Kenya didn't blame her one bit.

BabyRuth stared at Kenya for a moment. "Why, Kenya? Why would you do such a thing? On top of everything that we're going through, why would you even think of bribing a parole board member? That just doesn't make any sense to me."

"Mama, I had to do something. I just couldn't take a chance that Kevin would get out of prison. Mama, don't you understand? I feel responsible for what's happening to Dereka, and what happened to Serena. And it's eating me up inside. You told me that it's not my fault. But if it wasn't for me, none of this would have happened," Kenya cried.

"But Kenya, why didn't you talk to me? We could have worked through this. We could have gotten you counseling or anything you needed. But now look what you've done to yourself. Didn't you think of the consequences?"

"But we didn't think we'd get caught," Kenya pitifully responded.

"We?" BabyRuth said, surprised. "Who's we?"

"Ryan and I."

"You mean Ryan is in on this?"

"Yes. I talked him into helping me."

"Oh no, Kenya."

"I'll try to keep him out of it if I can. I didn't even tell Deborah about his involvement. I don't want him to get in trouble for trying to help me. It's my fault; I'll take the fall."

"This is a mess. One big mess. And I'm not going to even pretend to understand what you did. But I know in your heart of hearts, you thought you were doing the right thing. But it was absolutely the wrong thing to do. Preposterous," BabyRuth said, rubbing her forehead.

"I know, Mama. And I'm sorry. And I don't even know what went wrong. Mr. Kilpatrick must have changed his mind and turned me in."

"Well, it had to be him. No one else knew, right?" BabyRuth asked.

"I didn't tell anyone. Well, except Trevon," Kenya confessed.

"Trevon! Trevon knew?" BabyRuth asked, her eyes wide.

"Yes, I told him," Kenya admitted.

"Oh my Lord! I think Trevon had something to do with this," BabyRuth exclaimed. She jumped up, went to the living room, and got the two letters she received from Birdie. "Read these. I wanted to show them to you yesterday but couldn't reach you. The letters say someone close to you is deceptive and could harm you." BabyRuth waited impatiently for Kenya to read the letters.

"What's this about? And who's Birdie?" Kenya asked, confused.

"I don't know who Birdie is, but this little birdie was trying to tell me something. Now I think I know who these letters are referring to: Trevon. I've had my suspicion that he's been up to no good. If he knew about the bribery, maybe he turned you in."

"Trevon?" Kenya shouted incredulously. "Trevon would never do anything like that. No way. Either Mr. Kilpatrick changed his mind, or someone else found out and turned me in. But I guarantee it wasn't Trevon. I trust him completely," Kenya proclaimed.

"But that's always been your problem, Kenya. You're too trusting. And you sometimes trust the wrong people," BabyRuth said, implying that Kenya had also trusted Kevin Curtis years ago.

"But Mama, you're wrong about Trevon. Why would he do something like this?" Kenya asked.

"You know he has a criminal past. Maybe he did it for money or some other gain. I really don't know why he did it. But I plan to find out," BabyRuth asserted.

"Well, do what you have to do, Mama," Kenya said, getting up from the table and heading upstairs. "I'm going to try to reach Ryan and let him know what's going on. He's in Boston at a conference, so he may not know yet. I'd rather he hear it from me than on the news or something," Kenya stated sadly.

"Okay, honey," BabyRuth said as she watched Kenya go slowly upstairs. BabyRuth picked up the two letters from Birdie. "Yeah, I smell a rat," she said. "These letters are referring to Trevon. He's the deceptive person. I knew he was up to something. I don't know why he did it, but I'm going to get to the bottom of this. You just wait and see."

How Did You Know?

THE DAYS FOLLOWING the bribery scandal were brutal for Kenya and BabyRuth. Reporters knocked on the door at all times of the day and night, trying to get an interview. BabyRuth finally had to call the police, who warned the media against trespassing on private property. But they were still allowed to stay on the public street and sidewalk in front of the house. The phone rang constantly, and BabyRuth used her caller ID to screen the calls. And of course, social media was all abuzz with news of the prominent attorney's downfall. And while Kenya had her share of friends and supporters who rallied to her defense, she also had her share of haters who took advantage of the opportunity to slaughter her like a hog in the butcher's shop.

This morning, while cleaning up after breakfast, they heard a knock on the door. BabyRuth, thinking it was the media, peeped through the keyhole, ready to call the police back to the house if necessary. But her heart filled with joy when she saw Jasmine standing there. She yanked the door open and pulled Jasmine in. "Sweetie, what a pleasant surprise," BabyRuth said, embracing her.

"When I heard the news, I had to come. How's Kenya?" Jasmine asked.

"Not well. But she'll be glad to see you. Right now she needs all the support she can get," BabyRuth said, walking back to the kitchen with Jasmine. When Kenya saw Jasmine, she ran to her and hugged her tight.

"Thanks for coming," she murmured, her head down. Jasmine took her hand, lifted Kenya's chin, and looked her in the eyes.

"You keep your head up, girl. I got you. You hear me? You did what you thought you had to do, and I'm not mad at you. You did it for Dereka, and I can't fault you for that. So you keep your head up, sister friend. This too shall pass, and you'll be better for it," Jasmine assured. Her positivity, spunk, and comforting presence was just what the doctor ordered.

The three ladies then spent some time catching up on Jasmine's undercover work. And although she had nothing of note to report as far as finding Dereka, Jasmine was optimistic. "We're making progress, and we're rescuing girls. It's heartbreaking but very rewarding work. And we'll find Dereka. I know we will," Jasmine stated determinedly.

Later that afternoon, Kenya asked BabyRuth whether she wouldn't mind stopping by her office to pick up some of her personal items. Kenya had voluntarily taken a leave of absence from her job. When BabyRuth arrived at the office, Kenya's supervisor, Margaret Lovelace, and colleagues showered her with sympathy and kindness. "Let Kenya know we're rooting for her," one colleague shouted out.

Margaret walked BabyRuth to Kenya's office. "By the way, the police were here yesterday and confiscated Kenya's desktop computer and a few other items. But her personal things are still there. Take as much time as you need," Margaret stated, hugging BabyRuth before leaving her alone.

BabyRuth looked around and noticed Trevon was not at his desk in the front-office area. "Humph, I see he's missing in action. Probably hiding under some rock like he should be," she murmured under her breath. BabyRuth opened the door to Kenya's office and jumped in surprise. There was Trevon, snooping around in Kenya's desk, rummaging through her bottom drawer. He was startled when he saw BabyRuth.

"Oh, Ms. Jones. I didn't know you were coming here today," Trevon said, looking as flustered as the cat who ate the canary.

"I bet you didn't. And what are you doing in Kenya's office, going through her things?" BabyRuth responded, marching towards him.

"I was just getting some personal stuff to take to her later."

"Is that so?" BabyRuth said with her hands on her hips.

"Yes," Trevon replied, looking at BabyRuth strangely.

BabyRuth decided to lay all her cards on the table. "I know what you've been up to," she said, staring Trevon down.

"You do?" he asked.

"Yes, I know. I can always tell when someone is hiding something. You've been acting so suspicious lately. I know what you did," BabyRuth accused. Trevon stopped digging through Kenya's desk and slowly sat down in a chair. His eyes darted around as if he was trying to figure out how she had figured him out.

"But how did you know?" Trevon stated, stunned.

"I just know. I'm nobody's fool," BabyRuth said, crossing her arms across her chest. Trevon scratched his head.

"But how? I've been so careful. How did you know I am Birdie?"

BabyRuth's jaw dropped.

Will the Real Imposter Please Stand Up?

MEMPHIS SAT AT his home office desk waiting for his employee to arrive. When the doorbell rang, he looked at his watch. *Right on time*, he thought. Memphis opened the door, and in walked Ryan, with a big smile on his face.

"We did it," Ryan said, giving Memphis a half man hug.

"You did it, my man. You really came through for me on this," Memphis stated, motioning for Ryan to sit on the sofa.

"Well, I've learned from the best," Ryan responded, attempting to puff up his boss's ego. Not that it needed any further inflation.

Ryan was the true imposter, the one who had maneuvered his way into Kenya's world to spy on and deceive her. Memphis had met Ryan in Detroit, where Ryan was running a loosely organized gang of drug dealers in the Ninth Precinct in Detroit's East Side. What impressed Memphis the most about the young man was his cunningness. Ryan was one of the best con men that Memphis had ever met. And that's saying something. Ryan could talk himself into, or out of, almost anything. Ryan was a pathological liar who could make even the most obvious lie seem like the gospel truth.

When Memphis decided to hire someone to infiltrate Kenya's world, he knew Ryan was his man. Ryan was power-driven, handsome, charismatic, greedy, and devious—a winning combination in Memphis's eyes. Together they had fabricated a sob story about Ryan's past. A story that Memphis knew the bleeding-heart Kenya would fall for hook, line, and sinker. Ryan Young wasn't even his real name. Memphis changed it to Ryan when he hired him to work for him full time. And while Ryan was indeed raised by a single mom in Detroit's Islandville community, the rest of the story that Ryan had hand-fed Kenya was one big lie. Ryan's mother had not died of cancer as he told Kenya. She was alive and well, still living in Detroit's East Side. And Ryan had never gone to college, much less law school. He barely made it out of high school. Ryan only pretended to work as an attorney for a prestigious law firm. He had the fake ID, phony college and law school degrees, business cards, and monogramed briefcase to facilitate the façade.

Kenya had assumed that Ryan's lavish apartment, fancy car, and expensive clothes—all compliments of Memphis—were the result of his hard work as a top estate attorney. Whenever Kenya wanted to meet Ryan for lunch at his office, he'd always meet her either in the lobby of the office building where the law firm was housed, in the public café on the ground level, or at a nearby restaurant. The one time that Ryan had actually taken Kenya to see his office, he'd made arrangements with the pretty female receptionist, whom he slept with occasionally, to allow him to briefly show Kenya the office of a senior attorney who was away on vacation at the time. He choose to do his office showing late on a Friday afternoon, when most of the office staff had already left for happy hour or other Friday-night social activities. Ryan even had the receptionist temporarily replace the attorney's family photos with pictures of him and Kenya. Oh, he was good. A master at the game.

Memphis look at Ryan proudly, as a father looks at his son on graduation day. "I still can't believe you pulled this bribery scheme off, Ryan. It far surpassed what I originally had in mind for Kenya. My plan was for you two to be engaged, to have Kenya plan this huge wedding, and then for you to leave her humiliated at the altar. And while at the same time conning her into opening up joint bank accounts, and taking all her money. But then you approached me with this bribery setup. Man, that was pure genius," Memphis said, leaning back and propping his feet up on the leather ottoman.

"Well, it came to me when I was in the bed with Kenya," Ryan said, grinning from ear to ear. "She was reading the parole board members' bios and decisions in order to prepare their victim statement against paroling Kevin. And when she showed me the picture of this man who she said was the swing vote, I pretended to know him. I had his bio, so I just told her some of the basic info I saw in it. And then I joked about greasing his palms to swing his vote her way. I figured she'd go for it because of the way she feels about Kevin. She despises him. Of course I pretended I was joking, and pushed back on the bribery idea because I wanted her to have to convince me to do it. Make her think it was her idea, not mine."

And thus, the twisted plot for Kenya's downfall had begun. Ryan had not only tricked Kenya into believing that he knew Mr. Kilpatrick, but misled her into thinking he was holding private meetings with him. Ryan didn't know Mr. Kilpatrick from Adam's cat—had never laid eyes on or spoken to the man. During the times he was supposedly meeting with Mr. Kilpatrick, Ryan was actually meeting with Memphis to plan their next steps. They decided on the amount of $100K because Ryan knew that Kenya could get that amount relatively easily on her own, without any outside help from family or friends. Memphis used a crooked cop in the police department, one who had been deep in Memphis's pockets for years, to pose as Mr. Kilpatrick's accountant. They chose a public restaurant for the payoff and tipped off the media of the proposed bribery to ensure Kenya's utter public humiliation. They figured that the salacious news of a state prosecutor attempting to bride a public official would be momentous—just as it was.

Memphis retrieved an envelope from his briefcase and threw it on the table in front of Ryan. "That's a little extra bonus for your troubles."

"Thanks, doc," Ryan said, picking up the envelope and quickly counting the money. He often called Memphis "doc" because he admired his expertise in the criminal world and considered him to be at the top of his game. Ryan let out a low whistle. "Twenty thousand in bonus money. Not a bad deal. Thanks," Ryan said, elated with the extra bucks.

"Well, you deserve it. And the best part is that it's some of Kenya's money. I told my boy in the police department to only turn in fifty of the hundred thousand Kenya gave him. Of that extra fifty, you got twenty in bonus, and he got a few extra bucks. And there's nothing Kenya can do about it. If she complains that she actually paid a hundred thousand in bribery money rather than fifty, she'd look like an even bigger fool than she already does. Man, I got her right where I want her," Memphis said, laughing.

"That's why you're you," Ryan responded, putting the cash in his inside blazer pocket.

"Well, my man. You got a plane to catch," Memphis said, handing Ryan some documents. "You are no longer Ryan Young. Your new name is Jamal Ferguson. I'm sending you to Mexico City to work with one of my partners there. He's a top kingpin, and his operation is thriving. I'm sure you'll do well there. You have everything you need—driver's license, passport, airline tickets, and the like—in your envelope. Your old apartment is being cleared out as we speak. And I want you to leave your car here for disposal. Take mine to the airport," Memphis said, tossing Ryan his keys. "Park it in the usual spot. I'll have someone pick it up later."

Ryan took out his new passport. "Jamal Ferguson. I like it. Nice picture too," he said, placing the passport and other documents in his briefcase and heading for the door. Just as Ryan opened the door to leave, Memphis asked him to hold up for a minute. He took out his cell phone camera and aimed it at Ryan. "Why don't you throw your former fiancée a farewell kiss?" Memphis asked. Ryan, all smiles, was more than willing to oblige. He threw a kiss to the camera, and Memphis snapped the shot. And with that, the real imposter strolled out the door.

The Facts Speak for Themselves

WHEN BABYRUTH WAS able to pick her jaw up off the floor, all she could do was stare at Trevon with a flabbergasted expression on her face. *Trevon is Birdie? But how could I have been so wrong?* she thought. BabyRuth didn't know what to say or do next. But luckily Trevon kept talking and bailed her out.

"I should have known you'd figure it out, Ms. Jones. Kenya always talked about how perceptive you are. Said you could always tell when she's hiding something. I bet you figured me out that time you saw me in that restaurant, didn't you?" Trevon asked.

"Well...uh...hmmmm...that could have been it," BabyRuth stammered, truly at a loss for words. Her mind was still reeling from the fact that Trevon was Birdie—the one who was trying to help, not harm, them. *So that's why he's been acting so suspicious. That's what he was hiding from me. But if he's Birdie, who's the deceiver? Who's the person who wants to harm Kenya?* BabyRuth pondered.

Suddenly exhausted, she flopped down into Kenya's chair. One day she'd confess to Trevon who she really thought he was, and apologize. But right now she just wanted to know who was out to harm her daughter. "Trevon, who were you referring to in your letters? Who is this deceptive person close to Kenya?" BabyRuth asked. Trevon took a deep breath before speaking.

"I think it's Ryan," he stated. BabyRuth fell back in her chair. If she had not been sitting down, she would have hit the floor. "No. Not Ryan. It can't be Ryan," she stuttered, dumbfounded.

"I'm not positive, but I think so," Trevon said. He pulled a folder from his satchel. "I know it's hard to believe. And I didn't want to say for sure until I had all the facts. That's why I sent you the letters, Ms. Jones. I just wanted to warn you and put you on notice while I continued to gather information."

"But what makes you think it's Ryan, of all people? He's her fiancé. Why would he want to harm her?" BabyRuth asked.

Trevon confessed that he had always gotten a bad vibe from Ryan, from the first moment they met. Ryan just didn't seem legit. But Trevon shook it off, thinking that perhaps he was just a little jealous of the new man in Kenya's life, or was being overly protective of her. But when Kenya told Trevon that she and Ryan were planning to bribe a parole board member, Trevon's sixth sense went into overdrive, and he began to check into Ryan's background.

Trevon opened his folder and began to lay out some research he'd been able to do on Ryan. He was an excellent researcher. He'd used his criminal justice education, savvy computer skills, and attention to detail to gather extensive documentation regarding the so-called Ryan Young.

"It took me a while, but I think I got the scoop on this dude. First of all, I believe his real name is Walter Porter. He is from Detroit, Michigan, like he said. He graduated from Edison Public High. But I can find no evidence that he went to any college or law school in Detroit. And he has a criminal record for several charges for drug possession with intent to distribute. He spent about a year at the Brooks Correctional Facility before being released and placed on probation. Here's his prison mugshot," Trevon stated, handing BabyRuth a mugshot printout of Walter Porter, aka Ryan Young.

BabyRuth started at the mugshot, and there was no doubt in her mind that it was Ryan. "Lord, Lord," she said, shaking her head in disbelief.

"Walter Porter's trail in Detroit goes cold about three years ago. If I'm not mistaken, that's about the same time Kenya met him, right?" BabyRuth mentally calculated the time in her head.

"That's right. Almost three years exactly."

"So unless Ryan has a twin brother named Walter Porter, I'm thinking they're one and the same. And this morning I called the law firm when Ryan supposedly works, and was told there was no Ryan Young working there. It's all been a scam. And he's probably the one that turned Kenya in for the bribery scheme. He must have set her up."

"But why?"

"Someone must have paid him to. Someone with a beef against Kenya."

"Luther Curtis," BabyRuth surmised. "He's Kevin Curtis's father. He goes by Memphis. It had to be him."

"That's what I was just thinking," Trevon affirmed.

"Kenya will be absolutely crushed when she finds out about Ryan. She'll be devastated."

"I wish I could have put things together sooner. I didn't want to say anything without solid evidence, because I know how you all felt about Ryan. Kenya told me about the bribery plan, but she swore me to secrecy. And I didn't know when she was delivering the money. If I had known, I would have stopped her. I'm so sorry, Ms. Jones."

BabyRuth reached out and held Trevon's face gently in her hands. "You have nothing to be sorry about, darling. All you tried to do is help. And I thank you for it," BabyRuth said as she watched tears began to glisten in Trevon's eyes. He quickly wiped them away. BabyRuth stood up slowly, as if with great effort. "Now comes the hard part. Now I have to tell Kenya what we suspect about Ryan. Lord, help me, Jesus," BabyRuth said.

"Would you like me to go with you?" Trevon offered.

"Yes, thank you," BabyRuth gratefully responded.

As BabyRuth drove home, she was torn up inside. Now, Kenya had to endure not only the public humiliation of a bribery scandal but also the ultimate betrayal of someone she loved and trusted. How could

Ryan do such a thing? It just didn't seem possible. BabyRuth too had come to trust him and love him as a son. In her heart BabyRuth didn't want to accept that Ryan was an imposter and a deceiver, sent by the devil himself to wreak havoc, mayhem, and heartache. But BabyRuth had come face-to-face with the evidence. And as her late husband DJ used to always say—the facts speak for themselves.

Seeing Is Believing

WHEN BABYRUTH AND Trevon told Kenya about their suspicions regarding Ryan, she did not believe them.

"Ryan turned me in? That's absurd! Y'all must be crazy," Kenya yelled. "Why would you say something like that? That's absolutely ludicrous. You all should be supporting me right now. Not rubbing salt in my wounds. There is no way Ryan would betray me. No way in hell," she ranted. Kenya was appalled, bewildered, and angry with the messengers rather than the message.

"Kenya, I know it's shocking. But look at the evidence," Trevon said, spreading his research papers across the kitchen table.

"I don't have to look at no damn papers," Kenya stated, picking up the papers and flinging them on the floor. "I know Ryan. He's a good man who loves me. He would never do anything to hurt me. Never!" Kenya yelled, staring angrily at BabyRuth and Trevon.

Jasmine, who had been standing by wide eyed, watching the showdown, picked the papers up from the floor and began reading them. Her mouth dropped when she came across the mugshot of someone named Walter Porter who looked exactly like Ryan. "Oh my God. Kenya, you need to look at this," Jasmine said, holding the mugshot towards Kenya.

"Not you too," Kenya responded, shaking her head in disbelief. Kenya backed up against a wall and looked at her mama and close friends as if they were her archenemies. "I don't know what's going on here," she said. "But you all are wrong. Dead wrong."

"But honey, just hear us out," BabyRuth pleaded.

"No, Mama. I'm not going to stand here and listen to you all slander Ryan's name," Kenya stated. She turned and started to leave the room.

"Where is Ryan now? When was the last time you talked to him?" Trevon asked. Kenya turned around slowly and looked angrily at Trevon.

"For your information, Ryan is in Boston teaching a class. I left him a message telling him what happened just in case he hadn't heard. I also apologized for dragging him into it. Don't you see? Ryan could be in just as much trouble as I am. If he turned me in, he'd be turning himself in. Can't you see how bizarre that sounds?"

"Well, we don't have all the facts, but we have enough to ask Deborah and her team to have Ryan investigated. I also want to ask Detective Davis to look into his background," BabyRuth stated.

But Kenya forbade her mother from doing any such thing. She would not, she just could not believe that Ryan would deceive her. When she finally looked at the mugshot of Walter Porter, who was the spitting image of Ryan, she said it looked nothing like him. When Trevon told her he checked into Ryan's employment and discovered he didn't work at the law firm, Kenya accused him of lying. "I've been to the law firm, and I've seen his office with my own eyes. And I'm going to make a liar out of all of you," she said.

To prove them wrong, Kenya took them down to Ryan's office. Once there a senior attorney verified that Ryan Young didn't work there. But Kenya still didn't believe. Even when the receptionist, who was fired on the spot, confessed that she had lied to Kenya the day she visited, and had shown her someone else's office, Kenya didn't believe. She convinced herself that it was all part of some larger conspiracy against her and Ryan.

Even when Kenya's attorney, Deborah, informed her that Mr. Kilpatrick had never been contacted by Ryan about the bribery scheme, she didn't believe. As far as Kenya was concerned, Mr.

Kilpatrick was lying. He was just trying to cover up his own tracks so he wouldn't be prosecuted.

And although her repeated phone calls to Ryan went unreturned, she didn't believe. "He's just running scared," Kenya said. "And I don't blame him." Kenya and Jasmine stopped by Ryan's apartment a week later, after he was supposed to be back from Boston, and was told by the manager that the young man had moved out suddenly. But she still didn't believe. *There must be a logical explanation for all this*, she thought.

But finally one day Kenya received a text message that read,

Got u again. Ryan sends his best.
M

Attached to Memphis's text was the picture of Ryan, smiling and blowing a kiss at the camera. And when she saw, with her own eyes, Ryan's smiling face in a photo attached to Memphis's text, it was then, and only then, that she believed. Because seeing is believing.

Somebody's Sunshine

TODAY DEREKA HURRIEDLY finished her afternoon duties so she could visit Ms. Vee, whom she found resting comfortably in her bed. The kind old lady filled a void in Dereka's life, and she sneaked away to see her every chance she got. Ms. Vee's eyes twinkled with excitement when she saw Dereka.

"Hello, little one. I was hoping you would stop by today for a spell," she said.

"Hi, Ms. Vee," Dereka responded, kissing the old lady on her wrinkled cheek and sitting on the bed beside her.

On each of Dereka's prior visits, she spent time telling Ms. Vee something about one of the special women in her life, and how each of them had made her feel so cherished and loved. Telling Ms. Vee about them was Dereka's way of keeping them close in her heart. Dereka had already told Ms. Vee about her mama--about Serena's nurturing loving spirit, kindness, compassion, and gentle soul. She'd also told Ms. Vee about Grandma Ruth's godly love and faith, sense of humor, boldness, and positive outlook on life. "To this day my Grandma Ruth still calls me by my childhood nickname, Boogie Boo," Dereka had said, laughing along with Ms. Vee at the silly nickname. On her last visit, Dereka spoke of her Aunt Kenya's unconditional love, intelligence, strong determination, and her "throw caution to the wind" attitude. "My Aunt Kenya has the biggest heart," Dereka had said. "She treats me like her own daughter. There's nothing she wouldn't do for me."

"Which of your wonderful family members are you are going to tell me about today?" Ms. Vee said, her face animated with anticipation.

"My Auntie Jazz," Dereka said with a big smile on her face. Dereka went on to tell Ms. Vee about Auntie Jazz's sassy attitude, business savvy, zest for life, and pizzazz. "And Auntie Jazz walks like this," Dereka said, hopping off the bed to demonstrate her auntie's seductive strut, swinging her hips from side to side. Dereka sat back down on the bed after her humorous demonstration. "She's not really my blood aunt, but she may as well be. She's always been there for me, for as long as I can remember. She calls me her sunshine," Dereka said, her face aglow like the sun at the memory.

"Is that so?" Ms. Vee replied, her eyes twinkling with delight.

"And Auntie Jazz used to sing 'You Are My Sunshine' to me when I was a little girl. We would even do a pantomime of it together."

"Pan-to-mine?" Ms. Vee repeated with a puzzled look on her face.

"Yes, that's gestures that portray the lyrics. It's like performing the song. I'll show you," Dereka said, standing up to demonstrate.

"That looks like fun. Let me try," Ms. Vee responded, copying the hand and arm gestures that Dereka performed. Ms. Vee was a fast learner, and soon she and Dereka were dramatizing the entire song from beginning to end. Dereka's face glowed with joy, and she giggled like a small child as they performed the motions to the song 'You Are My Sunshine.' And for that brief moment in time, Dereka felt like she was six years old again, smiling her wide gap-tooth smile, with her fat pigtails bouncing, as if she were standing in front of her Auntie Jazz singing their song.

Afterward Dereka hugged Ms. Vee tightly and thanked her for performing the song with her. "It reminds me that I'm somebody's sunshine," Dereka said.

"And don't you ever forgot that, little one. You'll always be somebody's sunshine. Now you're my sunshine too," Ms. Vee pointed out.

Guilty, Your Honor

KENYA WAS DEEPLY wounded and felt like the ultimate fool for allowing herself to be conned into trusting Ryan and letting him into her heart. If it had not been for her strong support system of family and friends, she may not have survived. There were times she thought about taking her own life, as her brother Derek had taken his many years ago. But she couldn't do that to her mother. So Kenya carried on, more for her mother than herself, and with the hope of someday seeing Dereka again.

At BabyRuth's insistence, Kenya sought counseling from her pastor, who encouraged her to begin and end each day with scripture and prayer. Pastor Bobby reminded Kenya that Jesus said, *"In the world ye shall have tribulation: but be of good cheer; I have overcome the world."* He counseled Kenya on how to deal with adversities in life—through faith, long-suffering, patience, hope, and love. He told Kenya to focus on her love for God and her family. Because love *endures all thing, and never fails.*

When Kenya and BabyRuth met with Deborah and her team of investigators, they were told, as they already knew, the evidence against Kenya was overwhelming. The prosecutor's office had a video tape of Kenya entering the hotel and restaurant with the large black shoulder bag, an audio tape of her entire conversation with the policeman posing as Mr. Kilpatrick's accountant, her bank statements showing huge withdrawals of money just days before the incident, and the cash she gave to the officer. She had been caught red handed.

"We can fight this in court," Deborah said. "But it will be an uphill battle. It doesn't matter that the public official was not even aware of the bribe. All the prosecutor will have to do is prove beyond a reasonable doubt that you acted with corrupt intent to bribe a public official, regardless of whether the bribe was successful. That's why I think our best course of action is to work out a plea bargain. I'll do my best see that no prison time is involved, but there are no guarantees. But it's your decision, Kenya. We can go to trial, or we can work out a plea bargain. I know this is a tough decision, so I'll give you some time to think about it."

"I don't need time," Kenya stated without hesitation. "I want to work out a plea. I know what I did was wrong, and I'm willing to accept the consequences. And besides, I can't put my family through a lengthy trial. I couldn't do that to you, Mama," Kenya said, looking at BabyRuth with watery eyes.

"Don't you worry about me, honey. You do what you think is best for yourself. I'm here for you either way," BabyRuth responded.

Kenya found her mother's unconditional love and support truly astounding. "Thank you so much, Mama," she said, her voice choked with emotion. "But taking a plea is the right thing to do. Besides, going through a trial will divert our focus from finding Dereka. And I don't want anything to interfere with that. So I don't really care what happens to me. Let the chips fall where they may. I just want us to find Dereka," Kenya said, meaning every word.

"Okay. I'll get you the best deal I can," Deborah assured.

It didn't take long for Deborah and the prosecutor's office to negotiate an acceptable plea bargain. Kenya pled guilty to the felony offense of conspiracy to bribe a public official. She received a suspended sentence of one year in prison. Further, she was disbarred from practicing law, a profession that she loved. Kenya was also banned from working for the government and serving in any elected or appointed position. In addition she was fined $75K and ordered to perform four hundred hours of community service.

During the court hearing, Kenya stood beside her attorney as the clerk stated, "Court is now in session, the Honorable Judge Andrew Wellings presiding." Kenya knew Judge Wellings was tough and had a reputation for giving a harsh tongue-lashing to offenders in his courtroom. So she braced herself, held her head high, and tried to put up a brave front for her family and friends in the courtroom. But internally Kenya was humiliated and despondent. She had fallen hard from grace. She'd gone from her position as a prominent common-wealth attorney to that of a convicted felon.

"In the matter of *State versus Jones*, Ms. Jones, how do you plead?" Judge Wellings asked.

"Guilty, Your Honor," Kenya replied, her voice cracking a bit.

"Ms. Jones, do you know that by pleading guilty you lose the right to a jury trial?"

"Yes, Your Honor." The judge went on to recite the standard questions pertaining to the plea-bargaining process. As Kenya listened and responded to the judge's questions, she thought about how often she, as a prosecuting attorney, had watched defendant after defendant repeat the same words that she was now repeating. If someone had told her then that one day she would be on the opposite side of the law, pleading guilty to a felony, she would have thought they were deranged. But here she was, and it was mind boggling to her. *What a difference a day makes*, Kenya thought, recalling something her Grandma Leona used to say a lot. But as bad as things were for Kenya, she had no regrets about what she tried to do for her niece.

After the judge read the sentence, he went on a ten-minute tirade about Kenya's fall from public grace, calling her a disappointment and an embarrassment to the trusted public office she once held, and to the law profession as a whole. Kenya glanced behind her and saw her mother, Jasmine, Trevon, and others with forced smiles on their faces, trying to encourage her. She smiled weakly back at them and silently thanked God for them. They were her silver lining in the cloud, and she prayed that someday she'd make them proud of her again.

An Escape Plan

DEREKA SPENT HER sixteenth birthday as she had spent her three previous birthdays—in captivity. It was now three years and counting since Dereka had been violently snatched away from her family. Two of the older girls in the house, Milena and Gabriela, had been transferred to other sex houses and replaced with younger girls more fitting for La Casa de Placer. Dereka sensed it was just a matter of time before she too was moved to another place. Dereka had heard that some of the other houses were even worse than La Casa de Placer, although it was impossible for her to imagine anything worse. At *least here I have Jia and Ms. Vee to keep me going*, Dereka thought. *And if I'm moved from place to place, my family may never find me.* For those reasons only, Dereka preferred to stay put until her family came for her or she could find a way to escape on her own.

So Dereka tried even harder to prove her worth to the Tavaras brothers so they would not move her to another house. She cooked, cleaned, and catered to their needs until she was bone tired each day. And while she worked, Dereka was always on the lookout for information or anything she could use to help them escape. But she had to be careful. Mario didn't trust her as much as his older brother did, and would sometimes sneak up on her to try and catch her doing something wrong.

Today, as she cleaned their office, which she had only recently been asked to do, she decided to look in the desk to see what useful items or information she could find. First, Dereka peeked out of the door to see whether Mario or one of the guards were lurking nearby. Seeing no one in the hallway, Dereka hurriedly rummaged through the drawers, searching under papers, folders, notebooks, office supplies, and junk. When she got to the bottom drawer, she found an old cigar box. She picked it up, shook it, and heard a jangling sound. She lifted the lid, and to her surprise, the box was filled with loose keys of various sizes and shapes. *Oh my God*, Dereka thought. *I wonder if the basement door key is in here.* She knew that odd-shaped key well since she'd seen it used many times by her captors to lock and unlock the door.

Dereka placed the cigar box on the bed and peeped out the door again to make sure no one was in the hall. Then she dumped the keys out and frantically searched through them. She felt sweat roll down the sides of her face and her heart beating fast with the fear of being discovered. Dereka let out a small gasp when she found an odd-shaped key that looked identical to the basement key the guards used. She hastily put the key in her shoe and placed the cigar box back in the drawer, exactly as she'd found it.

Later that evening, Dereka breathed a sigh of relief as she placed the key in her secret place in the wall for safekeeping. She decided not to tell the other girls about the key until she had worked out a plan for escape. Right now, she didn't know how, when, or even whether she would ever use it, but she knew she'd seize the opportunity for escape if it came. So just having the key made Dereka feel more hopeful.

• • •

But Dereka's hope was soon dashed when a few days later, Mario and the two guards stormed into the basement. Mario ranted and raved in Spanish like a madman. *"La clave, la clave esta ausente,"* he shouted, his face contorted with anger. By now Dereka knew enough Spanish to know he was talking about a missing key. "You took it," Mario said accusingly to Dereka. She just stared at Mario and pretended not to know what he was talking about. The others girls looked confused and frightened by the mayhem.

"What's going on? What key? What is he talking about?" they murmured to each other. But Dereka knew exactly what he was talking about, and her legs trembled with fear.

Mario ordered the guards to search every inch of the basement for the missing key. They tore the place apart, flipping mattresses and bed frames and inspecting and throwing the girls' sparse clothing and other belongings around. They even turned over the trash cans and dug through the trash, looking for the missing key. *Suppose they find the place in the wall where I hid the key*, Dereka thought. She knew if they found the key, she would be severely punished. She could even end up in a trash bag like two of her friends. Dereka felt someone take her hand. She looked down and saw Jia looking up at her. *They may even send me away from Jia*, Dereka thought, placing her arms around the young girl and hugging her tight.

After what seemed like an eternity, Mario and the guards ended their frenzied search and went back upstairs. Mario didn't say a word to Dereka, but he gave her a menacing glare as he passed by, as if to say "I know what you did, and you will pay." The girls let out a concerted sigh of relief and began to put their place back together. Dereka immediately went into the kitchen and kneeled down beside the huge overturned trash can. She gasped when she saw that the loose concrete had been removed and all the items she had put in her secret place were gone. "Oh God, no. They found the key," Dereka murmured. *But why didn't they do anything?* she pondered with a puzzled look on her face. She stared at the empty space that had once been home to her valued treasures. And then she recalled how Mario had scowled at her before he left. So Dereka figured he must have found the key, and he wanted to prolong her agony with the unknown of when he would attack. It was his demonic way of torturing her mentally before exacting physical pain.

Dereka let out a low moan as she contemplated the agony to come. When she went back into the bedroom area, her friends looked at her in concern.

"Are you all right, hon?" Emma asked.

"I'm just a bit frazzled from all the commotion. But I'm fine," Dereka lied, not wanting to burden them with her problems. She was the one they looked to for comfort and encouragement. So for the most part, Dereka internalized most of her own fears and concerns, sharing them only with Ms. Vee whenever she could steal away to visit her.

Later that evening Dereka sat alone on her bed dreading the torment she knew would soon come. Jia sat beside her and held her two small fists in front of Dereka, signaling that she wanted to play her favorite game, Which Hand Is It In? But Dereka was in no mood for games. "Not now, Jia. Maybe later," Dereka said. But Jia was persistent and shook her small fists in front of Dereka. Dereka looked at Jia's face and saw the anticipation there as Jia waited for Dereka to choose a hand. Because so few things brought Jia pleasure, Dereka decided to put her own fears aside for a moment and play with Jia. "Okay, but just for a little while," Dereka said. She pretended to be in deep thought about which of Jia's hands to choose. "This one," Dereka said, tapping her right fist. And when Jia opened her hand, Dereka nearly fell off the bed. There, in the middle of Jia's palm, was the odd-shaped basement-door key. Dereka stared at Jia in shock, with her mouth gaping open.

Then Jia took Dereka's hand and led her into the kitchen area. She got on her knees and crawled under a small space beneath the big commercial sink. When Jia reemerged from underneath the sink, she had all of Dereka's treasures, including the angel soap figurine, Crystal's comb, and Esmeralda's rosary beads. During the chaotic search for the missing key, Jia had secretly slipped away, gathered Dereka's belongings, and hid them on a ridge underneath the sink where they would not be found. Dereka was so overcome with joy and relief that she broke down in tears and hugged Jia so tight she could feel the thin girl's ribs. "Thank you, sweetie. Thank you for doing this for me," Dereka said as she kissed Jia's cheeks. And for the first time since Dereka met Jia, she saw a tiny spark in the young girl's eyes and just the slightest hint of a smile on her lips.

The next day Mario changed the lock on the basement door and even added a second lock for extra security. Dereka disposed of her now-worthless key with the afternoon trash. And as she did so, she thanked God for Jia.

Live by the Sword

KEVIN CURTIS WAS being released on parole tomorrow, and he was as happy as a hog in slop. The parole board's vote had gone his way. He was getting out. He'd heard about Kenya's failed fiasco of trying to keep him in prison by bribing a parole officer. *Same old gullible Kenya*, Kevin thought when he heard the news.

Kevin sat in the TV room with his fellow inmates, laughing and bragging about his upcoming release. "Freedommmmm!" he yelled, mocking Mel Gibson's character in the movie *Braveheart*. Kevin slapped hands with his friend Parker. "When I walk out of this prison in the morning, that will be another win for me, my man," Kevin said. "And this one is sweeter than all the rest, because you made a promise to literally kiss my black ass. And I want you to do it in the morning in front of everybody in the chow hall."

"I know, I know. A deal is a deal. Lucky for you, someone got to Loco Larry before he got to you," Parker responded.

"It wasn't luck, my brother. It was fate," Kevin responding cockily, knowing full well that he was the "someone" responsible for Loco Larry's demise.

The following morning Kevin took extra time in the shower, shaving and primping, to make sure he looked good when he strutted out of the prison gate. He knew his father's employee was picking him up in a white limo. *My dad knows how to do things in style*, Kevin thought, picturing himself strutting out of the prison and hopping into the stretch limo.

Kevin was the last one in the shower room when his friend Parker entered. "You ready to kiss some serious ass?" Kevin asked, grinning from ear to ear.

"Yeah, I'm ready. So let's get this over with, mf'er," Parker responded.

"Well, I hope you've learned a valuable lesson from all this. Don't ever bet against me. You'll lose every time. Face it, bro. The better man won," Kevin gloated. He was so full of himself that he wondered whether it was even fair for mere human mortals, like Parker, to match wits with him.

"You're right. I shoulda known better," Parker said, smiling and bowing his arms towards Kevin in mock worship. Parker turned serious for a moment. "I hate to admit it, but I'm going to miss your crazy ass."

"Same here, my man," Kevin responded.

Parker held out his hand to Kevin and pulled him forward for a half man hug. Kevin was in such a state of euphoria that he didn't even feel the knife slide smoothly into his gut. But he did feel a slight burning sensation when Parker pulled the knife out. And Kevin fully felt the pain when the knife entered his body for the second and third times. He looked down and saw a huge blood stain on his shirt that was spreading rapidly by the second. Kevin stared wide eyed at Parker in disbelief. He toppled forward and tried to grab hold of his friend for support. Parker pushed him backward, and Kevin fell to the floor on his back. He tried to talk but could only make gurgling sounds. The last thing Kevin saw before he died was Parker looking down on him with a smirk on his face.

"Who's the better man now, mf'er?" Parker asked. "I told you weren't getting out of here alive."

• • •

BabyRuth and Kenya were shocked to hear the news of Kevin's death in prison, on the same morning that he was scheduled to be released. And frankly, BabyRuth didn't know how to feel about it. On the one hand, she felt relief that someone who caused them so much pain could not hurt them anymore. But on the other hand, a human being had died a violent death in prison. And that was nothing to celebrate. *"Live by the sword, die by the sword,"* BabyRuth said, referring to words Jesus told one of his disciples.

Kenya, although she didn't want to admit it out loud, was elated by the news. Deep down she knew it was wrong to feel this way, but the person she blamed most for Serena's death and Dereka's abduction was dead. Although his father, Memphis, had actually plotted and carried out the vengeful acts, Kenya blamed the son more than the father. After all, Kevin started everything years ago when he took advantage of her youthful naivety. *He got exactly what he deserved*, Kenya thought.

But then she reflected on something her pastor had said in one of her counseling sessions. He counseled her to let go of the bitterness in her heart. *Do not fret because of evildoers, nor be envious of the workers of iniquity. For they shall soon be cut down like the grass, and wither as the green herb*, Pastor Bobby had quoted. And that certainly turned out to be true in Kevin Curtis's case. So Kenya prayed for forgiveness because she knew she had to forgive in order to grow spiritually and move forward. And she'd already began putting the pieces of her life back together. After she was banned from holding public office in Virginia and disbarred from practicing law, her father's old law firm offered her a job as a legal consultant, which Kenya readily accepted. Although she was not practicing law, the job kept her gainfully employed in the legal profession which she loved. For that she was grateful, and she knew that with gratefulness came forgiveness.

• • •

But across town there was one person who was not, nor ever would be, in the forgiving mood. And that was Memphis. The news of his son's murder in prison enraged him nearly to the point of madness. He promptly ordered a hit on the person or persons responsible for his son's death. A few days later, the mission was accomplished. Memphis got the news that Parker had gone to meet his maker.

Undercover in Colombia

JASMINE SAT AROUND a conference table with her new team of undercover workers, discussing their next rescue project. Based on a human trafficking report an FBI agent stationed in South America sent to Operation Undercover, the team traveled to Colombia to continue their work to rescue sex trafficking victims. The report cited Colombia as a thriving industry for sex tourism.

Further, Detective Davis had also received credible information that young American girls had been abducted and sold to Colombian sex traffickers, who transported them from Miami to Colombia. It was possible that Dereka could have been among the American girls taken there. So Jasmine was hopeful that their rescue work would result in finding her.

"The exotic beauty of the young girls in Colombia attracts sex tourists like a magnet," Cliff, the leader of the rescue team, stated. The team consisted of five members, and Jasmine was the only female. She had worked with Cliff on a previous rescue effort and admired his integrity and commitment to saving children. "Resort cities like Cartagena and Medellin are hot spots for child prostitution rings," Cliff added.

"Cartagena? Isn't that where those Secret Service men got caught up in a sex scandal with prostitutes?" Jasmine asked.

"One and the same," Jorge, a Colombian American, chimed in. Jorge had migrated to the United States a few years ago, and his knowledge of the language, culture, and politics in Colombia would be vital to the team's efforts. "About a fourth of the 2.2 million citizens of Cartagena live in poverty. And it's estimated that around fifteen hundred children there are involved in child prostitution. It's a sad and shocking reality." Philip and Gene, the other two members of the team, nodded their agreement.

Cliff spent the next two hours briefing the team on their upcoming rescue, which was scheduled in a few days. He had already spent several months in Colombia working with local government, police authorities, and child protective services. The rescue would take place in a resort's penthouse suite, which the team was using free of charge, compliments of the resort's management. The four male team members would pose as American tourists on vacation looking to hire young girls for a wild sex party. Jasmine would wait outside with police in a nearby van and conduct surveillance of the video tape transmitted by the team's hidden cameras and microphones. By now Jasmine was an expert in identifying the verbal and physical cues the team used to signal when it was safe for the authorities to move in, when they should hang back, or when the team was in trouble.

"We'll be meeting with Miguel Suarez tomorrow afternoon at the pool bar. He's helping us find young girls for our so-called sex party," Cliff informed them. "I've met with him a few times already to gain his trust. This dude is real bad news. He's suspected of leading one of the largest child prostitution rings in Cartagena and has connections with pimps and madams throughout the area."

"He sounds like a real prize," Jasmine remarked sarcastically. Cliff smiled at her remark.

"Jasmine, the four of us will meet with Miguel at the bar, and I want you to sit nearby and listen in." Jorge handed Jasmine what appeared to be a cell phone with earplugs. "To the average passerby, you'll be just another foreign tourist listening to music on your cell phone. But this amplifier will allow you to hear our entire conversation," Jorge informed. Jasmine placed the portable amp in her bag, and Cliff concluded the meeting.

• • •

The next day around noon, Jasmine sat at a table in the pool-bar area sipping a Diet Coke. She had on a green sundress, sandals, a big floppy straw hat, and sunglasses. Although she was not a typical tourist, she certainly looked the part. The resort was gorgeous, with pristine white sandy beaches, azure waters, and swaying palm trees. It was a picture-perfect setting. Jasmine stared at the mostly foreign vacationers, who were eating, drinking, and splashing around in the pool with their happy kids. *Most of them have no idea of the despicable things that happen to children at resorts like this. Ignorance really is bliss. Or perhaps it's apathy*, she thought warily.

The male members of her team were already seated at the bar with drinks in front of them, laughing and talking while they waited for Miguel to show up. Jasmine instinctively knew Miguel when he first walked into the pool area. The hairs stood up on the back of her neck. He was tall and slim, with black hair slicked back, a thin black mustache, and deeply tanned skin. He was wearing a black sports jacket, a crisp white shirt, tan pants, and a straw hat. He strutted like a peacock towards the bar with a big smile on his face. One would have thought he owned the joint. Miguel headed straight to the team and greeted Cliff as if he'd known him for years. He didn't sit at the bar but instead ushered the men to another table off to the side, no doubt for privacy. Jasmine could only imagine how many times he'd done this type of thing before. She adjusted the volume on her amplifier and listened in.

"So, my friends, what do you think of our beautiful city?" Miguel asked.

"What's not to like? Look at all these sexy hotties," Gene said, pretending to be tipsy. The men engaged in a few minutes of senseless male-bonding sexual rhetoric before Miguel finally got down to business.

"Well, I understand you all need some girls for a party Saturday night."

"Yeah, that's right," Cliff affirmed, smiling broadly.

"Is it true that you, uhhhhh, specialize in really young girls?" Philip asked.

"Most are between thirteen and sixteen years old. But I got a couple that are twelve. And I just got one nine. A virgin," Miguel stated proudly. Jasmine felt her stomach knot up and her anger rise as she listened.

"Nine. Now that's what I'm talking about," Gene said, slapping hands with Philip. Jasmine knew that Gene was trying to ensure that if Miguel did indeed have a nine-year-old girl, as he claimed, he would bring her to the party. That way she could be rescued and taken to a safe place.

"And we want an assortment of delights. After all, variety is the spice of life," Philip added. He was trying to see whether Miguel had any foreign girls, perhaps even Dereka, among the children he prostituted without conscience.

"I can get you any kind of girls you want. We got girls from all over the world. But they don't come cheap, so I hope you gentlemen came with some cold hard cash."

"Do we look like we can't pay or something?" Philip asked, feigning offense. Miguel raised his hands in a sign of apology.

"I don't mean to offend. But most Americans who come here think our girls are cheap. But my girls are not your average run-of-the-mill street hookers. I got prime stock. But it will cost you. Three hundred for the virgin, and two hundred for the rest. I believe you want six to eight girls for the party. And what you do with them is totally up to you. We used to charge by the act, but that was too much trouble keeping up with who was doing what to who. So now it's just a flat fee. But you pay for the girls up front on delivery," Miguel stated emphatically.

"You'll get your money, you just bring the honeys," Gene responding, slurring his words intentionally.

"Then everything's set. We'll deliver the girls Saturday around nine. I like to bring them up two or three at a time. That works best. And I guarantee you won't be disappointed," Miguel said, standing and shaking hands with the men before leaving. As he strolled past Jasmine, he gave her an admiring glance and tipped his hat in greeting. Jasmine glared at him from behind her dark sunglasses, and it took every ounce of restraint to keep from kicking him in his stank behind as he swaggered by.

Scared to Stop

ON THE NIGHT of the rescue, Jasmine sat in a beige van in the resort parking area with five Colombian police from the Special Operations Command. They were parked by the front entrance so they could observe all the people coming and going from the resort. Another van with backup police was parked on the opposite side of the lot. It was Saturday night, so the place was extremely busy, with throngs of people milling about. Jasmine could see how it would be relatively easy for Miguel and the girls to blend in with the crowds of people staying at or visiting the resort.

Although by now Jasmine had been on several rescue missions, the work was never routine. Every nerve was on edge as she anxiously waited for Miguel and the girls to arrive. The surveillance equipment in the van was operating flawlessly, and Jasmine could clearly see and hear her team in the penthouse suite. To create a party atmosphere, they had liquor and beer bottles scattered about the place, pizza boxes stacked on a table, and a couple of them were puffing on Colombian cigars. They were playing loud music, which Cliff planned to turn off once Miguel and the girls arrived so that everything said would be clearly recorded on tape.

At 9:00 p.m. sharp, two SUVs pulled up in the parking lot. The driver in the lead SUV exited and walked around to open the passenger door. Miguel got out slowly and stood beside the SUV, talking to the driver. He appeared to be in no particular hurry. He lit a cigarette and leaned back against the SUV door. "He's looking around and checking things out," one officer commented. After about ten minutes, the driver opened the back door, and four girls exited. Jasmine could see only their silhouettes framed by the parking lot lighting. She could tell they were young and fit and dressed provocatively in short, tight clothing. Jasmine tried to see whether any of the girls resembled Dereka in shape and size, but it was impossible to tell from her vantage point. The girls appeared to be perfectly at ease in their environment, laughing and talking with one another. Jasmine learned from Jorge that in the poverty-stricken areas of Colombia, many young girls willingly prostituted themselves to make money. But the sex trafficking of minors was illegal regardless of consent because minors cannot legally agree to such acts.

Miguel flicked his cigarette on the pavement and motioned for the driver and the girls to follow him into the resort. The people in the second SUV stayed inside the vehicle. Jasmine called Cliff to let him know they were on their way up. Sweat beaded on Jasmine's forehead as she anxiously watched Cliff open the door a few minutes later. She was surprised when she saw Miguel and the driver enter alone. "The man of the hour," Cliff said, shaking hands with Miguel.

"So where are the girls?" Philip asked, taking a swig from a bottle of beer that was really nonalcoholic.

"Just outside," Miguel answered. "I make it a habit to check things out first before bringing in the girls."

"Well, check all you want; we got nothing to hide," Jorge stated.

"But be fast about it. We're ready to get this party started," Gene said, standing on top of a table and imitating vulgar sexual acts.

Miguel and the driver were not amused. They were all business as they walked around the suite, looking in every room and opening and closing doors. Jasmine watched as they slid their hands under tables, shelves, and lamps, obviously looking for hidden cameras. "You all don't mind if my man frisk you?" Miguel asked. The team didn't mind at all, because they were experts at concealing surveillance devices. Their high-tech equipment was hidden in high ceiling lights and mock smoke detectors—places criminals couldn't easily access without a ladder. In addition, the team was wearing sophisticated spy watches with night vision that looked like ordinary watches. After frisking the team members and thoroughly inspecting the premises, Miguel seemed satisfied that everything was legit. "You gentlemen ready to have some fun? We'll go get the girls," he said, smiling broadly and leaving the room.

Within seconds, the driver of the second SUV quickly sped away.

"Something spooked them. They're onto us," an officer said, pushing a button and speaking into his two-way radio.

"But how? They didn't find anything," Jasmine exclaimed.

"Some of these guys just have a sixth sense for this stuff. But don't worry, they won't get far. I just put a tail on them," the officer pointed out.

Soon Miguel, the driver, and the girls exited the resort. They were moving so fast the girls were having a hard time keeping up in their high stiletto heels. The police knew they needed to stop them before they entered the vehicle. They didn't want to engage in a high-speed chase that would endanger the girls' and others' safety on the road.

"Time to move in," the officer said. And things went into motion. Their van lunged forward and stopped within a few feet of the group. The police were out of the van in a flash, weapons drawn, and barking commands to the men to lie on the ground. Some of the police quickly surrounded the girls to separate them from their abusers. Miguel and the driver, knowing they were caught, immediately lay on the ground. They were handcuffed and placed in the back of a second police cruiser that had arrived.

Jasmine quickly walked over to the frightened, confused girls. Cliff and the rest of the team came down from the penthouse and joined her. The girls spoke only Spanish, so Jorge served as interpreter between the girls and the team.

"Don't worry. You're safe now," Jasmine said, looking intently into each of their faces. *My God, they're so young,* Jasmine thought, guessing they were between twelve and fifteen years old. Although the team had rescued many girls, some even younger than these, it was something Jasmine always found shocking.

"What's going on? Where are they taking Miguel?" one of them asked.

"We're with a group called Operation Undercover," Cliff replied. "We rescue girls like yourselves from child prostitution and arrest the abusers. Miguel is being arrested and will be transported to the local jail."

"But what will happen to us? Will we go to jail too?" asked one girl, who appeared to be the youngest. Threats of jail for prostitution was one of the ways their pimps kept them under their control.

"No, sweetheart. You'll be taken to a safe place tonight. We have another team who will ensure you get all the help you need," Jasmine reassured.

One of the police walked over to the group. "We're ready to transport the girls to the safe house now. And the perpetrators in the second vehicle have been captured. The other girls, including one who said she's ten, are being taken to the safe location as we speak." The officer turned to Jasmine. "All the girls in the other vehicle are Colombian. No American girl among them. I'm sorry," he said sincerely. Jasmine's heart faltered momentarily.

"Thank you," she mumbled. She'd known it was a long shot that they would find Dereka on their first rescue job in Colombia, but her hopes had been high just the same.

Jasmine watched as the police walked the girls to a waiting van for transport. One of the girls looked back, broke away from her group, and ran back to the team. "Thank you," she said, her eyes glistening with tears. "I wanted to stop, but I was scared," she confessed.

"God bless you, sweetie. I'll keep you in my prayers. You take care of yourself." Jasmine said as she choked back tears and hugged the young girl.

Anybody Out There?

ANOTHER AGONIZING YEAR crept by. Dereka was beginning to wonder whether anyone was still looking for her. *Is anybody out there?* she questioned in her mind. *Have they given up hope that I'm still alive? Have they gone about their lives and forgotten about me?* For four insufferable years she had been enslaved, unable to free herself from the pit of despair. And without cause, Dereka felt guilty and ashamed of her plight. Guilty that she had not been able to prevent her capture or break free, and ashamed of the disgusting things she was forced to do to survive. She never would have thought it possible if it hadn't happened to her personally.

Before her abduction, Dereka had heard a news story about three girls who had been held in captivity for ten years by a madman in Cleveland, Ohio. And if truth be told, Dereka had wondered how it was even possible for three strong, healthy young ladies to be imprisoned by one man for over ten years. She remembered thinking back then, *No way, Jose. No way that would have happened to me. I would have gotten out of there by any means necessary. Held and raped for ten years? Ain't no way.* But now that Dereka had experienced first-hand this type of bondage, she now knew that sex slavery, or slavery of any kind, has nothing to do with the weakness of the captive, but all to do with the brutality of the captor. It isn't about the servility of the enslaved, but the savagery of the ones who enslave. That's how entire races of strong, mighty people have been enslaved by other races, and how three strong, capable young women were imprisoned for ten years by one maniac.

And what's more, the captors have the advantage of the imaginings of a wicked mind, and the time and means to plot how best to snare their victims in their impenetrable traps. Thus, those enslaved are caught totally off guard by such wickedness lying in wait, and find themselves completely at the mercy of their captors. That's when their will to survive takes over, and they do anything and everything just to survive. Anything to avoid excruciating physical and mental torture, and even death, at the hands of their captors. Dereka now knew that her will to survive and live was greater than her will to rebel and die. Especially because she had something worth surviving for. She had her family.

But survival was a grueling and tiresome responsibility. Enduring degradation day in and day out chipped away at Dereka's strength and hope, until at times she felt she had nothing left. That's how Dereka felt today as she sat on the bed beside Ms. Vee and poured out her heart. Dereka's experience the previous night with a customer had been particularly brutal, and her body was still sore and throbbing with pain. Dereka laid her head on Ms. Vee's shoulder and wept.

"I don't know how much longer I can go on. Sometimes I don't think I'm going to make it out of here," she confessed.

"You'll get out of here, little one. I know you will. You're not going to die in this Godforsaken place. Not you, my dear," Ms. Vee reassured.

"But suppose my family has given up on me. It's been so long. Maybe no one's coming."

"Not a chance. From what you have told me about your family, they will never stop looking for you. You've just got to be strong until they come for you."

"But I don't know if I can."

"You've got all you need to survive because you've got traits of those four women you told me about in you. I see it. You've got your grandma's faith, your mama's compassion, your Aunt Kenya's determination, and your Auntie Jazz's spunk. Now how can you not make it with all that?" Ms. Vee stated confidently, winking and smiling brightly at Dereka. Somehow the elderly lady always knew exactly what to say or do to make her feel better. Dereka found herself returning Ms. Vee's smile. And in her heart Dereka knew her family would never stop looking for her. Their love was too deep, their bond too strong, and as long as they had breath in their bodies, they would never give up. So neither could she.

Biggest Lead Yet

WITHIN THE FIRST year of their work in Colombia, Jasmine's team performed several successful rescues in the Cartagena and Medellin area, resulting in the rescue of thirty-three children. Jasmine kept telling herself that the next rescue would be the one when she'd find Dereka. That's how she kept her hope strong. And just knowing that she was helping rescue other people's daughters, granddaughters, sisters, cousins, and so on was very gratifying.

Their biggest lead on Dereka's whereabouts came unexpectedly one afternoon while the team was having lunch at the hotel's poolside grill. An inebriated middle-age man, with a strong Australian accent, sat at the bar loudly bragging to another man about a good time he'd had with some girls on an adventure tour. The team's ears perked up because it was obvious from the man's mannerisms and flushed face that the good time he was referring to was sexual in nature.

Cliff excused himself from the team and sat in an empty chair next to the man. "How you doing, mate? Can I buy you a drink?" Cliff asked. The man readily accepted. Cliff engaged the man in friendly banter, and it didn't take long before the man was spilling his guts about a tour company that specialized in selling exotic young girls for sex with tourists. The man said it was a highly secretive operation run by some big-time Colombian crime organization. Before their conversation ended, Cliff had the name of the company, an address, and a phone number to call to arrange to take the tour.

"I wouldn't share this with just anybody," the Australian man said, leaning in close to Cliff and slipping him a card. "But you're all right. I like you. And I guarantee you won't be disappointed," he slurred, winking at Cliff, sliding off the bar stool, and stumbling away.

Cliff went back to the team and motioned for them to follow him to his hotel suite. "This may be our best chance yet at finding your niece," he exclaimed. "From what that guy said, this place has girls from other countries as well, and he believes he once saw a young black girl there who looked to be American."

"Oh my God. Do you think it could be Dereka?" Jasmine asked.

"I'm not sure, but it's our best lead yet," Cliff responded.

"If it's run by a Colombian crime organization, it won't be easy to set up a rescue," Jorge informed. "These groups are highly organized and ruthless. Even some police and government agents are afraid of them. It may take months, perhaps a year or more, to coordinate a rescue operation with authorities."

"But we don't have months or years. We have to do something now," Jasmine pleaded.

"I know you're anxious to find her, Jasmine, and so are we. But we have to do this the right way. This could be our most dangerous rescue yet, and we don't want to put ourselves in danger or risk the lives of those we're trying to rescue. We have to work within the system, and it could take a while. But I'll do everything I can to expedite things," Jorge assured.

"I understand. I've waited this long. I'll wait as long as it takes," Jasmine responded, letting her tears flow unashamedly down her face.

• • •

After months and months of meetings, paperwork, red tape, and negotiations, the rescue at La Casa de Placer was set to happen in a few days. The four male members of Operation Undercover's team, along with undercover FBI agents, had arranged to take the adventure tour. They would pose as wealthy foreign tourists from the United States, and much effort had gone into creating their fake identities. And since they had been approved for the tour, it appeared the effort had paid off. The Colombian police would assist with the rescue, and family services staff would be available to take the girls to a safe house. It had taken a lot of time, but everything had fallen into place. Jasmine had a good feeling about the rescue. She felt she'd find her sunshine.

Hanging On by a Thread

DEREKA CLOSELY WATCHED the white man enter the bedroom and slowly begin to remove his clothes. He didn't wear a mask to hide his identity, as some of the others did, but chose rather to reveal his face. He looked like any typical white businessman. He was similar in appearance and mannerism to the white male attorneys whom Dereka had met when she visited her Aunt Kenya at her office. He was of average height and build, clean shaven, with dark-brown hair parted on the side. He even smiled slightly at Dereka as he lay down on the bed beside her—the kind of genuine smile that Dereka had not seen on a man since her capture.

During his time with her, the man treated Dereka with tenderness instead of the lust-filled brutality she had become accustomed to. Afterward, as he was getting dressed, Dereka continued to watch him intently. She felt he was different from the others. She didn't know why, but she felt she could trust him. He looked as if he was from the United States. If so, perhaps he could get a message to her family that she was here. Dereka knew it was dangerous to speak to a customer. It was considered a cardinal sin, and if caught, she would be severely punished. So she agonized internally whether to say something—whether it was worth taking the risk. But when she thought about the bleak alternative of remaining in her current hellish situation indefinitely, she decided it was indeed worth the risk.

"Will you help me?" Dereka whispered to the man while he sat on the bed putting on his shoes. He stopped and looked at Dereka with a puzzled expression.

"Pardon me, did you say something?" he asked.

"My name is Dereka Jones. I'm from the United States. Will you help me?" Dereka repeated.

"You're from the United States? What are you doing here?"

"I was kidnapped and brought here. My family don't know where I am," Dereka stated in a hushed tone. The man looked as though he was shocked by Dereka's statement.

"I was told that all the girls willingly work here to make money for their families. They told me you're an Afro-Colombian girl from the poor Choco region. Not kidnapped from the United States," the man stated.

"Will you help me?" Dereka pleaded, her eyes involuntarily watering just at the possibility. The man put his finger to his lips to gesture to Dereka to stop talking. He walked to the door and placed his ear against it, listening for any sign of activity. Hearing nothing, he sat on the bed beside Dereka, reached into his jacket pocket, and retrieved a business card and a pen.

"Here, quickly write down the name and information of someone I can contact for you. Of course, I'll have to do it anonymously. You do understand?" he asked.

"Yes," Dereka responded as she hastily wrote down her Grandma Ruth's contact information on the back of the card. The man placed the card and pen back into his jacket pocket.

"I have to leave now. But don't worry. I will do what I can to help," he said, smiling at Dereka as he left the room.

Back in the basement, Dereka could hardly wait to tell the other girls that she had met someone who was going to help them. They hugged and cried, overcome with joy and hopeful expectation. But their optimism was short lived. The next morning before the crack of dawn, the girls were awakened by footsteps hurrying down the steps. It was Mario and the guards. They dragged Dereka out of the bed by her feet and dropped her on the floor. Mario bent down over Dereka and held something to her face. It was the business card she had written on and given to the man who was supposed to help her. It had all been a setup. Ever since the missing key incident, Mario hadn't trusted Dereka, and he'd finally convinced Diago to set a trap to test her loyalty. The white man was an employee of Los Chomas, hired to test the loyalty of the girls. He was hand-picked because of his average, nice-guy looks and trained in all the ways to gain someone's trust by appearing to be likable, genuine, kind, and sympathetic. Dereka took the rat's cheese from the trap and got caught.

She was taken to the shed for punishment. The windowless wooden structure was pitch black inside. Mario pulled a string, and a bare light bulb in the middle of the ceiling illuminated the room. The shed had an eerie, spooky feeling as if it were attempting to warn others of the horrors it had witnessed. The only furniture was a single wooden straight-back chair. Mario tied Dereka tightly to the chair with thick, coarse rope around her hands, torso, and legs. Dereka could tell by the glint in his eyes that he was looking forward to his gruesome task. He spent well over an hour exacting his torture, relishing in her pleas with him to stop and her piercing cries of pain. Finally Diago entered and put an end to her agony.

The guards carried Dereka back to the basement and dumped her onto her bed. The girls gathered around and attended to her as best they could. Dereka was barely conscious, and in excruciating pain. She was hanging on, but only by a thread.

The House Falls

ON THE NIGHT of the rescue, Jasmine rode in one of three dark-colored vans filled with heavily armed Colombian police. A dark-colored emergency medical mobile transport vehicle followed the police vans. As they moved slowly up the narrow, treacherous mountain paths, Jasmine was filled with a sense of dread as she realized it was likely the same path Dereka was taken on over five years ago now. *How scared she must have been*, Jasmine thought as she stared into the darkening night and listened to the wild sounds of the jungle nightlife.

They set up surveillance in the thick-jungled area surrounding the big gray stone house known as the House of Pleasure. Now it was just a matter of waiting for the tour bus to arrive. Jasmine used high-powered binoculars to get a close-up view of the huge building surrounded by a high barbed-wire gate. Although it was hard to see through the thick jungle bush, she did see one armed guard with a huge assault rifle draped across one shoulder. He was dressed in military fatigues and smoked a cigar as he loitered near the gate entrance. Jasmine closed her eyes and prayed, *Lord, please be with us tonight. We need you.*

Around eight o'clock the adventure tour bus arrived. The guard exited the gate and entered the bus. After several minutes he got off the bus and swung the gate open for the bus to enter. Twelve men, including the four team members, three FBI agents, and five unsuspecting customers, stepped off the bus. Once the men, the guard, and the driver entered the house, the lead officer in the van signaled to the others that it was time to deploy. For safety reasons Jasmine was instructed to wait in the van until the all-clear signal was given via the police radio. She watched as the heavily armed police silently crept toward the house. Although it was almost completely dark, she could still make out their shadowy figures staying low to the ground as they crept slowly toward the house. When they were within range, they used a high-powered long-distance laser beam to disable the outside surveillance cameras around the house. Once that was accomplished, they used sharp pliers to cut a hole in the gate large enough for them to slither through. Then they took up their positions at the front and rear entrances and windows and waited for the inside team to give the signal to move in.

The time Jasmine spent waiting in the van with one remaining policeman was agonizing. Minutes seemed like hours as she waited and listened for the all-clear signal. It took every ounce of her self-control to keep from bolting from the van to see what, if anything, was happening. The policeman tried to engage her in small talk to help pass the time, but to no avail. Jasmine rocked nervously in her seat, closed her eyes, and concentrated on taking long, deep breaths to steel her nerves. Earlier that day Jasmine informed BabyRuth and Kenya about the rescue. She generally didn't tell them anything until the rescue was complete, but she had such high hopes about this one. "I just got a good feeling about it. I think I'm going to find Dereka and finally bring her home," she'd said. Jasmine knew they were anxiously waiting back home for good news, and she could hardly wait to make that long-anticipated phone call.

The sound of rapid-fire gunshots startled her. Jasmine reached for the door, but the officer, in a stern tone, commanded her to wait. They heard more rapid gunfire in quick succession. Then all was silent. About twenty minutes passed before the all-clear signal was transmitted.

Jasmine and the officer moved quickly toward the house. Upon arriving they saw at least two men in military fatigues lying on the ground.

Both appeared to be dead. Another man was sitting on the ground surrounded by police. His hands were handcuffed behind his back, and he
was grimacing in pain from a gunshot wound to his left side. It was Diago
Tavaras. His brother, Mario, had also been wounded in the shootout with
police but had managed to escape in the dense jungle. One of the FBI
agents had suffered minor, non-life-threatening injuries.

Jasmine hurried into the house, which looked as if it had been
hit by a hurricane. Cliff took her by the arm and led her down some
narrow, steep steps. Because Mario was still on the loose, armed
and dangerous, the girls were being kept in the basement for their
safety until the surrounding premises were secure. Jasmine felt as if
she were entering a black hole to hell as she made her way carefully
down what looked to her to be a dungeon. It was dark, dank, and
dreary, and she couldn't even imagine what it must have been like
to be trapped down there. "Lord, have mercy," she murmured as she
continued her downward descent.

Jasmine saw a group of girls huddled under the light of a bare
bulb as they spoke with the police and team members. The girls were
in various stages of dress, with some fully or partially clothed and
others wearing only sheets to cover themselves. Jasmine quickly
scanned the group for Dereka, and her heart leaped when she said
a slim, brown-skinned girl with long, thick hair talking to Jorge.
Although the girl's back was to her, Jasmine just knew it was Dereka.
It had to be. Jasmine's heart raced with anticipation as she moved
towards the girl. After all this time, she was going to see her sunshine again. Jasmine reached out and gently placed her hand on the
girl's shoulder. The unexpected touch made the girl jump and spin
around in fear. Jasmine gasped. It wasn't Dereka. But it was another
young, frightened girl who needed love and support. Jasmine pulled
the trembling girl into her arms to comfort her.

• • •

The young girl Jasmine had thought was Dereka was actually Rhaelyn
Moore from Jacksonville, Florida. She was a runaway who had gone

to Miami for excitement and adventure and ended up with a pimp who had sold her cheap to a Colombian sex trafficker. She eventually ended up at La Casa de Placer. Thankfully, she had been there only about a week. Jasmine asked her, "Is there another African American girl here named Dereka?"

"I've heard of her. But she was gone before I arrived. They called her Angel Girl. Everybody really liked her."

"Do you know where she is now?"

"No, I don't, but some of the other girls may know. I heard she was very close to Jia. She took care of her," Rhaelyn said, pointing to Jia. Jasmine's heart instantly went out to the young, beautiful Asian girl staring at her with big sad eyes. She was sitting beside Cliff on a small cot, looking terrified by all the commotion.

Jasmine walked over and sat on the other side of her. "Hi, Jia. Sweetie, you're safe now. You don't have to be afraid anymore," Jasmine said soothingly taking the young girl's hands into hers. She could feel small tremors rippling through Jia's hand. *What horrors this poor child must have endured*, Jasmine thought, mortified. "I'm Jasmine, Dereka's aunt." At the mention of Dereka's name, Jasmine saw a wistful expression cross Jia's face, and her sad eyes glistened with tears. "I know Dereka took care of you. I'm going to take care of you now. I promise," Jasmine avowed, wrapping her arms around the young girl. Jasmine knew it was against Operation Undercover's protocol to get too personally involved with the girls they rescued. And she was certainly not supposed to make promises she may not be able to keep. But in that moment Jasmine couldn't help it. She felt a strong personal connection to Jia that she just couldn't explain. Perhaps it was because she sensed that Dereka cared for her so much.

Without a word, Jia got up, took Jasmine by the hand, and led her to the kitchen. A police officer followed them for safety. Jia reached under the sink, retrieved something wrapped in tissue, and handed it to Jasmine. Jasmine carefully removed the tissue and discovered three items—an angel carved out of soap, a hair comb, and rosary beads. "Dereka's?" Jasmine asked, looking at Jia inquisitively. Jia nodded slightly. Jasmine lovingly ran her hands over Dereka's items. Just touching them filled her heart with a mixture of joy and pain. "Thank you," she whispered to Jia, her voice cracking with emotion. She had just missed Dereka by about a week. *I'm sorry I didn't get here in time to find you,* Jasmine thought as she continued to caress Dereka's small treasures. *But I'm coming for you, sweetheart. You just hold on.*

Once the grounds were deemed secure, it was time to transport the girls to a safe house. Jasmine wanted to go with Jia, but Cliff prevented her. "But I promised I would take care of her," Jasmine protested.

"Jasmine, we talked about this. For now we have to let the proper authorities take it from here. She's in good hands. And I'll arrange for you to visit her in a few days," he offered. And while Jasmine didn't want to, she knew as a member of the team she needed to follow proper protocol. She held tightly to Jia's hand as she escorted her outside.

"You have to go with these good people now, darling," Jasmine said, looking directly into Jia's big eyes. "But I'll be by to see you real soon. Don't be afraid. I'm going to take care of you just like Dereka did. Understand?" Two tears rolled down Jia's face. Jasmine hugged and kissed Jia, and she also took the time to hug, kiss, and encourage each of the other girls before they got into the transport vehicle. Although Jasmine was extremely disappointed she hadn't found Dereka, she tried not to show it. There would be time for those emotions later. But for now Jasmine knew she had to be fully present for the young girls who were there and needed her love and support. And she was. *At least they're safe now*, she thought gratefully. *But where's Dereka?*

La Última Parada

MEMPHIS KNEW EXACTLY where Dereka was. He'd tried to get his grubby hands back on her ever since his son's death in prison. Kevin's death had driven Memphis close to the edge of sanity. After all, his son was the only somebody in the world that Memphis cared a hoot about. Memphis seethed with a red-hot hatred day and night as he plotted and planned his next vengeful attack against the Jones family. Through contact with the Tavaras brothers, he knew that Dereka had managed to survive at La Casa de Placer over the years. And Memphis had tried unsuccessfully since Kevin's death to get his hands back on Dereka so he could ensure her total and utter demise. But somehow the little darling had managed to endear herself to the brothers, especially the oldest one, Diago, who wouldn't part with her no matter what price was offered. Memphis couldn't understand why, because she was past the prime age that most of the perverts who patronized their place preferred.

So needless to say, Memphis had been thrilled when he received a call from Mario stating they wanted to accept his offer to buy back Dereka. Memphis didn't know or care what she had done to fall from their good graces. He was just glad that she had, and he wasted no time traveling to Colombia to settle the deal.

While Memphis had waited upstairs for the guards to bring Dereka from the basement, he wondered whether she would recognize him. But as soon as she saw him, he knew that she did, because her eyes widened in fear. "Hello, my love. I can tell you remember me," he said mockingly, with a sly smile. He stood up and walked around her slowly to inspect her. She was taller and thinner and looked worn and weary. And a solemnness had replaced the spunkiness she'd had when he first abducted her. But all things considered, she seemed to have fared well through her ordeal, at least better than he'd thought she would. "Well, Dereka, it's time for you to begin your next and final leg of the journey," Memphis said. He took her by the arm and led her out the door.

The next day Memphis left Dereka at what he was sure would be her final destination. The place was called La Última Parada, which means "the last stop." It was known as one of the crudest sex houses in the Brazilian criminal underworld. The place deserved its notorious name because it really was the last stop for the majority of the unfortunate sex trafficking victims that winded up there. And Memphis had no doubt that although Dereka had somehow borne her cross and persevered at La Casa de Placer, she would not survive La Última Parada. Few did.

Not My Mama

BABYRUTH AND KENYA waited late into the night for Jasmine's call regarding her latest attempt to find Dereka. Their hopes were high that it would be the call they had waited so long for. The call came around two in the morning. Kenya spoke with Jasmine while BabyRuth waited, with hope illuminating her face like a full moon. Jasmine had been so sure this was the one. After a few minutes, Kenya hung up the phone and looked sadly at her mother. She couldn't speak the words but simply shook her head no. Kenya saw the light fade from her mother's eyes and heard her make a soft whimpering sound as she slumped onto the sofa. Now it was Kenya's turn to be the strong one.

"It's all right, Mama. It just wasn't God's time yet. You always said that God's time is not like ours. We just have to hang in there a little longer, that's all."

"I know," BabyRuth sighed. She slowly rose to her feet. "I'm tired. I'm going to bed. See you in the morning, honey."

Kenya watched her mother's labored movements as she moved slowly towards her bedroom. Her shoulders were stooped as though she were carrying the weight of the world. It grieved Kenya tremendously to see her mother in such a state. "I love you, Mama," Kenya called after her.

"Love you more," BabyRuth responded as she entered her bedroom and closed the door.

Kenya started upstairs to her own bedroom but stopped in her tracks when she heard a loud thump come from her mother's room. "Mama, are you all right?" Kenya yelled, moving quickly towards BabyRuth's bedroom. "Mama!" she yelled again before opening the door and walking in. BabyRuth was lying on the floor next to her bed. She was holding her hands to her chest as if in pain and gasping for breath. "Mama, what's wrong?" Kenya cried as she ran and knelt beside her mother. BabyRuth's mouth moved, but no words came out. Kenya fumbled for the phone on the nightstand and frantically dialed 911. "Something's wrong with my mama," she shrieked. The 911 operator took all the vital information and stayed on the phone with Kenya while the ambulance was dispatched. Kenya held tightly to her mother's hand, comforting and reassuring her. "Help is on the way, Mama. Don't worry. Breathe, Mama, breathe. That's right. You doing great. You gonna be just fine. Hold on, Mama, please. Just hold on."

The ambulance arrived within minutes, and Kenya rode with her mother to the hospital. On the way the EMTs performed an electrocardiogram and asked BabyRuth several questions about pain, which she was able to answer with simple nods. After their preliminary diagnosis was complete, one of the EMTs called ahead to the emergency room and told them to prepare for a heart attack patient. When Kenya heard those words, her own heart nearly stopped beating. Mama? Heart attack? Those two things just didn't compute in Kenya's mind or heart. *Not Mama. Not my mama*, she thought in shock as she watched an EMT put a nitroglycerine tablet under BabyRuth's tongue, an IV line in her arm, and an oxygen mask over her nose and mouth.

Once at the hospital BabyRuth was wheeled away in a whirlwind of doctors, nurses, and technicians. Kenya waited nervously in the waiting room and called a few close family members, who informed her they were on their way. While Kenya waited, she did the one thing her mother had always taught her to do in times of trouble. She prayed.

An Unlikely Source

THE COLOMBIAN POLICE and FBI spent days at the house formerly known as La Casa de Placer, collecting evidence to build their case against the Tavaras brothers and the Los Chomas organization as a whole. They collected boxes upon boxes of drugs and drug paraphernalia, as well as a huge safe, computers, file cabinets, ledgers, and other documents. Every nook, cranny, and crevice of the house was searched for incriminating evidence. They even found hidden cameras in the basement that had been used to spy on the girls. And they were particularly horrified when they discovered the shed, which they quickly recognized, from the tools and weapons inside, had been used as a chamber of torture and torment.

It was clear from the truckload of evidence left behind that the brothers had been caught completely off guard. This was no doubt due to the meticulous planning and joint efforts of the undercover team, the FBI, and the Colombian authorities. Security was extremely tight at the scene, and it seemed like every police officer in Colombia was there. Authorities knew the crime organization was extremely dangerous, and with Mario still not apprehended, they were not taking any chances.

The Operation Undercover team stayed at a hotel in Cartagena for a few days, waiting to hear whether any evidence uncovered at the crime scene could lead them to Dereka's location. And true to Cliff's word, he arranged for Jasmine to visit with Jia at the safe

house. Jasmine was excited to see Jia, and she expected the same
from Jia in return. But Jasmine was caught totally off guard by Jia's
response to her. The young girl just sat quietly in a chair and stared at
Jasmine with her big sad eyes. What Jasmine didn't realize was that
Jia thought that Jasmine would abandon her just as, she thought
the others she loved had, including her mother, her sister Sun-Yu,
and even Dereka. It crushed Jasmine to see Jia looking so lost and
dejected. But it also made her realize that after so many years of
unimaginable abuse, it would take a long time, perhaps years, for Jia
to fully trust people again, if ever. Yet Jasmine was determined to
give Jia all the time she needed.

"Hello, Jia," Jasmine said as she sat down beside her. "I came by to
see you, just like I said that I would." Jia reached out a small hand and
touched Jasmine, as if to see whether she was real. Jasmine took the
young girl's hand and pressed it to her lips. "I'm here, sweetie. Don't
worry. And I'm not going anywhere," Jasmine reassured.

• • •

After a few days of waiting at the hotel, the team received a call from
the lead investigator, who had vital information about where Dereka
was. The information had actually come from an unlikely source, Diago
Tavaras. After recovering in the hospital from his wounds, Diago had
been taken to a Colombian jail. For his own protection, he was provided heavy security while in jail because it was not uncommon for
criminal organizations to order a hit on one of their own, either to
keep them from talking to police or as punishment for botching an
operation. And Diago had screwed up big-time by losing La Casa de
Placer.

So, knowing that he was likely a dead man walking, Diago suddenly seemed to get religion and willingly provided valuable information to the investigator interrogating him. He even mentioned that a
little black girl from the States had been at La Casa de Placer, and she
was sold back to the same man that sold her to them. Diago said the
man inquired about a place in Brazil called La Última Parada. Diago

assumed that's where he'd taken the girl. A few days after talking to the investigator, Diago was found strangled in his cell. So much for heavy security.

Fought the Good Fight

BABYRUTH SPENT OVER a week in the hospital recovering from her heart attack. Because her coronary artery was only partially blocked, she did not need invasive heart surgery. For that, she and her family were grateful. Kenya stayed at the hospital with her mother practically 24/7, going home only to eat and shower. And although BabyRuth was doing better physically, Kenya worried about her mother's mental state. The latest incident of not finding Dereka had taken a heavy toll on her spirit and soul. Kenya watched her mother sleeping peacefully in her hospital bed. It was early morning; the sun was just starting to peep through the blinds. When BabyRuth opened her eyes, she smiled at Kenya.

"Good morning, baby."

"How you feeling, Mama?"

"I'm feeling pretty good. Just ready to go home. Didn't the doctor say I could go home today?"

"They're going to do a couple of tests this morning first before deciding for sure. So we have to wait and see."

"Kenya, I'm ready to go home. I feel fine, baby. I want to go home."

"I know, Mama. But we need to be sure you're ready." BabyRuth struggled to sit up, and Kenya helped by raising her bed.

"I want to go home," BabyRuth insisted. "Suppose Dereka comes home and nobody's there?" Kenya marveled at her mother's resolve, determination, and enduring faith.

"Okay, Mama. I'll do what I can to take you home today."

The remainder of the day was filled with tests and waiting for results. Around six that evening, BabyRuth was discharged. Kenya helped her mother from the transport wheelchair into the car and, once home, settled her comfortably on the sofa. They didn't talk much but spent their time just enjoying being home in each other's company. Kenya kept a watchful eye on her mother for any signs of discomfort or pain.

Around ten o'clock BabyRuth indicated that she was ready to turn in. "I'm tired, baby. Help me to bed." She leaned on Kenya as they moved cautiously down the hall. Kenya helped BabyRuth into bed and pulled the covers around her. "Hand me those pictures," BabyRuth said, pointing to the family pictures on her nightstand. Kenya handed her several pictures, including one of her and her late husband, DJ; Kenya and her brother Derek as kids; Dereka in her basketball uniform holding a trophy; and a portrait of the Jones family females at Myrtle Beach. "We had some good times over the years," BabyRuth said, smiling as she gazed at each of the pictures. "We've had some difficult times. But the good times we've had were something special, weren't they, honey?"

"Yes, Mama. They sure were," Kenya responded, also smiling at the memories the pictures evoked.

When BabyRuth finished looking at the pictures, she asked Kenya to get her Bible. "Turn to Second Timothy, chapter four, verses six and seven." Kenya located the scriptures. "Read it to me, baby," BabyRuth asked as she stared upward into space. Kenya started reading.

For I am now ready to be offered, and the time of my departure is at hand. Kenya read the first verse and stopped.

"Keep going, honey," BabyRuth said gently.

I have fought a good fight, I have finished my course, I have kept the faith. Kenya continued reading as she fought back tears. She realized her mother was saying good-bye.

"I've kept the faith. I've done all that I know to do. And it is well with my soul. I'm ready," BabyRuth said, nodding her head in affirmation.

"No, Mama, you're not going anywhere. You can't leave me too. I can't make it without you. Don't give up now, Mama. We going to see this thing through together. Me and you, Mama. Pleaseeeeee don't leave me," Kenya sobbed as she knelt beside her mother's bed.

"It's in God's hands now, darling. His will be done. But no matter what, you've got to carry on. Be strong for Dereka. She'll need you when she gets home." BabyRuth paused for a moment before continuing. "Tell my sweet Boogie Boo that I love her more than life itself. And tell her that I always knew she'd come home someday."

"I will, Mama, but you'll be able to tell her yourself. Rest now. You're just tired. We'll talk in the morning. You're going to be just fine," Kenya stated confidently.

And then Kenya crawled into bed beside her mother, as she used to do when she was a little girl, and laid her head on BabyRuth's chest. She listened to the beat of her mama's heart and began to count the beats. *One, two, three, four, five*, she counted silently. The heartbeats gave her hope that all was well. So she listened to and counted her mother's heartbeats until she fell asleep lying on her mother's chest. When Kenya woke up in the morning, the heartbeats had stopped. BabyRuth was gone.

A Heartfelt Farewell

THE NEWS OF BabyRuth's passing sent shock waves through the Jones family and the city of Alexandria. BabyRuth had been a pillar of integrity, strength, faith, and service within the community for many years. People came from near and far to attend her funeral and honor the woman they'd come to know and love. Other commuters on the road who had to stop for the long funeral procession of cars inwardly marveled, some impatiently, about the deceased person who attracted such a magnitude of mourners. The pulpit, church pews, choir stand, vestibule, lower levels, and grounds overflowed with people of all ages, races, and religion. Jasmine flew in for the service, and she and Kenya huddled together on the front pew, crying their hearts out for the woman who had shown them nothing but unconditional love and support.

After numerous personal tributes and the eulogy, Pastor Bobby preached a stirring sermon from Hebrews 6:15, *And so, after he had patiently endured, he obtained the promise.* "Mrs. Jones endured a lot of hardships in her life," he preached. "And she endured them all with patience, grace, hope, long-suffering, and tremendous faith. And there's one thing we can rest assured of. BabyRuth has obtained the promise. She's laid down her burdens, and she's at peace with our Lord. Glory, hallelujah!"

The choir sang one of BabyRuth's favorite hymns, "Blessed Assurance," as the long line of family and friends filed slowly past her coffin. Many of the attendees were so distraught they had to be helped away. Kenya and Jasmine held tightly to each other for support, so overcome with grief their tears flowed like the mighty Mississippi. As Kenya bowed over her mother's casket and gazed upon her beautiful face, she could sense her mother's spirit whispering to her, "You stop all that crying, child. Don't fret over me. I'm fine. But I need you to be strong. You can do it. You're your mother's child, and God is on your side." And Kenya felt her mother's strength seeping into her body, and the hand of God straightening her bent back.

"Mama, I'll keep going. I'll be here for Dereka when she comes home. I'll take care of her, just like you took care of me all my life. I promise. I love you, Mama, with all my heart and soul." Kenya leaned over and kissed her mother good-bye.

Two Words

DEREKA LAY ON her back in the bed, waiting in dread for the door to open and the next monster to enter. The men at this place came at all times of the day or night, so there was no relief. And these men were not the wealthy, foreign tourists who patronized La Casa de Placer. At least those men were relatively clean and often used condoms. The customers here were the average, run-of-the-mill johns who spent a large portion of their weekly salary for a minimum fifteen-minute sexual tryst. The place seemed to be led by no one in particular but by several sleazy men jockeying for the top spot.

If Dereka thought La Casa de Placer was bad, the new place was a hundred times worse. At least at the old place she had the other girls as friends, Jia to take care of, and Ms. Vee to confide in. Here, she had nothing and no one. She was kept alone in a tiny windowless room. She was forced to relieve herself in a huge plastic bucket in the corner that was emptied once a day. Meager meals were brought to her twice a day, which she was forced to eat or be beaten. Sometimes Dereka took the beating, hoping that it would be her last. Each morning she was escorted to a tiny, filthy washroom down the hall to shower. That's how she discovered there were other females there. She would catch glimpses of them in the hall or hear them with customers behind closed doors.

How long have I been here? Dereka wondered as she stared at the dingy walls of the room. *One week, maybe two.* It didn't matter because time had no meaning for her anymore. She was simply wait-ing to die. *What's the use?* she thought. *Even if I made it out of here now, what kind of life would I have? I'm damaged goods. Damaged beyond repair.* So Dereka was okay with dying. Death had to be bet-ter than what she was going through. Her only regret was that she'd never see her family again. That fact was most unbearable.

Dereka's thoughts were interrupted by the door creaking open. Another customer had arrived. She closed her eyes tight, not wanting to see the face of the next demon. Dereka heard his heavy footsteps move closer to her bed. She cringed when she felt his hot breath on her face as he leaned in close to her. Then Dereka heard two words that made the hair on her neck and arms tingle. Two words that she hadn't heard for many years.

"Boogie Boo?" a deep voice said. Dereka kept her eyes shut, afraid to open them. Had she heard right? Was this some kind of trap? "Boogie Boo," the voice repeated, louder this time. Dereka cracked her eyes open and stared into the face of a middle-age Latino man. He sat on the bed beside her and whispered, "My name is Felipe Mendoza. I'm an undercover cop with the Brazilian Police Department. Are you Dereka Jones from the United States?" he asked. By now Dereka trusted no one, so she didn't respond. "I know you're afraid. So you don't have to speak. Just blink once for yes and twice for no. Are you Dereka Jones from the States?" he asked again. Derek blinked once. She saw relief flood the man's face. "Dereka, your family has been looking for you. Your aunt, Jasmine McKnight, has come for you. We're going to get you out of here," he said, look-ing intently into Dereka's eyes.

At just the mention of her aunt's name, tears began to roll down the side of Dereka's face and into her hair. But she didn't know whether to trust this strange man. The last man she trusted had betrayed her. *But how does he know about Auntie Jazz? Maybe that Memphis man told him. He knows Aunt Kenya. Perhaps he knows about Auntie Jazz and is playing a joke on me,* Dereka thought, her eyes darting around wildly. *But what about the nickname? How could he know about that?* she questioned in her mind. Felipe could tell Dereka was struggling to believe him. He reached into his pocket and pulled out a piece of folded paper. He carefully unfolded it and held it up for Dereka to see. She gasped. It was the smiley-face sun picture she'd made for Auntie Jazz when she was a little girl.

Dereka stared at the picture in amazement. She looked at Felipe through her tears and whispered, "Auntie Jazz is here? She's really here?"

"Yes, she's close by," Felipe responded. His own eyes misted slightly with tears because he was a family man with three young daughters of his own, and he couldn't fathom his girls being in such a despicable place.

"Dereka, listen to me carefully. This place is surrounded by police who will be moving in shortly. But first we need to make sure you and the others are safe." He scanned the room for someplace she could hide, but there was only the bed and a large bucket in the corner. "Dereka, can you fit under the bed?" She nodded yes. Felipe helped Dereka get under the bed. "I want you to stay here until I come back for you. You'll probably hear some loud noises, and maybe gunshots. I don't mean to scare you, but I want you to be prepared. You just stay under the bed until I return," Felipe instructed. Dereka really didn't want him to leave her, because she was afraid he wouldn't return.

"You'll come back for me. You promise," she said in a timid voice.

"I promise," Felipe responded, squeezing her hand before hurrying out the door.

Dereka curled herself into a fetal position in the cramped space under the bed. Her heart beat loudly in her chest, and sweat rolled down her face and back. She was terrified that Felipe wouldn't return and the sleazy men would find her under the bed, drag her out, and torture her. "Please, Lord. Pleaseeeee, Lord. Please, please, please, Lord," Dereka whispered over and over while she waited.

You Came for Me

JASMINE ANXIOUSLY WAITED in a police car parked about a block from the place known as The Last Stop. Along with her was a police officer and a social service case worker. It hadn't taken long to coordinate this rescue effort. Unlike La Casa de Placer, which was run by a highly organized criminal organization, this place was loosely run by a small group of low-level street pimps. A team of four Brazilian undercover cops and FBI agents were working with Jasmine's team members to conduct the rescue. The men were posing as customers, and once they secured the place, Jasmine and the others would be called in. Jasmine had given Felipe, the undercover cop in charge of the rescue, the smiley-face sun picture. That way if he found Dereka, he could show her the picture to let her know that she could trust him.

Jasmine was hopeful that they would find Dereka, but she was not overly confident, as she'd been in Colombia. She had not even told Kenya about this latest rescue, because she didn't want to disappoint her again. Besides, Kenya had enough to deal with, with the loss of her mother. Tears welled in Jasmine's eyes as she thought about BabyRuth, the woman who had become a mother figure in her life. *What a shame she didn't get to see her granddaughter again,* Jasmine thought sadly. BabyRuth had been so faithful, so positive and strong through it all. *Why, Lord?* Jasmine questioned in her mind. *Why wasn't her faith enough? Why didn't you answer her prayers to see her granddaughter again? I just don't understand.* But then Jasmine thought about something BabyRuth told her once. "God always answers prayers," she'd said. "Sometimes he answers yes, but sometimes his answer is no. We just have to be willing to accept it, no matter what it is. Because Father knows best." Jasmine smiled slightly. *That was one wise woman,* she thought.

Jasmine stared out the window at the crowded, narrow street located in Brazil's notorious red-light district in Rio. With prostitution being legal in Brazil, the street was overflowing with all kinds of men seeking sex for money. Some patronized the legal brothels while others drove around in their flashy automobiles, pulling over and rolling down their windows to proposition and cut deals with street prostitutes dressed in skimpy attire. Men came from all over the world to partake in Brazil's legal sex trade. But many also came to take advantage of the young girls who were either coerced or willingly sold their bodies, sometimes for as little as two dollars or a pack of cigarettes. Poverty, low social status, and a culture of disregard for females were said to be the primary reasons for the huge child-sex trafficking problem in Brazil. But the real culprit was the mass market of demented men who were willing to pay for sex with a child.

Jasmine checked her watch every five to ten minutes. The wait was excruciatingly long, with seconds seeming like minutes, and minutes like hours. She began to wonder whether something had gone wrong.

• • •

To Dereka it seemed like Felipe was gone for hours. Her body began to ache in its crunched position under the bed. She listened intently for any noise but heard nothing. She wanted to go listen at the door, but Felipe had told her to stay there. So she remained under the bed with only the dust balls to keep her company. And the longer it took for him to return, the more scared she became. Felipe had warned her that there may be gunshots. Suppose he, or even her Auntie Jazz, were hurt or killed. Dereka shook her head slightly, as if to shake away the negative thoughts from her mind. *Think positive*, she willed herself.

Suddenly, loud voices and footsteps running down the hall made Dereka jump in fear. She heard men's voices shouting, "Get down. Get down on the floor now." Then she heard three quick popping sounds, a pause, and several more pops. Terrified, Dereka moved as far back under the bed as she could, until her back pressed up against the wall. To her it sounded like World War III was happening outside the bedroom door. Loud voices, popping sounds, crashes, thumps, and such. Something large fell so hard Dereka felt the floor tremble beneath her. The pandemonium lasted only a few minutes, yet to her it seemed like forever.

When things finally quieted, Dereka heard muted voices of several people talking but could not make out what they were saying. Then she heard several footsteps coming down the hall toward her room. "Oh my God. Oh my God," Dereka mumbled as both fear and hope gripped her heart. She heard the door open and footsteps move toward the bed.

And then Dereka saw her beautiful face. It was Auntie Jazz. Dereka let out a shrill cry of pure joy as she reached for her aunt. Jasmine crawled as far as she could under the bed to get to Dereka. She took Dereka's thin arms into her hands and gently pulled her from beneath the bed. They stared at each other in wonder, each unable to speak as tears of happiness rolled like waterfalls down their faces.

Jasmine pulled Dereka's thin body, light as a feather, into her arms. They hugged and held on to each other for dear life, each crying so hard their bodies shook with their sobs. They touched each other's faces, arms, and hair, as if trying to make sure the other was real. Jasmine rocked Dereka gently in her arms like she was a small child. "Thank you, Jesus. Thank you, Jesus," Jasmine murmured over and over as they cried and embraced. This was the moment each of them had waited, hoped, and prayed so long for.

"You came for me," Dereka said through her tears as she gazed at her aunt with love and awe etched on her face.

"Yes, darling. Of course I came for you. I came for my sunshine," Jasmine replied as she kissed Dereka's face, arms, neck, ears, and hair.

Felipe stood off to the side and watched them. In all his years working as an undercover cop on the mean streets of Brazil, he'd never witnessed such a heartfelt reunion. He shook his head in amazement at the pure sincerity and depth of their love. It was times like this that made his job worthwhile.

The Call of a Lifetime

THE NIGHT OF the rescue was the end of the line for The Last Stop. Eight men, including two pimps and six customers, were arrested. Another pimp was shot and killed when he pulled out a gun in an attempt to flee. In all, nine girls, including Dereka, were rescued. They were all in poor condition, including Dereka, who had been there nearly three weeks. Four girls, who had been there for several months, appeared close to death. Jasmine wondered whether they would even survive and prayed that they would. She knew those girls likely had family and friends who were hoping for their safe return. All the girls were immediately transported to a local hospital for medical treatment. Jasmine held on tightly to Dereka's hand every step of the way and would not let go even when the hospital staff asked her to. "No," she informed them. "I just found her. I'm not letting go." So they tolerated her intrusion as best they could.

Dereka's initial diagnoses included dehydration, undernutrition, and pneumonia. Once Dereka was taken to her hospital room, she was hooked up to an IV infused with antibiotics, and given a sedative to help her sleep. Jasmine sat in a chair beside her bed, still holding her hand as she watched her sleep. *This is probably the first good night's sleep she'll have since she was abducted*, Jasmine thought. As a safety precaution, Jasmine had requested and received twenty-four-hour police protection for Dereka while she was in the hospital in Brazil. She feared Memphis might still be in Brazil. And as long as he was alive and free, Jasmine knew her niece would never be safe.

Jasmine stared at Dereka's face, still beautiful in spite of all she'd been through. But she was so thin and frail that her cheekbones, shoulder blades, and other skeletal bones stood out prominently. It made Jasmine sick to her stomach to think about what Dereka must have endured. "Lord, be with her," Jasmine said, shaking her head and sighing deeply. She stood up and kissed her niece gently on the forehead. "Sleep peacefully, my love. I'll be right outside the door. I have a very important phone call to make to your Aunt Kenya," Jasmine whispered. And she left Dereka's bedside for a moment to make the long-waited call to her dear friend.

• • •

Kenya couldn't sleep that night, so she went into her mother's room and sat in her favorite chair. It was a big, soft, comfortable blue chair with a matching ottoman. Kenya would often find her mother sitting there either reading her Bible, watching TV, or dozing. Being in her mama's room gave Kenya a sense of serenity and strength. It was as if she could feel BabyRuth's sweet aura in the air. Everything in the room was exactly as she'd left it. Kenya knew that eventually she'd have to pack away her mother's things. But right now she just didn't have the heart to do so.

Kenya heard her cell phone ringing and rushed across the hall to answer it. "Hi, Jasmine," she said after seeing her number on the screen.

"I've got her, Kenya. I've got Dereka," Jasmine proclaimed excitedly.

"You got Dereka?" Kenya asked, not sure whether she'd heard right.

"Yes, we found her in Brazil. I'm with her now. We're at the—" Kenya dropped the phone as her legs gave away underneath her. She fell to her knees and cried tears of pure ecstasy. "Thank you, Lord. Thank you, Jesus!" she uttered through her tears.

Kenya cried not only for herself, but she sobbed the joyous tears she knew her mother would have, if she were alive. Kenya looked towards heaven. "We found her, Mama. Dereka's coming home. Just like you said that she would," she shouted gleefully. Then Kenya stood on her feet and started running around the room, jumping and shouting for joy. She laughed, cried, hollered, danced, and praised God with all her might. She was so ecstatic she just couldn't contain herself, and totally forgot that Jasmine was on the phone.

Finally, when Kenya tired, she saw the phone lying on the floor and picked it up quickly. "Jasmine, are you still there?" she asked, out of breath.

"Yes, honey. I'm still here," Jasmine replied, reveling in the jubilance she'd overheard.

"How is she?" Kenya asked.

"She's...been through a lot. But thank God she's alive. Thank God we found her in time. The place where we found her is absolutely deplorable. It appears that Memphis took her there."

"Memphis! Hasn't he caused enough misery? Why don't he just go to hell, where he belongs?"

"He'll be there soon enough. Right now I'm at the hospital with Dereka. They gave her a sedative to help her sleep. She's got a long, difficult road ahead," Jasmine acknowledged.

"Poor baby. Poor, poor baby," Kenya said sadly. "Does she know about her mother and grandma?"

"No, not yet."

"Maybe you shouldn't tell her now. It may be too much for her. Perhaps wait until she gets home. What do you think?"

"I honestly don't know," Jasmine confessed. "I know she's going to ask about them. And if I lie to her it may just make things worse. So I may have to tell her, poor darling. Keep us in your prayers."

They spent the next thirty minutes or so making plans for Dereka's return home and the subsequent care she would need. Kenya planned to phone doctors and hospitals to arrange the best medical care possible. They knew Dereka would have to go through a barrage of tests, such as screening for STDs, including HIV/AIDs.

Kenya also planned to work with Detective Davis to arrange security for Dereka back home.

"I've got to go now," Jasmine said, anxious to get back to her niece's bedside.

"Okay, sweetie. Tell Dereka that I love her so much and can't wait to see her."

"You know I will."

After Kenya hung up, her thoughts turned to the two women, Serena and BabyRuth, who were not there to share in the joy of Dereka being found. *What a time we would be having together right now if they were here*, she thought. *How can I share this moment with them?* She looked around and saw the selfie picture that she'd taken at the mall shortly before Dereka's birthday. It was a picture of all of them, the Five Heartbeats, laughing and having a great ladies' day at the mall, their faces aglow with love. It had turned out to be one of the last happy moments they would ever share together. Kenya picked up the framed photo, went back into her mother's room, and settled into her mama's chair. She wrapped her arms around the picture and placed it against her heart. She fell asleep that way, with a serene expression on her face.

A Legacy of Love

WHEN DEREKA OPENED her eyes the next morning, the first thing she saw was Jasmine's smiling face. "Oh my God. You're really here. It wasn't a dream," she said, reaching for Jasmine. An explosion of emotions careened through Dereka's frail body, ranging all the way from gratefulness and joy to disbelief and awe. After five years of living in captivity in the most degrading conditions conceivable, it was hard for her to mentally and emotionally grasp the fact that her nightmare had finally ended. "Thank you Lord, thank you Lord," she said over and over as she held on tightly to Jasmine and sobbed.

"Let it out, darling. Just let it all out," Jasmine said soothingly.

When Dereka's crying curbed somewhat, her thoughts went immediately to her friends, who she assumed were still in danger. "There's a place I was at before. Called the House of Pleasure. There's some girls there who need help," she said, her voice rising in panic.

"They're safe. We've been there already and took the girls to a safe place," Jasmine assured.

"They're safe? They're really safe? Jia's safe?" Dereka questioned as if she could hardly believe it was true

"Yes, Jia's safe. They're all safe now." Dereka was so relieved that her friends had been found.

"What about Ms. Vee? Is she safe too?" Dereka asked. This was the first time Jasmine had heard of a Ms. Vee.

"Ms. Vee?" she asked, confused.

"Yes, she's an elderly lady they kept hidden away in a small room in the back of the house. Her real name is Victoria, and she was so kind to me. I don't think I could have made it without her."

"Well, I know the police searched every inch of the house and I don't think they found an elderly lady."

"Auntie Jazz, she may still be there. You have to find her and made sure she's all right." It was just like Dereka to be so concerned about others.

"Maybe they moved her before the rescue. But don't worry, I'll check with the police in Colombia and see what they know. We'll do everything we can to find your Ms. Vee."

Now that Dereka knew the other girls were safe, her thoughts were of her family. "How's Mama?" she asked tentatively. Jasmine looked away. While she didn't want to lie, she knew the truth would be so painful.

"Honey, maybe you should get some more rest now. There'll be plenty of time to talk later," she said, attempting to delay the inevitable.

"She's gone, isn't she?" Dereka sadly asked to confirm what she already knew. Jasmine nodded yes as she choked back tears. "It's okay, Auntie Jazz. I knew in my heart that she was gone," Dereka replied sadly. They were both quiet for a moment, each lost in their own thoughts of the woman they loved so much. "How's Grandma Ruth and Aunt Kenya?" Dereka asked.

"I spoke with Kenya last night. She's so thrilled that we found you. She sends her love and can't wait to see you."

"I can't wait to see Aunt Kenya and Grandma Ruth. I've missed them so much." Jasmine was thankful that a doctor and nurse walked in, so she didn't have to reply. She knew she'd have to tell Dereka about her grandma eventually. But she wanted to put it off as long as she possibly could. Dereka had already been through so much. Jasmine wanted to give her some breathing room to allow her to 'just be' for a while with any further heartache.

• • •

The next couple of days in the hospital were the most peaceful and restful days Dereka had experienced in five years. She spent most of the days sleeping a deep, sound sleep—the kind of sleep a three-year old child likely has after a long day at the playground. Sometimes Dereka would crack her eyes open and see her Auntie Jazz sitting beside her. Dereka would smile slightly, close her eyes and fall right back into a deep sleep. It was as if after five long years, she could finally let go.

Jasmine stayed right by Dereka's bedside most of the time, leaving only to grab a quick bite to eat in the hospital cafeteria. She showered in the small cramped bathroom in their private room and slept in a roll away cot the hospital staff provided for her. Sometimes Jasmine even slept upright in a chair beside Dereka's bed. She didn't care; she would have slept on the floor if need be.

When Jasmine woke up on their third day in hospital, Dereka was already awake and staring at her with a smile on her face. "Good morning, Auntie Jazz," Dereka said, reaching for Jasmine's hand. It was like she couldn't touch her aunt enough.

"Good morning, sweetheart," Jasmine replied, stifling a yawn. She had woke up several times during the night just to check on Dereka. "How are you feeling?

"Better," Dereka said softly. Dereka was still be treated for pneumonia, undernutrition, and several infections. Her more aggressive testing and medical treatment would take place when she returned home, and that was scheduled to happen as soon as she was well enough to travel. "Thank you again for coming for me, Auntie Jazz," Dereka stated sincerely. "Sometimes I wondered if I would ever see my family again. I thought maybe you all had given up hope of finding me."

"Oh, sweetheart. There was no way we could give up. Don't you know how much you mean to us? You're our heart, our world. We could never, ever give up on you."

"That's what Ms. Vee told me. She kept me going when I got discouraged. She reminds me a lot of Grandma Ruth. Always so positive and comforting. I can't wait to see grandma," Dereka said with an expression of longing in her eyes.

Jasmine found herself at a crossroads. *Should I tell Dereka now about her grandma's passing or wait until she gets home? It will be difficult no matter when she finds out, but which will be less difficult. What is the best time? Is there a best time?* Jasmine pondered.

Dereka saw something in Jasmine's eyes that told her something was wrong. "What's the matter, Auntie Jazz? Is Grandma Ruth all right?" Jasmine knew she had to tell her.

"Honey, I hate to tell you this, but Mama Ruth suffered a heart attack and passed away about three weeks ago. But she remained strong and faithful to the end. She never gave up hope you'd come home. She kept all of us going. She loves you so much," Jasmine said.

"Not Grandma too," Dereka cried. She had long suspected that her mother was gone, but she never imagined she wouldn't see her grandma again. Dereka took her grandma's passing hard.

Jasmine was desperate to do or say anything to comfort her niece. So she tried to lighten the moment by telling the story of the birthday cake fiasco. "You know Mama Ruth made a birthday cake for your fourteenth birthday?"

"She did?" Dereka asked, wiping her eyes.

"Yes, and it was a masterpiece of a cake. Stacked five layers high with that buttercream frosting you like so much." Jasmine saw the slightest hint of a smile on Dereka's face. So she went on to tell her how Kenya had accidentally run into BabyRuth and made her drop the cake on the floor. And how they'd been so scared that BabyRuth would be upset, but instead she had started a cake fight with the ruined cake. Dereka couldn't help but laugh at the vision of her grandma and aunts chasing and smashing each other with cake. It was just like her grandma to make the best of things.

"Grandma Ruth was something else," Dereka said, smiling with a faraway look in her eyes.

"Yes, she certainly was," Jasmine wholeheartedly agreed.

Two of the most special people in the world to Dereka were gone. But even through her grief she knew she was blessed to have had these amazing women as her mama and grandma. They left her a legacy of love.

The Takedown

MEMPHIS DROVE HIS rental car through the narrow cobbled streets of Mexico City. Lucky for him, he'd left Brazil a couple of days before the police raid on La Última Parada. He heard about the raid through a close contact in Brazil who managed several legal brothels there. And he also heard that Dereka was among the girls rescued. *That's one lucky wench who just refuses to die. But it ain't over till it's over*, he vowed.

Memphis was in Mexico City mainly to check in with his boy Ryan, aka Jamal, aka Walter. Since Kevin's death, Memphis considered Ryan as a kind of a quasi-son. And Ryan was really the only one in Memphis's inner circle of employed criminals that he trusted. Ryan was doing quite well in his new position and had already risen within the ranks of the Mexican drug cartel, which was also heavily involved in sex trafficking. *That's my boy*, Memphis thought, smiling as he pulled into the driveway of a big, beautiful house on the outskirts of the city.

Ryan strolled out of the exquisite wrought-iron front door and greeted Memphis in the driveway. He was dressed casually chic in a two-piece white leisure suit, shades, and a white straw hat with a black band. "What's up, doc?" Ryan said, slapping hands with Memphis.

"I see success agrees with you," Memphis said, looking admiringly at the surroundings.

"Well, I ain't complaining," Ryan said, grinning from ear to ear. He led Memphis to the backyard of the house, which was equipped with a swimming pool and wet bar. "Want something to drink, doc?"

"I'll take a shot of tequila."

"Coming up." Ryan poured two large shots of Milagro tequila, which the men downed without flinching a muscle.

"I've heard some good things about your work here, Ryan. Or do you prefer your new name, Jamal?" Memphis asked jokingly.

"Nah, you can call me Ryan. It brings back happy memories of my ex-fiancée, Kenya."

"Speaking of Kenya, did you hear about that raid that went down at that sex house in Rio, called The Last Stop?"

"Yeah, man, I heard about that sh*t. News like that travels fast."

"You know I had just moved Kenya's niece there a few weeks before that raid. The little bimbo had survived five years at that place in Colombia, so I thought for sure taking her there would be the end of her. But somehow she managed to escape death again."

"Maybe she's got her own little private Captain Kirk tucked away somewhere, and he jumps out and yells, 'Shields up, red alert!' whenever death comes her way," Ryan said, cracking up at his own lame joke.

"Well, she's got something," Memphis said, without cracking a smile. "But I'm not done yet. Not by a long shot."

"What you thinking, doc?"

"It's time to switch targets. I'm pretty sure security around Dereka is high right now. So I can't risk going after her again. But there's somebody I can get to. And that's Kenya."

"Kenya?"

"Yeah, Kenya, the true target of my revenge. All this stuff with her niece was just to get back at her anyway."

"You got a plan?"

"Don't I always? I'm taking the eight o'clock flight to Philly tomorrow morning. Flying directly into DC is too risky. I'll rent a car in Philly and drive to Alexandria. I know where Kenya works and where she lives. So it's just a matter of waiting for the right time. I plan to put a

bullet right between her eyes. That ought to settle the debt for losing my son," Memphis said, his jaws clenching in anger. Ryan let out a
low whistle.

"Yeah, doc. That ought to do it," he concurred.

When Memphis's flight touched down at the Philadelphia airport the following morning, he was relieved. It had been a turbulent
flight, and he was glad to be back on solid ground. Also, Memphis
was anxious to get his business with Kenya over with and head back
to Mexico, where he planned to lie low for a while. He grabbed his
expensive Italian-leather duffel bag from the first-class overhead
compartment and swaggered down the aisle. The flight attendant,
who had flirted shamelessly with him during the flight, blushed when
he passed her. "Thanks for flying with us, Mr. Jackson," she gushed
like a schoolgirl.

Memphis hurried down the plane's stairs and headed towards the
shuttle bus for transport to the main terminal. That's when all hell
broke loose. He was immediately surrounded by several police officers with their guns drawn, yelling commands at him. Shocked passengers scurried out of harm's way. Memphis was handcuffed, read
his Miranda rights, and taken into custody.

• • •

The news of Memphis's arrest sent shock waves through the criminal community, both nationally and abroad. His employees and peers
were dumbfounded that someone as ingenious and resourceful as
Memphis had been taken down. Crooks everywhere were all abuzz
with chatter about how such a thing could have happened. But there
was one criminal who was not the least bit surprised. And that was
Ryan. He'd tipped off the FBI that Memphis was on the Philly flight,
under the alias of Keith Jackson. And surprisingly enough, he'd done
it for Kenya. Sure, he had betrayed her himself. But since then he'd
thought a lot about her and realized that he'd developed feelings for
Kenya. He hadn't intended to, but it happened. After all, they had
spent a lot of intimate times together. But he hadn't realized just how

strong his feelings were until Memphis talked about taking her out with a bullet between her eyes. So Ryan took him down before he could take her down.

• • •

Kenya was at the office when she got a call from Detective Davis stating Memphis had been arrested in Philly. She let out a whoop so loud her coworkers came running, thinking something was wrong. After reassuring them that all was well, she called Jasmine in Brazil to give her the good news. "They got him. They finally got that heartless, hideous monster. They arrested Memphis this morning in Philly."

"Are you for real?" Jasmine asked, stunned.

"Yes, I'm serious. He'd changed his name to Keith Jackson. That maggot had been on the loose so long I was beginning to doubt that he'd ever be caught. But they finally got him."

"Praise God! This is wonderful news. Especially since I'm bringing Dereka home in a few days."

"Yes, God is good! First we find Dereka. And now Memphis is captured. Like Mama used to always say, you can run, but you can't hide. She was right about that."

"Mama Ruth was right about a lot of things. I think she must be up in heaven shaking things up, because the floodgates have opened and the blessings are coming down."

"Well, you know if anybody can stir things up in heaven, it's my mama."

Jasmine and Kenya spent the rest of their time talking about Dereka's upcoming trip home. Now, with Memphis in custody, they no longer had to look over their shoulders and worry about her security. Kenya had everything set for Dereka's medical treatment at Inova Women's Hospital in Fairfax, one of the highest-ranking hospitals in the area. Thankfully, Kenya did not have to spare any expense when it came to her niece's care. Her mother and father had planned well financially and left them a sizeable estate. Kenya counted her blessings to have had such loving and thoughtful parents. She'd be able to provide Dereka the best care possible. Kenya had promised her mama that she would take care of Dereka. And that was one promise she looked forward to keeping.

Going Home

DEREKA SAT ON the plane next to Jasmine, her heart filled with joy. She was going home. She still could hardly believe it. *Home, sweet home*, Dereka thought, amazed that it was really happening. She was grateful beyond words that this day had finally come. Grateful to God and grateful to her family, who never gave up on her. Dereka looked fondly at her Auntie Jazz, who was already laid back in her aisle seat, fast asleep. Her aunt had given up so much and risked life and limb to find her. And she'd barely left Dereka's side since. Dereka leaned over and kissed her aunt softly on the cheek as she snoozed. "Thank you, Auntie Jazz, for everything," she whispered.

But mixed in with Dereka's joy and gratefulness of going home was also a sense of sadness and anxiety. Sadness that her mama and grandma would not be there to welcome her home. Dereka knew her Grandma Ruth had been the glue that held it all together, standing faithful and strong until the end. She was like a tree planted by the water, that shall not be moved. And her mama, Serena, had given her own life for her. The Bible says, *There is no greater love in the world than to lay down one's life for another.* Dereka could literally feel her mama's and grandma's love covering her like a feather-down quilt on a cold winter's night. It was warm, comforting, and sure. A love like theirs transcended time and space.

Dereka was also leery about what kind of life lie ahead for her. Before her abduction her life had been filled with typical adolescent girly stuff, like hanging out with friends, school, parties, social media, hairstyles, clothes, and such. She wasn't naïve enough to think that she could just pick up where she left off. *How will I be treated now? What will my friends think of me? How do I start over after what I've been through?* she wondered.

Dereka stared out the window at the bright sun above and the fluffy clouds below. It was a beautiful sight. She reflected back on that frightening, pitch-dark night she was taken away on a small airplane. So much had happened since then. So many horrific things that she wanted to forgot but knew she never would. *If only I could forgot. If only I could blot it all out from my mind forever,* she thought wistfully.

Yet there was something that Dereka didn't want to forget, the only good memory from her horrendous experience: the girls and women who had become her friends and family by default. The ones who had loved, supported, and encouraged her as best they could under such deplorable conditions. She knew some of the girls rescued in Colombia had already been reunited with their family or guardians. But a few of them, including Jia, remained at the safe house. For Jia, so far the only family that had been located was her maternal grandmother, who was old, sickly, and living in a nursing home. No one was able to locate her mother, Lihwa, so far. Dereka was probably one of the few people who really knew what their mother had done. And if Lihwa never resurfaced, Dereka planned to keep that secret always, out of love and respect for Sun-Yu. Dereka was thrilled when Auntie Jazz had told her that she'd already inquired about adopting Jia and bringing her to Virginia to live. Dereka loved that little girl immensely.

Dereka's thoughts shifted to the girls who had not survived. Young, beautiful girls like Crystal and her dear friend Sun-Yu. They had both died in such dreadful ways. Their remains would likely never be found. Her eyes watered as she thought of them. Unlike her, they would never get to see their loved ones again.

Dereka reached into her carry-on, pulled out her small bag of treasures, and placed them in her lap. She was so thankful that Jia had given the items to Auntie Jazz. She ran her fingers gently over Crystal's comb, the angel soap figurine, and Esmeralda's rosary beads.

Such small items, but they meant the world to her. They were symbols of the beauty, love, and kindness that she'd found in the darkest of places. Seeing Esmeralda's beads made Dereka think of Ms. Vee. How she missed that nice old lady. Dereka recalled Ms. Vee's kind, wrinkled face and how her eyes twinkled when she smiled. Ms. Vee had often told her, "Don't give up, little one. Your family will come for you. You're going home." *You were right, Ms. Vee. I'm going home*, Dereka thought gleefully as she stared out the window at the blue sky and soft white clouds.

Joyous Reunion

KENYA EAGERLY AWAITED at the airport for Dereka's arrival. Other family members and friends had wanted to be there, but Kenya gently persuaded them not to come. She didn't want Dereka to be overwhelmed on her first day back. Dereka had been through such a traumatic experience, and Kenya knew they needed to take things slow to help her acclimate to a normal environment again. She planned to hold a gathering for family and friends to welcome Dereka home later. But only when she was ready. Kenya also planned to hold a press conference soon, primarily to thank the hundreds of people who had provided information, sent notes and cards, and prayed for Dereka's safe return. But all that would come later. Right now the plan was for Dereka to spend her first day or so at home in her own room and in her own bed, surrounded by love, joy, and tranquility. Then they would continue her hospital care.

Kenya watched the long line of travelers walking down the corridor toward the exit where she was standing. Her heart raced with excited expectation of seeing her niece again. Kenya had her mama's old, worn Bible in her hand. Inside the Bible she had placed a beautiful picture of Serena, her face aglow with love as she held and smiled down at baby Dereka, who was only a few days old at the time. Kenya brought the items along just to have something personal of the two of them with her. It was her way of sharing Dereka's return home with them.

Kenya craned her neck and squinted her eyes, searching through the crowd, trying to spot Dereka. And then she saw her, walking arm in arm with Jasmine. She was taller, much thinner, but still just as beautiful as ever. Kenya's heart swelled to bursting as she began to openly cry, not caring about the curious onlookers passing by. When Dereka saw her Aunt Kenya, her face lit up like a child's on Christmas morning. She ran as fast as her thin legs could carry her and leaped into Kenya's arms. They laughed and cried as they savored the pure jubilance of being together again. It was happiness in its purest form, and neither one of them wanted the moment to end. Kenya had not truly felt pure happiness since the day Dereka was abducted. And she had all but forgotten what it felt like—until now.

While Jasmine drove home, Kenya and Dereka sat together in the backseat. They laughed as each tried to wipe the tears from the other's face, finding humor in the fact that the more they wiped, the more the tears flowed. Jasmine glanced at them in her rearview mirror and prayed, "Thank you, Father in heaven, for returning our Dereka to us. Thank you, Lord." Kenya gave Dereka BabyRuth's old, worn Bible with the picture of Serena inside. Dereka took the Bible and picture and pressed them to her heart.

When they pulled into the driveway, Dereka did not move right away but sat and stared at the home she had not seen for five years. Both Kenya and Jasmine knew she was thinking about her mama and grandma. "It's okay, baby. Just take your time. Whenever you're ready," Kenya said softly. The three of them sat in silence in the car for a moment, each reflecting on how different things would be. They were now the Three Heartbeats instead of five, but their three hearts encircled the essence of the other two.

"I'm ready," Dereka said, smiling slightly at her aunts. When she entered the house, Dereka looked around as though she was in a trance. She moved from room to room, touching and feeling the furniture, curtains, pictures, and things. She even got on her knees and ran her hands over the shining mahogany wood floor. "There were times I didn't think I would see this house again," she whispered. For the rest of the day, Jasmine and Kenya pampered their niece, catering to her every need. "You all don't have to do all this. I can do things for myself," Dereka protested. She had gotten so used to slaving, serving, and taking care of others it was hard for her to relax and be taken care of. But her aunts continued to wait on her hand and foot. They drew her a hot scented bubble bath, shampooed her hair, gave her a manicure and pedicure, and ordered her dinner of choice—a sausage-and-mushroom pizza. "Thank you all for taking care of me, and mostly for not giving up on me," she told them over and over again. Dereka didn't take any of it for granted.

No One's There

LATER THAT NIGHT Kenya sat beside Dereka, who was lying comfortably in her bed. "Dereka, I'm so sorry for what happened to you. It should have been me, not you. You suffered because of something that happened to me long ago. I would have taken your place in a heartbeat. I'm so sorry," Kenya apologized, her eyes watering.

"It wasn't your fault, Aunt Kenya. You don't have to apologize. I never once blamed you. Not once," Dereka assured her.

"Thanks, sweetie," Kenya replied, rubbing Dereka's hair.

"It's so good to be home. I'm grateful beyond words," Dereka said, looking around her room, which was practically exactly how she'd left it. She continued, "I just hope the other girls are doing well. Especially Jia. We all went through so much together."

"I'm sure they're fine. Jasmine will be returning to Colombia soon to check on Jia," Kenya stated.

"That's good. I hope Auntie Jazz finds Ms. Vee. I'm worried about her. She took such good care of me. I'd like to find her and thank her for all she did. I think I would have lost it without her."

"Jasmine told me about Ms. Vee. Thank God she was there for you. We'll do everything we can to find her. I want to personally thank her for helping you. Now you get some rest, sweetie. It's been a long day."

"Okay, Aunt Kenya. Good night. I love you so much."

"I love you too, sweetheart. More than you'll ever know." Kenya kissed Dereka softly on both cheeks and her forehead before leaving the room.

Before going to bed, Kenya got on her knees and again thanked God for bringing her niece home safe. Dereka hadn't said much about what she'd been through. And Kenya and Jasmine had not asked. But Kenya could tell her experience had affected her profoundly and deeply. At times Kenya saw the pain and sadness reflected in her eyes. Before Dereka was taken from them, she'd been a bubbly, outgoing young girl without a care in the world. She returned to them a mature, sensitive, introspective young lady.

• • •

Kenya awoke early about half past five and decided to go downstairs for a cold drink. As she passed by Dereka's room, she thought she heard someone talking and laughing inside. Kenya stopped, put her ear to the door, and heard Dereka's voice. *Who in the world is she talking to?* Kenya thought, confused. And then she became afraid. Someone was in Dereka's room. Kenya pushed the door opened and saw Dereka sitting in a chair beside her bed, laughing, talking, and having the time of her life.

"Aunt Kenya," she said, a bright smile on her face. "We don't have to find Ms. Vee. She found me. Can you believe it? Ms. Vee came all the way here to find me." Kenya looked at the empty bed, and then back at Dereka. She gasped, *Oh my God*, when she realized that Ms. Vee only existed in Dereka's mind. The poor child had created this imaginary person in her head.

"Ms. Vee, this is my Aunt Kenya. Remember, I told you about her. Aunt Kenya, this is Ms. Vee," Dereka exclaimed excitedly, her face beaming with joy. Kenya walked slowly to the bed and sat down carefully on the edge.

"Nice to meet you, Ms. Vee," she said, while tears streamed down her face. Kenya didn't have the heart to tell Dereka that no one was there. There'd be plenty of time for that later, when Dereka got the help she needed. But for now, Kenya decided to allow Dereka the privilege and pleasure of being reunited with her dear friend.

Endurance

(Six Years Later)

KENYA SAT ON the church pew watching Dereka in the choir, leading a song in her beautiful soprano voice. Dereka had come a long ways but still had a ways to go on her road to recovery. Her years in captivity had taken a heavy toll on her, both physically, mentally, and emotionally. She'd been diagnosed with several STDs, including syphilis, which were successfully treated with penicillin and other medications. Thank God she tested HIV negative. She also had one of her kidneys removed due to deterioration from dehydration and traumatic injury. In addition, the doctors said she'd likely never bear children. Too much damage to her reproductive system.

And as if the physical impact were not bad enough, the psychological consequences were equally, if not more, devastating. Through therapy her psychologist discovered that Ms. Vee had appeared shortly after Sun-Yu hanged herself. Creating Ms. Vee was Dereka's way of coping with such a horrifying tragedy. Ms. Vee was a kind, older woman that she could confide in, someone to encourage, love, and support her. The kind older lady served as a substitute for Dereka's mother, grandma, and aunts, whom she loved and doubted she'd ever see again. With therapy, over the years Ms. Vee began to appear to Dereka less and less, until she finally faded away. But Dereka still talked about her sometimes as if she really existed.

Because to Dereka, she did. Kenya liked to think that Ms. Vee was an angel sent by God to help her niece endure her ordeal.

• • •

So much had happened in the past six years. Memphis had been tried and convicted of numerous felonies. Dereka had wanted to testify at the trial, but thankfully she didn't have to, which was probably best for her mentally and emotionally. Several other women and girls that Memphis had either coerced into prostitution or abducted and sold into sex slavery bravely came forth to testify against him. And because the notorious drug dealer had made a lot of enemies among the criminal elements in the illegal drug trade, some of his competitors and employees cut plea bargains with the prosecutor's office and testified against him as well. Memphis was convicted of a laundry list of offenses, including multiple counts of kidnapping, sex trafficking, contributing to the delinquency of a minor, drug trafficking, and money laundering, among other things. He was sentenced to life plus five hundred years.

There was little news over the years regarding what happened to Ryan. Authorities were able to track him to Mexico City, but from there the trail went cold. It seemed he left Mexico suddenly one night after stealing a huge sum of money from the drug lord he worked for, and no one had seen or heard from him since. With his cunningness and manipulative skills, he could be living in Bora Bora or anywhere under a fictitious name. Kenya received an anonymous text the year before with the words "I'm sorry." For a minute she'd thought it might be from Ryan, but quickly dismissed that thought. And even if it had been from him, it wouldn't have mattered. There was no amount of sorry in the world that could diminish the hurt his betrayal embedded in her heart.

In retrospect Kenya realized the signs of deception had been there all along. But she had ignored her intuitions and let her heart overrule her brain. Something she vowed would never happen again. Overtime she came to terms with Ryan's betrayal. It was difficult though. But Kenya was resilient. She had picked up the pieces and moved on. About two years ago, Kenya started her own legal consulting business, and her trusted friend Trevon was once again working as her assistant.

Jasmine was still with Operation Undercover but now as a spokesperson and fundraiser, sharing her experience on the front line of rescue operations. She had found her life's calling. Unfortunately, she'd not been able to adopt Jia as she'd hoped. It seemed Jia's paternal grandparents inadvertently learned of their son's daughters when they discovered some old letters postmarked from Beijing, China, hidden in a toolbox in their garage. Their son had placed the letters there years before and forgotten about them. A lady named Lihwa had written the letters, begging him to return to Beijing to help her raise their girls. When confronted, their son had admitted the truth.

The grandparents had located Jia at the safe house in Colombia. They were heartbroken to learn what had happened to the girls, and that their oldest granddaughter had not survived. After blood tests confirmed their relation to Jia, they were given temporary guardianship and took her to live with them in Bordeaux, France. The permanent adoption was finalized about a year later. The grandparents, a loving and considerate couple, were extremely grateful to Jasmine for all she'd done for Jia and promised that she could visit Jia whenever she wanted. Jasmine had already visited Jia several times and had plans to take Dereka to see her in the spring.

● ● ●

Kenya continued to watch Dereka singing with all her heart, swaying from side to side in unison with the other choir members. Her eyes filled with tears of pride and joy. She was so proud of her niece and the progress she'd made over the past six years. It seemed Dereka had managed to acquire the best qualities of the four women in her life who loved and nurtured her as best they could. She had BabyRuth's spirituality, Serena's humanity, Jasmine's tenacity, and Kenya's resiliency. She represented the best of them all rolled into one, and she was the epitome of the one trait they all shared in common—endurance.

Why Dereka had to suffer like she did, Kenya would never understand. She thought about the scriptures that state, *We are troubled on every side, yet not distressed; we are perplexed, but not in despair; Persecuted, but not forsaken; cast down, but not destroyed.* Dereka had lived through a hell on earth that, in all likelihood, should have been her death sentence. She'd been subjected to atrocities incomprehensible to most human minds. Yet she was still standing. By the grace of God, she had endured.

Author's Note

I hope this story stirred your emotions, edified your mind, or touched your heart in some way. This book is my attempt to portray the physical, emotional, and psychological trauma that child sex trafficking victims, endure. This story is not intended to be representative of all victims. It's simply the story of one young girl, who through no fault of her own, fell prey to a sickness flourishing in society—the sexual exploitation of our children.

I do not claim to be an expert on this broad, complex topic; not by any means. But in the course of the research I did as a foundation for writing this book, my eyes were opened to massiveness and atrociousness of this horrendous crime. No one is immune to this barbarity; it could happen to any family, anywhere, and at any time.

There are many reports with statistics about the millions of human trafficking victims around the world. However, these girls are more than just statistics in a report. So much more. They're our daughters, granddaughters, nieces, sisters, cousins, other family members, and friends. Having two granddaughters of my own, Reonna (my heart) and Iyonna (my sunshine), my heart truly grieves for the young victims of this monstrosity.

I pray *Endurance* helps increase awareness, and in turn, increase support to combat human trafficking. If you feel so led, please support a human trafficking organization, and help abolish this present day slavery. A reference list of organizations specifically designed to fight against child sex trafficking by rescuing and serving victims is included.

I love to hear from my readers. Please contact me at:

    Website: www.lifthimupproductions.org
    Email: lifthimup3@verizon.net.

Also, please review this book on Amazon.com or other book retailers' websites.

Thank you so much, and God bless.

Gwen Sutton

Please Help Fight
Human Trafficking

Because Every Child Counts

Following is a list of anti-human trafficking organizations you can support through donations, volunteering, increasing awareness, prayer, and other means.

Operation Underground Railroad, www.ourrescue.org, info@ourrescue.org
A front-line, nonprofit organization performing undercover work to rescue children from sex slavery and dismantle the criminal networks abusing them. You can become an abolitionist and help abolish child sex slavery for as little as $5.00 - $25.00 a month. All donations are tax deductible. Currently donations can be made online or by mailing a check to:
The Underground Railroad Project
700 N Valley St.
Suite B
Anaheim, CA 92801

LOVE146, www.love146.org, info@love146.org
An international human rights organization working to end child sex trafficking and exploitation through survivor care and prevention. Love146 was founded in 2002 when the group's co-founders went on an exploratory trip to Southeast Asia to see how they could better serve in the fight against child sex trafficking. As part of an undercover operation, investigators took several co-founders into a brothel where they witnessed young girls being sold for sex. The girls were given numbers of identification pinned to their dresses. One girl in particular stood out because she stared at them with a piercing gaze. One co-founder said, "There was still fight left in her eyes." Her number was 146. Thus, the name LOVE146.

New Haven Office   Houston Office
P.O. Box 8266,   P.O. Box 66253
New Haven, CT 06530   Houston, TX 77266
203-772-4420   979-476-2512

The Covering House, www.thecoveringhouse.org, info@thecoveringhouse.org
A place of refuge and restoration for girls who have experienced sexual trafficking or sexual exploitation. Services include therapeutic housing, out-client services, supportive adults program and reducing risk program.
The Covering House
P.O. Box 12206
St. Louis, MO 63157
(314)865-1288

Called to Rescue, www.calledtorescue.org
A non-profit, faith-neutral, worldwide organization dedicated to the rescuing of minor children from sex trafficking, violence, and abuse.
Called to Rescue USA
9709 NE 83rd Court
Vancouver, WA 98662
(360)356-3761
HOTLINE NUMBER: 1-855-646-5484

National Human Trafficking Resource Center, www.traffickingresource-center.org
A national anti-trafficking hotline and resource center serving victims and survivors of human trafficking and the anti-trafficking community in the United States. Their mission is to provide human trafficking victims and survivors with access to critical support and services to get help and stay safe, and to equip the anti-trafficking community with the tools to effectively combat all forms of human trafficking.
Hotline: 1-888-373-7888 (Call the hotline to report a human trafficking case or request services.)

Biblical Quotes and References

(King James and New King James Versions)

That the trial of your faith, being much more precious than of gold that perisheth, though it be tried with fire, might be found unto praise and honor and glory at the appearing of Jesus Christ. (1 Peter 1:7)

...it is more blessed to give than to receive. (Acts 20:35)

Ask, and it shall be given you; seek, and ye shall find; knock, and it shall be opened unto you. (Matthew 7:7)

...but this one thing I do, forgetting those things which are behind, and reaching forth unto those things which are before, I press toward the mark for the prize of the high calling of God in Christ Jesus. (Philippians 3:13-14)

We are confident, I say, and willing rather to be absent from the body, and to be present with the Lord. (2 Corinthians 5:8)

My help comes for the Lord, Who made heaven and earth. (Psalm 121:2)

Be still, and know that I am God; I will be exalted among the nations, I will be exalted in the earth! (Psalm 46:10)

And the peace of God, which passeth all understanding, shall keep your hearts and minds through Christ Jesus. (Philippians 4:7)

Jesus Christ is the same yesterday, today, and forever. (Hebrews 13:8)

The Lord is my shepherd; I shall not want. He maketh me to lie down in green pastures: he leadeth me.... (Psalm 23)

God is our refuge and strength, a very present help in trouble. (Psalm 46:1)

But he who endures to the end shall be saved. (Matthew 24:13)

Looking unto Jesus, the author and finisher of our faith; who for the joy that was set before him endured the cross, despising the shame, and is set down at the right hand of the throne of God. (Hebrews 12:2)

And the Lord will make you the head and not the tail; you shall be above only, and not be beneath, if you heed the commandments of the Lord your God,.... (Deuteronomy 28:13)

Ye are of your father the devil. ...for he is a liar, and the father of it. (John 8:44)

I returned, and saw under the sun, that the race is not to the swift, nor the battle to the strong,.... (Ecclesiastes 9:11)

The Lord is my light and my salvation; whom shall I fear? The Lord is the strength of my life; of whom shall I be afraid? (Psalm 27:1)

But they that wait upon the Lord shall renew their strength; they shall mount up with wings as eagles; they shall run, and not be weary; and they shall walk, and not faint. (Isaiah 40:31)

For he shall give his angels charge over thee, to keep thee in all thy ways. (Psalm 91:11)

In the day of my trouble I will call upon You, For You will answer me. (Psalm 86:7)

And he arose, and rebuked the wind, and said unto the sea, Peace, be still. And the wind ceased, and there was a great calm. (Mark 4:39)

...In the world you will have tribulation; but be of good cheer, I have overcome the world. (John 16:33)

Bears all things, believes all things, hopes all things, endures all things. Love never fails.... (1 Corinthians 13:7-8)

For Jesus said to him, "Put your sword in its place, for all who take the sword will perish by the sword. (Matthew 26:52)

Do not fret because of evildoers, nor be envious of the workers of iniquity. For they shall soon be cut down like the grass, and wither as the green herb. (Psalms 37:1-2)

For I am now ready to be offered, and the time of my departure is at hand. I have fought a good fight, I have finished my course, I have kept the faith. (2 Timothy 4:6-7)

And so, after he had patiently endured, he obtained the promise. (Hebrews 6:15)

Greater love has no one than this, than to lay down one's life for his friends. (John 15:13)

We are troubled on every side, yet not distressed; we are perplexed, but not in despair; persecuted, but not forsaken; cast down, but not destroyed. (2 Corinthians 4:8-9)

Songs Reference

(From Wikipedia, the free online encyclopedia)

"Amazing Grace" is a Christian hymn published in 1779, with words written by John Newton (1725-1807), an English poet and clergyman. The song is based on his personal experience. After leaving the Royal Navy service, Newton become involved in the Atlantic slave trade. During a violent storm he called out to God for mercy, and survived. He wrote the first verse of "Amazing Grace" while his boat was being repaired. Newton continued his slave trading career until around 1755. Ordained in the Church of England in 1764, Newton began to write hymns with poet William Cowper. "Amazing Grace" was written to illustrate a sermon on New Year's Day of 1773, and debuted in print in 1779. It is one of the most recognizable songs in the English-speaking world.

"You Are My Sunshine" is a popular song recorded by Jimmie Davis and Charles Mitchell, and first recorded in 1939. However, while Davis and Mitchell are the credited songwriters, Davis was never known to actually claim authorship, as he bought the song and rights from Paul Rice and put his own name on it, a practice not uncommon in the pre-World War II music business. Some early versions of the song credit the Rice Brothers. Descendants and associates of Oliver Hood, a Georgia musician who collaborated with Rice, claim Hood wrote the song in the early 1930s, first performing it in 1933. The song has been covered numerous times — so often, in fact, that it is "one of the most commercially programmed numbers in American popular music.

"Going Up Yonder" was released in 1975 by Walter Lee Hawkins (1949–2010), an American gospel music singer and pastor. The song featured his wife, Tramaine Hawkins, as soloist. Bishop Hawkins started his career in one of his brother's chorales, "The Northern California State Youth Choir" of the Church of God in Christ. Later, he accompanied his brother Edwin and founded The Edwin Hawkins Singers. This collaborative effort produced the hit song "Oh Happy Day," which became one of the first gospel songs to cross over onto mainstream music charts.

"A Brighter Day Ahead" is a traditional gospel song written by Margaret Aikens-Jenkins in 1958. Raised in Chicago, Ms. Jenkins, along with her sister Celeste Melton Scott, joined Robbie Preston Williams to form the Ladies of Song gospel group. Ms. Jenkins, a gifted songwriter, wrote most of the songs for the group. Her songs were also recorded by several other artists, including the great Mahalia Jackson who was one of the group's biggest supporters. The multi-talented Ms. Jenkins, along with Ollie Lafayette, formed Mag-Oll Records in Chicago. (This information is from multiple online sources including, Uncloudy Days, The Gospel Music Encyclopedia.)

"He's Got the Whole World in His Hands" is a traditional American spiritual first published in the paperbound hymnal *Spirituals Triumphant, Old and New* in 1927. In 1933, it was collected by Frank Warner from the singing of Sue Thomas in North Carolina. Frank Warner performed the song during the 1940s and 1950s, and introduced it to the American folk scene. He recorded it on the Elektra album *American Folk Songs and Ballads* in 1952. The song made the popular song charts in a 1958 version by English singer Laurie London with the Geoff Love Orchestra, which went all the way to #1 of the Most Played by Jockeys song list in the USA, and went to number three on the R&B charts. Mahalia Jackson's version made the Billboard top 100 singles chart, topping at number 69.

"Blessed Assurance" is a well-known Christian hymn written in 1873 by blind hymn writer Fanny J. Crosby to the music written in 1873 by Phoebe P. Knapp. Crosby was visiting her friend Phoebe Knapp as the Knapp home was having a large pipe organ installed. The organ was incomplete, so Mrs. Knapp, using the piano, played a new melody she had just composed. When Knapp asked Crosby, "What do you think the tune says?" Crosby replied, "Blessed assurance; Jesus is mine." The hymn appeared in the July 1873 issue of Palmer's *Guide to Holiness and Revival Miscellany.* It is not certain that this was the first printing of the hymn, but it certainly helped to popularize what became one of the most beloved hymns of all time.

Coming Next from Gwen Sutton

RESTORED

THE JONES FAMILY SAGA CONTINUES.

Made in the USA
Charleston, SC
19 November 2015